CHASING AMBULANCES

A NOVEL

TOM NILSSON

Copyright © 2023 by Tom Nilsson

Paperback: 978-1-963050-18-9
eBook: 978-1-963050-19-6
Library of Congress Control Number: 2023922010

All rights reserved. No part of this publication may be reproduced, distributed, or transmitted in any form or by any electronic or mechanical means, without the prior written permission of the publisher, except in the case of brief quotations embodied in critical reviews and certain other noncommercial uses permitted by copyright law.

This Book is a work of fiction. Names, characters, businesses and organizations, places, and events are fictitious and a product of the author's imagination. Any similarity to people, places, or events is entirely coincidental.

Ordering Information:

Prime Seven Media
518 Landmann St.
Tomah City, WI 54660

Printed in the United States of America

To Monica – for continuing to believe.

Every loss is different, yet there's a ghastly sameness in the anguish. Death is loss and loss is never easy. People get that. Yet it's grueling to comprehend the sudden and unexpected change to your world and your perception of it. You doubt everything you've ever known and all you've ever loved.

That's to be expected.

What's isn't, however, is your reaction. It's as personal as the loss itself.

You're helpless. There's this wandering, a bewildering endless stream of contradictions. You want to talk about it, but you don't really want to talk about it because you want to be alone, but you don't really want to be alone. You're starving even though you don't eat. You're exhausted but can't sleep. You're haunted by questions begging for answers, infuriated by not-knowing. The only remedy for your ache is time.

But time never hurries; it drags its own slow march.

Consider yourself lucky if you're yet to experience such grief, but it's coming. Eventually, loss finds us all. For some, it's coming hard and fast. Be alert, for the reaper will not be timid when he comes for a loved one. Loss snaps on you with a sudden and stunning ferocity, an ineffable finality.

Death may take only one life but affects many. It blindsides survivors in a manner not understood despite being an unknown inevitability. Rarely do those left behind have time to plan or prepare. You simply react. There's no *How-To* manual detailing ways to cope, describing how to grieve. Only the cynic would read it anyway since contemplating death goes against human nature.

You respond individually, looking for ways to properly handle grief. You'll rely on others, knowing lesser persons found the necessary means to soldier on. But how? Had they surrounded themselves with the comfort of friends and family, discovering the true strength often found only in numbers? Or was there some other unknown method to alleviate this madness?

The reaction is as distinct as the person reacting. Well-meaning people will tell you grief is personal, that there is no right way or wrong way. And while they may mean well, people can be idiots; such advice bullshit, echoed solely because a silence requires filling.

Case in point is our protagonist, my friend, Eric McKegney, Esq. His way was decidedly wrong. He drank, or drinks. His alcohol of choice is Scotch Whisky, a Scottish libation for an Irish lad. He's become a bit of a Scotch snob, drinking only twelve-year-old single-malt and never blends. He's not particular providing there's enough, for in a pinch any booze will do.

But it is said: Alcohol is never the answer . . . until it is.

And like the problem which prompted it, his solution too snapped on him hard and fast.

Not only does he feel the pain, he also fears it for his monsters are real. They scare the shit out of him. Unable to peacefully coexist, he hides in a bottle.

In a way drinking is like having financial problems. It's gradual, then all of a sudden, more like the slow creep of a flood. Eventually the water's so high you're in over his head. Unable to tread water, the walls close in. The floor falls away. You're in free-fall, finally splashing down in a tumbler of whatever.

Liquor became Eric's crutch when the knees wobbled, or his feet slipped out. From there it became mind-numbing steps from mourning to boozing, from wanting to remember to needing to forget.

Alcohol is destroying him, leaving his cold fears combating the warming tingles. He's outmanned and outgunned, so he surrendered peacefully.

After not-enough time passed, his strength and purpose relatively regained, auto-pilot was disengaged. Agony and dread remained, magnified by tangled guilty ironies. Instead of answering the unanswerable, he ignored the questions by trying to drown the demons asking. The end-result was complete desolation, a yawning void of nothingness. Like a black hole, he was being swallowing from the inside.

When the casserole Pyrex was returned, his friends wrongly assumed he was healed. They had lives to get back to and it was time for him to do the same. It was then booze went from crutch to companion, someone to share his loneliness and hopelessness. Soon alcohol dominated him, holding him upright while cutting him down. Drinking became as constant as gravity. He felt like a five-hundred-pound man.

Whiskey became the lens through which to view life. If the world looks dark, booze shines a light. If something good happens, drinking is a celebration. Alcohol is his hammer in a world populated by nails.

It was only a matter of time before his solution became problematic, but in drinking he found comfort, almost acceptance. Sure, he's infected. He craves his medicine, the fix. It's a simple trade-off, empty bottles for his own torturous emptiness.

A bullet ripped through his heart and soul, the bloody carnage evident and exposed for all to see. His scars prove the damage. Yet no one understood the unseen gaping self-inflicted exit hole. Nobody ever would, so he withdrew. And into that bottomless hole, his eternal void of guilt, he continually pours the drinks like his liver is ablaze and he's a one-man bucket brigade.

So now as he sits in the exquisitely appointed legal conference room resting one elbow on the polished mahogany table, his shakes barely perceptible as he rubs at his eyes. He refills a water glass from a matching decanter, exposing a gold cufflink. He wears an expensive watch without a functioning battery conveniently set to five o'clock since he's not without a sense of humor. His white shirt is lightly striped and heavily starched, his suit dark and not off-the-rack. The

Windsor knot of powder blue silk is so crisp and impeccably dimpled you'd never guess it's been six months since he'd touched a tie, let alone tried to tie one.

If not for the slight beads of sweat visible above his freshly shaven lip and the redness bleeding into his dark eyes, you'd never guess it's been three hours since drinking lunch.

He studies the etched drinking glass, wishing it contained something else. While it occupies his hands, its contents slake none of his true demons.

To his left is a wall of four windows each with heavy wooden slatted blinds to keep prying eyes from peering in. The other three walls are wainscoted with dark wood matching the blinds plus an ornate door off to the right. The floor is a burgundy carpet with khaki-painted walls rising to crown molding made of the same dark finish. Twelve chairs surround a long table, each with its own recessed light in the ceiling above. This lighting serves a purpose not intended by the ornamental chandelier over the table. It's solely for pretention, like his watch and stylish round-framed eyeglasses with no prescription.

The room harbors a wafting of power and intimidation, mingling with the expensive scent of the leather chairs. There's skeletons in this room, fifty years of deals struck, others killed, arbitrations won and souls crushed. It's like every legal conference room Eric's ever been in.

Except, like loss itself, it isn't. He's anxious, in over his head. He's from the other side of the lawyerly tracks, a *downstate* attorney in an *uptown* world. He's a coach lifer flying first-class for the first time, or maybe even private. With every sip he feels more like the conference room is a zoo cage. He's on display for all to see and it's feeding time.

Everyone peering into the cage knows his story. He heard the whispers, sensed the empathy. They're aware of his baggage, as certainly is Mr. McGraw. But for almost thirty minutes now the man who will determine his future is further taxing his resolve and his eagerness to get back in the legal game.

The wait isn't due to meetings running long, or something similarly lame. Initially he thought his former associate, Teddy Grimes, had arranged this afternoon out of charity. It's now apparent the conclusive interview is yet another test. He should expect nothing less from the firm's Managing Partner based on reputed pomposity alone. But Teddy had cautioned him J. Tyler McGraw would be the final meeting and would likewise have the final say.

Most lawyers would never tolerate such maltreatment. But Eric is no longer like *most lawyers*. His membership in that club died too on that day eight months back. He doesn't fully know this new as-of-yet-undefined version of himself, but he knows if he reaches for the flask in his pocket or gets up to head to a bar, he'll not be asked back. He has no idea of any topics to be discussed, or offers to be offered, but it's time to get back to work. Eight months is a long time with no paycheck and expensive single malts as a wingman.

I've often thought Eric's story to this point has a beginning, a middle and an end, like a play written in the three-act structure. In his life, there's the lead up to the loss, what dramatists refer to as the *Setup*. Act II is the *Confrontation*, which in his case is the loss itself. Immediately thereafter my character was introduced. It was the middle yet feel I know his story well enough to tell.

Finally, after his hundredth sip of water, the conference room door swings open. Our protagonist rises to his feet, brushing the dark hair from his forehead and self-consciously adjusting the frames of his fake glasses.

With little fanfare, the curtain rises on the final act, what playwrights call the *Resolution*.

So begins the end.

You'd better hang on.

ennings Tyler McGraw, Managing Partner at *Donaldson, Clements, Blaine & McGraw* is second generation on the masthead. His father founded the firm in Springfield, Illinois after clerking at the Nuremburg Trials. His were a huge pair of combat boots to fill, but J. Tyler holds tightly to those reins and has grown the firm exponentially since taking the big corner office. Don't think the top job was achieved by nepotism alone. He's led a colorful and distinguished legal career defending the private and public alike, companies with homes on Main or Wall Street. He's both a colleague of the heavyweights in the gilded class and the champion of those gazing up at them.

But while his accomplishments are lengthy and flamboyant, he's personally neither. He's smug and short, the hackneyed little man, small in stature, hoping to appear larger with an inflated self-importance. He enjoys being J. Tyler, but why shouldn't he? As he sees it, the world lay at his size-six shoes. He's a well-respected family man and long-time pillar in the community. An elder at his church, he sits on the boards of banks and charities, generous with both time and treasure. He's a *Type-B* personality surrounded by *Type-A's* who do the lifting. He thinks himself a great leader. This belief and his stature inspired the running joke among the local bar that Napoleon himself suffered from a J. Tyler McGraw complex.

So, when he entered the conference room dressed in a tiny three-piece suit which originally came with short pants, clip-on bowtie in place, Eric popped his cuffs and reached out a hand. I kid about the man's clothes solely to pile on about his diminutive size. In fact, his tie was ditched, his sleeves rolled to give the impression he toiled in the trenches even though he'd not set foot on any of the firm's lower two floors in three years.

Eric towered over the much older man as they shook hands, gazing upon his liver-spotted bald head. The strength of his grip belied his apparent frailty.

"Eric McKegney, it's a pleasure to finally meet you."

His voice too was surprisingly vibrant as he brushed aside formalities and introduced himself simply as "J. Tyler."

In the same throaty baritone he added, "This is Jillian Stennet. She's a senior associate, the true rising star in our litigation department."

I know from experience that when it's been some time since Eric's had a drink, he gets completely out of sorts. Things become tough. He begins to feel as if he's under water, fighting to find air. I recognize this because I've seen it often. His hyper-focus on one individual causes tunnel vision at the expense of others. People on the periphery become barely noticeable.

That's the only reason he failed to immediately acknowledge Ms. Stennet's presence, because despite her demanding deportment, she's a joy to behold. She strode in purposefully, commanding whatever chunk of the room had not already been chewed up by her boss.

She's an exotic beauty, somewhere maybe in her thirties, dark and hourglass shapely in a tailored hound's-tooth blazer with a tight pencil skirt accentuating long legs. She wears a frilly ivory silk blouse unbuttoned enough to draw stares and display a strand of matching pearls. Her hair is a dark wavy brown, knotted back in a casual chignon with a few rebel tendrils escaping over her right ear. She gracefully sweeps them back as she takes the chair on Eric's right.

It was late in the workday, but she looked amazingly fresh, bright lipstick, brighter teeth, perfect mascara, a cup of coffee in one hand. She's all purpose and businesslike as she set down the mug next to a folder and crossed her legs.

Eric simply nodded in her direction, obviously not seeing her. McGraw took the seat immediately to his left. After a quick exchange of pleasantries and a meaningless comment or two about the weather, Eric hustled to the heart of the conversation by thanking them for taking time to meet at the end of the day.

"Happy to do it, my boy."

At this McGraw paused and opened a manila folder, spreading sheets of paper on the table. Before Eric commented on this latest delaying ploy, the old man spoke in a slightly bemused manner.

"I've followed your career, enjoyed your TV commercials. Or at least I did before . . . Sorry."

Eric had to wonder when Mr. McGraw was either awake in the middle of the night or home in the middle of the day to see his old firm's ads. He'd never liked his role nor how he looked on TV, but according to the ad agency, the claim he personally investigated every case was believable. The ads worked. Research revealed clients often indicated TV as responsible for the business.

McGraw, regaining composure after his initial misstep, added, "In my day, you'd never see an attorney shilling himself on TV. Shows what a relic I am."

"You have to go where the clients are," Eric acknowledged in a quiet voice, repeating a line he used in defense of being *a lawyer who advertised*.

"That you do," McGraw said, continuing the pretense of studying his paperwork.

Finally looking up, he said, "If I looked like you, I'd get my face on as many TVs as possible. And billboards."

With nothing to say in response, Eric simply forced a tired smile, wondering when McGraw was going to get to the point so he could get to Happy Hour.

"I've paid attention to you, what you do and how well you've done it, long before young Mr. Grimes came to work for us. He speaks very highly of you."

"Thank you, Sir," Eric said softly before adding another remark solely to fill time. "Teddy's an able attorney. He'll be a tremendous asset to your firm."

"Ahh yes, but we are not here to discuss Theodore. We're here to discuss how you may be able to help us. And if we can reach an accord."

He again shuffled through the papers, making a dramatic show of apparently perusing every word on each. Hurry up and wait tactics grow annoying to a man desperately needing a drink. Eric drew a deep snorkel-like gasp from under the water and tried not to think about his flask, keeping his focus solely on Mr. McGraw. Soon the man was humming softly before speaking again.

"As mentioned, I know a lot about you and your successful Personal Injury practice. I was sorry to see it close. What I didn't know about you before today, I've learned from visiting with those to whom you've spoken."

He made a show of holding up several of the pages from his folder.

"I apologize for keeping you. Call it due diligence. These are samplings of a few recommendations on where *Donaldson, Clements* might best utilize your legal talents."

It was never his intent, but Eric scoffed at the comment.

"Sir, my talent is going after insurance companies. I appreciate your attempt to dress it up, but I was an *Ambulance Chaser* before. Now? I'm not sure . . ."

McGraw smiled at this blast of unbridled honesty, not seeing it as intended, instead brushing it off as an attempt at self-deprecating humor.

"Just the same, we have numerous possibilities for your services. I'd like to discuss one scenario with you, but first there are housecleaning items."

He asked, "Is your license to practice law still in good standing?"

"Yes," Eric said matter-of-factly, having earlier checked on-line.

"Are you caught up on your CLE?"

This is Continuing Legal Education. It's professional education and training for attorneys after initial admission to the bar. Subjects include ethics, diversity training and the like, needing to be updated biennially. There's also a module on substance abuse which might be calling his name.

McGraw didn't wait for a response, recognizing no answer as a *No* answer.

"I'll have someone check online to determine where you stand. I can't imagine it to be an impediment.

"Moving on to a new topic. Lawyers don't have conversations. Friends do. Attorneys don't. Now, we remain attorneys. To protect all involved, I trust you will have no problem signing an NDA before we go any further."

He gestured across the table and like magic a single 8-1/2 x 11 typed sheet of paper slid into Eric's circle of vision. He turned to discover its mysterious source and found himself staring into an incredible pair of smoky grey eyes. He squinted hard and subconsciously cocked his head as if to silently ask, *how long have you been sitting there?*

Jillian Stennet for her part seemed none too amused and held out a pen. Eric barely noticed; he was too busy giving her the once-over and doing a horrible job of disguising it. Here was a woman accustomed to stopping conversations in mid-sentence. He gazed into her eyes to the point of discomfort but couldn't get himself to look away. He was drawn to them the way men stare at rubies or pearls. They were similarly lustrous, a light grey, closer to silver. They offered both opaque nothingness and translucent possibilities. He was mesmerized.

Yet while they were a pleasure to gaze upon, he immediately did a mental one-eighty, curious as to what they might see when turned on him. If they were appraising, what did she see?

With no change in her indifferent expression, she wiggled the pen the way you'd gesture to an inattentive waiter to get your check after a tedious meal.

"We can go no further until you sign the NDA, *Ambulance Chaser*," she said, adding the nickname as a pejorative.

Eric completely missed the slight and continued to gaze upon her. She was phenomenal. Her complexion was dark, whether from the sun or the product of incredible genes, he couldn't tell, nor care. He thought about how her caramel coloring might contrast with any number of silk sheets. And what a body. She had curves so clearly dangerous you'd have to downshift to keep from losing total control. He wondered why she didn't come with a flashing warning sign.

Something was almost hypnotic about her, however, beyond her stunning appearance. She had a sublime toughness, a pouty edge. Whether natural or manufactured, it was like part of her wanted to smile, but wouldn't so it could never be misconstrued you had a chance with her. That was the first time he noticed her ability to both attract and repel. Of course, he completely missed it and would only recall it later when I reminded him.

His eyes then went to her pen. He'd not only forgotten his name, but also how to sign it. Her hands were beautifully dark, her fingers long and slender with French-manicured nails. Then he spotted the missing flashing warning sign. A huge diamond ring consumed her left-hand resting on the table. He realized then that the metaphorical door of possibilities was never even slightly ajar. Potential flicker doused. Highway crash averted.

Defiantly taking a Pilot pen out of the inside pocket of his suit jacket, he signed without even making a show of reading one word. He'd seen countless boilerplate non-disclosure agreements and knew this would be similar.

Once signed, he slid it back toward Ms. Stennet, expecting she'd get up to leave, her role seemingly concluded. He anticipated watching her walk out. Instead, she leaned back and crossed one remarkable leg over the other lightly bouncing her right strappy high heel up and down. The elaborate presentation was a treat unto itself.

Her expression quickly returned to disinterested, however, telegraphing the notion that she wasn't thrilled in the least with what was coming.

"Great. Thanks," McGraw said, as he slid his papers and the folder off to the side. Like Ms. Stennet, he leaned back in his chair folding his hands in his lap. His subtle smile suggested he was about to enjoy this more than his associate across the table.

"Now then, let's get to work."

Their offer could be best summed up in these few words: They wanted him to be an investigator. Contrary to the earlier theatrics and posturing about ways to use his legal talents, and all that doubletalk about his license and CLE, they didn't want him to practice law. He was being recruited as an investigator in a case McGraw himself was to defend and Ms. Stennet would manage. They wanted him part of their *"Dream Team."*

Despite Eric's protestations, McGraw kept referring to his former personal injury practice and the commercials about personally investigating every case. It wasn't quite blackmail, no implication if he didn't agree then something untoward might happen. It was meant to compliment while penalizing.

Eric mentioned he lacked an investigative license. McGraw replied none was required. Eric countered with why the firm couldn't use their normal investigators so he could be a lawyer. McGraw too was ready for this objection.

He explained that since it was years since he'd led a defense, only doing so as a favor to a long-time client, it was beneficial to have an additional set of lawyerly eyes going over everything. Ms. Stennet's gorgeous luminous grey pair would be the lead. This approach would also ease him back into the legal world without throwing him in headfirst. It all seemed to make perfect sense to McGraw.

Then Ms. Stennet took over and was forthright and firm, laying out the chain of command and Eric's place in the basement. She reiterated she was never in favor of this half-cocked idea but would work within its confines out of respect for Mr. McGraw. She conceded maybe a former attorney investigating could benefit the defense team. He would be allowed to offer opinions when asked but rarely invited to strategize. Her closing summation was if he didn't like it, there was the door, pointing to it with her damned pen.

She was probably the mean cheerleader in high school.

At this, McGraw smiled a crooked little smile and laughed almost proudly, "Juries just love her."

The case was a trumped-up conspiracy to commit murder charge brought by a local Federal Prosecutor who McGraw referred to more than once as an "eager and ambitious bitch." The founder of a local agricultural technology startup stood accused of conspiring with unnamed persons to do a bunch of nefarious stuff which may or may not have included murder. Eric could see the man's mouth moving but had drifted off long before. He'd be hard pressed to recount anything germane except for the abbreviated wording "Ag-tech."

For his part, McGraw had been less than forthcoming with the pertinent details anyway, choosing to read Eric in only after he'd officially joined the firm. That would happen the next morning with on-boarding and orientation.

In general, McGraw laid out the legal strategy they'd employ. I'll put this in normal English for all of you non-lawyers who might be reading. The plan was to mount an affirmative defense, in that they not only hoped to clear their client but also bring forth allegations against others. Since a conspiracy is an incomplete crime -- and there will be much more about this later -- it's hard to prosecute without using circumstantial evidence with broad inferences.

Conspiracy prosecutions involve numerous dots and how they do or do not connect. Therefore, the defense has to investigate them all, deciding which are vulnerable to attack. McGraw used a few flanking analogies and looking for soft spots and the dreaded *House of Cards* metaphor, saying they only had to determine the weakest card of the prosecution's case and when to yank it.

Eric feared they were positioning him to be under it when it fell and had this vision of his body on the ground, chalk outline around him, a sea of playing cards covering him. There was McGraw laughing and Ms. Stennet sticking her damned pen in his dead eye. But he couldn't get his flask into the metaphor.

But these concerns seemed superfluous. He was a personal injury attorney, not an investigator. And it didn't take a genius to understand he'd be reporting to Ms. Stennet. His initial read on her was "ball-buster." She had a genteel air and polished demeanor, brassy attitude with incredible looks. Eric knew without having yet seen her in action, that she got wins both in the courtroom and the bedroom. You don't become a rising star in a prestigious firm's litigation department at her age without results. Plus, McGraw probably specifically chose her solely to make himself look good.

Regardless of whether he was attorney or investigator, he'd work for her. It was going to be difficult to thaw the ice princess with the magnificent eyes and diamond ring. What was he wading into?

It was then he glanced toward the door, to where her pen had indicated, wondering if fleeing remained an option.

Yet at the same time, working directly on a trial with J. Tyler McGraw of *Donaldson, Clements, Blaine & McGraw* – Yeah! That McGraw -- would look great on his resume' regardless of the outcome. I knew it would get him back in the game, and based on the offer letter in the folder, they intended to pay him handsomely to be an investigator.

Ms. Stennet seemed disappointed he hadn't fled when given the chance. She set the boundaries. She'd never let a smooth pretty-boy lawyer disrupt the firm's hierarchy. Litigating a case with these two was fraught with problems. She'd hold the hand of the Managing Partner and babysit the *Ambulance Chaser*. She was the meat in this defense shit-sandwich and neither piece of bread had been inside a courtroom in at least eight months.

For Mr. McGraw, it might as well have been eight years, or maybe eighty. Local lore had it he was a lawyer's lawyer, the consummate negotiator who even at the height of his prowess rarely went to trial. He'd never seen a plea deal he couldn't sell to a client, or a settlement offer he couldn't settle.

And a former Personal Injury attorney would be more of the same. These two would be the biggest challenge of her career. If she could pull a rabbit out of this hat, Equity Partner with double stock options should be on the table.

When the meeting was over and no more questions, McGraw surveyed the faces in the room and realized if his *Dream Team* had any hope of success, these two would have to at least get along. He knew Eric was on board. His prized litigator, however, seemed to be wavering. She looked like she'd rather be any other place while assigned to any other case. But she was his glue. Without her, the whole arrangement falls apart.

She didn't have to like him. He didn't care if she could barely tolerate Eric, but he needed her to guide and manage him. But most importantly he selfishly needed someone to watch over his newest investment because he'd just offered a shit pot of money to a functioning alcoholic.

At the door, McGraw stopped and turned. Eric had earlier noticed the man had a way of asking a question to which he already knew the answer, and a unique tilt and dip to his chin to convey that fact. It had been on display during their meeting.

It was McGraw's subtle way of saying, "I know you understand exactly what I'm saying."

He did this little tilt and dip toward Ms. Stennet when he said, "No working late tonight. Why don't you take Eric to dinner?"

Dinner? The word exploded in Eric's ears. He didn't want dinner, and he certainly didn't want to have to sit and eat with this she-devil and her huge diamond ring. Even her name sounded pretentious. *Jillian?*

He needed alcohol and had never been opposed to drinking alone. It was odd, but he and I had learned that the longer the drought combined with the closer he got to getting his next drink, the more anxious he became. And now, here he was on the verge of finally coming up for air only to be going to dinner to be belittled.

For her part, she acted dismayed by the boss' suggestion.

"Tonight, sir?" Her tone implied there would never be a good night.

"Yes. Tonight. Now." Then McGraw's tone changed. "Why don't you two kids get out of here and get to know each other. We'll see you both back here in the morning."

Eric saw a man who seemed overly satisfied with this outcome. Was it because of his newly assemble *Dream Team*, or something else? Whatever, his expression seemed kind of creepy.

When McGraw was finally gone, Eric glanced again to see Ms. Stennet's jaded expression had returned. She waited long enough for the door to swing closed, guaranteeing privacy before speaking more to the room than to Eric.

"I guess we're going to dinner."

Then she turned those incredible eyes on him and swept those few unruly hairs behind an ear. Through a dangerously provocative squint and in a devious tone seldom used inside this building, she couldn't help but laugh. She had tried to stifle it, but a tiny squeak had escaped.

"If the firm's buying though, we're drinking dinner. You okay with that, *Ambulance Chaser*?"

It was like she'd offered him a scuba tank for Eric once more could breathe.

TWO

On their way to a little corner bar called Alford's, a tavern full of downtown denizens, there was little interaction. Ms. Stennet was on her cell, speaking about something pertaining to one of her cases to someone back at the firm. She adroitly navigated their path through the crosswalks, pointing and nodding with clipped directions. She would cover the receiver and say, "Left here," or "Cross now."

Entering Alford's, again with only a gesture, she motioned to two empty stools near the elbow of the L-shaped bar. She liked giving directions,

Still with the phone to her ear, she again covered the receiver with her other hand and said, "Order what you want. I need to finish this."

With this she walked toward the skinny back portion of the bar near the kitchen door for additional privacy.

As Boz Scaggs warned of a "Breakdown Dead Ahead," Eric watched her, as did every other guy in the bar. She remained professional, which reinforced that the call was business. All the while on the phone, she stared back toward him, as if he were the topic of conversation. He could imagine her whining to whomever about "Having to entertain the new dolt from the firm."

When the call was over, she arrived at the bar coincidentally right as the bartender set two drinks in front of Eric. She immediately reacted the way any liberated career lady lawyer might.

"Wait. I didn't ask you . . . I can order my own drinks. Moreover, I . . ."

Here her tone trailed off with the realization that neither were for her. In the large mirror behind the bar, she noticed the painful grimace on Eric's face. He'd been found out. She was unsure how to feel. She'd initially overreacted to his presumptive chauvinism but instead stumbled into something altogether messier. As she calculated how best to address this new situation, she quietly took her stool next to him and ordered a drink of her own.

The night was already off to a rousing start, the first few minutes providing all the evidence needed to confirm the office gossip. After being hopefully skeptical, she was left with no choice but to regard those whispers as fact.

She weighed her options as she watched a waitress set down a plate of wings on a bar table, the smell reminding her she'd worked through lunch. Deciding to approach this very casually, she ordered a glass of the house Merlot, asking if it was Happy Hour with *twofers*.

Not waiting for a reply, she added, "But I'll do mine one at a time, please."

The bartender either had years of experience or tremendous perception. She looked at Eric who shrugged sheepishly. She proved herself to be fast on her feet, nodding toward Ms. Stennet.

Michael McDonald's soulful baritone filled the silence as they waited for her drink, both trying to determine the best way to deal with what had occurred. Their thought processes trod down similar newly exposed pathways.

Eric, who was yet to touch either glass, felt embarrassed and guilty for being outed so quickly. How could he have been so stupid as to order two drinks at once? That was his go-to move when drinking alone. He realized now that he'd never have kept his secret from her but would've liked to retain some mystery. He had little recourse but to hope she'd be able to see it for what it was and assess it on a professional level.

Ms. Stennet realized her initial reaction added new layers of complexity. Was she a babysitter or A.A. sponsor? But this was the prearranged plan to have drinks rather than dinner to determine the extent of his problem. She felt more like his enabler. Whatever her role, there was this little thought forming in the back of her brain that this may be her way out of this sordid arrangement. If she reported the scope of the problem, she and Mr. McGraw could both rid themselves of the *Ambulance Chaser.*

But was that what she genuinely wanted? The whispers about his drinking had been proven true. So what? Did that also mean the stories of the recent tragedy endured would be likewise? She tried to smile and looked over at him, still staring into his drinks, yet to touch either. It was like maybe he thought they might bite, or worse yet, more sadly they already had. She felt no derision for him, only compassion and sympathy. And she vehemently denied it when I asked later, but there was this tiny part of her somewhere that thought she might be the one to save him from himself.

So, when her glass of wine arrived, the bartender again confirmed her prescient powers by not hanging around to chat. Ms. Stennet absentmindedly swished her wine before lifting it to make a toast.

"To good times at *Donaldson, Clements, Blaine & McGraw,*" she offered as they touched glasses.

"No. To you," said Eric, before adding, "Thanks."

"For what?"

She knew he meant her downplaying the whole *new hire is an alcoholic* thing, but nonetheless felt the need to play coy.

"You know."

"You want to talk about it?" she asked, slightly turning on her stool.

He took a big slug of Glenfiddich, with no more reaction than if he were drinking something as benign as iced tea. Her eyes were incredible, almost a dark grey now in the dim bar light as they beseeched him, waiting patiently for him to tell her how he'd sunk so low, begging him to relive the worst day of his life. He regarded all the ways telling his tale could go with no desire to drop this unseen curtain between them.

"Isn't there something else to discuss?" he finally said. "Maybe the case?"

"Sorry," she said almost immediately. "That's not why we're here. The boss wants us to get to know each other."

"But to do that, you'll have to know my story, right?" he said with another gulp of single malt.

She regarded his question, seeing the bartender bring new margaritas to the couple to her right, and then said with a grin, "How about I'll start then."

"Kind of an *I'll show you mine then you show me yours*?" he said as a mix of humor and deflection.

"Exactly," she said, smiling demurely. She checked her reflection in the big mirror behind all the bottles and swept those same few strands of dark hair behind her right ear.

"Where to start? Born in Naperville. Big family. High School valedictorian. Graduated Northwestern with honors. Top of my class at University of Chicago Law. Joined *Donaldson, Clements* right after graduation. Passed the bar on the first try. Currently Senior Litigation Associate with an eye on Partner within two years."

Very self-satisfied with her performance and how her bona fides always sounded regardless of the setting, she sipped her wine somewhat arrogantly and challenged him with, "Your turn."

"Me? My story's pretty much word for word the same. Replace Naperville with Carlinville, Northwestern and Chicago with Eastern and Southern Illinois. Oh, and I eventually passed the bar after a few tries. Plaintiff's Attorney for seven years. Now I'm a big-time investigator for *Donaldson, Clements*."

"You're right," she said, watching her own haughty expression and the blooming of a sardonic smile in her reflection in the big mirror. "Almost word for word. How have our paths not crossed before now?"

"I'm younger than you." He slid his empty glass out of the way, watching her sarcastic laughter in the mirror. "I am," he stated in a forceful manner. "I just turned thirty-four. You're four years older."

"And just how did you deduce that, Mr. Big-time Investigator?"

He let her worry for a beat and then unveiled his talent for deduction.

"Making Partner by age forty is one of those benchmarks proper attorneys use to validate themselves. In personal injury it's judgement amounts. You said you want to be there in two years. That's a specific plan. Five years would have been more of a generic goal, like a couple. But you didn't say "a couple." You said, "Two." Two sounds like a plan. I do the math. Forty minus two equals thirty-eight."

She had to acknowledge his ability to connect a few randomly spaced dots was impressive, but she hung onto her noncommittal expression. So instead, she nodded somewhat approvingly and lightheartedly placed her left hand with the French manicured nails and the big diamond on his right forearm as it rested on the bar.

In a playful tone, she admitted, "That was good, but now let's test your powers of observation. Tell me something about me, Mr. Holmes."

He knew he was being played. Any laudatory comment or literary detective reference was dubious at best. Nonetheless he smiled, accepting her challenge. He spun on his stool and considered how to deliver a response in terms of political expediency. Did this call for over-the-top fawning and flattery, empty praise for its own empty sake?

He removed his fake glasses and looked her up and down slowly and deliberately, thoroughly enjoying the journey while nibbling on an earpiece of the frame. She sat still and professional, almost as though posing for a photo or portrait, hands in her lap, legs crossed.

"You want me to be honest?"

"I'm a big girl," she said, with a flirtatious grin. "What've you got?"

When he began his theories and possibilities about her, she was equally amazed by his thoroughness of forethought as his candor and accuracy. He held nothing back.

"My impression of you back in the conference room is different because I've now seen you away from work. I'm thinking you're so formal and serious in the office because it's expected. Your walls are always up, especially there. You're the ball-buster like you were with me. And you're good at it; you play the part well. You're an incredibly good-looking woman in a man's world, so you hate that everyone sees your lofty status as a result of your perceived skills while on your back."

"You really just said that?" she half laughed, half gasped but with no hint of embarrassment.

"You wanted honesty," he said with a smile.

"Yeah, but more of a PG-13 version. There are other people around."

Eric chuckled at this, noticing that there were indeed other men at the bar and seated at nearby tables suddenly paying an inordinate amount of attention to their conversation.

"My apologies. I'll tone it down a bit. But this does lead me to the ring. I don't think you're married, only engaged. If you were married, you'd also have a gold band. Plus, I doubt the puritanical Mr. McGraw would have asked a married woman to take me to dinner. Nor would a married woman have turned it into drinks. Maybe you were married before and your job ruined it.

"Nope. I'm sticking with engaged and possibly to someone not in town. I'm guessing maybe it's a long-distance thing and that's why you often work late. He hates it that you can't be together, but you have high-powered careers, so you do what you must. Besides, you're only thirty-eight. There's plenty of time to be together."

"I have yet to admit to that being my age," she protested with a great deal of conviction.

"Lastly, you strike me as the kind of woman who will hyphenate her maiden and last names when you do get married. That way everyone can continue to connect you to the accomplished person with the achievements and accolades you so proudly mentioned. You know, like Jillian Stennet-McKegney."

She jolted upright on her stool and said, "Aren't you getting a little ahead of yourself?"

"No. I'm sorry."

He quickly scrambled into damage control, awkwardly turning back to the big mirror, his face the picture of humiliation. After a beat, he swept the dark hair from above his brow and added, "I threw that out as an example of a hyphenated last name. I truly meant nothing by it. I was not implying . . . It was stupid. I apologize."

She laughed at his embarrassed reaction. "That's okay. Call it my way of getting even for your speculation about my horizontal career skills."

After a beat she asked, "Are you always so serious?"

He exhaled audibly at this and watched a wide smile spread across his face in the mirror. He had been *so serious* because he was noticing clues and cues, and logically linking them in a coherent stream. And then she busted him. He liked a girl who could give as good as she got. The bittersweet memories of one such girl turned his expression more forlorn.

She saw this transformation in the big mirror and asked softly, "You okay?"

"Huh? Yeah," he said, before adding, "I thought for a second there I may have screwed this up. I'm thinking tonight might be fun . . . That working with you might be too. I hope you're not offended."

"Not at all. And without inflating your ego, you were close on almost everything you said."

He instantly perked up again. "Really? What did I miss?"

Rather than answer, she smiled flirtatiously over the rim of the goblet in her right hand while once more patting his forearm with her left. Whether it was to console him or simply to remind him of her big diamond he'd never know.

She took another quick sip for the added courage and plunged ahead. "Let's talk about you. If half the stuff I've heard is true, you have my sympathy."

"I appreciate that," he said quietly and humbly.

She turned and intently studied his profile, again with a hand gently on his arm, she said, "I'd like you to tell me what happened."

He finished his second drink, again reacting as if it had been nothing more biting than warm tap water. Without turning to look at her, he confessed to the big mirror, "I didn't always drink like this."

The mirror spanned the length of the bar, the edges trimmed with two gold lines about the thickness of painter's tape that crisscrossed in a geometric pattern high in the corners. He stared at them, regarding those lines and his story to be like a Mobius strip. Where did it start? Where might it end?

He normally tried to lighten the mood with woeful attempts at humor to duck and dodge the truth about his drinking. Tonight seemed different, so his approach was likewise.

"It's humbling that something can totally control you the way this does. Something inside me is broken with no idea how to fix it. It's like I'm smashed into a gazillion pieces. Liquor is the glue holding me together, keeping more pieces of me from falling away. I feel as though I have no control over it."

Jillian would tell me later that his remark both amazed and saddened her. She didn't see humility in him, however. Nor was it shame or embarrassment. She said it was honesty, more of an acceptance of a fact.

"I want to understand how you got here," she whispered.

He turned to face her and to gaze into the shimmering depths of those eyes. In the light reflected off the mirror they now appeared almost to be light silvery blue, like the color of a chlorinated pool at night. Maybe it was time for a late-night skinny dip. But to do that he was going to have to be stripped naked.

"What've you heard?" he whispered, beginning to metaphorically undress.

She never intended to tackle the enormous elephant at the bar one rumor individually addressed at a time. Confirmed or denied. She wanted to hear it directly from him, a free-flowing narrative in his own words. This wouldn't happen in a question-and-answer format like a deposition. She decided she could hopefully get him started, like pulling the chord on an outboard motor to see if he might sputter initially before churning straight ahead with the details.

Drawing a deep breath, she yanked by asking, "Erin Haynes was your fiancé, right? The girl from the DA's office who was killed?"

THREE

I've been there on many occasions when Eric retells the story and it's never easy. Nonetheless the telling and retelling have become rote to him, divorced from any emotion or feelings because that's how he gets safely through it. He acts as if it happened to someone else, like he'd witnessed it from a detached, third-person distance. He'd flip to autopilot and continue to drink on cruise-control as the story vomited itself out. All he needed was someone to hold his hair.

But not tonight. She was engaged and involved, interrupting with questions as if he was on the witness stand. He should have expected nothing less from a fellow attorney. At first he hated the intrusions because he had intended to just spew out the whole story like always. Jillian would have none of that. She displayed empathy and understanding, and Eric recognized right away she was curious and concerned more out of sympathy than merely filling in any missing slats in any *Donaldson, Clements'* rumor mill.

"Erin died eight months ago in a car wreck on a Thursday night. She was resigning from the DA's office to join my firm. Then that Saturday night, the first one in September, we were to be married."

"How awful," Jillian whispered.

Eric grabbed for his new drink – he was ordering them one at a time now. He took a sip and said, "When she and I started dating, she'd just broken it off with Patterson Ritter, the lifestyle reporter for the local paper. The guy was good-looking and ran in all the right circles because of his job. I could tell Erin still had something for him even after two years, but it could be more about the places he could take her. They would see each other every now and then and she'd tell me about it, so . . . Anyway, she'd agreed to marry me. We were just two days away."

After another thought filled sip, he said, "He was driving the car."

"I'm not sure I understand," Jillian said.

"That night I get a text from Erin." This next part of the story never wavered. He solemnly recited her message verbatim. "Don't hate me. Just have to do this one last thing. Then yours forever. Love you."

"I'm still not following."

"Ritter was the one last thing she had to do."

Jillian tried not to react in any way he might notice, for she'd heard much worse, but this bit of frank news caught her unawares.

Eric continued, "The accident happened on one of those county roads out south of town. Are you familiar with the motel called Sangamon Suites? I guess it's a notorious *no-tell* motel with hourly rates. Ritter was rumored to have been there previously. They crashed just down the road. Where else could they have been going then? It was still evening. Toxicology showed that they were drunk when the crash happened. State Troopers called Erin's father. He called me."

Jillian was astute enough to realize in the previous eight months of telling this tale the obvious first objection would be to question facts not in evidence. Was that truly where they were heading and why? What proof was there? If it had truly been a sexual liaison, why not go to either of their homes? How did he know their actual destination? Her list went on.

Whether he'd jumped directly to the conclusion, she saw no reason to argue this supposition. He'd had eight months to reinforce this position. Questioning his beliefs now would benefit no one.

"Her text came at 6:30. She texted instead of calling so she wouldn't have to supply details. I'm guessing it was sent right about when they were leaving Café Fernando. I later found out they'd been drinking pitchers of margaritas."

The similarities were eerie in a way Jillian might never be able to explain. Here sat the two of them currently in a bar. It had to be approaching 6:30. This too was a Thursday night and the couple to her right were drinking margaritas. It was either fate at best, or a fateful anniversary at worst. Rather than bring any of these parallels to his attention, she chose a different tact.

"Were they both killed?" she asked in a whisper.

The question initially surprised Eric. He assumed everyone knew the Patterson Ritter portion of the story as it had been continually carried in the State Journal-Register. The man had barely survived, having been life-flighted to St. John's Hospital to undergo hours of brain surgeries. The newspaper kept up a daily vigil until he was finally out of critical condition.

Somewhat angrily, Eric snapped, "He's still alive, but a vegetable. He'll never walk again."

His visceral tone stunned Jillian. Nothing she witnessed to this point led her to believe he was capable of such loathsome thoughts. It tested the bounds of her empathy. She felt the need to give him an opportunity to detract what she hoped was simply an intoxicated comment.

"Is that really how you feel?"

Very soberly he replied, "It is. I hate him. I hate what he did. I'm glad he's suffering."

"Wow," she said more loudly than intended, her disappointment in him hard to mask. Was this the scotch talking?

She leaned in more closely to ask, "You have no compassion at all for him or his family?"

"He's paying for what he did."

She thought hard about this and weighed her next remark carefully and dropped the hammer.

"It appears you are too," she said in an evenly spaced cadence.

"With every drink," he said without hesitation, regarding her forthrightness as if it hadn't been yet another affront to his civility.

She needed to give him room to reign in his animas, but the geography, their tight confines of the bar, made that almost impossible. The only concession she could grant was time, so she took as much as she could, hoping he would return from this dark place. Right now, she didn't care much for him.

Eventually after some raucous laughter in the seating area of the bar had subsided, she asked, "Is there no forgiveness in you at all?"

Slowly he turned toward her and shook his head bitterly.

She regarded this and said, "Carrying around this much hatred is not good for you."

Eric exhaled in exasperation. "It's all I got."

Jillian considered that the loss of a loved one, combined with the timing and this level of hatred, could cause anyone to have a few drinks. And now, here they were eight months removed and those few drinks were a full-blown issue. Before she could dwell further, he began to drunkenly ramble about something which at first appeared to be totally disconnected.

"Then her family treats me like a leper at the funeral. They always liked Ritter. I hated him. They felt sorry for him. The man killed their daughter! It was a mess. I started having a few drinks just to get me through that first week. I didn't know my place, or if I even had one. Was I still part of the family or just an interloper? Would I ever have been part of her family?

"They had each other and I had no one. Oh, I had lots of friends and people checking on me and bringing me casseroles. But they quit coming by. They couldn't figure out why I couldn't just flip a switch and get back to my life.

"I completely lost my place. Life became hard. I was walking around with this paranoia I couldn't shake. It was like waiting for the next bad thing to happen. So, I drank to drown those irrational fears only to have it turn out the next bad thing to happen to me was the drinking.

"I got drunk all the time. Then once I finally got past the blackouts and the puking and the hangovers, all my friends drifted away because I went from being the funny drunk to a sarcastically mean one. And my work went to hell right when my life did. I completely dropped the ball on one of my cases and screwed it up.

The client sued. My Errors and Omissions coverage had lapsed. I tried to countersue because I'm hard-headed and that's what I do; I sue people. Then soon my lack of E&O took the business. Ritter took everything from me, and Erin had turned out to be his accomplice."

"That's not fair," she protested, mindlessly rushing in to defend someone she didn't know, doing so more out of sentimentality than fact.

His defiance had dimmed when he softly asked without attitude, "Isn't it?"

She watched him down the remainder of his third Glenfiddich and motion to the bartender for another. Somewhere and somehow his alcohol-fueled fall from grace made sense if she chose to give him the benefit of the doubt. The timing and the circumstances alone would be a double gut-punch unlike most could weather. That alone, not counting the loss of his business, would cripple many. Yet he'd survived, staying upright, although severely medicated.

What was she missing? Everybody loses somebody. Why then did this feel so different, so unlike any other loss she'd encountered? It was eight months. He was no better now than back when it happened. In reality, he was worse. She couldn't help wondering why he'd been unable to trudge forward when others in similar situations before him had.

Then he told her something he'd never before admitted to anyone but me.

"Weeks before the wedding I had doubts and jitters. I was scared. Marriage and snakes I guess are two things I'm scared of. Was I doing the right thing? What will happen if I mess it up . . . when I mess it up? Was I good enough for her, or her family? I actually considered ways to get out of the wedding. One of the possibilities I actually thought about was . . ."

There it was. He felt responsible. He'd been unable to finish the comment, sniffling back tears and stemming them with the thumb and forefinger of his left hand. Jillian reached for his sleeve, feeling his turmoil, having seen her fair share of heart-wrenching confessions.

She knew he didn't possess the power to affect events, either for good or bad. But obviously Eric didn't see it that way. He'd selfishly negotiated for ways out and offered a few bargaining chips. The price for his freedom was too steep to pay. Yet he continues paying.

It made sense on a straightforward level, but she realized Eric himself could not yet understand. Maybe it was his closeness to the forest. Regardless of why he'd started drinking, it was now this guilt that caused him to continue. His drinking, in an ironic sort of twisty way, was his safeguard, ensuring that the guy foolish enough to once have bartered with God could never repeat the sin. A constantly inebriated Eric McKegney could never again betray anyone the way he perceived a sound and sober one had.

Yet even understanding the problem's root got her no closer to fixing it in the way that just knowing the disease's cause never immediately guarantees a cure. So, she wrapped her arm through his and drew him to her while trying to imagine herself in his shoes eight months ago. Would she have reacted any differently? He was a captive to his addiction, a prisoner to his remorse. Events never in his control had forced him near the cliff's edge, but it was guilt which had thrown him over.

Eric welcomed the warmth and tenderness of her gesture and the nearness of her fragrance. He leaned his head onto her shoulder and breathed her in, sniffling hard and dabbing at his eyes. He found comfort in her hold on him. He offered himself, bare, exposed, vulnerable and honest, and she responded with solace and kindness, and now a gentle upper arm embrace.

Never had his retelling of the story included this last brutally candid portion. He'd added it because he needed for her to hear his full confession. He wanted her to realize that any strength remaining was only as strong as his weaknesses, his emotional chain having many worn links. He appreciated her sympathy but didn't need it. Her understanding was more important, but not a requisite. And even though he was in no position to ask, he would admit to me later that he was seeking help. Anyone's help.

She stared at the two of them in the mirror and smiled to herself at the sight. She had her arm through the arm of a man she'd met only two hours before. They made quite a curious picture, the workaholic lawyer and the alcoholic investigator. And that's when the idea hit her.

She said his name in an urgent whisper as if waking him. This caused him to look up as she pulled away from the hug.

"Did you investigate the accident, like for all your clients?"

"That was just a line in those commercials," he argued curtly, as he had in when McGraw referenced his previous investigative experience.

"That's not . . ."

"And learn what?"

"Discover what really happened."

His tie had been ditched since they walked in and his glasses were still on the bar, so he looked disheveled and sounded worse. But at this new topic of conversation he righted his posture to where he looked almost lawyerly.

"I tried but it was too soon. I couldn't distance myself." He let this thought hang there and then explained, "What's the first thing we tell clients? You need an attorney to look at this rationally, without emotion. I could never get past that to examine it judiciously."

"It's been eight months. Look again. You're a big-time investigator now."

He regarded her idea for a second or two and said almost as if thinking aloud, "And I'm pretty much out of emotion."

"There's your distance," Jillian said with an encouraging grin.

"Okay. So, what then am I looking for?"

She wondered if he was serious. "The truth, for what happened."

"I was going to say that," he laughed, dabbing at the last of the tears in his eyes. "Eventually, once I incorrectly guessed *Somebody to sue* and *Some way to profit*, I was going to guess that."

Her hand with the big diamond was back on his forearm when she smiled and said, "Maybe Mr. McGraw has given you a tremendous opportunity by asking you to be an investigator. Maybe you're now far enough removed to gain some perspective and do some good."

Jillian's suggestion came right when the bartender delivered another single malt to Eric and her second glass of Merlot. She thanked the girl and noticed that Eric did not immediately reach for his scotch even though his other glass had been emptied for some time.

"Maybe so," he said somewhat pensively, having given her idea a great deal of consideration.

In his mind, he was running over how best to proceed, and which evidence might have survived the eight months. There were plenty of old dots, but which might still connect, and which might be a waste of time. This was beginning to sound a lot like McGraw's strategy for the conspiracy case he was hired to work. But for all the similarities, there was one huge difference.

Maybe he didn't want to find the truth. Maybe his personal belief of what had transpired and *why* was all he'd ever need. He'd come to tentative grips with it for the past eight months. What if he discovered something different? Then suddenly would he not feel the guilt which had consumed him? Would he not miss Erin? Would he be able to hate Ritter any less? Would he be strong enough to relive the last eight torturous months of his life?

Jillian watched his inner battle in the mirror. She realized if she were going to help him at all, she'd need to keep him occupied. Idle hands would be stirring drinks. At present, there might not be enough on the ag-tech conspiracy case to keep him busy, but also investigating Erin's accident might. She would just have to continue prodding him.

He glanced at her smiling face, the perfect teeth, the dark complexion, and couldn't believe that his newest friend would turn out to be a woman, nor that she would look like this. Her eyes had been incredible all evening, but he had gained a new-found appreciation for the person behind them. Those mirrors to her soul were nearly translucent, but Ms. Stennet was not. There was substance and depth to her that reminded him a lot of Erin. That recognition saddened him yet made him smile at the same time.

Eric raised his new cocktail as a toast. He spun on his barstool and offered, "To the future *Mrs. Stennet Hyphen Somebody*. I completely misjudged you. For that I am sorry."

"Apology not necessary, but accepted," she said with a wide grin.

"It's necessary. Thank you for tonight. For the drinks, the friendship. You're an amazing woman."

They touched glasses and Eric added, "*Mr. Somebody*'s a lucky man."

She gave him an expression he'd not yet seen, maybe somewhat forced, almost uneasy or unsure he thought. She nibbled subconsciously on her lower lip almost as if lost in thought. Then, as quickly as it had flickered, that spark of indecision was gone, the gorgeous eyes again widened.

Proof that her sass and attitude were back, she tilted her head to the right and said, "He knows."

Eric studied their reflections again in the big mirror wrestling with a new dilemma. On a night when he had unburdened himself, telling her everything, why had she apparently chosen not to reciprocate in kind?

FOUR

*I*t was almost 11:00 by the time they leisurely strolled the lighted downtown streets of the Illinois capitol back toward the firm. There was already a warmth in the air for the first week of May, the quarter moon gliding through a cloudless sky promising the blast-furnace of Midwestern humidity only a few calendar rows away.

And just as the seasons were changing -- and there was nothing any of us could do about it -- Eric felt euphoric that the same could be said about his life. He thoroughly enjoyed the night, for after months on the sidelines, he was finally back in the game.

Yet at the same time, while on the topic of change, he knew things between them would be different in the morning. Their respective worlds had collided, one veering from a controlled and comfortable planetary orbit and the other from whatever would be considered the complete contrary trajectory. It had been both random yet measured, quite unlike opposites attracting, even though they were opposite in many ways. And dare I say, attracted in even more. It went without saying, however, tonight was a one-night thing; when the sun came up, they'd be back to lawyer and investigator.

And there was nothing we could do about that either.

They sat and drank, singing along with George Michael and Billy Joel, Queen and Foreigner and other bands whose names neither could remember. There were also country songs and drinking songs, the few remaining patrons singing in unison.

They moved the fun to the more secluded confines of a vinyl booth. It wasn't like they had any intention of doing anything untoward. It was just that with each goblet of Merlot, the louder and looser she got. Her chignon had surrendered, her hair down past her shoulders, wavy loose and luscious. Soon the hound's-tooth blazer had been folded next to her and the ivory blouse was a bit more unbuttoned and untucked from the tight black skirt. The shoes were off in the booth, and somehow one was missing.

She'd never gotten out of control or flirted with the edges of propriety. It was nothing like that. With all her laughter and sexy confidence came added unwanted attention from Eric's competition around the bar. It was like *Ladies' Night,* and she was the only girl.

She was having a type of fun long overdue. Tonight, her feminine energy took over so she could enjoy herself. She no longer had to pretend being one of the guys, a woman in a man's world. It was as if her true self had been hidden behind her masculine energy lawyer persona for too long. Once a few drinks drug it out, it was *Out!*

I couldn't determine which was enjoying themselves more.

Not that she requested nor expected it, but with her getting to be *the girl,* Eric became *the guy,* playing her protector. With this new-found responsibility came a level of tortured quasi-sobriety.

Normally his drinking takes him from *zero-to-sixty* in mere minutes until he eventually sets the cruise around *one hundred.* Think of it this way. If *zero* is stone-cold sober and *ten* is the drunkest you have ever been, Eric McKegney lives life at *seven-and-a-half.* Tonight, though, wasn't about him. Alcoholism, by definition, is selfish, similar to suicide or masturbation. On this night, he sensed something much bigger was in play.

These events had combined to strike him curiously. They were still relative strangers regarding the clock, yet there was some kind a deep-down connection rarely formed in a mere few hours. Whether it was to be classified as new boss to new employee, new friend to new friend, or even novice drinker to skilled drunk, if she felt the same mattered little. If she felt anything was not relevant at all. She still wore the big diamond, and for tonight at least, he'd had her back. He rather liked the way chivalry fit.

Once seated by the window and away from the prying ears and eyes of the others at the bar, they ordered food as the kitchen closed.

Jillian switched to coffee, but it didn't hamper the fun nor damper the conversation. They talked about growing up wide-eyed as opposed to being bloodshot-eyed grown-ups. There were stories of college life in the bars regarded in hindsight as dangerous and reckless by present members of the bar. They talked about their friends and families, their hopes and dreams. And they talked about Erin.

No topic was off the table, save for one. Every time Eric would dance around *Mr. Somebody*, she would deflect and distract.

Jillian has an amiable relationship with words, as do most litigators, and she was adept at fending off questions while offering nothing of significance. It was like a fencing match. He'd thrust. She'd parry. He'd thrust again only to be parried again. Nobody scored any points and soon they were laughing about a completely different subject.

There was a healthy lawyerly competition to their stories, an unstated game of legal one-upmanship. They bragged about courtroom victories and inflated their respective won/loss records. Eric mentioned judgements won on behalf of his clients and Jillian judgements averted defending hers. It got to the point where I found it to be almost laughable. If Eric had a story with a judge in it, Jillian's next story would have two. If Jillian told a story that took place while snowing, Eric's next had taken place in a blizzard. I thought they'd argue about who walked farther to and from the courthouse in the snow uphill both ways.

But now there was no snow as they walked side by side on a level sidewalk. He sped up a step and gracefully turned to dance a few backward steps in front of her. She giggled at the sight as it reminded her of a Michael Jackson video in terms of the visual, certainly not the choreography. Jillian's prim self had returned, blouse re-tucked, blazer on, except leaving the hair down. And she'd found her missing shoe, but rather than put them back on, she walked barefoot and carried her heels by the straps.

"What are you doing?" she asked, watching him with a sense of delighted exasperation.

She thought he was cute in a floppy-eared lost puppy kind of way. Maybe he'd eventually find a home at *Donaldson, Clements*. She'd be okay with his sticking around after this first trial was over. He seemed sharp and relatively harmless. She liked the fact that he had not made a pass, notwithstanding the "skills on her back" comment. But in the eyes of HR, that was closer to sexual harassment than an overt pass. And he could certainly make her laugh, a luxury thought to have been left behind long ago.

She also appreciated the way he seemed to be watching out for her. She told me she noticed, finding it comfortable with a guardian. And he'd been nothing if not polite, a true gentleman. She expected more of the same upon parting in a few minutes, and likewise if questioned in the morning.

"Why is the estimable Mr. McGraw personally handling this case?"

The question surprised her, but not to the point that she couldn't answer. "The reason he told you is not one-hundred percent accurate."

"About the ag-tech CEO being his friend?"

"Are you familiar with Thomas Gradeen?"

"The CEO of Agri-Illinois, big holding company for farms and chemical companies? He's a real civic heavy-hitter around here."

"That's him. Mr. McGraw claims they're friends, but I get the sense of late that maybe things aren't so rosy between them. It's actually his son, Jameson, who's our client.'

"Wait! Jameson, like the Irish Whiskey? I might be perfect for this."

Jillian couldn't help but giggle at his enthusiasm.

"Yep. He's a tech whiz kid. The federal indictment is against him."

"Federal? Why federal? Murder is a state crime."

"It's murder-for-hire. Under *18 U.S.C. 1958(a)*, it becomes federal when you cross state lines with intent. Conspiracy violates the same statute."

This is commonly referred to as the murder-for-hire statute, which makes it a federal crime. And thus enters Mr. McGraw's protagonist, Federal Prosecutor Cynthia Forrester.

Jillian pointed upon entering the pedestrian gate to the garage. "This way."

There on the ground floor of the immaculate garage were two cars – a 2015 BMW 640i four-door Gran Coupe convertible, Alpine white with black moon-shadow ragtop, and an older nondescript pickup parked right by the elevator. As identified by a decal on the door, it belonged to the janitorial service. This meant the $65,000 BMW was hers.

As they walked the distance to her car, Eric's voice echoed in the concrete parking structure when he asked, "Do you litigate trials with the partners?"

"Most are solo, or with James Petrie. He's General Litigation Partner and my direct boss. Every strategy, every decision, every plea offer goes through him. He signed off on my new arrangement."

She unlocked her car with the key fob, the high-pitched beep ringing off the concrete walls.

He said, "Mr. McGraw running a defense at this stage of his career is rare. You as second chair for any partner except your boss seems odd. Throw me into this mix as an investigator." Here he surrounded the word with air quotes, and said, "We're miles outside the box."

She flashed an incredible smile, one widening her amazing eyes instead of squinting them, and tilted her head to one side.

"You sure you want to be a part of this?" she asked.

He never wavered in the least. "I need a job," he said with a shrug.

"I'm glad." She looked away and then back, realizing the *Visitors* parking spaces were vacant.

She asked, "Where did you park?"

He blushed a bit in embarrassment while saying, "I don't drive too much anymore. Let's just say I have a problem which doesn't mix well with driving. And it's not texting."

She respected the remark on two levels. He was responsible enough not to get behind the wheel but also assure of himself enough to joke about it. This drew a smirk of appreciation from her.

"Do you need a ride . . . or something?"

She'd later tell me how stupid the question must have sounded, wondering why she felt the need to add "or something."

But there was *something* about this guy that unnerved her, threw her off balance. She wasn't sure how she felt about that. Eric McKegney turned out to be fun and was certainly handsome, and therefore dangerous.

He smiled and answered, "You know what? There's nothing I'd like more than a ride in that car. You need to get home and I must be at work at 9:00. Lately I don't get up that early unless I have a tee time."

"Are you going to take an Uber or walk home? Do you live nearby?"

"No. I take cabs. A lot of cabs. I have a standing deal with Springfield Cab Company. I get frequent rider miles redeemable for merchandise."

"Springfield Cab Company has merchandise?" She leaned against her car door, suspiciously looking him over. "Tonight was a lot of fun. Thanks."

"No. Thank you. Thanks for listening and not judging me."

"Oh, I was judging you."

He dug his hands into his suit pants pockets and said, "I think you know what I mean."

"If talking about Erin helped, I'm glad," she said. "She sounds amazing."

"I appreciate your saying that."

She smiled and shrugged without saying anything further.

"Look. I know I have a long way back, and it's not going to be easy. You helped me take a big first step tonight. I really appreciate how delicately you handled it." Here he smiled and wiped at the hair on his forehead. "And I too enjoyed myself."

"Maybe tonight was good for both of us," she said almost as an afterthought.

Eric stuttered the beginning of his next line, struggling with the blending of several metaphors.

"I have my share of demons yet to slay. Every day for the past eight months has been like wandering aimlessly through a mine field. I'm a fragile man, a damaged man. I'm the butterfly with the broken wing, but tonight it felt like I got to be the old me again. And with a girl."

Neither could help but react to this comment. She laughed at his sour facial expressions while delivering it and he at the ridiculousness of the line itself.

She stepped away from the car and stood right in front of him, looking up and regarding the dark eyes blinking back from behind the glasses. His long brown hair was mussed and the stubble from a long day was thickening. He was easy on the eyes, but there was likewise a sincerity about him that she liked even more. He pulled no punches. He'd been truthful in his perceptions of her and even more brutally candid about himself. He was who he was, and while not proud of this latest version, she found his earnestness and decency welcome in a world where she experienced little of either.

Still in her bare feet, she bounced up on her toes and gave him a peck on the left cheek.

"I think we might make a decent team."

"I hope I won't let you down."

She turned to open her door, but rather than getting in the car, she hung there, the car door and her shoes in her left hand, the big diamond on display for all to see. Her keys were in her right.

"Let's you and I make a deal, kind of a parking garage pact. We both know Mr. McGraw is up to something. So no games, okay? No secrets between us. We're on the same team."

Never giving it a second thought, he replied, "You bet."

She reached out her right hand for Eric to shake and realized the keys would make that an unsafe proposition. She sheepishly weighed her options. Finding none, she smiled sheepishly. Soon she was behind the wheel, her keys in the ignition.

"You sure you're okay to drive home," he asked. "I could call my friends at the cab company."

"I'll be fine. Besides, what would I do with cab merchandise?"

"Oh no. You misunderstood. I'd still get the points and the merchandise."

The car was idling, the driver's window lowered. "Thanks again. I needed this, and I really enjoyed myself. And with a boy."

She mocked his earlier sour expression with one of her own causing them both to laugh.

From behind that million-dollar smile, she said, "I look forward to working with you."

"Me too. Thanks."

As she pulled away, the last thing she said through the open window was, "Same team. Right?"

"Same team," he said back loudly to be heard over her squealing tires.

As the sleek Beemer pulled up the ramp leading out of the parking garage, I remember thinking that neither of them had any inkling of how vexatious it was going to be sticking to their little pact.

In case you don't know, that word means *troublesome*.

FIVE

One time, when asked in my presence after golf how one gets from a few drinks to having a problem, Eric used yet another poorly-constructed metaphor, this one dealing with cough syrup. Bear in mind he remains adamant about the stark difference -- and great distance -- between a few cocktails and a problem. He'll never deny the linkage, however, nor dispute the steps are connected, for he's proof. Having traveled that distance, he's been shackled by that link for the past eight months.

But back to the analogy. He said it all starts with a tickle in the back of the throat which soon develops into a scratchy cough. You hope it goes away on its own, but when it doesn't, you treat it with cough syrup. Finally, you get to the point where the medicine allows you to sleep, because not sleeping is the worst part of having a cough. And after the cough is gone, soon you realize you mentally need the cough syrup before you can ever fall asleep again. You rely on it. You can't function through life without alcohol any more than you can sleep without cough medicine. When that *want* turns into *need*, it's too late.

So, for roughly the past eight months, his every day has begun with that little tickle in the back of his throat. And normally he treats it with a cough syrup that comes from Scotland, or Ireland or even Tennessee. Sometimes it's straight and other times in coffee. On this morning, though, he tried something different, for he wanted to attempt a relative level of sobriety for his triumphant return to work.

The liquor bottles above the refrigerator in the gourmet kitchen of his high-end townhouse called to him, but he ignored their siren song by lashing himself to the mast of keeping busy. I apologize for the overblown literary device, so let's just say he showered and shaved, picked out another tailor-made dark suit and even polished his cordovan Italian loafers. He made coffee and ate toast, without any hint of alcohol as part of his new temperate approach.

Now while he awoke overly optimistic because he wasn't hungover, he wasn't misguided enough to think he could just stop drinking because he'd decided so. Maybe 7-1/2 months ago this idea had merit, but now he had both a psychological and physical addiction; neither was going away just by play-acting neither existed. So, he prepared for his contingencies.

The flask would be in the inside pocket of his suit jacket. He knew he could visit a men's room and the privacy in the stalls. There would be a half-filled Glenfiddich bottle under the front seat in his car, and countless bars and liquor stores within walking distance of the firm's offices. His goal was to make it to lunch, but he knew even in a perfect world, it would be an hour-by-hour fight.

At 7:45 he backed his Jeep Cherokee out of his underneath garage to head into town. He never closed on the home he and Erin were moving into after being married, and he'd sold the home he lived in while engaged. He missed that place's proximity to downtown. He likewise missed the comfort and power of the late-model Audi Sedan leased by his firm, returned to the dealership when the business went away.

The streets in downtown Springfield are named for our early presidents. There's Washington, Adams, Jefferson, Monroe, and Madison, but not in chronological order. But while the streets are named for the founding fathers, most of the buildings and attractions have a connection to Springfield's favorite son and our sixteenth president. Abraham Lincoln's life and history in the city are hard to miss.

Within walking distance of any surface parking lot are six of the seven most-visited of his tourist sites. There's his Presidential Museum and Library; his humble home and his church; the Old State Capitol and Lincoln-Herndon Law Offices; and the Great Western

Depot or Lincoln Depot where he began his journey as president to Washington. The seventh is north of the town, Lincoln's Tomb at Oak Ridge Cemetery, the second-most visited cemetery in the nation after Arlington National.

But his influence doesn't end there. There are statues and monuments, walking tours and driving trips. His silhouette from the penny is everywhere, on billboards and banners, buses and cabs, while his name is on hotels and parks, restaurants and diners. It's not tricky to tell which *Springfield* you're in.

Springfield, Illinois is Lincoln; Lincoln is Springfield.

The firm *Donaldson, Clements, Blaine & McGraw* sits in a sprawling rectangular building on Adams that controls a whole city block of downtown. The firm is not the only tenant, but the largest, taking up the top three floors of the seven-story structure. Eric announced himself to the well-dressed men seated behind a huge desk in the lobby that looked like something out of mission control. They checked a video screen, as had been done the day before, and directed him to the elevators down a marble hallway just off the spectacular glass atrium. And like yesterday, one of the guards, decked out in a uniform of grey slacks, white shirt, red tie, and navy blazer rode up with him, so he could use his security credentials to operate the elevator.

He arrived early, beginning life at the firm filling out paperwork in the main reception area on *Five*. The onboarding went fast, the orientation faster. Both were handled proficiently by firm staff, yet Eric had contemplated reaching for the flask before barely one hour.

A dour looking lady who may have been old enough to know the original Mr. McGraw, handed him a thick three-ring binder, the firm's policy manual. There was a sheet to sign acknowledging he'd read and understood everything. She expected it back by the end of the following week. Good luck with that.

He was provided an Apple iPhone and an HP Pavilion laptop, plus a security badge on a lanyard to wear when in the building. It already had his photo on it. How'd they manage that? He recognized the photo as his headshot from his old firm's website. He was told these credentials would also get him into the offices on nights and off-hours.

When finished in HR, security escorted him up a back stairwell to the top floor where yesterday's meeting with Mr. McGraw and Jillian had been, the *Executive Level* and his new home. The young guard, whose nametag identified him simply as *Smith*, led him to a room at the opposite end of the expansive floor. This one was all glass, a window to the outside world on oner side and glass showing the inner offices on the other. The spacious room would be his office.

Even though it seemed large, it was Spartan and metallic, almost stark and antiseptic. The rich woods from yesterday were now rusting metals and the thick carpet a Berber looking though it could wear equally well indoors or out. The room appeared to be more storeroom than an office, the wall of the inside glass neatly stacked with banker's boxes. There were fifteen to twenty, all labeled in black marker with some innocuous numbering.

The guard stood patiently in the doorway while Eric unpacked, using a smudged glass table for his desk. He found floor sockets to plug in his laptop and charge his new phone while testing the rolling chairs to find one without a missing wheel. There was a metal cabinet with pens and legal pads and assorted supplies, plus a large rectangular white board on an easel.

Once Eric was situated, the guard asked if there was anything further he could do. Smith carried a precise military manner about him, complete with the buzzed haircut and clipped cadence to his speech. He wore an earpiece, but thankfully no sunglasses.

Eric thanked him for his help, and the guard nodded in return. His place in the room was taken by a bearded guy in his early twenties about half Smith's size. This guy didn't look like security, nor did he dress the part. He wore an untucked white short sleeved shirt ill-fitted to accommodate a necktie, but he'd tried even so. He introduced himself as Shane West, overseer of information technology and cyber security. He did look *that* part, with the scraggly beard and taped horn-rimmed glasses, like he walked right out of central nerd casting.

But Shane West undeniably knew his stuff and explained the importance of informational security in today's legal world. He connected Eric's laptop to the firm's virtual desktop infrastructure and set up his email. He took the iPhone to show where all the firm's employees were grouped in *Contacts*. Lastly, he downloaded an app on the phone which randomly generated sequential number and letter passwords to get on the web.

"Wait," Eric said. "My password changes?"

"Not technically," West replied without looking up from the HP's keyboard. "VDI basic encryption protocol mandates your logon changes every time. Your password only changes monthly. Our security apparatus also identifies who's on-line, when and what he or she might be doing."

"Kind of *Big Brother*-ish, isn't it?"

"Most definitely."

"What if I need to email someone outside the building?"

"You'll be able to do that. Internal firm to firm email need no encryption. Things sent externally should not have unencrypted attachments."

"Okay, but you also said you can tell what we're doing on-line. Who exactly is watching?"

"All information is gathered down on *Five*."

"Is that where you are?"

"Yep. IT is on *Five*."

Eric watched him play the keyboard like a piano virtuoso. Then he laughed to himself and asked, "So if I'm watching porn up here somebody down on *Five* will know?"

West never looked up from the laptop. "Can't happen. All of the good sites are blocked."

"The good sites?"

Eric glanced at his watch to see how he was doing on his sobriety goal of getting to noon. It was still two hours away. He realized he was never going to make it. First it had been the monotony of HR and now this guy who banged on the laptop keyboard so loudly that the click-clack echoed in his head. It had gathered quickly on him, closing him in, sinking him underwater.

He needed to come up for air.

He excused himself and ducked into the men's room, moving urgently like a guy with bladder issues. Luckily the bathroom was empty, no need for introductions or small talk. Once behind the securely locked door of a stall, he poured two gulps of single-malt smoky smoothness down his throat.

The heat spread throughout him, warming his insides. It was like a blanket had been thrown over his shoulders, the comfort, the relaxation enveloping him and further stoking the fire to generate added warmth. He sighed and let his body go limp, shaking out his arms to speed the coziness to his extremities. He no longer felt claustrophobic, sensing the room had expanded around him. His breathing slowed, his hair no longer so close together, as every worry in his world had seemed to be righted.

No matter how at-peace the booze made him feel, he couldn't escape the feelings of disappointment in self. And the guilt. He's a weak man; he'd failed almost too easily. He was only trying to make it to noon and he'd barely lasted three hours. This disheartened him, reminding him of the torturous length his road back would travel.

He splashed water on his face and stood motionless, calming himself with paper towels pressed to this face. He heard the bathroom door open and froze perfectly still, almost as if hoping no one could see him since he could not see them, like peek-a-boo played as a baby.

"Sir, you're good to go," said a voice he recognized as the IT technician.

"Huh? Great. Thanks for all of your help."

He finished drying his face, wadded up the many paper towels and tossing them into a large waste container right by where West stood. He then checked his tie in the mirror and straightened the security badge lanyard.

"I was coming back. You didn't have to come looking for me."

"You just looked a bit overwhelmed. I know the firm's VDI, and security can be a bit much. I get that. I'm just down on *Five* if you ever need me."

"Thanks. I'm sure I'll be taking you up on your offer."

"I can get you released, but I need you to pass a little test for me. Send me an email. Remember: everything starts with your phone. Get a password to get on the VDI and then check for my address in the contacts. If you can do that, then you're good to go."

West fell in line behind him as they headed down the immaculate hallway back to his office. The walls looked as if they had just been painted, with large and brightly colored artwork making it feel as if the bathroom was in an art museum.

West was still talking. "Once you send that email, you can get to work on the boxes."

Eric partly turned over his shoulder and asked, "What boxes?"

"Those seventeen banker's boxes in your office. Isn't the Gradeen case yours? As I understand, that's why Mr. McGraw assigned that room."

Seventeen boxes? Eric almost returned to the bathroom for another swig. He was to read and comprehend seventeen boxes of files? There wasn't enough booze in his flask or under the seat of the car for one box, let alone seventeen.

"Not to worry," West was saying, as they continued to walk together. "All of the case information has been scanned and electronic versions of everything will be available to you."

This was a relief. "Then what's in the boxes?"

"Photos or documents too big to scan, videotaped depositions and corporate reports, things like that."

They arrived at the door, Eric stepping back into his office and studying the boxes, while West hung back. How close were they to trial that they'd already accumulated enough discovery to fill seventeen boxes?

"All cases are retrieved from our intranet by the case number, but you will need the code I'll send you to view the electronic versions of info specific to your case. No one can access cases they're not working."

"This cyber security thing is pretty serious, isn't it?"

"Everybody else is doing it."

"What other security systems do you have? Are there cameras? And what's with the muscular security guys in the blazers? Do they work for the firm?"

West waited as if not sure the questions had finished, then smiled and said, "We have cameras, but most are in the common areas." Then less convincingly, he added, "I think they are monitored by security."

"Do they work for the building or the firm?"

"Yes and no. They work for the building, but the building is owned by the partners of the firm."

While Eric considered the extent of this, and the ramifications, West again cocked his head to the side and stared at him.

"These measures are in place for your protection. You attorneys say it's done to protect us, not to prosecute us."

Eric groaned at this because it sounded exactly like something stupid some inane attorney would say. While West apparently found the line amusing, he didn't appreciate how something so unoriginal gives every attorney a black eye. As if there aren't already enough lawyer jokes.

"You never know who might be listening and what they might do with that information."

Shane West was talking about people outside of the building trying to hack their way around the firm's firewall to steal information. For some reason, Eric seemed more suspicious of the prying eyes of those already on the inside.

SIX

O n many a late night, Eric and I have discussed his personality at length, more specifically whether it might be considered clinically addictive. It's safe to say, regardless of our diagnosis, there's a problem and he needs help. It's just that it seems as if he angles in that direction more out of expediency, or as an excuse.

In his mind, having an addictive personality would lessen his perceived weakness and resulting embarrassment. It would also serve as the basis for his susceptibility of having fallen so hard, so far. It's as if he wants to be regarded as sick and then pitied for it. It would be much more advantageous for him if that were indeed the case.

Now, bear in mind, I have no formal training, but I've spent time around people in his position. It's currently estimated only 10 to 15% of the population carries a personality trait that makes addiction more probable. These are people who don't know when to stop, when a few drinks equals drinking. That's not Eric. As I've mentioned, he's aware of the distinction. It's just some nights he can't tell. Plus, I can find nothing in the stories of his past that would indicate he's part of that percentage. And from everything I have heard about Erin, she'd never have tolerated his being addicted to anything but her.

Eric McKegney is a walking example of someone without a psychological bent toward addiction to become lethally hooked, nonetheless. His addiction is purely physical, in that his body would get deathly ill without booze. Now, knowing he'll suffer tremendous withdrawal when he does quit adds the mental component, the psychological dependency. It's as if he got his steps crossed, went in the wrong order. It wasn't a trait that led to his addiction; it's the other way around. Now, once addicted, he exhibits addictive personality traits.

I sometimes think of it as more of a superstition. This might be a cavalier description of a serious problem but think about it. He can function when he drinks, so he continues to drink so he can continue to function. It's survival. Being a superstitious guy, he continues a behavior which ensures continuation.

This and the personality trait discussion is more than my untrained mind can process. There are a handful of interrelated concepts with which addictive personalities -- or superstitions -- must deal. I added the superstition part to bolster my earlier argument. The personality trait list includes patterns, habits and impulse control, but Eric deals with, and has surprisingly almost mastered, another. And that is compulsion. Since he's become an alcoholic, he can throw himself headlong into new things without being overwhelmed.

He did it first with golf. He started reading books over the winter and soon had completely reconfigured his swing and began hitting the ball cleaner and scoring better than ever when spring arrived. Granted, golf has been called a drinking man's game, but it became compulsive to him. And for the better.

Three hours into *Case # 75-93654 US v. Agribotics Technologies* this was happening again. He dove into the electronic files and boxes of information and had yet to feel the need to come up for air. He was immersed and intrigued and deeply absorbed. This was all new to him, and while he'd never admit as much aloud, it was highly informative and almost fascinating.

He began by reading an overview of the modern-day Agricultural condition. With the estimation that today's world population of 7.3 billion will balloon to 9.7 billion by 2050, and the demand for organically-grown foods also rising, farmers are increasingly under pressure. Add to this the push to make farming and the planet greener, plus the fact that arable farmland is shrinking, the challenges are readily evident.

This is no new phenomenon; men down through history have battled with one version or another of this problem. One he came across, English cleric and scholar Thomas Robert Malthus, had argued back in the early 1800's that food supply grows arithmetically while the population multiplies geometrically. According to Malthus, whenever food supply increases, the population also grows in proportion to eliminate any abundance. Even today his principles factor into the overall equation.

Feeding the world is hard and only getting harder. It's time for technology to come to the rescue.

On that topic, Eric stumbled across the intriguing phrase *Swarm Farm* and searched the web for a definition. This is the hypothetical combination of two robotic technologies, namely sensors and agbots. Already available on the market there are air and soil sensors, crop sensors and equipment telematics which alert farmers to upcoming mechanical failure in farm machinery. And these machines, whether for tilling, plowing, planting or harvesting can be operated as agbots.

The air and soil sensor element of the *Swarm Farm* is already scientifically viable, and, as mentioned in a few of the publications, will begin to return investment dollars later this year or early next. Adding the robotic component with automated tractors and sprayers will not be financially viable for another ten years. This *Swarm Farm* platform is being pioneered by – Guess who? – Jameson Gradeen's *Agribotics Technologies*.

Their annual report was a perfect-bound, glossy book the size and shape of a catalog. It was professionally designed to make the shareholders feel secure about their investments with enough info to hopefully attract new stockholders. The flowery prose spoke of a company on the brink of breaking through the numerous barriers to profitability, while the financial statements buried near the back promised a different story, one of restraint and patience. They might be near the brink, but maybe loitering there for an extended period.

There was a full color professionally staged photo of Jameson Gradeen, a pretentious looking thirty-something with jet black hair and prematurely grey temples. He had a look both professorial and whiz kid, with the round wire-rimmed glasses of an academic and one of those ridiculous soul patches of a hipster. It looked like Hitler's moustache on the wrong lip.

His credentials, however, were no joke. University of Illinois undergrad with Agriculture Science major and Finance minor. He somehow also found time at U of I to get an Environmental Engineering bachelor's degree before going to MIT where he received a master's in engineering, with a concentration in Robotics. And if that wasn't enough, he then earned a Doctorate in Robotic Technology from the University of Michigan.

Eric searched *Agribotics Technologies* on the web and the first few hits came back about the pending legal action against their founder. Ironically, while this was the reason he was researching the company, he wasn't quite ready to get on that expressway yet. He felt the need to traverse a few more of the less-traveled contextual backroads.

There were stories about the father and son and their respective companies, *Agri-Illinois* and *Agribotics Technologies*. The two individuals and companies had made a personal impact on farming life in the United States, and Central Illinois more specifically. There were opinion pieces and editorials, most praising their business acumen and their willingness to test new products and technologies on surrounding farms free to the farmers. Father and son were magnanimous and not profit-driven, doing what was best for the farmers at the expense of what was best for their companies.

He found a specific three-year-old article about Jameson that compared him to the father, Thomas. Here was also a photo of the father. He had close-set eyes in a weather-worn face below a severe, graying widow's peak with fluffy hair on the sides. Think Grandpa Munster goes to Miami Beach.

The story was a puff piece from the State Journal-Register, lauding both as visionaries and philanthropists, yet contrasting their upbringing. Thomas had started as a family farmer in nearby

Edinburg and over the years bought other troubled area farms. Soon he had grain elevators. From there he acquired a chemical company for his pesticides and soon had built *Agri-Illinois* into an agricultural and chemical conglomerate. Because of this success, Jameson was a silver-spoon baby, who began working with his father when still in his teens. The experience gave him the drive to equal the father's success. The father's hardships and struggles were never visited upon the son.

The story went on to detail Jameson's educational bona fides, so the reader never got the inference that the boy had blindly followed a path the father had blazed. This would have been the simple approach, but Jameson was described as someone choosing difficult over the easy. His was a story of resiliency, of getting knocked down only to get back up. His chosen field was untried and untested, so there were several failures and resets, yet Jameson Gradeen and *Agribotics Technologies* were somehow still upright.

The piece was enlightening and well-written, in a style that stood apart from all the technical journal tripe of the other publications and other websites. There were insightful quotes from each man to give a better understanding of the firm's clientele. Both spoke to the future of farming, intending to be a driving force shaping it.

These intentions and dreams had been quoted during a charity event. That's when Eric first got that feeling like something had shattered his pelvis. He knew without looking that the story's byline belonged to Patterson Ritter.

Seeing the man's name sent him into an emotional spiral and soon he felt himself losing all focus. He did some quick math with the article's date only to realize Erin would still have been with Ritter when it was written. She'd more than likely been at the event on Ritter's arm. But strangely, these thoughts didn't anger him as much as they made him feel thirsty.

On his way to the men's room, he considered that there was still hatred for Ritter, but to a much lesser degree, now surprisingly tinged with admiration for his writing ability. He'd never say it aloud, but the guy was talented. He had a literary flair which may have been wasting away as the newspaper's society guy. And as a journalist, it appeared he was solid at gathering and organizing information, while his questions were profound and intuitive enough to elicit the responses quoted in the piece.

He thought back to one of the first times he ever saw Erin. Ritter had been there. It was right outside a courtroom across the street from the bathroom in which he now hid to drink scotch. He was on an errand to check out Erin Haynes, sent there by her sister. We'll get to all of that later, but Erin had been approached by this handsome guy who stood in a manner that demanded the whole world gaze upon him. The pretentious ass turned out to be Ritter.

And now as Eric returned to his office, the clandestine reinforcing ritual complete, he recalled how before Erin told him about her previous boyfriend, he took an immediate dislike to the man. He purposely went out of his way to avoid any of his articles or pay the man any attention. Before now he hadn't realized Ritter had talent, nor had he wanted to consider it.

A wise man once said. "Fate has a way of not letting you move forward without a reminder of where you've been, of not letting go until it's sure you know where it all began." Okay. I say that. I'm that wise man.

Eric turned a corner to see someone waiting for him outside the door to his office/storeroom. It was his former associate at his old firm, Teddy Grimes. Welcoming the distraction, Eric dashed ahead a few lively steps and shook Teddy's hand like long-lost friends. About my earlier *fate* over-romanticizing, here again was a vivid reminder of his past.

"You look good, Ted. How are things treating you around here?" Eric asked, glad to see a familiar face.

It had been months since they'd in fact seen each other, but they'd stayed in contact. Remember: Teddy's responsible for setting up yesterday's meetings. He looked like the harried attorney he was, with a stack of papers either on his way to or from a copier /

scanner. It was early afternoon, but his tie was already ditched, his long sleeves rolled up to the elbows.

Teddy was older than he appeared, his youthful blonde and blue-eyed look being somewhat of a detriment to his litigation career. But Eric knew him to be a baby-faced assassin. The kid was sharp, ruthless and borderline unscrupulous. They'd made a lot of money together because of this lethal combination.

While nodding, Teddy said, "I'm good. Thanks."

"You on this floor?" Eric asked.

He laughed at this idea. "Nope. Rainmakers only up here. I'm a floor down. I got a nice little set up, cubicle is on a major thoroughfare so lots of good-looking paralegals passing by. You know, the big firm perks."

"What are you working on?"

"Contracts." He had said this in somewhat of a disappointed tone. Then he explained as if reciting what he had been told numerous times, "All juniors start with the excitement that is contractual law."

Eric laughed at the intended sarcasm, and Teddy leaned casually against the door jam.

"That is except for you, of course. You land on *Seven*, working on the firm's biggest case with the firm's best-looking lawyer." Then more seriously he said, "You deserve something good, man. It's great to see you back in the trenches again. So how are you doing? Really?"

Eric smiled at the genuine sentiment. "Good. I'm glad to be working again."

"But not as a lawyer? Now you're Thomas Magnum?"

He passed through the door and slowly returned to his chair at the glass table, wondering if there were no surprises around this place. In less than twenty-four hours that was already grist in the rumor mill.

"You want to come in and sit down? You have time?"

"Hardly. They keep me hopping. Word is you took the investigator gig."

Sighing heavily, he said, "Honestly? I'm not thrilled about it. In my mind, I'm still an attorney, still an *Ambulance Chaser*. If they want to pay me to investigate, I'll take the money. I'm hoping if I prove myself, I can get back to practicing law again."

"You'll do great at whatever they want you to do. I'm sure. Somebody once told me that there is nothing more dangerous than a lawyer with something to prove."

Eric smiled, fully aware he was the source of such wisdom.

"So how's life in the big firm?"

Teddy had a blunt manner about him. If you wanted sugar-coating, you asked someone else. If you wanted the truth you asked him because he would not hold back.

"Shit, man. I spend eighty hours a week around here and have yet to see the inside of a courtroom. I write legal opinions no one reads, let alone presents. I read case files and log hours. I miss what we did, man."

"Me too, but this new gig might be good for me. I need the discipline. Who knows? I might end up liking it here. It's still a bit too early to tell."

"It would be fun working with you again."

Teddy switched positions, leaning now against the other door jam. His expression drew serious, as if he were about to reveal the real reason for the surprise visit.

"Dude, you go out for drinks with Ms. Stennet last night?"

It was increasingly apparent it was going to be nearly impossible to keep a secret at *Donaldson, Clements*. What *Big Brother* couldn't discover, gossip seemingly would supply.

"She's the biggest enigma around here," Teddy was saying. "Last night has got the firm talking. Somebody said they saw her smiling and even whistling this morning. You do that? You've already achieved legendary status. No one can recall ever seeing her out. And never with a co-worker."

"Really? A legend?" Eric asked with a laugh.

"So, spill. What's the scoop on the lovely Ms. Stennet? She's crazy-hot. Any chance there? I don't know her. Don't think I've ever heard her speak. Does she have an English accent?"

Eric regarded the question as way off topic and quickly replied with a questioning tone. "No?"

"All I know is if she did, then she'd be pushing up against a ten. Even without it she's nine material. That lady makes me harder than third grade."

"Wait. What?" Eric believed he may have misheard the line, but understood it was certainly something Teddy might utter. He smiled with appreciation at the remark and then fired back a suspicious, "Third grade was hard for you?"

"What?" Teddy asked in confusion. "No. It's a humorous axiom."

"I get it, Ted. I would have said law school, or even the bar exam because those truly were hard."

"That's why it's funny. Third grade isn't . . . It's funny because it's ironic."

Eric chuckled at this and considered that he could hang Teddy out there even further on this thread, but instead said, "I have missed you."

"Right back at you, man."

An awkward silence descended between them until Teddy broke it by asking, "So? What's the scoop on her, man?"

Eric shrugged. "She's American, I guess. At least, she talks like one. What do you want me to tell you? She's almost more fun to talk to than to look at, but she's with someone and I'm still not over Erin. So, no chance. No scoop."

"That's too bad, man." Teddy then knitted his brow. "You know I miss Erin, too. I was seriously looking forward to working with her. At least grant me this: Is she as cool as her?"

"Very easy to talk to. She reminded me a lot of her."

"Well, man, the gossipers are not going to be satisfied with just talk. Too passive. We need some action verbs. Work on that, will you?"

He shuffled the papers he had been holding and changed the subject.

"You know before when I mentioned all the cute paralegals on *Six*? They're as interested in the guy from those commercials as all of us are in Ms. Stennet. I mentioned that you and I were former associates . . ."

"And that means you are not here just to say hello and spout humorous axioms? Your ulterior motives disappoint me."

"You know it's nothing like that. You and I go way back, so you know I care about you. A lot."

"I do," Eric said in an almost fatherly manner. "Therefore, I will help you impress your harem of paralegals."

"It's not yet officially a harem," he said with a wide grin.

"Let's impress them more with tales of your legal accomplishments than me or Ms. Stennet. Okay?"

Teddy smiled in appreciation, glanced quickly at his watch and said, "I've got to run. It's great to see you back up on your feet."

But he didn't turn to leave. He hung there almost as if suspended, wondering whether he should say something more before departing.

Finally deciding, he turned resolute and said, "I'm sorry I couldn't keep the firm afloat when Erin died and you . . ."

"No, Teddy. Don't do that. You were the victim. Please don't hang that on yourself. A lot went down that was out of your control. I self-destructed. You got burned. I'm the one who should apologize."

"You did. You have," said Teddy.

"I'm glad you landed on your feet here. And I can't thank you enough for getting me in here too. Who'd have thought you and me working together again? And at a big firm."

"I did nothing, man. Don't give me any credit. All I did was call you like Mr. McGraw asked. He actually approached me about you."

"You didn't go to McGraw asking him to bring me over?"

This puzzled Teddy. He squinted hard and glanced around while running his teeth across his bottom lip.

"Not that I wouldn't have done that, man, but it was the other way around. He called me to his office initially about two months ago with questions about you. Then Tuesday he called me back in to ask if I thought you'd take a position as an investigator."

"Why didn't you tell me that when you called me?"

"Sorry. Didn't think it mattered. Did I do wrong?"

"No. You did good. Thanks," Eric offered less than convincingly.

So, all the meetings and the conference room drama from the day before was a complete charade. Why go to such lengths and to what end? Eric didn't like the idea of being played any more than he liked sneaking into a stall in the men's room for a drink. But some things were out of his control.

And the flask was out of scotch.

SEVEN

Eric's present kept smacking up against his past. While I continue to believe that your past portends your future, where does your present fit into the time equation? And how long is *the present*? *Right now* is already over; it just ended. Does that then make it *the past*? And as you read this line, it too becomes history. So, then for the sake of this story, let's think of it this way: the previous chapters were the past, and the next will be the future, so then, by default, this one must be the present.

Regardless the answer, the previously distinct walls he was trying hard to build between his old life and this new one continued to blur. First it was the well-written piece in the State Journal-Register that had elicited memories of Ritter and Erin. He hated that those two would always be linked. One was so good, while the other took her from him. They were a pair, joined at the hip by events. He loved one and loathed the other.

Then Teddy stops by. It was great to see him, even though he too was a reminder from the good times of the past. Now that they were again working together, this fact further muddled his attempted clean start. Teddy and those memories might haunt him also.

It was that last part about McGraw, however, that concerned Eric most. The night before he and Jillian had come to an agreement, a parking garage pact, that they'd be on the same team. Had she intended for it to be the two of them against McGraw, for McGraw was looking like an adversary? What was with all the theatrics the day before?

And where did Jillian come down on any of this? Was she aware of Teddy's involvement? What might her part in all of this be? Where was she, by the way? It was almost the end of the day on a Friday, and she hadn't stopped by to check on him or even say hello.

Rather than defensively dwell on questions outside his control, he decided to go on the offense and re-engage in his research about the future of agriculture and the place of Jameson Gradeen and *Agribotics Technologies*. It was time to focus on robotics.

The first article was a position paper from a European university. It began with a premise I'll paraphrase; it went something like this: While farming in and of itself is vulnerable to the impacts of climate change, it's also one of its causes.

It too touched on the expected population explosion and reinforced the need to produce higher quality food with sustainable cultivation becoming essential. It also cited labor losses in the agricultural world as people leave the profession for other pursuits. To accomplish the first and change the second, we needed to turn to the "exciting high-tech" world of farming with agbots.

As Eric read further, *exciting* might not have been a proper portrayal, but *high-tech* fit. In crop and fruit farming, robots already autonomously navigated their environments and performed activities at set locations. The article spoke of the ease with which this is achieved in greenhouses because of limited size and rectangular construction. It was the section about getting similar results outdoors in farm fields where this became thought-provoking reading.

Since fields are rarely laid out as squares or even rectangles, there are few manageable angles. Agbots either work by receiving a preprogrammed plan with set locations to visit or use GPS positioning and a closed-loop control to keep it on track. A third option is to use a drone to help the agbots find their way to follow unknown trajectories, like a winding crop row.

This is where Eric was first introduced to the Chinese Postman Problem. In a branch of mathematics called graph theory, the Chinese Postman Problem looks to find the shortest closed path that visits every edge of an undirected graph. This is also sometimes called the Route Inspection Problem, so as to not disparage mail carriers in China.

This was a whole new area of math for Eric, full of references to Eulerian circuits and polynomial time, so it diverted him down an internet rabbit hole. It turns out a Eulerian circuit is a path within a graph where every edge is visited exactly once, starting and ending on the same vertex. The name goes back to 1736 when Leonhard Euler first solved the *Seven Bridges of Konigsberg* problem. Such a path or circuit can then be plotted as an algorithm.

Really. Why would the internet make up something that's not true?

Polynomial time matters because it's a measurement of time taken to solve an algorithm or run the path. Basic functions such as addition and subtraction, multiplication and division, are said to be solvable in polynomial time since they are calculated "fast." Even square roots and logarithms are polynomials.

Right now you're probably asking, "So why does all this matter?"

It all goes back to the idea that few fields have right-angle corners, so tilling or spraying a field in a tractor is much more complex than merely turning right or left. Even without remote control or robotics, the most fuel-efficient path must be determined beforehand to ensure no resources are wasted.

Think of it like mowing your lawn. As you cut the grass, you don't want to take a route going over areas already mown.

Farmers have comparable concerns.

The most effective path is then calculated by an algorithm whether the tractor is being steered by a human or an agbot. In the case of the latter, the predetermined path must be conveyed to the machine, and this too has been accomplished in a variety of ways in the short history of ag-tech. The first to market was a laser-guided concept where multiple transponders are placed at the vertices of the field. Lasers on the front of the tractor bounce signals off these receivers and turn until they can pick up the next transponder. It's a lot more intricate than this, with radio frequencies and off-site controllers, but this gives you the general idea, like a laser-guided bumper car bouncing off the transponders.

A more modern idea, and the one currently being researched and developed by *Agribotics Technologies,* involves dropping navigational markers within the plotted algorithm. The tractor then is guided by a software program to turn or perform a farming activity at these predetermined locations. This process can also be watched over by the eyes in the sky of drones.

And while other companies have marketed comparable software or similar drones, to date only Jameson Gradeen has developed the interface which allows all these technologies to communicate with each other. It's the *Swarm Farm Platform* which has inched *Agribotics Technologies* to the aforementioned brink of profitability. But like all companies in the R&D business, the costs to get to market can be crushing to the bottom-line. This concept, however, might be the light at the end of the long and dark tunnel.

Before Eric could finish jotting down all of this on the second of his legal pads, he found himself off on another tangent. You would think the personal injury lawyer in him would have gotten here sooner, but what about the safety and liability aspect of agbots running wild? According to another semi-arid position presentation, this one published from a University of Illinois study, this lack of regulation is both a blessing and curse for companies entering the agbot field.

Let's look at these one at a time, but safety first. See what I did there?

Agbots must detect what's going on around them and react accordingly to protect humans, wildlife, and themselves. An out-of-control robot can do much more harm than any good done by one staying in control. Safety versus output cannot be viewed as a trade-off.

Crashes then give rise to liability questions. This was right up his alley. Who bears the responsibility for injuries or damage caused by an autonomous robot? The manufacturer or the end user? Would agbot cases be adjudicated like auto cases? There is no precedent. Can you chase an ambulance through a cornfield?

Regardless of the solutions to the safety and responsibility concerns, the study stated that currently there's no legislation or regulation dealing with agbots, either here or abroad. Living in Springfield, the legislative capitol of Illinois, Eric understood that laws and rules would soon be forthcoming. That's what people around here do. Soon some state rep from the farming areas would stand up on the floor of that big building not far from here and try to define and implement the right degree of autonomy for agbots.

And when that happens, attorneys at *Donaldson, Clements* and countless other firms from here to Chicago will profit from either agreeing or disagreeing with the rulings while defending or prosecuting for their respective clientele. Each new law is a win one way or another when it comes to billable hours.

But agbots are here. As he continued spinning through the webpages, he read about automated milking machines in use in the Netherlands which allow cows to be milked when they want, not the farmer. These machines also gather data to help the Dutch monitor the herd for problems or improve milk yield.

There was a project recently finished that developed a fleet of tractors and aerial robots with sensors to distinguish weeds from crops and apply chemicals as necessary. These same sensors are helping to reduce overspray of herbicides and pesticides by directing them onto specific target areas as opposed to spraying indiscriminately.

Lastly there's a company marketing a smaller agbot to make farm solutions safer, with more reliability and added productivity. The smaller size also then avoids what is referred to as "soil compaction." This happens over time because of larger tractors and robots continually navigating the same paths through the same fields.

So then, what did any of this mean regarding the pending litigation against *Agribotics Technologies*? He wasn't sure but knew that his time spent had not been wasted. He considered he had to be thorough on context and background as most investigators are.

Oddly, that had been the first time he had viewed himself no longer as an attorney.

Back to *Agribotics Technologies*. Their name had come up numerous times in his research, so it appeared as if they were out there on the bleeding edge of this technology. And he found himself to be fascinated by Jameson Gradeen. Was he the agriculture ambassador, the good-will visionary as reported in some stories? Or was he the proverbial mad-scientist/evil genius who might conspire to kill to protect his secrets?

Reminding himself "innocent until proven guilty," he'd make no premature determinations and review all his background notes at home under the watchful eye of single-malt. He'd start examining the case in the morning.

EIGHT

Eric's existence for the last eight months was more than just grieving and drinking. There was also golfing and drinking, weather permitting.

But seriously, there were also a lot of mistakes and several bad decisions which led to many more mistakes. While booze became his crutch, it also served as rationale for the stupid choices he'd made, plus the repercussions of those stupid choices. It was a convenient way to deflect blame by putting everything at the fault of his problem.

But don't we all rationalize and make excuses for the stupid things we do while looking for something to blame? Or, in his case, some*one*?

And while discussing excuses and their convenience, I don't know about you, but I don't quite buy the idea that Erin was going with Ritter to have one last fling. I wasn't around then, so I can only go on what I've been told.

Eric remains adamant since we were first introduced that was the reason for Erin's text, and for the two of them being together at the time of the accident. He was being two-timed. I see that story more as fitting his narrative. It's convenient for him to cast her as the bad half than to bear the responsibility and guilt himself. Like he confessed to Jillian, he was looking for feasible ways out and had considered his fiancé's untimely death as a possibility.

I never met Erin, nor do I know anything differently than what he's said. But what kind of woman does that to her fiancé two nights before the wedding? Oh, sure, there are stories of harlot brides and fiancés with second thoughts who jump the bones of some guy willing to jump back. But nothing I've learned about Erin hints toward this.

She was a devout Catholic girl who was so fervent in her beliefs that she had demanded he go through the steps to convert. Think about that. Catholics may have flaws, but commitment rarely is one.

Here's another thing: even if Erin had been a bit loose in the morals, would she go to bed with an old boyfriend? Whether he might still be hung up on her or not, if she does that before her wedding, is she ever ridding herself of the guy? I've never met Ritter either. The stories don't strike me as him being the kind of guy who's going to screw a girl right before her wedding and then quietly disappear. This whole thing is hard for me to understand.

While I'm at it, and then I'll return to the story, if Erin had second thoughts about what she was doing enough to sleep with another man, why would she leave a great job at the D. A.'s office to chase ambulances with Eric and Teddy?

None of it makes sense, other than *his* version is convenient for *him*.

I'm convinced he's wrong about Erin and has been the entire time, but he refuses to listen. He blames it on the curse of the *McKegney men* because he'd seen it happen to his father.

Eric was born in Carlinville, maybe fifty miles straight south of Springfield off Interstate 55. Dad was a mechanic at the only Ford dealership in town on weekdays and under a shade on weekends. Mom taught elementary school. As Eric describes his childhood on many occasions, "Dad liked getting his hands dirty and mom didn't." He gravitated towards the books and away from grime.

He would always say that his parents seemed happy even though he could feel his dad's sense of disappointment for being unable to provide better for his mom. His dad always seemed tired, whether from a hard day's labor or the endless footrace to stay a step ahead of the bill collectors. His dad loved him and his older sisters, but with the benefit of hindsight, he now questioned if he loved his mom. He assumed he must have at some point, but . . .

His mom liked things his father seemingly couldn't afford. When Eric left for Eastern Illinois she left for someone who could provide those things. She always lived on the edge; she liked to dance with danger. Oftentimes it took the form of needless purchases or worthless men. His father tolerated being cuckolded because small-town Illinois offers little recourse other than the admission of shame.

The silver lining was with Eric being the youngest of three kids, she hung around long enough to see each child get out on their own. He sadly told me once he hadn't seen his mother since his father's funeral seven years ago. He does get Birthday and Christmas cards from his older sisters, and while both planned to be at his wedding, neither attended Erin's funeral.

So I tell him, "Just because your mother cheated on your father doesn't mean Erin planned to cheat on you."

He won't listen.

One time he did listen, however, has also turned into a stupid choice. I will take sole responsibility for this one. Her name is Lorrie Ann Rosenthal, and maybe twenty-five. She moved into Eric's condominium complex about two months ago, across the small courtyard. The area is called Matthews Place and it boasts high-end townhomes south of downtown by Lake Springfield. There are four groups of four two-story walk-ups atop garages laid end to end, four across from four two times, beautiful landscaping and winding sidewalks between the units. Most residents are professionals of one sort or another because of the price.

Lorrie Ann, however, is the exception. She was married at nineteen and divorced four years later and lives with her two small children. She doesn't work, unless yoga and constant exercising are considered paying jobs, and let's just say that she's not shy about flaunting her body of work. She wears tight outfits, or maybe they appear tight because her after-market parts are roundly firm in all the right places. She's considered afternoon-at-the-strip-joint pretty, brown hair and eyes, a sultry gap-toothed smile. With that body in those tight clothes, it's always afternoon somewhere!

The ex comes on Wednesdays and every other weekend to pick up the kids. They seem amicable enough. Without judging, it's easy to tell that the ex could never afford to live at Matthews Place, but he's doing the best he can.

On a weekend when the kids were with dad she knocked on Eric's door. It was my idea to let her in. She seemed very pleasant, said she'd heard the story about his fiancé from the neighbors and asked if there was anything she could do. They shared a bit of common ground which comes with loss, she explained. Eric lost his fiancé. She lost her marriage. He knew they weren't comparing apples, or even oranges to apples, but he was lonely and adrift and tired of drinking alone. By stretching this shared circumstance and flavoring the mix with a great deal of liquor, soon they were kindred spirits.

She was not good with alcohol, but it turned out she was good at other things when drinking alcohol. One of those she enjoys doing is a certain thing men enjoy having done to them. And that is how it all started with Eric and *The Girl from across the Courtyard*.

It's a repugnant relationship, more of a dirty liaison. They never set foot on the second floor of his condo together and she never spends the night. They're just adults doing the sordid things intoxicated adults do behind closed doors. The trysts are never at Eric's prompting, nor do they ever interfere with her parental duties, never scheduled, nor planned. They happen spontaneously.

For Eric's part, he knows it's wrong. But what harm's being done? While functioning during the day, he's mostly an obliterated mess by dark, often to the point where he wakes the next morning wondering if he'd dreamt the whole thing. He never gets excited when she knocks, nor disappointed if she doesn't. Most of the time he has no idea what night it is, so it's hard for him to feel anything in advance of their rendezvous.

They made no promises to each other; they owe nothing, no expectations, never any resentment. It's two ships continually passing on Wednesday and every other weekend nights. These are two wayward ships, neither with a true heading or purpose, just floating through loneliness together.

So, when her signature three little knocks sounded on the glass panes beside his front door on this Friday night, he got almost irritated. His reaction worried him, for he was quite drunk, yet not drunk enough to be void of a reaction.

He'd spent three hours at his kitchen table with Scotch Whisky, cataloging all the day's research notes into a Word doc on his office laptop. And like earlier when doing the research, he was on a roll. He'd had enough to drink to feel a laser-focus and a new feeling of achievement he could appreciate. He didn't want to stop, regardless of the reason.

The clock on the lower right of the laptop screen told him it was almost 10:30. There was maybe an hour's worth of work and a quarter bottle of scotch to finish. The last thing he wanted was to stop now to be entertained by *The Girl from across the Courtyard*.

He got up and went to the door, opening it slightly but blocking any possible attempt by her to enter.

"Tonight's not a good night," he said bluntly.

Lorrie Ann's dark hair fell loose across her face, her lipstick smeared and her cheeks aglow, all recognizable signs she'd been drinking. The box of White Zinfandel she held by the handle confirmed this. She was dressed in heels, a tight miniskirt and blouse apparently missing most of its buttons. She looked as though one time during the night she was dressed for dancing. He was afraid to guess what she might be dressed – or practically undressed – for now.

"Come on," she pleaded. "Don't make me stand out here. Let me in."

"We can't do this tonight. I'm working."

"On a Friday night? Come on. One drink and then one little . . ."

She playfully pawed a hand at his belt buckle.

He batted it away and said decisively, "Lorrie Ann, listen to me. I can't do this tonight. And come to think of it, I don't think we should do this again."

"You always say that, but then here we are again."

This was true. These two had done this little dance on his doorstep countless times. Every time she'd take the lead and he'd follow to the point of eventually relenting and giving in.

But for some reason tonight felt different. He was on a mission; there was a purpose tonight which was missing during the other dances.

"I have work to do."

"Let me in."

"Tonight's no good. I have work to finish."

He knew he was repeating himself, but he had to stay firm and resolute. His history had proven he was his own worst enemy with her and the things she liked to do. And their positioning was not helping his resolve. Being taller and a step higher out on his stoop, the angle made it easy to look right down the front of her open blouse. She was wearing a black lace bra that looked to be working overtime.

She pawed again for his belt buckle. "But I do the things you like. You always tell me that."

This time he made no attempt to push her hand away. "Tonight's not going to work," he said suddenly much less convincingly.

One last time he said no, but it's earlier force and firmness was missing as he began to erode and collapse. It was as if the concrete base of his fortitude had been worn down to sand by a relentless tide of her persistence. He could feel the water carrying it out from under his feet. He was crumbling further with every glance down her open blouse, every thought of her smeared lipstick.

But what about the work to finish for tomorrow? The thought embarrassed him, for it had turned out to be weaker than his self-discipline. He didn't just have a drinking problem; he had a compulsion problem. He didn't know when to stop any more than he knew how. He was a weak man with many failings.

Opening the door to his mistake, he considered how every other time with Lorrie Ann he'd closed his eyes to pretend she was Erin.

Tonight she was going to be Jillian Stennet.

NINE

Early on Saturday morning, entering the lobby, Eric noticed there were fewer security guards behind the mission control desk. He flashed his ID badge and then used it in the elevator to get up to *Seven*. The floor seemed deserted, so he made himself a coffee from the Keurig in the little kitchenette after setting up and logging in on his laptop. While he waited to get into the firm's system, he poured scotch from a flask into the white ceramic coffee mug bearing the name of the firm.

Let's change our focus to basic *Law School 101*. Whether you received your Juris Doctor from a law school at the top of the rankings like Jillian Stennet, or one from the other end like Eric, one of the first lessons is the concept of *Incomplete Crimes*. This basic legal principle is at the heart of all conspiracy cases, such as *Case # 75-93654 US v. Agribotics Technologies*.

If you think about criminal acts, oftentimes you assume an actor's intentions have been carried out, like someone was killed, the bank was robbed, the drugs were sold. But some crimes fall short of the final act of commission, or completion. These are *Incomplete Crimes*. They include *Attempts*, *Conspiracy* and *Solicitation*, and fall somewhere among the middle steps in the process of committing crimes.

As I learned at Happy Hours with attorneys, Jerome Hall in *General Principles of the Criminal Law* wrote about the six steps in the commission of a crime. Drumroll please.

They are: 1.) getting the idea for the crime; 2.) evaluating the idea to decide whether to proceed; 3.) deciding to go forward with the idea; 4.) preparing for the crime; 5.) beginning the crime, and 6.) completing the crime.

People are not punished for any of the first three, because having nefarious ideas or making illicit decisions are not against the law in and of themselves. At the other end, #6, the completion of the crime, is most definitely punished. But activity happening in steps #4 and #5 can be punishable as one of the three *Incomplete Crimes*.

Let's start by reviewing *Attempts*. An attempted crime is one that wasn't finished. It failed to reach Step #6. There are two types of *Attempts*, and they are *Complete* and *Incomplete*. A *Complete Attempt* is when a defendant does everything he or she set out to do only to fail. Say you want to kill someone. You buy a gun and lay in wait, but you fire and miss.

On the other hand, if you want to kill someone and do all those same things, but get stopped by the police before you shoot, it is considered an *Incomplete Attempt*.

Without getting too deeply into the jurisprudence weeds, a person can only be convicted of attempting to commit certain crimes without seeing it through. The determining factor is *intent*. When watching movies or TV, you may have heard the phrase, "mens rea," Latin for "guilty mind." This speaks specifically to *intent*. And, as it seems with everything else to this point, there are also two types of intent – *specific* and *general*.

Specific Intent goes to the defendant's state of mind, which is to achieve the result the criminal statute prohibits. This differs from *General Intent* which requires only the completion of the physical act. For example, murder is *Specific Intent* because the prosecutor will be required to show the defendant intended for the victim to die. Battery by definition is *General Intent* because all the prosecutor must prove is that the defendant purposely hit the victim, not trying to specifically cause a certain injury.

Many of these *Intent* crimes are quite similar in that it is hard to differentiate between the two kinds. One determining factor is the statute of the crime itself, in that the definition includes the requirement that the actor does -- or does not -- intend the result.

So, what then constitutes an *Attempt*? You must take a concrete, substantial step toward furthering your intent to break the law. Here's one for you: An *Attempt* is an act of *perpetration*, not *preparation*. Or numerically from above, #4 not #3. For example, buying a gun in and of itself is not an *Attempt*, while pointing it at somebody and firing is.

The punishment for *Attempts* has changed over time. Before the 18th century an *Attempt* was not a crime unless successful. After that for a while an *Attempt* was considered a misdemeanor. Today almost all *Attempts* to commit a felony are themselves felonies. And here is another one for you: If you have completed a crime, you have also attempted it, so you can be *charged* with both to give the jury a choice. You cannot, however, be *convicted* of both as the attempt "merges" with the completion of the crime.

This then brings us to *Conspiracy*. This *Incomplete Crime* is an agreement, explicit or implied, among two or more people, to commit a criminal act. This definition is vague at best, making the crime of *Conspiracy* very controversial when it comes to determining between a mere idea and an agreement to break the law. But an agreement alone does not constitute a *Conspiracy* without a stipulation called an *Overt Act*. This is a step taken by the actors toward the furtherance of their goal, or as detailed above, an *Attempt*. But there's one place where it differs since a *Conspiracy* involves more than one person. The *Overt Act* taken, or *Attempt* made, by one member of the conspiracy suffices to prosecute all members, even members who join the conspiracy after the *Overt Act* has taken place.

But how do prosecutors prove the existence of such agreement, let alone a *Conspiracy*? As a rule, a *Conspiracy* is a tenuous arrangement. The agreement can be established with circumstantial evidence alone, from which juries then draw broad inferences as to the plan. One way to identify whether there is a *Conspiracy* is to determine if the resulting crime was "choreographed." This too is ambiguous, however, and open to argument – a lawyer's paradise full of plea bargains and settlement offers.

Lastly, unlike the crime of *Attempt*, there is no "merging" in a *Conspiracy*. All defendants can be charged for both crimes, the conspiracy to commit the crime *AND* the crime itself.

Against this backdrop, what defenses are available against a *Conspiracy* charge? Or more specifically, how does *Donaldson, Clement* intend to defend the pending charges against Jameson Gradeen? We'll get to that in a bit, for now there is one more *Incomplete Crime* to discuss. That's *Solicitation*, and it's not just for ladies of the evening anymore.

Solicitation consists of inviting, requesting, hiring, or encouraging another person to commit a crime. You can solicit felonies, as well as misdemeanors. The prosecution need only prove the defendant intended the other person to do what the defendant suggested. No crime need be committed, or even attempted, to be convicted of *Solicitation*. This makes it conceivably the most incomplete of these three *Incomplete Crimes*.

So, without completely glossing over all the previous legalese and *italics*, all that *Law School 101* on the topic of *Incomplete Crimes* for this story can be summed thusly: A *Solicitation* is an *Attempt* to form a *Conspiracy*.

This leaves Federal Prosecutor Cynthia Forrester with multiple bullets to fire at a solitary target. The "eager and ambitious bitch," can formulate a three-front attack plan without tipping her hand as to where she'll wage true war. The defenders then spend an inordinate amount of time fortifying against all three, all the while knowing two-thirds of their effort is in vain. Don't weep for the defense, though. This is why law firms take exorbitant retainers and charge by the billable hour.

On his second cup of Scotch Coffee Eric turned his attention to the facts and suppositions of *Case # 75-93654 US v. Agribotics Technologies*. There was a detailed timeline of the convoluted events leading up to the Conspiracy to Commit Murder charges filed against Jameson Gradeen. It was page after perplexing page of names and places which made it ridiculously hard to get a clear picture without a white board with arrows detailing their connections.

The Cliff's Notes summary goes something like this:

In July of the previous year, Channel 6 TV news personality Ann Flannery was found murdered in the parking lot of *Faces*, a local Springfield nightclub, late one Friday. Her companion, Patrick Weathers, was also shot, but survived. His statement to the police noted the gunman wore a Cinderella Halloween mask and asked Ms. Flannery if she was the "Lady from the news?" prior to firing.

Looking for motive, immediately the police began investigating any stories Ms. Flannery was working. But she was an anchor, a newsreader, making it difficult. Nothing in Mr. Weathers' past revealed any reason he was targeted.

The next morning, another female reporter from the same station, Olivia Jacobsen, received a phone call from a man identifying himself as the hired gunman, informing her she'd been the intended target. Killing Ms. Flannery was in error, and he now feared for his own safety from the people who hired him. Few further details were revealed.

SPD detectives, working in conjunction with Ms. Jacobsen, began looking through her stories. They focused on a Dr. Arthur DeBisshop as a person of interest. DeBisshop was COO and Head of Research for a local company called *Agricultural Chemical Group* currently under investigation by the station for allegedly dumping toxic waste into local creeks. It was their "Sweeps Week" lead-in, but nothing on the dumping ever materialized nor was any report ever filed by Ms. Jacobsen. DeBisshop was eventually cleared of any wrongdoing, and any suggestions the reporter was targeted because of her story were also dropped.

Springfield authorities were baffled until a fortuitous event a week or so later in St. Louis, thus turning this case federal and bringing in the FBI.

There, a man named Freddy Steinhauer was found dead, two shots from a small caliber handgun straight to the heart. Such a shooting, in and of itself, wouldn't raise red flags, except for the fact that a Cinderella mask was found nearby. Mr. Weathers was shown the mask and confirmed it had been worn by their assailant because he remembered a crack in the plastic above one eyehole.

Witnesses testified Steinhauer was from Springfield and had in fact been in town on the day of Ann Flannery's murder. A check of his cell revealed calls with a Springfield area code. The time, date and a triangulated location of one happened to be a hotel in downtown where Jameson Gradeen was the keynote speaker at a luncheon.

This was the first time his name surfaced in the investigation.

At the time, Gradeen was yet to be considered, but nonetheless he was put under surveillance; the police were hard-pressed for suspects. This introduced the federal authorities to many of his better-known associates. One, a shady character named Randy Fuller, was followed to a late-night meeting with a dark sedan registered to a security firm employed by none other than *Agricultural Chemical Group*. Fuller's role was never fully developed; he was viewed simply as a middleman. *ACG* and more importantly DeBisshop, however, were now back on the radar because of the clandestined meeting. Couple this with the fact the police had few other actionable leads and DeBisshop became the focus of the Grand Jury probe.

Search warrants on phone and email records of a research farm operated by *ACG* were authorized. Emails uncovered a relationship between DeBisshop and Gradeen through a secret cipher the two used when communicating. It was also discovered the farm in question was the original family farm in Edinburg, Illinois owned and operated by Thomas Gradeen's family prior to hitting it big. Tenuous at best, yet circumstantial at worst, all these coincidental connections could not be ignored. Still, no one could interpret their little code, nor guess at the underlying motive why any of this happened, or if in fact int actually had.

Detectives struggled to form a coherent storyline. They speculated Ms. Jacobsen had gotten close to something which might harm DeBisshop, and then by connection also Gradeen. This was less than flattering to Ms. Jacobsen, an experienced investigative reporter, who apparently failed to recognize reasons making her a threat. Because of this humiliation, she's changed her on-air name and moved to Moline, Illinois as a weekend anchor on Channel 8.

The police narrative went like this: Fearing they were about to be exposed for something, for anything, DeBisshop and Gradeen conspired with Fuller to hire Steinhauer to kill Ms. Jacobsen. When he then killed the wrong reporter, it is alleged the two corporate titans again conspired to have Fuller find and kill Steinhauer. He caught up to him in St. Louis. What has since happened to Fuller was never fully theorized. DeBisshop and Gradeen were labeled as conspirators and considered responsible because of their secret code.

Initially the prosecution convened a Grand Jury in late November, intending to charge DeBisshop because they could establish no discernible connection between Ms. Jacobsen, the alleged target, and Jameson Gradeen. Plus, it was determined, and seemingly rightly so, that DeBisshop would flip on Gradeen more likely than vice-versa. If they were to eventually get Gradeen, they'd have to shoot through DeBisshop.

But then DeBisshop disappears and is since presumed dead. The time and effort the prosecution spent to bring the case had to be charged off somewhere. It was directed toward Gradeen. Rather than shooting through DeBisshop, they would fire straight at Gradeen.

A new Grand Jury was convened in February. They went along with the charges, because it was alleged Gradeen had been the mastermind and now the sole-survivor. There was nowhere else to point the finger of blame.

Eric regarded all he learned and realized he must have missed something. This was the textbook circumstantial evidence, but as we have just learned, flimsy or not, it alone can be utilized to convict on conspiracy. But still there was no smoking gun, nor even one in the non-smoking section. This case had more holes than a pair of fishnets. Where was DeBisshop? Fuller? What proof was there that Fuller shot Steinhauer? How do we know it was not a robbery gone awry?

Why would anyone bring these charges solely on this evidence? Even the "ambitious bitch" must realize she can't win based on what Eric just read. This was the classic King of the Hill prosecution. Only one guy got to the top, so it must have been at the expense of others.

What was he missing? Charges should never have been filed, so why would the accused retain a firm with the reputation of *Donaldson, Clements*? An overreach by the prosecution can be defeated by a capable lawyer regardless of the law school. Was this more about seeing justice done, or about seeing Cynthia Forrester's face on the news or perhaps political posters?

As he considered all of this, she'd leaned in the doorway of his storeroom office watching him work. He reminded her of a DJ sliding between turntables. He'd flip through a legal pad on his desk and then turn his attention back to the screen of his laptop. He'd jot down a note on one of the yellow pages and spin his chair to bang on more keys. She liked the way he worked as well as the way he looked. Unshaven and without glasses, dark hair long and mussed, he looked hard-working yet casual in an open-collar golf shirt and a pair of khakis, Topsiders and no socks. It was the way she'd hoped he might look if their paths happened to cross today.

She'd read his background research from the day before, so she knew he'd thrown himself into this. She appreciated his attention to detail and enjoyed the few sporadic snarky comments peppered in. It was obvious he was taking this assignment seriously, regardless of his views on investigators.

He printed the word "Overreach" on his yellow pad in all caps and circled it, inhaling with a hand over his mouth when he saw her. In perfectly creased black slacks and a starched pinstriped blouse, hair up and slightly tousled with dangling earrings, and the big diamond ring, she looked dressed for client meetings. It was the calculating smile with a nibble on her bottom lip, however, that first drew his attention.

"Hey," he said as if it had two syllables. "You're wearing glasses. You really look good in glasses."

"And you're not wearing yours."

Hers was a statement of observation, while his was more of a come-on. But who could blame him? With the black-rimmed rectangular eyeglasses and loose bangs flipped to one side, a twirling pen playing across her bright red lips, her look gave off a naughty librarian vibe. It was dangerous.

He leaned back in his chair and placed both hands behind his head. Without small talk, he got right to the heart of the matter.

"What am I missing? How could anyone logically build this case without first knowing the root cause of everything?"

"Are you casting aspersions on the federal prosecutor?"

"Ms. Forrester? I guess I am. I'm trying to determine what the lady reporter may have stumbled onto to set this chain reaction into motion. She apparently doesn't know. Connecting the dots, it's hard to delineate the ensuing dots if the point of origin is missing."

More as a statement, she asked, "You're a dot theory proponent also?"

"Or a *follow the money* person."

"I read your research. I'm impressed with your commitment to all this."

"Thank you." He accepted her compliment with a wry smile and said, "That doesn't answer the question. Why doesn't this add up logically?"

She considered this and, and like a learned law school professor, came back with, "Tell me why you think it doesn't."

"Really? Okay. For starters, there are assumptions and leaps in this line of reasoning that a first-year law student could destroy. There's no Point A from which all the subsequent points flow. And whether there was ever a substantial case built against DeBisshop or not, you can't just cross out his name and pencil in the name "Jameson Gradeen" and take it to trial. It doesn't work that way."

"I owe you an apology," she said in a complementary tone. "I told Mr. McGraw you'd never grasp the complexities of criminal law."

"And how about this? I doubt if you could get Steinhauer on *Manslaughter* based on this."

Jillian nodded her approval at his summation of the facts. "So, you think we have a pretty good case?"

"I do. And clearly so does McGraw. You wouldn't march down from on high for an uncertain verdict. It better be a case you can't lose."

He waited patiently for her to say something, but she didn't, instead staring off to a point in the distance above his left shoulder. He felt as though she was trying to tell him something without telling him something. The facts didn't add up for conspiracy charges, and now she was also apparently withholding something from him.

"What else am I missing?"

When his question failed to illicit a reply, he repeated it.

Her gaze strayed from the invisible spot above the windows behind him and then through a squint, their eyes met. In this contact he felt the apprehension and concern in the absence of normal sparkle in the gorgeous translucence of her grey eyes. Suddenly he understood.

"Oh, my God," he said, the words evenly spaced. "He's guilty. Gradeen's behind this."

Almost like a robot, she slowly and methodically turned her head to one side as if to glance back over her shoulder and then back to face him. Her expression remained clouded with unease, her dark brows bunching together.

"Are you hungry?" she asked.

"What? Am I what?"

"It's almost lunch time. Are you hungry? Let's go grab some lunch."

He pushed off from the glass table, the chair rolling back. Soon he was on his feet following her down a hallway to the elevators. They were leaving to have a conversation that could never happen within the hallowed halls of *Donaldson, Clements,* for these walls apparently had ears.

TEN

*J*illian used her credentials to operate the elevator, punching the illuminated "G" for ground near the bottom of the panel denoting the numbered floors.

"Why am I even here?" he asked, as the elevator jerked its descent.

Her eyes widened dangerously, and a long slender finger went to her lips, part of a relaxed motion to adjust her glasses. He immediately understood her insinuation, regarding how *Big Brother* had the capability to listen to elevator conversations. He glanced at the ceiling, looking for a camera or a microphone, but if either were present, they were well concealed.

Sixth Floor. So, he turned his attention to Jillian. She was in profile as she stared forward at the mirrored panel on the closed elevator door. With her hair piled on top, and the same strands from Thursday night persisting in rebellion, he got an unencumbered view of her perfect outline. Her delicate nose, pouty lips and smooth chin all looked as if sculpted by a master, but it was the glasses that didn't leave his thoughts. They were like matte-black picture frames for the flawless artwork of her eyes and the dark fullness of her lashes.

Fifth Floor. In the reflection, she observed him staring intently at her, as he ran a hand through his unruly hair. What was it about this guy that intrigued her more than ever intended or imagined? Based on what she read from his research the day before, and then now with his quick and concise deductions about the state of her case, was her interest only in his work? Or was there more to this guy than just an ambulance chasing past chock-full of heartache and loss or a present soaked in alcohol?

Fourth Floor. Wouldn't he like to be there when she removed the glasses and shook down that hair? Would she let him unbutton her blouse, or did she not realize how much men enjoy that simple pleasure? Her legs in the black slacks were long and ramrod straight, crossed right over left, as she leaned with her perfect butt against the corner. She continued to look straight ahead, and he would have given anything to know what she was thinking at that instance.

Third Floor. He'd referred to himself as a butterfly with a broken wing, but that wasn't the whole story. Sure, he seemed damaged, but irreparable? He had issues and problems, but too many to fix? She couldn't shake the thought of him as a lost little puppy needing a home. What if she rescued him, took him in? How could that turn out any way other than trouble? And once inside, could she get him out again?

Second Floor. Teddy called her as "The biggest mystery around this place." What was the mystery? She was incredibly pretty and a pleasure to be near. This didn't include the delight of her scent. It filled the elevator. He greedily breathed it in, dreaming of nibbling near the spots she'd dabbed the fragrant perfume with her slender fingers with the flawless French manicured nails.

Ground Floor. Impatiently she reached for the "Open Doors" button with her left hand and there it was, her big diamond ring which had so conveniently slipped from his mind on the journey down. He felt embarrassed and guilty. He was not *that* kind of guy; nor would he ever be. Patterson Ritter was. Look at the lives that bastard changed. Eric didn't know anything about *Mr. Somebody*, but he knew better than to insert himself into the relationship. Unlike Ritter, he had respect for her ring and the promise it carried.

The doors opened, and she leaned close to whisper, "Wait until we're completely outside."

He nodded but wondered why the stealth and secrecy remained necessary in the lobby. Did *Big Brother* have eyes and ears here also? There were two military-looking men seated behind the lobby desk and Eric understood. He'd been told by the IT guy that the security people work for the building, but the building is owned by the partners of the firm. So, then by extension, they were all in the same bed, and there was possibly informational incest going on; you had to be careful who knew what.

Two men decked out in the same uniform as the day before, navy blazers, red ties and all, jumped to their feet upon Jillian's approach. Cordially she acknowledged both as she passed, while Eric eyed them suspiciously. It was apparent they knew who she was while paying him little attention.

Once outside in the bright sunlight, Jillian immediately veered to her right down the sidewalk, showing no second thoughts as to where they were heading. He hustled to catch up, watching her, waiting for her to say something to indicate that they were finally in the clear to converse.

After a few purposeful strides, she turned to him almost in exasperation and said, "We can talk now."

"Where to start?" he asked with a half-laugh. But where does anyone ever start anything? At the beginning, of course.

He sighed and said, "What in the hell am I doing here?"

From that jumping off point, he led her through a maze of questions needing answers and concerns begging to be addressed. It began something like this: If Gradeen's guilty, why do you need me? Since the prosecution won't be able to prove his guilt, why do you need me? What's the origin point of the whole conspiracy? He realized the answer to the last question answered the others.

He asked about DeBisshop and Fuller's whereabouts. When was the last time they were seen? Could someone have planted the Halloween mask on Steinhauer to frame him? And what was up with their secret email code? Were the Feds making any progress on it?

When he'd run through those and other holes in the case, he pivoted to the firm itself. Did she know McGraw approached Teddy Grimes two months ago about his willingness to work as an investigator? What was / is McGraw up to?

He ranted and railed to the point that he was still raging against the world when they ducked into a small diner a few blocks from the firm.

The only thing he didn't ask was how she might feel knowing he'd pretended to be with her the night before.

The diner was dark and dank, looking to be old and rundown, with the vinyl bench seats cracking or duct taped. There was doo-wop music to give it the feel of the Fifties, but many of patrons appeared old enough to have broken bread with Lincoln. Were they going for the 1850's? It sported several pungent odors. There was coffee and bacon from the kitchen and the antiseptic smell of a cleaner recently sprayed on the tables.

Once seated in a booth, a disinterested waitress dropped laminated menus between them. He picked his up to peruse his options, but Jillian pressed it back on to the tabletop.

"My turn," she said.

She began to dissect his worries one at a time, beginning with their client, the esteemed Jameson Gradeen himself.

"As defense counsel, you never ask your client if he's guilty. One, it doesn't matter, and two, chances are he's lying anyway. Guilt is immaterial. Your job is to exonerate your client."

"Did you anyway?" he asked.

"No. We never asked. Like I said, it doesn't matter."

"But you think he's guilty." It had not been phrased as a question.

She considered this and finally came back with, "Let's just say there are reasons to believe he is. His father, who is footing the bill, is extremely anxious. It's as if he knows things he's not telling. Something is going on. On the other hand, the son is noncommittal, stone-faced, relaxed. Too relaxed. I'd hate to play poker with him."

"Can they tie him to Fuller? Any evidence he sent Fuller to St. Louis to kill Steinhauer? If so, there's solicitation and conspiracy right there."

"But as you said earlier, Forrester lacks hard evidence to get him on either."

He liked how she pronounced the last word with the long "I" sound as if it were part of her everyday English, and not the pretentious pronunciation some are prone to enunciate. She had a way of making *The King's English* sound as if she were superior to you yet wasn't speaking down to you.

"Maybe Forrester has Fuller. Or even DeBisshop," Eric offered.

"Unlikely. We think Fuller may still be alive, but chances are DeBisshop's in one of Gradeen's fields."

They waited to continue with the sensitive theme until the waitress took their order -- Rueben Sandwich with chips for him and Tortilla soup and half a Club Sandwich for her. They both added iced-tea.

"So why me?" he asked once alone again.

She pondered this, whether to find the words to explain it or to rationalize it to herself. She chewed her bottom lip contemplatively in a move he'd come to recognize as indecision or concentration. When she spoke, there was doubt and hesitancy so unlike her.

"Not sure, but there's something you need to know."

Here she paused just long enough for him to become concerned about what might be coming.

"Mr. McGraw and I ran a game on you. I was initially uncertain about your involvement. Mr. McGraw was insistent on your participation. I do know the offer to you was long in coming. He checked you out through several people, and even with your issues, he wants you on board. The other night's little game was to gauge how bad things really are."

While the idea bothered Eric, he appreciated her candor. He knew the wait in the conference room had been a test, so why not more? If the roles were reversed, and he'd heard damaging info, he too might have continued testing.

"But he's the one who suggested dinner," Eric said with confusion.

"I know. You were being good cop - bad copped."

"Which were you?" he asked dryly.

"The good cop of course," she replied in an upbeat tone. "You have to ask?"

She shrugged at this with a flirty tilt of her head as if to apologize or explain, or maybe both. Eric wasn't offended by the game, but she knew he'd be concerned about her role in it.

He proved this at once, by asking, "So what about the parking garage pact? By then, you and McGraw had basically already been working me."

She nibbled deliciously on her bottom lip.

"And I feel rotten about that. It's just that after spending time with you I started to see things differently. Don't take this the wrong way, but it turns out I kind of like you.

"I knew if the other stories were true I'd feel sympathetic toward you, but it was something more. I didn't see you as the third wheel any longer. Suddenly that was Mr. McGraw. Rather than him and I against you, it just looked like my better option would be to align myself with you. You and I being on the same team. I doubt we will actually be working against him, but . . ."

"So everyone in our little triad is being played except you?"

She laughed with this realization. "Yeah. That's about the size of it."

"And that's the way it's going to be?" he asked with a raised eyebrow.

The waitress brought their iced teas and two paper coasters without a word and set a small plastic container with sugar and sweetener packs between them. Jillian tore one of the pink packets open and stirred it in while she waited for their privacy to return.

"While I appreciate you being honest with me," he said, "none of what you told me explains my involvement."

"We want to find out what really happened, to discover whether Gradeen set this machination in motion. And *why?*. That remains the missing piece in our defensive puzzle. You called it the origin point. I'm assuming this is why Mr. McGraw brought you in."

As he took the first sip of his tea, Jillian continued. "You investigate this case as if you're prosecuting it. Then whatever you learn, we'll defend."

He regarded this and came back with, "Why all the games? Why not just level with me in the conference room?"

At this she smiled widely and said, "For one, my initial plan was to run you off. And a funny thing happened on my road to getting rid of you."

"You kind of liked me," he said with a wry grin.

"And now I regret telling you that."

This time her gorgeous eyes squinted, her smile dazzling.

"But no. It turns out you're quite good at this. I'm impressed by your words and powers of observation. Plus every word of your research. Mr. McGraw too. I forwarded it to him when you downloaded it to the case files this morning. So maybe we didn't need the game. I'm glad we didn't run you off."

He regarded this and said, "I guess I am too, to an extent."

"You got to the "Gradeen is guilty" days ahead of what we expected."

Eric considered this and changed the subject.

"It wasn't so much the evidence. I got there by two and two equaling five. There's not enough to convict, which I'm sure you've informed your client, but he's staying with the firm and paying the exorbitant fees nevertheless because he needs to. Innocent people don't do that. That leaves only one conclusion I could draw."

"See? That's what I'm talking about. That's deductive logic."

He formed a cheesy grin. "And that's why you kind of like me."

She too had to smile at his remark. And I could tell that there was something about this lost little puppy that was growing on her more all the time.

ELEVEN

Right toward the end of lunch, Jillian posed a question which redirected their conversation from a discussion of things past versus future.

"Tell me about the steps in your investigation," she said.

Okay. So maybe it wasn't so much of a question as much as an invitation for information.

He contemplated her statement and came back with a question of his own. "The way I see it, you have three vital areas of concern, right?"

I know what you are thinking. That's not much of a question either; it's more of a request for an affirmation of a fact. Don't mind me. I'll just get out of the way for a while.

"The three potential problems I see are DeBisshop," he said this with a raised index finger. "Fuller." Another finger joined the first. "And the cypher. If either of the first two are found still alive and willing to testify, or if they break their secret code, our client's situation changes."

She liked the fact that he was direct and succinct, a cut-to-the-chase kind of guy in a world full of bloviators. He made no pretense, enumerating the loose ends straightforwardly.

"Grand Jury transcripts reveal a Forrester guarantee of the deciphered code by trial. Then they have that added evidence."

"So, that bit of prosecutorial bluster, plus the circumstantial evidence got Forrester her indictment?"

"You do understand Grand Juries regularly return what the prosecution has asked of them. It's never an exceedingly high standard."

He grinned at her condescension and said, "Yes, Professor. I did eventually pass the bar, even though rarely does an *Ambulance Chaser* convene a Grand Jury. Tell me about the cipher and the Feds."

"Here's what I know. The FBI exclusively utilizes software and computers to crack codes, ciphers, and encryption nowadays. They can backdoor into the myriad of internet sites that encode and decode messages. It's apparently not that. They have access to years of history of military and diplomatic codes. It's not that. They have the smartest hackers available, and the highest tech money can buy, and yet have come up with nothing."

"Maybe the code is old-school, maybe even back before computers. Sounds like something out of a John Le Carre novel. Is it numbers or letters?"

"Numbers. We've been told the FBI has every book downloaded and can run combinations of pages and paragraphs yet can find no pattern."

"Every book?" There was more than a hint of skepticism in his tone.

"I'm just telling you what we know."

He took a swig of tea and said, "New topic: Might it be worth a trip to the old family farm in Edinburg?"

"That's unexpected, yet interesting. What are you hoping to find?"

"I don't know."

She sighed at this and laughed, "I thought you were going to say some trite and predictable line from movie dialogue. 'I'll know it when I find it.'"

She had lowered her voice a few octaves to mimic his deeper register and puffed up her chest to mock his self-importance as an investigator.

"You know I don't sound like that," he said with a mouthful of chips. "And I hope I don't look that pretentious when I talk either."

She considered this with vivid grey eyes squinting behind her black frames. She asked, "So if you make fun of my impression of you, aren't you really just making fun of yourself?"

"That's not how it works."

"I think it is."

"Okay then, but I have no problem making fun of myself." He accepted her terms too easily.

"But you're thinking I do?" she asked with a concerned grimace. "You think I'm too serious all the time, don't you?"

He never once paused. "I saw you Thursday night. Plus, if anyone had just seen that awful impersonation, they'd know you can poke fun at yourself."

"Was it that awful?" she asked self-consciously.

"Nooo," he drew out, rich with sarcasm. "Like looking in the mirror."

They both laughed at this little exchange and shared one of those almost sickeningly sweet moments, the staple of romantic comedies. When this story becomes a movie, the director will bring up the music and pan the camera back for the audience to see the other diners enjoying their little exchange. But they were basically alone in the diner, and I knew that he was not thinking in terms of romance any more than she was looking at this as a comedy.

"I am too serious," she said almost as if talking into her glass of iced-tea. Then she looked up and her eyes danced while she said, "Maybe I should spend more time around you. You're good for me. Thursday night was fun, and you do make me laugh."

"Then do you want to come with me?" he asked.

It took a second for the question's context to register before she asked, "To look at the farm? When are you thinking of going?"

His delay implied he'd not given his schedule any thought.

"I'd like to research it on-line first. It shouldn't be too hard to find info since its renown in the Gradeen family history."

"You like doing research, don't you?"

"Always have. I think it's good to know what you're walking into."

"I'll tell you what. There's a status update meeting first thing Monday morning with Mr. McGraw. Let's see what he thinks. If he green lights it, I'd love to go with you."

"I'd like to look at a working *Swarm Farm*. That has to be where they're testing the idea."

"Maybe a trip to the farm would be time well spent."

"Great. I'd like it if you came with me."

"Me too."

This conversation had gotten a bit too cute, too quickly, and we all realized it at once. They scrambled clumsily for their respective over-wing exits.

Eric bailed out first, "So you can introduce me to the players at the farm."

Jillian was down the chute right behind him.

"Right. After this long, it's time I got a look at what's happening out there."

Despite her inelegant attempt to backpedal, we picked up on her bringing up their spending time together. Were we reading too much into this? If there was any inference or insinuation in the remark, though, it lacked reinforcement by a smile.

After an awkward silence, she asked, "Do you know anybody at the SPD?" This was the commonly used acronym for the Springfield Police Department.

"In my previous life, I knew traffic cops and accident investigators. Don't really know too many detectives."

He took a sip of tea and asked, "What are you thinking?"

"I know DeBisshop's disappearance is being investigated as a murder, even without a body. I believe Fuller remains a missing person case."

"Are you thinking that rather than being dead, he's fallen off the grid?"

"That's the hope. Forrester wants to find him and offer immunity."

"Because Gradeen's the kind of person who might tie up loose ends?"

"I feel we have to continue to defend him based on that supposition. Both DeBisshop and Fuller have disappeared since the Federal investigation kicked into overdrive earlier this year."

Here she looked from side to side to ensure they were not being overheard.

"I'm not convinced Jameson Gradeen is the criminal mastermind he'd like to be perceived, but somebody more than likely sent Fuller to St. Louis to take out Steinhauer. That would be out of self-preservation."

"Do we have a copy of that police report?"

"We do. It's in the on-line case files with everything else. There are police reports, bios and last known whereabouts. Also depositions and Grand Jury testimony. There's plenty in there to keep you busy."

"I'll get started when I get back and then work on it tonight."

She wiped a paper napkin at a bread crumb on the corner of her mouth and set it on her plate, signaling lunch was over. She then tilted her head to one side and stared at him intently, her brain spinning with questions, her silence making him uneasy.

"I don't mind. I like feeling productive. I used to work a lot of weekends."

Again, she fell silent after this remark. The nibbling on the bottom lip was back, as was her timid smile. Then her eyes widened gloriously as it hit her, as it all fell into place and finally made sense. She understood why the new guy was outworking everyone on this case. It came back to her *idle hands* reflection from the other night.

"You've come to realize you need to stay busy, haven't you?"

Hers was not an accusatory tone. This was purely observational, asked and answered, making sense to both. He'd never considered it in those exact words, but he knew it to be the truth.

Softly he said, "My demons tend to prey on boredom and loneliness."

She knew his demon only as alcohol, but he was also regarding the she-devil across the courtyard who often visited. Those trysts with Lorrie Ann were wrong and embarrassing, and never would have occurred before the booze. Did he and Lorrie Ann have anything in common? Did he know anything about her outside of her kinky likes and her custody schedule?

He didn't want Jillian to learn about her, vowing right there to do whatever necessary to keep them apart. He had his failings, of which Jillian was fully aware. If Erin had left scars, Lorrie Ann remained an open wound. She was more than a mere shortcoming. *The Girl from across the Courtyard* was a weakness bordering on another addiction.

It was, in a way, his old life versus this new and improved life. Was it Lorrie Ann then and Jillian now? Or Lorrie Ann now, maybe Jillian in the future. But his two worlds had collided the night before in a lascivious way which neither could know, for the girl from last night's fantasy was sitting in his booth.

He felt mortified for not telling her, but too ashamed to admit it. How would she react? How was mentioning anything about it not degrading at most and sexual harassment in the least? Lorrie Ann would remain a secret. She was the nightmare, whereas Jillian might be the dream. Even though she was engaged.

She said, "Maybe back at the office we can work on this together."

It had been at least eight months since a woman had flashed signs or given him signals, so it would be no surprise if he were to miss them. By my count, this was now her third or perhaps even fourth overt overture. Or was I maybe misreading the situation? But if I was right and he failed to acknowledge these flirtations, would this chance ever present itself again?

She was an amazing woman, both in terms of looks as well as actions, but his hands were cuffed by situation. He understood any possible advances in return would be rebuffed by the force-field created by her huge diamond ring.

Although, if *The Girl from across the Courtyard* happened to knock again tonight, he and I both knew who would be in his head.

TWELVE

*H*ours later, the storeroom office looked like an Illinois farming community the morning after a tornado, open banker's boxes everywhere with folders and documents strewn around the glass table and stacked on shelves. Maybe a better analogy would be that it looked like the boxes had detonated, throwing lids and exploding their contents apparently into undistinguishable heaps. Yet in this mess, somehow Jillian maintained order, for she knew no other way to function. She was as organized as she was beautiful, as thorough as she was enjoyable to be around.

Their first interaction, working together as professional colleagues, was eye-opening for Eric. There was a way about her that seemed both exhaustive and demanding. She could grab a document or file from a box and in seconds have read and comprehended the main thrust. Based then on the topic of her discovery, the evidence or whatever, was sorted into piles. She worked at a furious pace, leaving him with little room to keep up, let alone compete.

Jillian understood the importance of this. If she didn't, he'd begin to drift. She needed him right at her elbow, diving into the boxes and coming up with information. It would be beneficial to the case while also being for his own good; she wanted to make sure those hands did not become idle.

They began their research at what she referred to as, "The bottom of the food chain." This meant the first pile would belong to Frederick R. Steinhauer.

At first blush, Freddy seemed anything but the ideal hitman. His life from childhood could be considered disposable, so on second thought, maybe the earlier conclusion was premature. Maybe a throwaway hitman was perfect in this situation. But he'd proven to be a bad choice, an unprofessional, because of allegedly killing the wrong target. And to make matters worse, he then called the intended target to warn her.

Freddy was a local boy, the product of the underfunded Springfield Public School system and a disinterested juvie program. He made it through ninth grade, dropping out sometime in his sophomore year. He bid farewell to formal education and hello to the court system before his sixteenth birthday. He later tried and failed to acquire his G.E.D. But he had an aptitude for cars, the son of an auto parts store clerk who served time for the distribution of meth out the back door of the store. Freddy followed in Edward Steinhauer footsteps. When he was found dead in St. Louis at the age of twenty-eight, he was working as a janitor at a local auto parts warehouse. Ex-cons with felony drug convictions had a six-month probationary period prior to being promoted.

There was not much in the files about the circumstances of Freddy's arrest or drug trial. He was assigned a public defender who, according to the recent police interview transcripts, had a hard time remembering Steinhauer without referring to his notes. Steinhauer was nabbed in a wide sweep of an inner-city area known for drugs and prostitution, sentenced for possession with intent to distribute. Freddy served one and half of the three-year hitch.

Friends and associates characterized Freddy as "different" and at the same time "distant." A neighbor in a run-down apartment complex mentioned he had many cats. Co-workers at the warehouse barely knew him, while most of the attendees at his funeral turned out to be men he'd met in the joint. The section of North St. Louis where his body and mask were discovered is a well-known area for meth and pills, so speculation was that upon realizing his mistake, the miscast hitman fled there looking to hide.

There, he attempted to contact a woman originally from Springfield named Cindy Wright. Their association went back to the neighborhood of their youth and then through his limited run with school. Ms. Wright was familiar to the St. Louis police with prostitution and drugs on her sheet.

A colleague of Ms. Wright's had been the last to see Freddy alive. During questioning, she stated he claimed to be in St. Louis for almost a full week looking for Cindy. His movements and whereabouts in that interim remained unknown to this day. The Feds showed her photos of everyone suspected of being involved, but she testified that she'd never seen any of them. But if the prosecution theory is to be believed, Fuller somehow tracked this loose end to St. Louis. But how? Was Cindy Wright somehow in this deeper than as a cursory witness?

Did Forrester and the Feds know something the defense didn't?

At the bottom of the Steinhauer pile was an interview with James Hoover, an overworked parole officer assigned to Freddy's case when released from prison. It appeared Hoover was responsible for the janitor job at the warehouse. His handwritten notes stated that after their initial meeting, "Steinhauer is at crossroad. Wants to rehabilitate with a great fear of recidivism. Will monitor. Could be the model parolee."

The last two words had been underlined for emphasis.

So, while the system seemingly had failed Freddy, the same could never be said for Randall Fuller. He too was a local product, but his path to disrepute wound through parochial schools and the U.S. military. After graduating high school, Fuller enlisted in the Illinois Army National Guard, assigned to the 2nd Battalion, 103rd Infantry. In 2005 he fought inside the Sunni Triangle in both Ramadi and Fallujah alongside the 2nd Marine Division before rotating home.

He joined the nearby Decatur, Illinois police force, but quickly developed a reputation for excessive and unnecessary force. After numerous complaints, the most severe of which had come from fellow officers, Fuller was terminated for cause. He sued the city, losing in a long and drawn-out mess and returned to Springfield to work for Sentry Security. Here again his propensity for rough stuff surfaced after he beat a would-be robber within inches of his life.

The story goes like this: Sentry Security ran an armed courier service for several businesses making small to medium cash bank deposits. On one of the runs, Fuller and his partner were accosted by a homeless man looking for a handout. Fuller drew his company-issued revolver, pistol whipping the man in view of bank employees and customers. Sentry Security, to save the face, fired Fuller. Again, a lawsuit was filed for wrongful termination, and again, Fuller lost. But it was the notoriety of this trial that apparently popped Fuller onto Jameson Gradeen's radar.

The circumstances of how they met remain a mystery, or if Gradeen himself had a hand in the hiring, but soon Fuller was an up-and-comer at *Agribotics Technologies*, rising quickly through the ranks of company security. When the top job of Security Chief opened, Fuller got the job over several longer-tenured candidates with better qualifications.

Jillian revealed they questioned Gradeen about Fuller's hiring on numerous occasions only to have him reply something along the lines of "Fuller nailed the interview."

As Head of Security for Gradeen's companies, Fuller was never too far removed from the boss. That was the Fed's connection. There were cell phone links from Steinhauer to a *burner* Fuller used while with Gradeen at a luncheon. It was a stretch, an unsubstantiated link at best, but linkage, nonetheless.

"The connection was established after the fact," Eric said. "Do we have any evidence of whether they knew each other before. Are we assuming Fuller solicited Steinhauer?"

Jillian looked up from the stack of papers on the table in front of her, the hair piled atop her head now hiding a pencil.

"We've been unable to uncover a connection."

"What if . . ." Eric began, bouncing a fingertip off his nose as he considered this. "What if their paths intersected when Fuller was a cop? The timing would be about right."

"That's good," she said with a slight tilt to her head. "We can look for his footprints over in Decatur to see if he's in their system. Well done."

"Thanks. Now let's talk about where Fuller might be, presuming he's still alive. We either need to find Fuller, or we make sure no one does."

She seemed surprised by this. "You do realize of course that we cannot do the latter? There's that little thing called obstruction of justice to consider."

"I get that, but how about this? If we regard Fuller and the National Guard the way you and I think of college or law school, wouldn't you have someone from back then to take you in and hide you, no questions asked?"

"No questions asked?" Her tone was uncertain, her expression amazing.

"Maybe this is more of a guy thing." When her look changed to questioning, he clarified by saying, "I'm sure there are any number of guys from your past who would love nothing more than your showing up unannounced and looking for help. They'd be stupid to not take you in."

"Oh, right," she laughed. "And why not make it at night in a rainstorm so I'm all wet and quivering? I'd look helpless, mascara running with my tears."

While thoroughly appreciating the visual produced by her comment, he had to chuckle at how quickly she could fire right back at him. She gave as good as she got; she was taking no prisoners in their battle of wits. And her performance wasn't quite finished.

She pouted her lips and made a despondent and pathetic face. While batting her perfect lashes, she said, "Eric, can you help me? I've nowhere else to go."

"Come in," he said almost reflexively, swallowing hard.

She laughed aloud at this, tossing a sheet of paper across the table at him. He grabbed it up and returned it to its assigned pile, hoping to busy himself straightening other piles while trying to compose himself.

"So, you'd let me in?" she asked in a tone as flat as if she asked about the weather.

They both understood that she was in fact toying with him. Likewise, they both knew he was unable to do anything about it.

"But even if Fuller wasn't all wet and vulnerable, and didn't look like you, wouldn't an old army buddy take him in and help him?" he asked.

She took off her glasses and gazed across the table at him. Very confidently she said, "He would if Fuller had saved his life in Iraq."

"That's perfect!"

Eric got up and went to the white board on the easel. On it in red marker were two lines. The first was "Farm in Edinburg." Below was "Decatur." And finally, as denoted by the number three, he printed "Fuller's Military Platoon."

She leaned back and threw her long perfect legs up onto the glass table, crossing the right over the left. She wore a pair of strappy heels like those from Thursday night. He watched as she rubbed those remarkable eyes.

"Let's take a break before we start on DeBisshop," she said, craning her neck from side to side.

"You sure? If you will excuse me, I think I will run to the little boys' room."

She opened her eyes and stared up into his. "Don't do that on my account."

He could tell by her stern tone that this time she was playing no games. He was busted. But as the man he'd become, guilty of nothing and willing to admit to less, he tried on an unconvincing smile.

He asked, "What? Go to the bathroom?"

"Come on. Really? When you went to the bathroom right after we got back from lunch you took your backpack, and I'm assuming you're doing the same now. Either," and here again she had said with the long "I" pronunciation. "You don't trust me not to look inside, or there's something in there you need."

He considered beginning his practiced dance of avoidance and evasion, of hemming and hawing, but he knew he was dead. He could accuse the accuser, question the questioner, or scream about his lack of privacy, all of which had worked at one time or another in the past. But that was his past. This was his present and to fulfill any hopes for the future, whether working with her or this firm, he had to come clean. He looked at his hands, surprised they weren't red for he was caught.

She got to her feet, glasses back in place, feet spread with hands on her hips and arms akimbo.

"Listen," she began in an unsympathetic voice that fit her posture. "Have enough respect for me to know that I get it. Okay, you have a problem. I can't fix it, but I'm willing to work with it or around it, whichever, because you are good at this. We have a job to do. And I like this."

Here she motioned a hand back and forth between them.

"Me too," he said barely above a whisper.

"I like working with you. At times, it rarely feels like work. Today has been fun. I feared I may have forgotten how to have fun. You've injected passion back into my work. Thanks for that. But please don't lie to me. Never hide things from me. If you're going to the men's room to have a swig from your flask, then tell me. I'm a big girl. Or do it right here. I get it. Okay?"

He stood silently rooted to the little piece of Seventh Floor carpet also supporting the easel and white board. Outside the wall of windows, clouds danced across the blue sky in total disinterest as he considered her words. It was as if he hadn't comprehended the last things she said or feared what the next out of her mouth might be. Was that last part a challenge? Was she daring him to pull out the flask?

But while all of this played in his mind, he realized she was waiting for him to make the next move. He watched her body language soften, feet now closer together, hands clasped at her waist. But it was those silvery grey eyes, again beseeching him. Somehow, once again he felt he could tell them anything.

"For the past eight months," he began slowly, looking for a footing. "I've lived in this claustrophobic little bubble of my own creation. I drink to drown the ghosts of my nightmares. I then drink to kill my hangovers. I drink to forget because I cannot forgive. I drink to feel pain while at the same time hoping to feel nothing. I drink simply to exist, to function. And every day it embarrasses me more, so I've become conditioned at hiding it without realizing I'm doing it. I don't want anyone to learn the true extent of my problem."

She flashed a sad smile and softly said, "You know I'm here. I'll help you any way I can. I don't know what that may be or how that might look. And I fear you may not have figured that out either."

"Not yet. I'm sure I'll have to check myself into a program eventually, but you don't realize how much your saying that means to me. It's good just to get this out in the open. And good to not be alone in this anymore. Thanks for just being here and listening."

Before she could reply, he added, "And I apologize for the position you find yourself in. First, I did this to me and now I've also done it to you. There's no excuse for that. If at any time you feel like . . ."

"No. I've never."

"I can be gone and out of your hair. Just say the word."

"I don't want that. . ."

"Good, because neither do I."

"You are particularly good at this. From a professional perspective, you will be a great help on this case. You see things differently than we do."

"Thank you."

Here she paused and flirtatiously nibbled on her bottom lip. "And from a personal angle, I haven't quite figured this out yet."

Again, she motioned her hand back and forth between the two of them. But unlike before, this time it was the hand with the huge diamond ring.

"Friends?" he asked in response to her indecision about the status of their relationship, before adding the caveat, "I hope. I've been doing this and dealing with this all alone for so long. It feels good to have someone on my side. I needed a friend. I also needed a job. You've given me both."

"So, we're friends and coworkers?"

"Is that okay?" he asked with a touch of worry in his voice. When she failed to immediately respond, he asked the question for a second time.

She turned away from him and then back, placing her left hand in the left pocket of her perfectly creased black slacks. Whether this was done to take the huge diamond out of his sightline he'd never know, but he noticed the move. She confessed to me later that she hadn't realized she'd done it.

When she again spoke, it was as if I could see the relief in her face, like a great weight had been lifted from her.

"I felt I needed to confront you. I hope you don't mind."

"Not at all."

He shuffled his weight from one leg to the other and laughed quietly, self-consciously.

"I'm like a helium balloon, just bouncing all over the place, close to disappearing into the sky for good. Mr. McGraw grabbed the string initially. He handed it to you. I appreciate the way you wrapped it around your finger, still holding on. There's comfort being around you, knowing that, at least for now, you get me and have me tethered. And since you confronted me about my problem, it's better . . . more honest."

"Good. I wasn't sure how you'd react. Frankly, I was a bit concerned."

"No need for that. You've been perfectly honest with me. I will be the same with you. I owe you that. I apologize for any earlier deceit and disrespect."

"Good. Great."

His hand started moving back and forth between them, the gesture the same as hers from earlier.

He said, "And *This*, whatever *This* might be, I like it too. And I can't thank you enough for including me."

She later admitted to me this little impromptu exchange hadn't gone exactly as intended, but she was nonetheless satisfied by the result. She'd been angling for somewhat of a tradeoff; an ear for an ear. Get him to confide things in her so she could do the same in return. You know, tell a total stranger things that you'd never unload on a friend.

Yet it never got to that point; she never got her turn because the roles were changing. Her total stranger was beginning to feel more like a friend.

And this friend had entrusted her with the ribbon string of his metaphorical balloon. For now, she had to make sure she maintained a firm hold.

THIRTEEN

A wise man once said, "When there have been missteps in your recent past, corrective steps are required in your immediate future."

Okay, that too was me, but it fit Eric's mood and outlook as he prepared to go jogging on Sunday morning. That's right. I said jogging. It had been a long time since throwing on the Nike's and heading out, but this was part of the first step in his rebirth.

The weather was overcast and spitting rain, fitting for central Illinois in late spring. It would've been the ideal morning to sleep in, but he'd resolved the night before to go running, and neither hell nor high water had yet arrived. He stretched his hamstrings and calves on his front steps, plotting in his head the route he'd attempt. He wasn't overly optimistic about his stamina, hoping determination alone might suffice. He reminded himself there would be no shame in walking back if he went out too fast.

He adjusted the jogging phone case on his upper left arm and tuned into the *Incubus* station on his phone's *Pandora* app. The band reminded him of high school. Plus, more than once back then he'd been told by girls that he resembled Brandon Boyd, the band's lead singer.

He rammed in the wireless earpieces and cranked the volume, pulled down hard on his ballcap. After a deep breath, he started off on the paved sidewalk crossing Lake Springfield over to Lake Park by the zoo.

His pace began slow and controlled, easy strides, one foot in front of the other. Right-left-right-left-right-left, in rhythm with an *Incubus* song called "Summer Romance (Antigravity Love

Song.)" Check it out. You'll like it. It's from their 1997 CD called *S.C.I.E.N.C.E.*, their second album, which some of their hard-cores swear is their best.

As he ran, raindrops bouncing off his cap and nylon pullover, he thought back to the many missteps of his last eight months. He wasn't going to fix the drinking with willpower alone, or in one night. He had, however, successfully fended off his drinking's collateral damage. While rarely would you ever admit to hiding in your condo not to have sex, that's what he'd done. He'd purposely doused all the lights and retired to his bedroom with his laptop. Granted he had one of the *Glen's* for company, but he hadn't gone to the door when *The Girl from across the Courtyard* knocked.

This was a victory, small in stature, but victory nonetheless. When he awoke, he felt a pride of accomplishment in that place normally reserved for hangovers. He'd promised himself he was going to do something – or in this case, not do something – and he'd seen it through. And now, just as he had also sworn to himself the night before, he was running.

Toward the end of the *Incubus* song is a saxophone solo, which is surprising on an *Incubus* track, but it's great sax. And as any sax is wont to do to most men, it made him think of women, or more specifically one woman: Jillian.

Here running through the rain, his mind flashed on the mental image of her at his door in a similar downpour, crying, drenched, shaking. She referred to it as "quivering?" The word had naughty connotations. He'd let her in.

So, how many of these new leaves being turned over were for her benefit? And how many were her responsibility? He knew avoiding Lorrie Ann was definitely because of her. Whether or not the future held any shot of true friendship or more with Jillian, Lorrie Ann had to go. There was always the possibility that *The Girl from across the Courtyard* might reappear, but he'd temporarily dodged a bullet which wouldn't be loaded again until Wednesday.

So, there was good from hoping to impress the impressive Jillian Stennet. Was he then also running because of her, or for himself? Did it matter?

He could not stop thinking about her, but the dichotomy of their situation was torturous. On one hand, she continued flashing less than subtle signals, flirtations, and seemingly evident advances, while on the other hand was the huge diamond ring. It was like simultaneously pulling him close and straight-arming him away; what she said rarely matched her nonverbal cues. It was like her words and her body were speaking a different . . . language.

Was she doing this, or was it his imagination? If she was, did she realize it?

Or the better question: Was she doing anything, really? Had he somehow imagined the whole thing? She was a fun, amazing woman, the total package – personable, gorgeous, confident, successful. The future Mrs. Stennet – *Somebody*, Esq. Why would a woman like her bother to waste her precious time toying with an alcoholic former lawyer turned investigator?

But it wasn't like she was wasting her time on him. It was more like she was investing it in him, bringing him along slowly, patiently cultivating him. If he was clay, she was his sculptor. But what was the final product to be? Was he investigator or attorney? Just friend or more?

He'd been out of the game for a while, but not so long that he'd forgotten the rules. Yet he couldn't get a read on her. Like late yesterday, they completed the background of Dr. Arthur DeBisshop. It was already gaining on six o'clock. They'd again worked great together, playing off each other's suggestions and suppositions, sometimes even finishing each other's thoughts and sentences. There was even the time when she playfully pushed him aside at the white board so she could finish a list he'd started. As with everything else about her, her penmanship too was flawless.

The work was all business, but also enjoyable. They fleshed out additional connections between Gradeen and DeBisshop personally and professionally. Their respective companies also intersected in ways previously not considered. It was mutually agreed that if Gradeen was at the hub of this case around which all the players wheeled, DeBisshop was closer to being on the inside than out. Eric used a tire metaphor to which she laughingly suggested DeBisshop was a lug nuts.

As they prepared to leave for the day, he noticed she looked tired. Other tendrils had joined the few rebellious strands of hair, as she again removed the glasses to massage her incredible eyes and rub the bridge of her nose. He hadn't wanted to let the fun stop any more than he wanted to be alone for the remainder of the evening, so he had casually asked if she was hungry.

"Do you want to get something to eat? My treat this time."

It was a harmless request. They'd earlier danced around Saturday night plans. She'd been her customary ambiguous self at best and noncommittal at worst. He'd intended no hidden meaning, no allusion that it might be a date. It lacked insinuation or agenda. There was no subtlety or smoothness.

Thinking back on it now, he considered it to have been almost caveman-like in its approach. There was never any intention to club her over the head and drag her back to his cave, yet it had been a blunt one-two combination of questions.

You hungry? Wanna go eat?

"I'm not sure that's such a good idea," she'd replied, void of any positive or negative indicators.

In doing so, she'd once again been so vanilla in a response void of any explanation that it produced more questions than any answers. This time it had to be on purpose, for nobody can reply with so many double meanings without trying. Like the true lawyer she was, she could answer "Yes" and/or "No" to the exact same question and be believable in both.

Even now, running in the rain, a *Linkin Park* song in his headphones, he still couldn't reconcile her answer. On a night when she apparently had no plans, why was dinner not a good idea? Was it the dinner aspect or the person proffering the invitation? Did that then make it a bad idea? If so, when was eating ever bad? Was it because of the huge diamond? Or did she now see him as a threat to the promises made with the acceptance of said ring? Could it not being *such a good idea* be somehow construed as being good for him?

Regardless of these answers, he never aimed to be the next Patterson Ritter. He wouldn't inject himself into anyone's engagement. Period. So maybe she was right after all.

Her curious response prompted him to concede defeat at once. He wasn't in the mood for games. Question asked and answered. Time to move on. Time for single-malt.

Placing his laptop in his backpack, he said in a somewhat distant voice, "Maybe some other time."

At this, her expression had clouded over, and her face noticeably fell, the disillusionment deeply etched. He failed to notice, but she was disappointed he accepted the knockdown so easily without any counters. She was in the mood to spar, or at least trade jabs. She wanted to play, to be pursued, to let herself be worn down by his persistence before eventually agreeing. She wanted him to work for it. But surprisingly, she got none of that. He was down for the count and apparently staying there.

His unwillingness to chase surprised and saddened her. Where was that guy who previously refused to believe she was out of his league? Didn't he get his teeth on something and then refuse to let go? When had all that changed? What happened to his determination? Did she wish to remain unobtainable?

All this newfound self-doubt left her with limited ladylike alternatives. She imagined stepping over to the white board and listing her possible responses: 1.) Reconsider the dinner offer; 2.) Counter with drinks rather than dinner; or 3.) Do nothing.

"Are you leaving now? I'll walk with you down to your car."

Having said this, Eric made the choice for her. Shockingly it was #3.

After gathering up their belongings, they left together in relative silence, neither saying much of anything of importance. And that's neither with the long "I" sound. When they got in the elevator, they looked like two boxers mid-bout, each retreating to their neutral corner. But this bout was already over, and their reflections in the mirrored door made them both appear to be losers.

"Security in the lobby can see me to my car," she said as a means of ending everything right there in the elevator. "We have an 8:30 Monday morning with Mr. McGraw. Remember, punctuality is important to him."

He said, "I remember. Thanks for today. I enjoyed it."

"Me too."

The elevator door opened on *Three,* and he stepped out where he'd parked. Their day together was over, just like that. There would be no holding the doors open for lingering good-byes, no second thoughts, no second guessing. He'd ripped that Band-Aid clean off.

As Pandora switched to "Dark Necessities" by *Red-Hot Chili Peppers,* he played in his mind how things may have gone. What if he'd not stepped off the elevator? What if he had just manned up and asked her why all her games? Why was he afraid to ask for specifics on *Mr. Somebody?* Why was she hesitant to offer any, or anything about herself?

Often times people choose careers where they get to ask questions, so they don't have to answer any. I have no basis of fact for this notion, but I did feel it to be very insightful, nonetheless. If true, she's the poster girl.

He looked around now and noticed not too many others as determined or as stupid to be running in this weather. The other thing he realized was that he was already a long way from his home. He thought about it like reading books as a kid. You find yourself turning the page without any idea what you just read. In that same way, he'd made it halfway around his loop without knowing how he got here. If he stopped now, it would be as far to get home continuing forward or going back. It was time to get back to moving forward.

Jillian remained a mystery in the same way Erin had been straightforward, grey in the way Erin had been black and white. If it had been Erin toying with his affections in such an obtuse way, he'd have called her out on it, for she had never been much of a game player.

Erin Haynes had been a prosecutor, and by all accounts, a damned good one, always on offense, moving forward toward a verdict. Erin would get directly to the heart of the matter based solely on the facts. That's also the way she lived, right versus wrong in a world were right was rewarded and wrong demanded punishment. She laid her cards out on the table for all to see, good hand or bad. When she won, it was always beyond a shadow of a doubt.

Jillian, on the other hand, from the defensive side of the aisle, oftentimes sidestepped charges if not strategically stalled and/or dragged, or other dilatory tactics. She didn't need facts, or even right or wrong. She wanted wide open spaces where the whites of truth and the black of lies blurred together into a muddled grey. You never got to see her cards. As he knew firsthand, she wasn't afraid to bluff with a bad hand, for somewhere in her version of poker the best hand holds the reasonable doubt card.

The best example of the variances between them could be illustrated by an old lawyer joke. It goes like this:

The defense counsel in a murder trial, let's call her Jillian, is wrapping up her closing argument. She tells the jury that the man her client is accused of killing will walk into the courtroom in five seconds. As she dramatically counts down from five, every member of the jury turns to look toward the door.

"There's your reasonable doubt," she announces to the jury. "Everybody in the courtroom turned to look."

The prosecutor, let's say her name is Erin, stands up and points out that, "Everybody in the courtroom did look, except for the accused."

Smoke and mirrors versus fact. Reasonable doubt as opposed to beyond any doubt. Professionally they were different because their respective sides of the aisle dictated such. But they could have traded places, along with the resources and tactics, and both been equally successful. Lawyers pick their side of an argument and fight to the death. Tomorrow it may be the exact reverse. They will passionately defend their new position as if it had been theirs all along.

Coming from Erin's side as a plaintiff's attorney, proving and prosecuting, he could gravitate more toward her in the professional sense. Theirs was a world of absolutes. I will prove to you what happened so there is no doubt in any of the twelve jury members. He liked the straightforwardness.

But now, suddenly involved in his first criminal defense, he could also see the value in Jillian's methods. Instead of facts and proof, there was punching holes and what-ifs. Instead of twelve buying in from the jury box, there only had to be one who wasn't. Hung juries are considered wins to the defense.

Two women from different sides of the aisle had their pluses, both their minuses. Both had jobs to do. Neither better than the next. Two interchangeable women. Two interchangeable approaches.

Next up on *Pandora* was "Everything You Want" by *Vertical Horizon*. It was more of a sing-along song rather than a driving rocker, so he settled into a comfortable stride. As the rain pelted holes in the lake to his left, he wondered what might have happened if Erin and Jillian had ever met.

Outside the courtroom, could they have been friends?

Both being professional women, they'd initially have been cordial, if for no other reason than politeness, or mutual respect, woman to woman. Jillian had a few years on Erin and definitely made more money. Here again this was no reflection on ability. It was because Erin had worked as a county prosecutor, a civil servant, while Jillian had been with her firm since law school. She drove a $65,000 BMW whereas Erin had a used Honda Accord. Jillian had pedigree with a lengthy and impressive resume'. Erin was just a girl from the area who sought to find equal justice under the law. But while Jillian remained a mystery or an illusion, the two in the bush, Erin had been his bird in the hand. She was real.

He thought about her last text on her last day, and almost as if by rote, it again played through his head as if written in iambic pentameter. There was a flow or rhythm to her words.

"Don't hate me. Just have to do this one last thing. Then yours forever. Love you."

The lines had fit perfectly in the little blue text bubble, almost as if she chose what to say based on spacing and right-justification. Five lines evenly stacked and perfectly punctuated with only the bottom line not spilling all the way over to the right.

Rather than dissect each word, every period, or any grammatical deficiency, as he was prone to do when warm and dry, today in the rain, soaked and out of breath, he was reduced to only one thought.

Erin was to be his wife.

FOURTEEN

*T*he initial cursory investigation of Dr. Arthur DeBisshop the day before had revealed little more than the man's veneer. Born in Horsens, Denmark after World War II, his biography included bullet-points -- a graduate of both the University of Copenhagen and the Technical University of Denmark, master's degree in chemistry at the former and mathematics and engineering Doctorates at the latter. He was a tenured college professor in Denmark before emigrating to Central Illinois with his now-deceased wife in 2007. There were no children. He went to work for *Agri-Illinois,* reporting to CEO Thomas Gradeen, who sponsored his work visa. He stayed there for five years before leaving to head up research and assume the role of COO at *Agricultural Chemical Group.* He's been missing and presumed dead for the last four months.

Nowhere mentioned in his bio was the name Jameson Gradeen until the recent investigation and their consequent legal troubles. It's assumed they met while working for *Agri-Illinois.* Ironically, they'd left within months of each other.

This seemed odd. Everyone was working off the assumption the nefarious association had been between DeBisshop and Jameson, but he'd first worked for the father. Had others missed this tenuous connection, or was there nothing to it? It made sense based on age that he'd have had a relationship with the elder Gradeen. Did the fact that they both left at basically the same time -- DeBisshop for ACG and Jameson to start *Agribotics Technologies* -- mean anything?

It was on a deeper dive that Eric stumbled upon something remarkable. Back in 1995, Dr. DeBisshop published an article in a Danish trade publication about "Control Architectures for Autonomous

Mobile Vehicles." In the paper, he discussed the inclusion of separate layers of abstraction for handling both deliberation and reactivity in a hybrid architecture, something, something, agricultural something in the route plan for autonomous vehicles.

This was heavy science and even heavier vocabulary for Eric, but he got the gist of it: Ag-bots.

Over twenty years ago, DeBisshop had postulated about the application of mathematical principles of graphing movements of agricultural machines traversing arable land. This was primitive "*Swarm Farm*" theory.

The coincidences were too many to be discounted, the discovery prompting a whole new line of questioning. Had Thomas Gradeen brought DeBisshop to America to help his son's company still five years from formation? Unlikely. There are men of vision, but had Thomas Gradeen been able to see that far into the future? Or had there been another purpose for bringing the Danish scientist to Central Illinois? If that were the case, what was Thomas Gradeen up to in 2007?

At first blush, DeBisshop appeared to be the one lab accident away from becoming the axiomatic mad scientist. Okay. A bit of a stretch; I wanted to use that line I saw on a T-shirt, so I wedged it in here.

More to the point, DeBisshop was maybe only one more episode away from being classified as an environmental terrorist. As a consultant for a Danish Ag-chem Conglomerate, he was reputed to have been responsible for faulty design of a burst silo in Frederica Harbor which leaked several tons of liquid fertilizer into the water. Sparks from the silo's collapse then caused palm oil from a neighboring tank to catch fire, resulting in the evacuation of a one-kilometer radius area. Firefighters fought the blaze through the night. Clean-up crews scraped liquid fertilizer residue off everything the water touched in and around the harbor.

In the investigation, DeBisshop testified in front of the Associated Danish Ports Authority, willing to scapegoat anyone to protect himself.

He placed the blame for the burst silo on either a malfunctioning crane or the crane operator. This denial of responsibility didn't sit well with the Danish Environment and Food Minister, Peter Kjelle Swensen, who officially censured him.

The Copenhagen newspaper *Metroxpress* savaged him, describing him as hypersensitive and vindictive. The paper then embarked on a campaign of their own, advocating for the revocation of his tenure at the Technical University. Before he could be censured again, DeBisshop was quickly on his way to America. Eric thought this might be worth discussing at the Monday meeting.

Another person of interest might be Thomas Gradeen himself. Was there a link to this outside of strictly paternal? There had to be a reason for bringing Dr. DeBisshop to Illinois almost ten years ago, but what? Why would one of Springfield's most distinguished corporate citizen stick his neck out to bring a disgraced Danish eco-terrorist to work in his company?

Against these unknowns, Eric looked more closely into the background of the *Agri-Illinois* CEO. He'd learned the day before about the man's humble beginnings on the Edinburg farm and his climb to the top of the local civic ladder, stepping up on the rungs of struggling local farms and small Agri-chem companies. He'd read about his philanthropy and his causes, seen the photos of Gradeen with various politicos and local celebrities. His was the tried-and-true rags-to-riches story, the kind they write songs about. Or at least books and movies.

But books and even movies need controversy and there appeared to be none in the past of Thomas Gradeen. He was born on the Edinburg farm and worked it with his father and brother until outliving both. Eric thought it would be great if he murdered his brother or something as bloody? Okay. Maybe *great* was a poor choice of words, but if he'd been a Cain and his brother an Abel, it might explain a lot. Maybe his father died under mysterious circumstances. Had Cain maybe also murdered Adam? Was there biblical precedent for that?

Hardly. Thomas Gradeen had no formal education after high school yet had somehow managed to turn one farm into an empire. Had he done it alone? Was there someone in his past to guide him or to trod upon? Was his rise to the top at the expense of others? Were there bodies buried in his past like the ones alleged to be in his son's? Could this be a Gradeen family trait?

If all the stories were true, that he got to where he was by doing everything legitimately, had there at least been a burning bush moment which inspired him? Perhaps a fork where he may have taken the road less traveled? Rarely does a common man achieve this level of greatness without a trigger, whether positive or negative.

That trigger, or event from his past if it did exist, remained a mystery. Eric dug and delved, read and reread, finding scant about Thomas Gradeen which might contradict the rosy tale. Magazines loved him; the area newspapers sang his praises. He was almost too clean.

About then he stumbled across a book titled *Thomas Gradeen: Titan of the Prairie. An Unauthorized Biography*, written by local author R. J. Harris, and published by Python Publishing. They were listed as a self-publisher with a Chicago address. A search for a local store where he might find the book came up empty. A paperback copy could be ordered from Python Publishing, but it would take two weeks.

The author's name revealed similar results. That search spun him right back to the biography and the publisher. It was like he found himself in a do-loop. Look for the book and get the author. Search the author and you get directed to the book. R.J. Harris apparently was not prolific; there were no other titles associated with him. Nevertheless, his name was added to the list to discuss in their morning meeting.

As he gave second thought to the Thomas Gradeen angle, he realized that tangent represented a rabbit hole quite possibly not worth visiting. Plus, if the senior Gradeen and McGraw were indeed personal friends, and apparently that relationship remained open for discussion, would a firm's partner let them make a run at Gradeen? It might be worth dancing around with McGraw, but it would have to be from a safe distance.

Next on his list was to peruse the police reports scanned into the office data base. Being a personal injury lawyer, he was more astute at reading accident reports and viewing diagrams of who hit who and where. These were even more mundane, if possible. The reports were little more than transcribed narratives of interrogations of the players. Most had taken place with either Jillian or an underling present, so little of any substance or import had been revealed to the detectives.

A distant faint buzzing interrupted Eric's attentiveness. It was coming from his backpack on a kitchen chair. I recognized it as the vibration of a cell phone, but it took him some time to make the connection. When he withdrew the firm-issued iPhone, he saw a text from a number identified as Jillian Stennet. Was everyone's contact info preloaded into the phones?

"How's your day? Got time to talk?" her text read.

It was my idea, and after some convincing he reluctantly agreed to play along. He quickly typed back, "New phone. Who dis?"

She immediately responded with, "Funny."

"What are you wearing?" he texted back. I must take the credit for this one too. I'm like that. Besides where has all the fun gone if you can't do a little obscene texting between friends?

Then the phone in his hand vibrated with an incoming call, signaling their little reindeer game had ended before going too far. He thought she might have given him a little more rope, but she showed little patience.

He answered it by saying in a short burst, "*Donaldson, Clement, Blaine & McGraw.* Eric McKegney's phone."

"That's funny too," she said in a mocking tone. "It's not even four o'clock on a Sunday afternoon. Are you drinking already?"

Her comment offended him. Just because he answered in a frivolous manner didn't necessarily mean he was drinking. Was she implying there's no place for silliness while sober? He looked to the bottle of Glenfiddich and the half-filled glass leaving a condensation ring on the legal pad next to his laptop and lied to her.

She said, "Something has come up we need to discuss."

"Everything okay?"

Here she hesitated before coming back with, "Are you doing anything now? Can you meet me so we can go over this in person?"

"Really? You bet." Regardless of the potential level of calamity, he'd get to see her.

"I'll even let you buy me dinner."

It was only getting better. He was already on his feet, heading to the shower with a half-filled glass of Glenfiddich.

"When and where?"

She looked amazing in the oversized white-with-black-trim Nike drawstring pullover, with accenting – and incredibly snug fitting – black yoga pants. She sat alone at one of the four or five outside tables on the patio of the little Italian eatery, hair in a ponytail, sunglasses on, right leg crossed over left, hot pink running shoe steadily bouncing up and down. Nibbling absentmindedly on a breadstick from a plastic basket full of them, she was reading something on her phone as Eric neared.

She glanced up and smiled adorably, yet almost embarrassed. Here she was in sweats, having made no real attempt to dress for dinner while he put forth an effort. He was wearing a pair of light blue Levi's and a navy shawl-collar sweater, hands in the side pockets on his approach. His long dark hair appeared damp. Since the rain had stopped hours before, it didn't take Miss Marple to deduce he showered. He hadn't shaved though, the dark stubble inviting to maybe spark a bit of friction.

It was enjoyable just being around him. She'd be hard pressed to define it because she didn't fully understand it herself. She liked that he was different than the stuffed-suit attorneys dealt with daily. He was a breath of fresh air on an otherwise stale *Seventh Floor*, exhibiting life among the moribund, fun amidst the fun-haters. And tonight, again there was no pretense, no trying to be something he's not. He was here, he was handsome, and he'd be hers, uninterrupted for the next few hours.

They exchanged small talk about little or nothing except the changes in the day's weather. Rain in the morning and now cloudy with a brisk nip to the air. The waitress stopped by to drop off menus and take drink orders. Eric scanned the small patio, five other tables with red and white checked linens and Chianti bottles with candles as centerpieces. The smell of freshly baked bread filled the air as instrumental music provided the background soundtrack.

He mentioned he'd never eaten here. Jillian explained she'd represented the owners many years before. Nowadays she visited solely for the Caesar salad.

He looked from side to side and asked with an animated expression, "You represented the family that owns this place. Is this a mob restaurant?"

"I can't tell you that," she said dryly and with no facial expression.

"Anybody swimming with fishes?"

When she only answered with a patronizing smile, he shifted in the seat and started down a new road we rehearsed on the drive over. He wanted to explain himself from the night before. I thought he should lead with empathy called for by their current circumstances, a woman and a man working closely together with potential possibilities inherent in similar situations.

You know, the *Will they? - Won't they?*.

Then once groundwork was laid, go for the truth about *Mr. Somebody* and the huge diamond. I was adamant that tonight he does not settle for side-stepping. Tonight presented a fantastic opportunity to get to the truth. After all, she invited him.

Apparently, I'd wasted my breath. He began by seeking forgiveness for his actions. This bled into an extremely misguided, one-sided discussion about boundaries. It sounded lame when he'd role-played it aloud in the car. It was worse now.

"Thanks for calling," he said. He began slowly, for his intent was to build momentum.

"I was worried I overstepped last evening with the dinner invite. I intended nothing more than a meal. I promise. I hope I didn't mess this up because I wouldn't want to do that."

He gave her a wide opening to jump in, to say something, anything. When she chose silence, he nervously kept talking, gradually building speed.

"Things got kind of short and strained last night when we were leaving. That was my fault. I'm sorry. It seemed that I did something untoward, and I never intended to be the thing that comes between our friendship."

She considered this last comment and tilted her head to one side, her all-seeing eyes still hidden by the dark shades.

"That's a unique way of looking at it. Your coming between us," she finally said in a tone he recognized as a sort of confused approval.

Third gear now. "You're engaged. And all I know about the guy is that he's a lucky bastard. Then there's me, a drunken *Ambulance Chaser* who just met you three days ago. You're my boss. The fact that we are sitting here together at all makes us one of the odder couples ever."

It was time to kick it into overdrive. "So now, all that being said, please rest assured I know my place. In it I shall stay. We work together. That's it. We're colleagues and I won't do anything to compromise that implied trust."

She took all of this in with a knowing grin. "So, let me get this straight. You won't be asking me to dinner ever again?"

This had been asked with that deviously coy smile that simultaneously drew him in and pushed him away. There may have been mock disappointment in there too, but either way he stood rock solid.

"Never again. Unless there is a mutually agreed upon business purpose."

She tilted her head to ask, "So then it would be a business dinner?"

"Right. Business dinners will be okay."

He was really tripping all over himself now, groping to establish invisible parameters between personal and professional.

She didn't seem bothered in the least by all his histrionics and stumbling. She reached across the table and placed her right hand on his left forearm.

Calmly, she whispered, "No worries. You and I are good."

"Thanks." It was time. I prodded so he asked, "You want to talk about you?"

When she hadn't fired right back with some sassy remark or a response dripping in sarcasm he was surprised. She looked to her left toward a large hedgerow of evergreens that offered a semblance of privacy to the diners. At this he got his first look at her eyes behind her sunglasses, the bright white and smoky grey in sharp contrast to her dark lashes, which were incredible from this angle, long and full, curling perfectly upward. When she turned back to him after more than a few beats, she spoke in a tone somewhat foreign to him. It was distant and mysterious in that he'd not heard anything like it previously.

"My current situation is complicated," she said almost in a whisper.

The waitress arrived to save either of them from further proceeding down this uncomfortable road. As she placed a glass of red wine in front of Jillian, he looked at her and got this eerie feeling. She seemed to stiffen. There were secrets buried inside her, and he could tell by her expression, regardless of his prying, they weren't spilling out tonight.

He raised his scotch and toasted, "To a successful business dinner."

Her smile returned before the glasses touched. After a sip, she announced it was time to get down to business, immediately demonstrating she intended to be in control. She began by chronicling the work already done on her supposed day off. Mr. McGraw had called her shortly after noon when he had returned from Sunday service and brunch at the club with the wife. She'd praised Eric's progress in developing new avenues in the investigation, those white-board topics from the day before.

"I've got a few new ones, too," he said, interrupting her flow.

"More? Anyway, Mr. McGraw thought it best to get you some help. He wants one of our investigators to assist you. The man will be at the meeting tomorrow morning."

Tentatively he asked, "Are you then out of the loop? Will I report to this guy? Is that why we're meeting? You wanted to dump me in person?"

His last question had been accompanied by a sardonic grin.

"No one is being dumped. The only change is that you now have someone below you." A light smirk accompanied this remark, for she did revel in her elevated spot in their command hierarchy.

Then it hit him, and there was a part of him that considered not asking, but I convinced him to trot it out there, let her know that he knew and put it on display to see where it might lead.

"You could have told me this over the phone," he said matter-of-factly. "Instead you invited me to dinner."

"That's right." She tried to brush his remark off as immaterial.

"Is that because you kind of like me?"

I was proud of this question. It was almost as if I was working his mouth.

"Didn't we already have that discussion?" she asked with a disarming grin. "Remember: Business dinner."

"We did. My apologies for forgetting."

"Yes. We could have done this over the phone, but then you wouldn't have this chance to tell me all about the new angles you've discovered in the case."

Wait! Oh, she was good. She'd almost gotten away with it, too. Eric missed it completely, but I hadn't, so I pointed it out.

"You didn't know anything about that until I got here," he protested.

"Didn't I?"

Now this was getting too surreal. With her stone-faced expression and those damned dark glasses, she looked like a cold-blooded assassin, or a spy. This made a part of him believe she already knew what he uncovered. But how? Was his new firm-issued iPhone bugged? The only way anyone could know would be to have remotely checked the web pages he visited on his firm-issued laptop. He'd never put it past them, but was that something the firm could do?

And now thinking about the security apparatus at the firm, Eric's attention was drawn to the arrival of the only other patron on the outside patio. He was a large man with a military style haircut seated caddy-corner from their table closer to the hedges. He sat with his back to Eric, facing in the same direction as Jillian, so he was unable to see his face. Was he firm security? He had the physique for it. Were they being followed?

Was it possible the firm could access his web searches on the internet and follow him? She'd mentioned the name of the restaurant, Piozzi's, during their call over the firm-issued iPhone. What if someone was listening in? Was he losing his mind? And what was she up to now?

It had started slowly, the blank expression cracking a faint grin which then bloomed into a gorgeous smile. Her giggles soon became full-blown laughter, and by the time her hand came up to her mouth, it was so contagious he couldn't help but join in. She'd fished him and easily set the hook. She hadn't known about any new discoveries any more than she could guess what they might be, but she'd delivered the line so coldly and believably that he had to consider the possibility.

But her bluff never answered our initial question. Why hadn't she just told him all of this on the phone? Was it presumptuous to think that maybe she did kind of like him? I would have to give this more thought.

Moving on, he told her about the connection of Dr. DeBisshop in Denmark and America. In the old country, he was an early *Swarm Farm* theorist and eco-terrorist. Over here he was charged with conspiracy to commit murder and had since disappeared. He also mentioned to her about the unauthorized biography of Thomas Gradeen, written by R. J. Harris.

"We need to add the name to our list to investigate," he said in conclusion.

"And we need to get our hands on a copy of that book," she added.

This brought him to yet another crossroads, those proverbially converging at Thomas Gradeen.

"I think he's involved much more than McGraw is willing to admit."

Jillian scrounged up her incredible face as she regarded this idea.

"His fingerprints are all over this. He sponsors DeBisshop's emigration from Denmark long before Jameson forms his own robotics company. Why? And for a disgraced Danish chemist? Then DeBisshop leaves *Agri-Illinois* the same time Jameson does. Is this because Thomas forced them out, or was this the plan all along? And then DeBisshop's research farm turns out to be the original family farm. Whether these are connected or simply coincidence, I don't think the father should get a free pass."

She regarded this further, knowing it to be an avenue McGraw would wish to avoid.

"Regardless of their current relationship, that's going to be a tough sell. I've told you he and Mr. McGraw go way back. I know he's in more than one photo hanging on the wall of the big office."

"I get that. But what if Forrester has been going after the wrong Gradeen?"

She leaned in close to whisper, "The father is not our client."

He glanced over his shoulder to ensure the other patron was not listening and replied also in a whisper.

"Wouldn't the son take the rap for the father? Whoever is charged will walk on this. Plus, you said that Thomas Gradeen is paying the firm's retainer."

While she continued to consider all these likelihoods and the ramifications of each, he asked another question.

"Does *Attorney/Client privilege* extend to the person paying the bills? Can we tell Thomas we are investigating him in order to defend the son?"

"Or are we prohibited from divulging to Thomas what we may learn?"

"That too. Is the retainer payor entitled to know the goings on in the case?"

As their Caesar salads were delivered, and they proved to be as delicious as Jillian had promised, I decided to let these two eat and carry the story myself.

For those of us without law degrees, let's quickly review the articulation of the *Attorney/Client privilege*, or *ACP* as the pros call it. There are four basic necessary elements to establish its existence. #1.) A communication; #2.) Made between privileged persons; #3.) In confidence; #4.) For the purpose of seeking, obtaining or providing legal assistance to a client.

The rules for third-party payers are detailed in the *Rules for Professional Conduct*, or *RCP*. Under Rule 1.8(f) a lawyer is permitted to accept fees from a third party provided #1.) the client consents, #2.) the lawyer continues to protect the client's confidential information, and #3.) the lawyer recognizes the third party is not the client and as such should never direct the representation.

Jillian swallowed a mouthful of salad and said, "Even though the third-party payer rules seem pretty clear, there's still serious ethical issues. Confidentiality and evidentiary are two since the payer's need to monitor the progress must be considered. Whether third party or not, all payers want accountability of our spending."

"I get that. I know I would if I was writing the check." He stabbed his fork in his salad bowl and said, "Does the client have any say in what's disclosed to the third-party payer? Can Jameson dictate what we can tell his father?"

"That's the true essence of the ACP. It keeps us from telling anyone what Jameson might tell us. That includes the authorities, other defendants, or even his father. We have to control those who know any of the pertinent facts. This would certainly include Thomas. I'm guessing he knows everything. Jameson probably told him himself. That's maybe why he seems anxious."

"I know husbands and wives can't, but can a father be compelled to testify against his son?"

"Yes, but the judge could rule it all hearsay and therefore inadmissible."

Thinking aloud, Eric said, "Because Jameson would have told Thomas."

"Exactly." Here she paused with a fork full of romaine lettuce inches from her mouth. "But you're asking if we have any obligation to inform Thomas if we decide to turn our investigation in his direction."

She put the fork in her mouth and thought about her dining companion. He saw things differently and from angles no one on the *Seventh Floor* had yet to consider. His thinking was linear, dot to dot, point to point, much more logical than legal. She'd been contained so long inside the little box that is *Donaldson, Clements* that it was refreshing to meet someone free from of its constraints, someone peering into the forest from outside and not only seeing trees.

He'd hit upon a unique courtroom strategy, though one fraught with legal entanglements both the aforementioned confidential and evidentiary. While she was thinking through the steps and progression something like this would take, he said it aloud.

"Can we establish the innocence of our client by proving the guilt of the person paying for our defense?"

As Jillian watched the only other patron on the patio get up from his table and take his check inside to pay, she understood that this new angle was going to be difficult to sell. Regardless of the relationship between the two men, whether old or new, good or bad, based on just the short sample size of success thus far in Eric's investigation, Mr. McGraw was not about to turn him loose on Thomas Gradeen.

She could foresee nothing good coming from that for anyone involved.

SIXTEEN

*D*arkness had fallen. The small patio of the bistro was partially illuminated with white lights strung across its top like six loose and unevenly spaced guitar strings, leaving Jillian and Eric in relative dimly-lit seclusion. Most couples would have romance foremost in their thoughts, the ambience of candlelight and Italian folk music adding to that presumption.

These two, however, continued carrying out the business dinner charade to an other-worldly level. All through their entrees of spaghetti and meatballs for both, a shared bottle of red wine and now with the arrival of desert, the dinner conversation had steered clear of the above-mentioned taboo topic and became more of a contest. It was as if they were trying to outdo each other, a perverse battle to see who might blink first and slip in a hint of attraction. They resisted personal stories because that might redefine this as a date. Neither apparently outwardly wanted that.

I guess I was the only one who could see they were fooling no one. So as I grabbed a butter knife to cut through their crap, the pretense continued.

They debated the merits of digging into the Thomas Gradeen connection and what further might be learned by speaking to the author of his biography, or at least reading the book. They bounced back and forth the slim chances of DeBisshop still being alive and how difficult it might be to extradite him from Denmark if he turned up there. They speculated what connection they might uncover between Fuller and Steinhauer with a deep dive in Decatur.

They then began to discuss attorneys and judges they know in common, or those either may have encountered in the courtroom, which weren't many. While both practicing law in the same medium-sized metropolis, it was their chosen specialties which presented obstacles to their crossing of paths.

The topic then meandered and floundered, finding no real landing spot until Jillian steered him toward the staff of the District Attorney's office. Once at the front door, it was just as easy as turning the knob to get to Erin Haynes.

Jillian had blinked first, having downed enough vinted courage to bring up his former fiancé. It was purposely a circuitous journey, for she intended to cover her tracks if necessary.

Cautiously she said, "Are you okay if I ask how the two of you met?"

"Actually, I met her sister first. I was with a friend, another attorney, and we were having a few drinks. He was an associate of mine at my firm. It was Teddy Grimes. Do you know him? He's now at *Donaldson, Clements*."

"I don't think I know him personally."

"You should get to know him," Eric replied reflexively without recalling Teddy's *third grade* remark from a few days prior. He shook the comment away and said, "He's going to be a great attorney, and already a better guy. He's down on *Six*. He was extremely interested in what we did Thursday night, by the way. You're apparently the firm's mystery lady."

All of a sudden she began to nervously fiddle with the drawstring at the neck of her pullover and asked, "What did you tell him?"

There were so many ways to play this, but he decided against any games and told her the truth.

"Not a thing. You shall remain a mystery to us all."

"I told you it's complicated," she playfully whispered, her smoky eyes widening, her dark cheeks rosy from the red wine. "Now back to the story. You and your friend are having drinks."

Again, she'd refused to nibble on any bait, to provide closure to any of the open-ended scenarios. With only a reverent nod to her almost godlike ability to continually evade and avoid, he gladly re-engaged in his tale.

"Anyway, I'd interviewed Teddy to join my firm and I can't remember if we were still negotiating, but he spots these two girls at a nearby table and starts sending them drinks. Soon we join them, and Teddy's firing with both barrels on the younger of the two."

"Wait," she interrupted. "He did this during a job interview?"

This question surprised Eric. As the only woman in the firm's hierarchy he would have thought she might be familiar with such tactics. Or maybe because, being a woman with an incredible resume', she'd never be considered under such mundane standards. When her face remained blank, he tried to explain.

"You never want an associate who isn't aggressive and self-assured, maybe even borderline cocky. I got to watch him work his charm, his magic. He set a goal and moved on it. Depending on the job, sometimes it's the best way to interview."

He shifted his weight in the chair and tried another approach.

"It's the same reason prospective salesmen are frequently asked to bring their wives to job interviews or dinners. Sure, the boss wants to meet the wife to gauge if she'll fit in at events and parties, but how good looking the wife is can tell you a great deal about how good a salesman the guy is."

She'd never regarded any of this and felt embarrassed for having missed it. It made perfect sense in a chauvinistic way in this chauvinistic world. She lived it every day of her professional life from the wrong side of the curtain. The misogynistic old boys' club, no doubt, had their own specific way of recruiting prospective members. He'd just tipped their hand to her.

She shook her head and said simply, "All men are pigs."

He laughed at this and got back to his story.

"It turns out the other girl, my girl, is Sara, Erin's older sister. These two are down from Chicago, in Springfield for meetings or training or something. Sara is happily married and just out for a few drinks to relieve the boredom, humoring her single friend, whose name now I can't remember."

"Where were you?" Jillian asked, her words slurring a bit.

"There was an old bar downtown that closed. We called it Stones."

"Stepping Stones," she corrected.

"That's the place. Sara and I were watching our friends getting all cozy and disgusting right at our table, so we went to a booth. Our role as wingmen, or wing persons, was accomplished. We were like two proud parents watching our kids hooking up."

Jillian interrupted. "That's a bit incestuous. You referred to them as your kids. You should not be proud, that they are going to . . ."

When she chose not to finish her thought, playfully shrugging her shoulders instead, he couldn't help but smile. It was as if suddenly, she was a young innocent girl, too embarrassed to bring herself to even consider that their behavior might lead to sexual activity, let alone voice the possibility. The only other possible explanation would have been that she remained too good, too proper, but any modesty on her part had disappeared with her half of the wine.

Treading delicately, he said, "Can you just be quiet and listen? Do you have to interject? This isn't a cross examination. It's a story. You asked to hear it."

"You're right. I'm sorry. No more."

Here she pantomimed locking her lips with a tiny invisible key then tossing it over her shoulder. She then sat up straight and folded her hands into her lap under the table.

The story continued. "Sara told me about her husband and kids in Chicago and was not interested in me the way her friend was interested in Teddy. That was evident early. Sara is cute and fun, but it was apparent that she and I were still there only because of our friends. Teddy and his girl left, and to be honest, I have no idea where they went. Still don't to this day. Don't care. Sara and I wondered whether they would be back or if we should wait but decided to give them some more time.

"I told her I was a lawyer and she told me her sister worked for the DA's office. She asked if I knew Erin. She decided she would try to hook us up, me and her sister. She sent Erin a text right there, saying all these great things about me, how Erin and I should meet for a drink or something."

Here Eric's mood darkened, turning to face the row of evergreens to hide his eyes. Sounding a bit choked-up, he relayed something which I had initially pointed out to him.

"It's amazing that a text from her sister started the whole romance thing and then one from Erin herself ended it."

He struggled with the last part, the irony of one simple fact still raw after eight months. Jillian, for her part, remained silent true to her word, choosing instead to raise one hand back up onto the table to place it atop the sweater on his forearm.

"I'm sorry, Eric," she said, barely audible above a whisper.

"Thanks," he said with a sniffle. "But this is a happy story. It is. So, that night Sara had somehow gotten it in her head that Erin and I were perfect for each other. She showed me some photos of Erin on her phone, and I was like, let's set this up. One in particular was this candid head shot of her, taken from a slight angle. She was all blonde hair and big brown eyes, with this expression like she was totally amazed that anyone would waste the time to take her photo. She wasn't quite smiling, but it was either the end or the start of one. She looked breathless. Does that make sense? It was an amazing photo, almost professional quality for looking completely spontaneous, but the two-dimensional version didn't do the real Erin's appearance justice.

"That same night, Sara took my photo right there in the booth and sent it to her sister. My tie was ditched, my hair was all over the place. I had my glasses on, but Erin texted back to give me her contact info. The only explanation I have is that the lighting in that bar was horrible. Funny thing. Erin kept that photo on her phone and even on the day she died it would have come up on her screen if I called her.

"We tried to meet, but Erin was hard to pin down. She'd say it was work, but I suspected there was someone else. Sara, however, refused to relent. From back in Chicago she called her sister and texted me to call her too. We finally agreed to meet for a drink solely to placate Sara. We had set a time and a place, but something came up and it didn't happen.

"Then one day sometime later, I was at the courthouse. Keep in mind, plaintiff's attorneys are rarely at the courthouse. Most of my work was done in settlement conferences. So, I'm at the courthouse for no reason other than to maybe bump into Erin, and there in the hallway I hear someone holler out her name. I turn and there she was, standing right next to me and she was amazing. It turned out it was Patterson Ritter who called out to her."

He took a sip of coffee and continued the story.

"I already knew who she was and a great deal about her from her sister and our brief conversations and texting. Maybe it was the anticipation, or the wondering if we were ever going to see each other in person, but I was floored. She's not stunning like you. She was cute, adorable. Blonde hair and enormous brown eyes, and it was like the whole world had gone into slow motion."

He regarded everything he had just said, brought a hand to his eyes and said, "I'm sorry. I shouldn't be . . . Does this make you uncomfortable?"

Jillian almost giggled at this. "Not at all," she fired right back. "That's the second time tonight you've referred to me as stunning. Besides, I asked."

"You kind of are. Do I need to apologize again?"

She sat there for a split second, head tilted to one side, wearing a look of condescension. A light breeze tugged at her hair causing her to sweep a few strands back behind her left ear and then adjust her ponytail with both hands above her head.

Then she fiddled again with the pullover's drawstring and said, "So, don't leave me hanging. You're standing there with Erin and Ritter."

"Right. I'm standing next to her, and Ritter is coming down the hallway. Up until that point I had no idea who he was. I say "Hi" to Erin and introduce myself and mention her sister. I see the recognition in her eyes, but she kind of anxiously jumps at this and glances back quickly over her shoulder. When she turns back to me she smiles and then goes into total professional mode."

Let me jump in here and take over the story telling. I've heard it enough times and it will be a lot easier than trying to let Eric tell it. Hopefully I can eliminate all the *Who said what?* pronoun confusion and any punctuation and quotation dilemmas which would pop up while trying to write it like that.

The first thing I need to do is clarify his last statement. Erin's professional mode would better be described good-naturedly as *bitch-mode*. Supposedly she would explain it to him later, but on that day, she shut him down completely.

Ritter was on the two of them before Erin could say anything or try to warn him about what was coming. He sidled up to her and kissed her on the cheek, instantly asking Erin, "Who's this?"

"This?" she asked without hesitation or even a stammer. "Eric McKegney. He's opposing counsel. Eric, this is Patterson Ritter. Patterson is with the State Journal-Register. He's at the Lifestyle desk."

As Ritter reached to shake Eric's hand, he quickly gave him the once-over and said, "Actually, Love, I'm the Chief Entertainment Reporter." He then looked up into Eric's eyes and said, "It's a pleasure to meet you. Rick, was it?"

Eric tried to correct him. Ritter easily deflected it away like a bothersome insect. While Eric wondered what the Chief Entertainment Reporter was doing at the courthouse, Ritter was focused solely on Erin.

"It looks like both of us are free for lunch. What say I buy you that wedge salad in the cafeteria downstairs you so enjoy?"

Erin said almost dismissively, "That would be great. Do you mind running down and ordering it for me? I'll be right there. I need to discuss trial timelines with Mr. McKegney."

Ritter wasn't buying it. Eric would come to learn the man, despite the good looks and poised exterior, was one of Springfield's more insecure males. He wasn't about to leave them alone, regardless of the reasons.

Erin noticed this. In what could be called an Oscar worthy performance, said to Eric, "We don't have enough time to do this now, but I need to get you on my calendar. Can you call my office? Better yet, call my cell."

Here she produced a business card from an inside pocket of her jacket, turned it over, jotted a number down in blue ink and handed it to him.

"Will do," Eric replied, amazed at her improvisational skills. He thought she didn't remember they'd spoken several times. It was just that convincing.

"Great. Thanks. I'm guessing, based on the document load, we may need a few hours. Can you find that much time for me, Mr. McKegney?" Here she smiled and mouthed the word, "Sorry."

"I told her that I'd see what I could do about the scheduling and to enjoy her lunch."

Eric was now back to telling his story.

"So, a week later we met for that elusive drink. Two weeks later we had dinner and were officially dating. Maybe a month later she told Ritter, but he didn't go easily. That Christmas we spent with Sara and her family in Chicago."

"That's a happy story," Jillian said. "Do you stay in touch with Sara?"

"No. Not since the funeral. It's too hard." He finished his coffee and went on. "She feels responsible, when all along I've done this to myself."

Jillian would hear none of this. "Come on. Think about that. It's not your fault any more than it's hers. It's nobody's fault. It was an accident. Accidents happen. She did a nice thing for you. Don't forsake her because it didn't turn out the way either of you had hoped."

He mused aloud, "Tennyson penned, 'Tis better to have loved and lost . . .'"

Jillian sat bolt-upright and stared intently across the table. Why hadn't she thought of this previously?

"What if Ritter thinks that way too?" she asked quickly, excitedly. "That maybe it's not better to have loved and lost? Eric, have you ever considered that maybe he wanted to make sure you never got married by killing Erin and himself, like driving off Lovers' Leap?"

Granted, I wasn't anywhere around when the accident happened, but I've never heard him suggest such a thing aloud. He had to now, however, because it made too much sense not to.

illian began digging into this vein of their dialog, her excavation continuing all the way through the paying of the check and the walk to their cars through the darkened parking lot. Eric was embarrassed for never considering the possibility before. He'd been too much of a basket-case back then with all his grief and guilt that he never stopped to contemplate this idea. He'd hung his hat on *Unfaithful Erin* because it explained the unexplainable. More importantly it made him the victim.

As I've mentioned numerous times to him, and to you, to me *Unfaithful Erin* was purely out of expedience. Blaming Erin absolved him of all sins and pinned every portion of the fault on her. She'd been the one unsure about their future together, not him. It was her decision, her actions which led to her death. Not his. No more questions, your honor. Case closed. Insert crack of pounding gavel here.

But now this brand-new theory comes along. Was it remotely possible Ritter could have wrecked the car intentionally to kill them both? Murder–suicide? Had Ritter gone off the deep end, completely losing his mind? Or was he the *If I can't have her no one will* kind of guy?

This too worked for Eric. If Ritter deliberately drove into that telephone pole, then Eric somehow still remained the victim. Erin was still dead, perhaps killed by a scorned lover. Even if this were the case, was it possible to hate Ritter any more than he had for the past eight months?

Hell Yes!

Think about it. By trying to bed Erin one last time, he'd only been trying to steal her away, something which over time could've been forgiven. But if it was instead murder-suicide, then he was trying to take her for good. Maybe it's *torpedo-torpodo,* but there's a distinct difference when it comes to intent, in that the latter would be *Specific Intent.*

I'm sure you all remember that from a few chapters back, so we don't need to go through it all again. If you're confused, spin back a few pages for a quick refresher. We'll wait. . .

Okay, so Jillian and Eric's examination of the facts in evidence, and all the wild resulting supposition in Erin's death had gone back and forth between them like a prosecutor deposing a witness. It flew in the face of everything the witness believed. They started at the beginning, debunking every theory about what happened and why. They began with her text, looking at each line, every word, differently and maybe even seeing it for the very first time for what it might truly be.

Don't hate me. Just have to do this one last thing. Then yours forever. Love you.

"What else could she mean by *this one last thing*?" he asked defensively.

"And why would she have not wanted you to hate her for doing it?"

He said, "See? It's those lines that made me think she didn't want me to hate her for having one last fling with Ritter."

The pace of the interaction was measured, unhurried and deliberate, like their questions and answers when conferring about the two Gradeen's. There was never urgency. Instead their play off each other had an evenly restrained cadence which had mirrored the relaxed and purposeful pacing through the parking lot.

"Do you remember anything else you guys may have talked about back then? Anything else to which she may have been referring?"

He regarded her questions and thought hard about those last few days.

"All I can remember talking about that caused friction would have been the wedding and the arrangements."

"Nothing else? No steps or number of steps leaving *one last thing*?"

"There were some last-minute issues with the details. I wouldn't have hated her for changing the color of the cake frosting. I didn't even know what color it was supposed to be. White, I guess."

The defense attorney-turned-prosecutor paused as if to gather her thoughts, before coming back with another line of questions. She began with, "She was leaving the DA's office, right? Any chance *this one last thing* had something to do with her work?"

"I did ask around about that. Work had been winding down. Her cases had been reassigned. Her last assignment was as local liaison for a Department of Defense investigation, or something Federal like that. Anyway, she was easy to replace on that. She was sticking around just to help in any way she could. She told me she played a lot of computer solitaire."

"And she was joining your firm?"

"She was. We were going on a honeymoon to the Caribbean and then she'd come to work when she felt like it, or when she eventually got bored."

"Do her parents know about the text she sent you?"

"I don't believe so. Why?"

She found this to be incredulous, so she repeated, "Why?"

Then he began to answer his own question. "Because they may know what *the one last thing* could be."

"Yep. But how do you explain that it's taken you eight months to ask?"

Hers was a great point. Again.

She asked, "Did you get a copy of the original police report or an accident reconstruction?"

I know his reluctance had stemmed from his fear the report's findings may not fit his narrative. But now that his version had been brought into question, I was glad to see him agree to be proactive. After eight months on his heels, it was good to see the change she could foster in him.

"I can probably get by the police station sometime tomorrow," he said.

"What does Erin's family think she and Ritter were doing?"

Damn! She was good at this. He'd been too ashamed to discuss any of this with her family working off the assumption they were going to that shady motel to do the nasty. How could he explain that to her parents? Yet, here again, this might all be changing.

This was the cross-examination he should have subjected himself to months ago. The eight months, however, would give him the distance he claimed to need to investigate. Now with a different perspective and the buffer of time, maybe it was time to move this back to the front burners. Yet dredging up all these memories would cause pain to everyone asked as much as to the asker.

Sensing his hesitation, Jillian redirected her line of questioning yet again.

"Okay. Let's look at something else. Where did Erin think they were going? Why would she get in the car with him?"

"I never doubted what they were doing."

"Fair enough. Describe for me their relationship as the wedding approached. Better yet. What about you and Ritter? Did you ever see him? When would the last time have been?"

He thought about this, his mind swiping through memories like photos on his phone.

"There was an engagement party at Erin's parents' house."

"Ritter was there? And the wedding was scheduled for the end of summer?"

"Uh-huh. Labor Day weekend. Ritter was there. Mr. and Mrs. Haynes liked him and had invited him over Erin's objections. I remember that. I spoke to him briefly. It was weird between us, but now that I think back, he was cordial. Almost nice. He always told me how happy he was for both of us. I never would have suspected that he might lose his mind and murder Erin."

They were to her car now. Jillian leaned against the door of the white BMW the way she had on that first night. With her hands, she motioned like she was tamping something down.

"Keep in mind we don't know if that's what happened or not. I only threw it out there as something worth considering."

He laughed under his breath, more at himself than things recently discussed. He said, "It's odd how for eight months I never thought about any of this. Now I want him in the electric chair."

This was somehow funny to her also. She moved her hand away from her mouth and played with the pullover strings under her chin.

"What can you tell me about the relationship between Erin and Ritter prior to the wedding?"

"I know for a fact they were drinking margaritas the night she was killed, but not much else. I guess she saw him, but it was never anything she really talked about. I know they'd tried to remain friends."

Jillian glanced around to see that theirs were the only two cars left in the lot. She realized her work for the night was over. There was only so much she could do. She could lead him to the water, but . . .

"Thanks for all of this," he said somewhat shyly, embarrassed that he'd not gotten here earlier.

"Thank you for another fun evening. And thanks for dinner. I'm awfully glad we did this."

"So am I."

"Good night, Eric. I'll see you in the morning for the early meeting."

Almost afraid to ask, because of where it might lead, but at the same time dying to know, he ventured forth.

"Why do you care so much about this? Why does it matter to you that I'm wrong about Erin?"

She pondered this for a beat and said, "You know what I think your problem is? Your problem is that you've spent eight months obsessed with Erin's text, preoccupied by only the first two lines."

He thought about this, picturing the perfectly spaced and evenly justified lines of type in the text bubble on the screen of his phone.

She bounced up on her toes and lightly kissed him on the cheek. As she opened her car door and stepped inside, she said, "You need to pay more attention to the last two."

The last two lines were ingrained in his memory and would be for all time. He could almost hear her saying them now.

It was Erin reassuring him, "Then yours forever. Love you."

EIGHTEEN

The 8:30 Monday morning meeting was set to get underway around the round conference table in J. Tyler McGraw's spacious corner office. From where Eric sat, his back to a wall and facing into the office, he wondered if he could hit a sixty-degree wedge all the way to where the diminutive McGraw sat at his desk on the phone. The ceiling height seemed as if it might allow that much loft on a club. How was it possible that there were not only ample square feet, but an inordinate amount of cubic feet? Or did it only seem so large because its sole occupant was so small? He thought of how the building appeared from the street and realized that the corners and various outcroppings were raised at the top floor like castle turrets to repel invaders.

Eric also noticed that the trappings of being Managing Partner were on full display. As McGraw was fond of saying, "It's good to be king."

There were floor-to-ceiling windows covered with expensive pinch-pleat draperies on two sides, and wooden walls with expensively framed and matted photos of local celebrities on the others. This must have been the wall of photos Jillian had mentioned when asked about Thomas Gradeen. Eric wasn't sure which one might be him because there were so many. There was McGraw in a hard hat at groundbreakings as well as in a tuxedo at balls and charity events. Many contained politicians, either in groups or in one-on-one handshake poses. It was apparent from the people in these photos that McGraw chose only to associate himself with democrats, but anybody who matters in Illinois politics must lean hard to the left. There were also photos of McGraw with more than a few of the former Illinois Governors who currently sit in Federal prison.

This must have posed an interesting dilemma for the lifetime lawyer, pitting personal friendship against a system of laws he'd been sworn to uphold and a lifetime defending. It was these photos, however, that gave Eric hope that maybe by comparable logic, the Managing Partner might allow him to take a run at one other gentleman somewhere on that wall.

As they waited, Jillian, looking even more extraordinary than previously, if at all possible, had introduced him to the investigator, George Harrison. She'd referred to him as "Sarge," prompting Eric to wonder if the nickname was derived from a military or law enforcement past. The man's paunch suggested years of doughnut abuse, tipping the scales toward police.

Sarge, a large and gregarious African-American with thinning white hair and a tight white beard, told Eric he went by the nickname, "So no one would confuse me with the Beatle."

Despite the numerous dissimilarities of race and not being dead, the man laughed heartily at his own line, prompting Eric to do the same out of politeness. The quick descriptive was that the surviving George Harrison was a former desk sergeant with SPD who claimed to be an expert background investigator, "knowing where all Springfield's bones are buried."

Still, neither investigator seemed to be overly interested in the other because their attention was focused solely on Jillian. In a perfectly tailored grey suit coat and skirt, with a royal blue blouse again opened teasingly at the neck to show a color-coordinating necklace, she sat cross-legged at the table, right foot bouncing up and down. Her thick dark hair was casually up and her head was down, as she read from sheets of paper in a manila folder on the table. She inattentively spun an expensive fountain pen in her right hand as she flipped through the pages with her other.

They'd first seen each other earlier outside the office when she asked him if he was ready. She had then added, "I think you should take the lead."

"I'd planned to," he had responded confidently.

The truth be told, he was conflicted going into this meeting. He'd spent the weekend researching and organizing his thoughts and strategies, enumerating the steps necessary to prove Jameson Gradeen's innocence, or perhaps his father's guilt. Whichever, he felt prepared. Then it all changed the night before. All he could concentrate on this morning was the possibility that Ritter had murdered Erin with malice aforethought.

During his early morning run – That's right. Two days in a row – while he listened through his headphones to *Deftones* and *Perfect Circle*, all he could hear was Jillian. She'd somehow become the voice in his head when it came to Erin. Any irony fans out there? Think about that. Of all people, she's the one steadfastly clinging to the idea Erin was not culpable in the events leading up to her death. She defended her honor, which was no surprise because defending is what she did.

While running, and panting and sweating, but not stopping, he kept going back to Jillian's parting comment from the night before. She was right. Again. He'd spent the past eight months focusing only on the first part of Erin's text and not the ending. Erin had had every intention of being with him forever and she'd loved him. She'd continually told him as much. It was, by all accounts, the last thing she ever said to him. Yet he'd chosen either not to believe her or not to pay attention. He owed her so much more than that.

And to pay her back, all he could think about was getting even with Ritter for what he may or may not have done. Coma or no, the bastard deserved to fry for taking Erin. Vengeance wasn't yet consuming him, but it would be his . . . eventually. Insert evil laughter here.

"You look very nice this morning," Jillian had said, commenting on his dark suit while straightening the Windsor knot of his bright pink tie. Then in a whisper, she added, "Last night was fun."

As he let her pass to enter the office, and get a whiff of her fragrance, he replied, "Maybe we can do it again. Soon."

She had blushed and playfully patted him on the upper arm.

Now as he sat at the small table, both he and Sarge continuing to stare at her across the coffee service, he pondered that same old question. Who was she? He felt he knew more about her than most in the building, but it still wasn't a lot. When Teddy referred to her as a mystery, he'd nailed it.

McGraw hung up the phone already on his feet and began the meeting on his long trek to the conference table.

"I expect formalities have been concluded and everyone knows everyone. I want to reiterate Mr. Harrison's involvement is subordinate to your duties, Eric. You remain the lead. George understands his role. I want you out front. Sarge will be your researcher."

McGraw pulled out his chair between Jillian and the older investigator and looked at his watch as he sat down. Looking around the table, he said, "I have Mrs. Brubaker to record our meeting."

As if by magic, an unseen door in the wall behind them opened and a matronly lady who reminded Eric of his kindergarten teacher appeared. She took a seat, somewhat removed from the conference table behind McGraw in a leather chair that seemed to be part of a living room arrangement in the huge office. With a steno pad in her lap, she nodded that she was ready. The meeting was now officially on the record.

McGraw began by complimenting Eric on the progress he'd made in just a few short days.

"Jillian has vaguely communicated to me the approaches you'd like to take. It was their sheer magnitude which prompted Sarge's involvement. I've read him in on background as we did for you, so I'm hoping he can follow along this morning. If there are gaps, we can fill them in later. Fair enough?"

Sarge nodded, as he reached to refill his coffee from the sliver pot on the table and said, "Yes, sir."

"Young man, the floor is yours."

Jillian glanced up from her notes in the folder and smiled at him, her gorgeous silver eyes widening with encouragement.

From the folder in front of him, he withdrew four stapled copies of notes and strategies. Standing to deal them out like playing cards, he said, "I apologize, Mrs. Brubaker. I didn't make enough copies."

"No problem, Dear."

She even sounded like his kindergarten teacher, while dressed more like someone's grandmother. Nonetheless Eric couldn't help wondering how many times McGraw may have chased her around his big desk throughout their years together.

Eric remained standing and began, "By definition, a criminal defense is for all intent and purposes reactionary. I'm not telling you anything new. We're tasked with defending Jameson Gradeen, and to do this we have several paths. The actions of the prosecution will dictate which path needs fortification. We need to preemptively identify our weaknesses and readiness.

"You do this for a living, so I'm not going to waste anyone's time telling you things you already know. What I'm hoping to accomplish this morning is to read you in on the facts we already know, those we already know we don't know, and how best to move forward based on those knowns and unknowns."

This made sense to Jillian and McGraw as evidenced by their nods of assent. Sarge was a different story. Whether it was strictly terminology or he had been unable to follow along was not quite clear when he said loudly, "Whoa! I know you three are attorneys and I ain't, and you talk your own lawyer-speak. Tell me how we can know what we don't know?"

"Sorry, Mr. Harrison," Eric said.

"Whoa again. Appreciate your manners, *Young Gun*, but call me Sarge."

Eric quickly said, "You bet."

Then by way of explanation, he continued, "I may have emphasized the wrong words. Think of it as a police investigation where there is evidence or facts of which you are not aware. It benefits you to understand that you will need to learn them. These are the unknowns. When you become aware of them, you know your unknowns."

"Okay," the big man said with an exaggerated nod of his head. "I got that now. It's just that for a second there I thought the *Young Gun* here might be running for office. All that doubletalk started sounding downright political."

They all got a good chuckle at this before Eric was back on point.

"So, the info in front of you is a breakout of our knowns and unknowns, without calling them such."

"Much obliged," Sarge interrupted with another hearty laugh.

"And the plan I wish to attack." Eric paused here just for a beat. "Whereas criminal defense is just that, defense, I want this investigation to be the offense. I want to force the issue. I want to dictate how the Feds prosecute this trial."

"How do you plan to achieve this?" McGraw asked without taking his eyes off his copy.

Eric turned to face the Managing Partner and said, "Simple. We need to beat them to the punch. We need to present an affirmative defense by finding either Fuller and/or DeBisshop before they do."

Sarge slapped an open palm on the table. "I like the *Young Gun's* style, J. Tyler. Beat them to the punch."

Here Jillian interrupted to clarify, "But if we find them, we nonetheless turn them over to the authorities. He's in no way suggesting we find them and hide them. Are you?"

Here he smiled sheepishly and admitted, "I had considered that until I was informed by more learned counsel that we aren't allowed to do such things."

"But I'm not sure finding them will benefit us." McGraw let this hang for a tick, long enough for all around the table to question his meaning.

Then he asked, "What if they testify against our client?"

"We can handle that," Jillian said. "Part of the original justification for the conspiracy charges included the presumptive deaths of both DeBisshop and Fuller. If either is still alive that card no longer holds up other cards."

"Point well taken. How do we go about finding them?" McGraw asked.

Eric quickly wrested back control.

"The prosecution steers us where to investigate and the leads to follow. I have listed eight such areas on the sheet in front of you that I believe might have either been overlooked completely or paid little attention. They are not in any particular order."

The sheet read: 1) Fuller's Decatur Police career; 2) Steinhauer in Decatur; 3) Fuller's National Guard Platoon; 4) Edinburg Farm; 5) James Hoover; 6) Olivia Jacobsen; 7) R. J. Harris; and 8) last, but not least, Thomas Gradeen.

He then led them through each one in much greater detail.

#1 & #2 The possibility existed Fuller and Steinhauer first come in contact during Fuller's employment as a Decatur police officer.

#3 Fuller's National Guard Platoon mattered because if Fuller was still alive, he may have sought shelter with someone he served with in Iraq. Or better yet, as Jillian had postulated, someone whose life Fuller may have saved.

#4 The old Gradeen family farm in Edinburg was apparently where research into *Swarm Farm* theory was taking place. This was also reportedly the last place DeBisshop was seen alive.

#5 James Hoover was Steinhauer's parole officer. Was he possibly the link between Fuller and Steinhauer, or had that link been established prior to Steinhauer's being in the system?

#6 Ms. Jacobsen was the alleged intended target of Steinhauer in the murder of Ann Flannery which triggered the alleged conspiracy. She had to know more than she was letting on or why had she been targeted?

#7 R.J. Harris was the author of the Gradeen unauthorized biography, *Titan of the Prairie*. He had to be a great background source, plus he might be able to shed light on why DeBisshop and Jameson Gradeen left *Agri-Illinois* within weeks of each other.

It was about here in the discussion, before Eric could further elaborate on why the as yet unmentioned Point #8 mattered, when McGraw began to shake his head. The man glanced at his watch and scowled.

McGraw had remained relatively silent and listening intently as Eric, with an occasional assist from Jillian, laid the investigative importance of each numerical heading on the sheet. His only out-of-the ordinary reaction was a quick discussion of the folly in reading the Gradeen biography despite Eric's assertion that it might add vital background information. McGraw had implied that the book could be a total waste of time.

Be that as it may, before any further discussion of *next steps*, McGraw was apparently shutting down the meeting after the preordained thirty minutes.

Now the Managing Partner sighed heavily and those around the table deferred to him. With both hands on the table, he pushed his small frame up out of his chair. Eric knew this gesture meant that this meeting was over, ending before he could get to what he really wished to discuss. He looked to Jillian for moral support. She was doing a pitiful job of pretending to read something in front of her. He then glanced to Sarge. The big man was staring intently at McGraw like the next words out of the Managing Partner's mouth were going to be the most important he'd hear all week.

"Eric, I applaud your efforts and all this hard work. Jillian, thank you for your stewardship of our newest employee. Sarge, these two will divide up the tasks, and you will report your findings to either or both. Thanks to each of you this morning. Mrs. Brubaker will transcribe her notes and email a copy to each of you before day's end. Here's to a good day and a good defense."

With what we'd come to learn was his trademarked phrase now delivered, the little man turned to take the long walk across his office back to his desk. Despite Jillian silent imploring for him to do nothing, and a firm grasp on the sleeve of his suit jacket, Eric stood.

He asked, "What about #8, sir? What about Thomas Gradeen?"

McGraw turned slowly, deliberately, almost like a gunfighter ready to draw. His expression was sour and his tone aggrieved. Almost in a murmur he asked, "What about Thomas?"

Eric watched Jillian bury her face in her folder, but he soldiered on.

"Sir, I think he's in this thing up to his elbows. There's enough to suggest he may be pulling the strings. I believe you might also think so. If we're seeking the truth here, as is our legal mandate, he may be the key."

"Is that truly your assertion, Mr. McKegney?"

McGraw had said this with that tilt and dip of the chin which implied Eric should already know this answer. But the fact that he had used his last name scared him, causing him to question this approach.

Regardless, Eric was already so far out over his skis that the fall was going to kill him anyway. How much deader would he be if he kept pressing?

Standing firm, he said, "I believe it is, sir. If nothing more, Thomas Gradeen is the linchpin between his son and DeBisshop. He deserves to be investigated."

McGraw weighed this and flashed a crooked grin. Whether out of pride, or maybe conspiratorial no one in the room dared guess. Eventually he again did that thing with the dip of his chin and said, "Then I'd move him up from #8. However bifurcate the father and son. Jameson is our client."

He accompanied this last remark with a scissors gesture of his two fingers as if maybe hoping to help define that big word for Sarge.

"Yes, sir," Eric said. "Thank you, sir."

McGraw wasn't quite finished. He stopped and spun back and announced, "Anything and everything you uncover on Thomas goes through me or Ms. Stennet first. Agreed, *Young Gun*?"

Eric didn't appreciate the new nickname, but nodded, nonetheless.

"Agreed, sir."

NINETEEN

By noon that same Monday, the eight items on Eric's list had been divided between Sarge and himself. Jillian had explained she had commitments which would occupy most of her time for the week, but she'd be available to help any way she could today.

An additional laptop was set up and secured in the storeroom office for Sarge. He and Eric were loudly banging away on their keyboards. For relative strangers before that morning, they'd fallen into an easy rapport, both thinking aloud and talking on occasion to only themselves. The only time they weren't talking back and forth was when one or both were on the phone.

Sarge volunteered to search for members of Fuller's National Guard platoon from Iraq. As it turned out, he'd been an army sergeant too. He also had a knack for finding bones outside of Springfield, for after just a few strategically placed phone calls, he'd received a faxed list of soldiers in Fuller's unit. He was busily searching the web, primarily military and VA databases for phone numbers or other pertinent information. It was monotonous work, but already he'd whittled seven names off the list of almost forty possibilities.

As preordained, Eric went right after Thomas Gradeen. He called Python Publishing to get the contact information for the author R. J. Harris. They were more than happy to provide it, thinking that whatever the reason for the call, books might be sold because of it.

R.J. Harris' answering message turned out to be a woman with a throaty voice that probably came from years of smoking cigarettes and dripping ash into her typewriter. Eric left a message inquiring about a meeting to discuss the Gradeen biography and possibly getting a copy. He was waiting to hear back.

When this was done, he easily found a phone number for James Hoover, Steinhauer's parole officer. He called to set up a meeting for the next afternoon. It was scheduled for Hoover's office over at Police HQ, a trip which would also give him the chance to get a copy of Erin's accident report.

He thought about the accident report and wondered how much single-malt might be required in his future to get through it. And he considered how little alcohol was in his present. Was it, as Jillian had speculated, the busier he stayed, the less would be required to function? Outside of two Bailey's and Coffees for breakfast, he was relatively sober.

As he considered the implications of the flask in his inside pocket, Sarge looked up from his screen across the table from him and flashed a wide smile.

"You loving on the lady lawyer?" He seemed to delight in his spontaneous alliteration and added, "She your lady, *Young Gun*? That ring from you?"

Eric regarded the timing of the question to be odd, and the crux even more outlandish.

"What? No. I didn't give her that ring."

"Seriously?" Sarge asked. "I'm sorry then, man. I just thought that the way you two . . . My gut missed awful on that. My bad."

At this, Eric got up from his side of the table and walked around to make sure the door was closed tightly. Still facing the door, his back to Sarge's back, he said in a very calm manner, "First, I answer directly to her on this case. And secondly, we just met the other night."

Apologetically, Sarge held both hands up in front of himself as if to ward off a forthcoming invisible attack.

"Brother, forgive me overstepping. I've seen it happen quicker. It's just that it looked to me that she was sparking on you."

Eric came back with, "I think you're way off base."

"You mentioned something about last night. Last night was Sunday." Then he laughed and added, "Sunday ain't a normal workday."

"Business dinner." His comment even sounded feeble to him.

"You're right. Very clumsy attempt at humor. My bad, man."

Eric planted himself on the table right in front of Sarge, one leg on the floor the other dangling.

"Let me enlighten you about my situation since we'll be working together, and I think we can be friends. My fiancé was killed in a car wreck eight months ago. Not sure yet, but it might have been that an old boyfriend deliberately drove the two of them into a telephone pole two days before my wedding. Since then I fell off the deep end. I'm an alcoholic. And alcoholism is a full-time job, a commitment not a convenience; you can't just be a drunk in your spare time. Frankly, if it were easier, more people would do it."

Sarge smiled at the humor in this despite the fact that Eric had deadpanned the delivery.

He continued, "And yet, Ms. Stennet and Mr. McGraw have given me this opportunity to turn my life around and contribute again. They're easing me back into the legal game by letting me start investigating this case. Someday, if I prove myself worthy, there may be an opportunity to join this firm as an attorney. Nothing has been promised."

Sarge, who had leaned back in his chair when Eric's diatribe began, looked up at him and said flatly, "Man, you didn't just say one thing I didn't already know."

This confounded Eric even further. Almost as if pained to ask, he said, "Then, why would you . . .?"

"*Young Gun*, look. You can deny it all if that's your thing, but that pretty lady is giving you the signals that she's open for business. One of us needs to go shopping, but I'm guessing your credit is better."

"Why would I mess up my new situation by making a run at her?"

Having said this, Eric then regarded Sarge's comment. In a long, drawn out, roundabout way, this may have been the finest compliment one man could pay another. What could be more flattering than one dude thinking that the amazing Jillian Stennet might be interested in him? That's what he meant by open for business, right? That shopping line was a little creepy. And, by the way, Eric's credit was awful.

"We're just co-workers, working toward being friends." This line seemed plausible the evening before, but now it just sounded foreign. To add some proximity to it he added, "Like you and me."

"Is that what you call it, or her? My third wife was my co-worker."

"Wait." Eric took exception at this and asked with a wry laugh, "I'm taking relationship advice from a man who's been married three times?"

Sarge held up and wiggled four fingers.

As he returned to his chair, Eric sighed. "Someone who's been married four times is going to lecture me about women?"

"No lecture. Just saying I recognize when a woman shows interest."

Eric sighed again. "Because you've seen it four times?"

"Why else you think a man at my age is still working? Alimony." He had pronounced it as if it was a man's name. *Al E. Mony.* "It's just that I know firsthand from *Wifey #3* that office romances can be a bitch."

"Thanks for the advice, Sarge."

"Just know the company pier is a no fishing zone most places for a reason."

Eric couldn't help but laugh at this. Sarge was going to keep this loose and fun. He should have expected as much. His new co-worker hadn't proven thus far to be big on subtext. He was about as subtle as a two-by-four to the forehead. He may never hint at anything, ever, but he could make you laugh. And all early indications were that Sarge might be a lot of things, but boring was not one of them.

Nonetheless, Eric didn't want to turn this whole perverted exercise into locker room gossip. Hoping to close this chapter, he said, "We've got work to do, Sarge."

"Okay. Okay. One last question about the lovely lady lawyer, okay? Last one. I promise."

Eric hesitated before relenting. "One last question."

"Is the smoking-hot Ms. Stennet one of your knowns or unknowns?"

Both men again smiled at this, as Eric's earlier ambiguity had returned full-circle and with full-force. He considered how best to answer the question, only to come back with Jillian's similarly flimsy reply when put on the same spot.

"It's kind of complicated, Sarge."

"Then uncomplicate it."

He made it sound so easy, so . . . uncomplicated. Dying to ask how to go about that, how to take all the complications and complexities out of the Jillian Stennet mystery, Eric instead chose the higher road and said nothing further. Instead he went a different path, the one which led back to their work.

"How do you suggest we handle Olivia Jacobsen?"

Sarge hesitated before asking, "We'll get to that, man, but we good?"

This was Sarge guy-code for making certain he'd not offended Eric with the talk about Jillian. The big man reached a fist across the laptop screens hoping to bump knuckles, a gesture to confirm no offense had occurred.

Eric left him hanging and asked with a laugh, "Did you earlier say that she was sparking on me?"

"I did. You know, like one of those Zippo lighters from my day, with the wheel and the flint. It had to spark up first before that fire got lit. You know, click-click-click. Spark it up."

Now he touched his fist against Sarge's and asked, "She was doing that?"

"Ask J. Tyler if you don't believe me. Ask Mrs. Brubaker, or better yet, ask the lovely lady lawyer. *Young Gun*, she straightened your tie and love-patted your arm. I saw her."

Eric's smile told Sarge that everything between them was fine. Then he asked, "And what's up with this *Young Gun* nonsense? If you want to give me a nickname, they used to call me *Muck* or *Kegs* in college."

"Where's any creativity in shortening a last name. What? You don't like it? *Young Gun* just seems to fit you, quick on the draw like in the old west, fanning with both barrels."

Sarge made a gun with one hand and repeatedly banged on the thumb with the palm of his other hand.

"If I had known I was only getting thirty minutes, I'd have fired faster."

"But you got what you wanted and I got to ogle the lovely lady lawyer the whole time."

"I thought we were done talking about her."

"Oh, we are," Sarge said apologetically before adding, "You got me kind of sparking on you too now."

When they were both done laughing at Sarge's latest gem, Eric returned his focus to his laptop. It was time to decide how best to handle the newswoman. As they debated whether she merited the two-and-a-half-hour drive to Moline or if substance might be gathered over the phone, he did background Google research on her. It appeared as if due to the notoriety -- or maybe closer to infamy -- from her stint in Springfield she was now going by the on-air alias J.J. Jacobs at her new post.

Eric tried to put himself in Steinhauer's shoes. He's hired to kill Olivia Jacobsen but mistakenly kills a different newswoman. Remember: he asked Ann Flannery if she was the woman from the news prior to pulling the trigger. So, he knew he was to murder a newswoman, but *why?* Had anyone explained the situation to him? Why would they? Steinhauer was pretty far down the food chain, a cog in a much larger wheel. At the same time, however, the reasons behind the hit on Olivia Jacobsen might have forestalled any confusion, thereby eliminating the mistake.

What if he hadn't gotten the two confused? But he had, right? He'd admitted as much to Jacobsen. Eric felt as if he was missing something. What about this continued to confound him?

"Sarge," Eric said in a curious manner which caused the investigator to look up from his laptop.

"You were a cop. How quickly would the focus of a homicide investigation change if it were discovered that someone else had been the intended target?"

"Almost immediately I'm guessing. Didn't do too many homicides. What you getting at, *Young Gun*?"

"Not sure." Eric ran a hand through his hair as he pondered all this. "How likely is it that an investigative reporter could be completely unaware of what she might have learned that made her dangerous?"

"You think she's hiding something or protecting someone?"

"I don't know," Eric said, his voice showing frustration. "I need to mentally work on this a bit more."

"Maybe you could wrestle with it on a two-and-a-half-hour drive to Moline. That reporter lady might have answers for you."

"I also feel we need to take another look at Ann Flannery."

"Positively or negatively?" Sarge asked. When Eric failed to respond, Sarge elaborated, "You know she was one of us, right?"

"One of us?"

"African-American. She was a sister, probably one of the more prominent ones in town. Nobody wanting to desecrate her memory. She was one of our queens, being on TV and all."

Before he could ask if Patrick Weathers was also African-American, or if it mattered, there was a light tapping on the door as it opened slowly.

Jillian stepped halfway in and said in a tone of excitement, "Mr. McGraw got Jameson Gradeen to agree to meet us at the Edinburg farm for a *Swarm Farm* demonstration. He's there now. I'll drive but we need to leave now."

"Seriously?" Eric asked, the excitement in his tone hard to disguise.

"Grab whatever you need. We have to go now because we'll need to GPS it on our phones."

He was already on his feet, unplugging his laptop and gathering up the chord to put both and the mouse in his backpack, as Jillian waited impatiently in the doorway.

Sarge said, "It don't take forty minutes to get to Edinburg."

Eric said, "You keep working on your list of soldiers. If you need me, call me. I'll see you back here either later today or first thing in the morning."

"You two kids have fun. I'll be here working the phones."

"Thanks, Sarge. I'll start formulating a list of questions we need to ask about Ms. Flannery."

Jillian paused at this and turned to Eric. "Ann Flannery's back on your list?"

"I'm still working through that. I'll explain on the way."

Sarge glanced over his shoulder to the lovely lady lawyer and then back at Eric. He smiled widely and said simply, "Click-click-click."

Left alone in the storeroom office, a gratified Sarge overheard Jillian's voice in the hallway.

"What was that about?"

He had to smile to himself when he heard Eric reply, "I have no idea. That guy's different. Lots of fun, and good at his job, but different."

TWENTY

Edinburg, Illinois sits barely twenty-five miles due southeast of downtown Springfield. As Sarge had suggested, it would only take forty minutes under normal circumstances traveling the diagonal Highway 29. Today, however, was not normal.

Unbeknownst to Jillian, behind the wheel of her BMW 640i convertible with the 3.0 liter 6-cylinder, 6-speed manual transmission, Eric had overridden the GPS on his phone and purposely sent them on a more ninety-degree route. They traveled straight south on Interstate 55, turning east on Illinois Highway 40. This two-lane meandered through beautiful Illinois farm land with its flat-as-far-as-the-eye-could-see fields, a horizon only broken by an inordinate number of silos or grain elevators in every direction.

This route, dotted with the occasional stop sign or marker post, allowed Jillian to power shift the performance Gran Coupe. She found great enjoyment in the car's power and her ability to harness it, to make it respond. There was something inertly sexual about it. She wasn't just driving. She was *driving!*

They slowed considerably to pass through downtown Edinburg, a farming community of maybe a thousand residents, none of whom were visible on this Monday. Farther east, past the Dairy Queen and Food Barn, the gas station and the pizza place, they crossed Highway 29. Jillian recognized the route he'd navigated wasn't flown by crows. She'd looked at him suspiciously but said nothing.

This meandering route allowed them to discuss what could and couldn't be addressed. They agreed since they were meeting with Jameson no mention of his father should be made. As Jillian constantly reminded him, the younger Gradeen was their client.

Soon they came to a stop with a small sign listing Agricultural Chemical Group Research Farm being one mile ahead. The next sign with an arrow directed them maybe a quarter mile down a nondescript unpaved gravel road and through a forestry hedge row. About the time both wondered if they were lost, they emerged to find a gate fortified with concrete bollards and armed guards in ballcaps and army fatigues. It seemed like they'd taken a wrong turn from reality. This secret entrance in the middle of nowhere, manned by men with semi-automatic weapons slung over their shoulders, looked more military base than farm, more Iraq than Illinois.

Jillian gave their names to the guard with mirrored shades, despite the overcast day. He asked for their driver's licenses and they were handed over without issue. He then checked the names against his clipboard for effect only, since the reflection from his glasses revealed his clipboard held no paper. This was just an exercise in appearances. Besides, how many visitors might they get on a Monday that they'd need a guest list?

The guard then told them, "Mr. Gradeen is already on property. Follow that Jeep. It will lead you to your meeting. We'll hold your licenses until you leave."

Jillian glanced over to Eric with a quizzical expression, then turned back to thank the guard. She then pulled the $65,000 BMW Gran Coupe in line behind the battered military-style jeep and followed for another half mile. In the jeep was a driver and a passenger who continually looked back over his shoulder as if to ensure they were still behind them. It wasn't like they could get lost or go anywhere else. The corn stalks on both sides were already so high it was like they were traveling through a canyon.

Soon they could see farm buildings up ahead, three or four barns, numerous silos, and a large two-story house. Everything was painted the same shade of brown, the buildings, the road, the fencing, and now that they noticed, even the jeep ahead of them. While they could come up with no reason for it, they did discuss the color. Jillian thought it to be mahogany, or cappuccino, like she was naming brunette hair shades. Eric just called it odd. To him it was like they'd entered the surreptitious lair of a Bond villain, or a UPS hub.

The brown jeep stopped on the brown pavement in front of the brown house. Jameson Gradeen stood on the porch flanked by guards dressed and armed like those out front. He waved as all three of them came down the steps to greet them. They stopped, still in formation, like they were preparing to welcome a new batch of prisoners to *Stalag 17*.

Jillian threw the car into park and turned off the engine. She placed her right hand on his left arm and turned to say, "I know this is weird, but I have to assume it will be okay."

Looking around, Eric said, "I know you got that first part right."

"Just remember: We are on his side."

As they approached, walking side by side, Jillian staring straight ahead, Eric looking all around, Gradeen stepped away from his detail to offer the official greeting.

"Ms. Stennet, always a pleasure to see you. You look as wonderful as ever," he said smoothly, yet politely. He ignored her outstretched hand and went in for a side hug with a light kiss on her cheek.

Nonplussed, Jillian replied, "Thank you, Jameson. And thank you for agreeing to see us. This is Eric McKegney. He's new to the case, but I assure you he is up to speed."

Gradeen turned to Eric and said, "Welcome. You must enjoy getting to spend time with Ms. Stennet. I know I do when good fortune allows."

Where another guy might have been able to make that line sound somewhat natural, this was not one of those times. It was downright creepy, but Jillian's expression didn't budge. She'd heard it all before, if not worse.

She'd mentioned a few times on the drive out that Jameson was an odd duck. She used the old dictionary line about looking up the word "pretentious" and finding his photo. She'd also remarked that if you wipe away the rather pleasant exterior you will expose a downright cad.

Jameson Gradeen's exterior in person looked like an older version of the photo Eric had seen during his research. His hair was a bit shorter, his sideburns a little greyer, different glasses and the doofus hipster soul patch gone. He wore a starched dress shirt and a pair of creased khakis and hiking boots. Outside of the creepy innuendos aimed at Jillian, at first blush the man seemed to be genial while exchanging small talk.

He gave them the nickel tour of the grounds, walking with Jillian while Eric was forced to follow in front of the two guards, like they were playing a two-one-two zone. Gradeen spoke of the farm's need for privacy and secrecy, that they were doing things his competitors would love to discover. He claimed that was also one of the reasons everything was brown.

"Satellite imaging has a difficult time distinguishing depth and definition within variations and shades of brown. From on high, we appear to be nothing more than a plowed field."

As they continued to walk and talk, he added, "To a certain extent, the same can be said for planes and drones."

Jillian, who rarely missed anything, proved it by asking, "You said that was one of the reasons. What might the others be?"

Gradeen nodded a compliment and said, "Patience, Ms. Stennet. Patience."

Their next stop was in the nearest of the brown barns, but it was not full of hay or horses. Instead it was a state-of-the-art communications center. There were four or five workers in ballcaps and fatigue pants with army issue t-shirts and headsets monitoring ten to fifteen large screens. The image on most was a static shot looking down at an acute angle of some field, but on two, the image filmed from slight altitude was moving. These had to be from his drones.

A man got up from his station and walked to join them. Gradeen introduced him as Robinson and everyone shook hands. Robinson barked out something and Gradeen directed their attention to the large screen closest to them. On it they watched Jillian's white car pull off Highway 40 and into the drive and then disappear in the hedgerow. Soon it was back on the screen, traveling across a brown road and stopping at the main gate.

The adjacent screen next to this one came to life and there was the same image only the background was black instead of brown and the car was barely outlined. It was as if the image was filtered. There were two orange blobs next to each other within the outline, looking like the letter "U".

"Heat signatures of the two of you arriving," Gradeen announced.

They stood, silently watching as the two orange blobs began to follow two other orange blobs up the black road. This seemed odd that they would employ such sophisticated security measures. What were they protecting? And from whom?

Eric's attention was drawn to the blob that was him. He could see fidgeting, shimmering slightly, and knew his anxiety while pulling up the drive had caused him to consider reaching into his inside pocket for his flask. He'd decided against it out of courtesy to Jillian. But here was documented proof that he shook when needing a drink. He fearfully looked to those around him but no one else seemed to notice.

"This way we ensure nothing or no one is hiding in your trunk."

Gradeen had revealed this, gazing intently at the screen, one finger to his bottom lip where the soul patch had been. My only thought was that thankfully they didn't have such technology at drive-in movies.

All four of the orange blobs now stopped, and in what would have been Jillian's BMW, the left blob extended across to the right blob, joining them for an instance into one orange blob that resembled a barbell with a short bar. Eric glanced to Jillian whose worried expression mirrored his.

Then over a loud speaker, they heard Jillian's voice. "I know this is weird, but I have to assume it will be okay."

Eric's voice: "I know you got that first part right."

Jillian's voice: "Just remember: We are on his side."

Gradeen stood there with a gratified look that suggested any minute he might cough up canary feathers. The fingertip now tapped lightly under his lip in a self-satisfied, professorial manner.

Jillian reacted with indignance. Whether it was what they'd just watched and heard, or the smug way Gradeen had displayed it, we didn't know. Yet, being a professional, it was her words, not tone, which made her point.

"Where do you draw the line between security and invading privacy rights?"

"That line disappeared the minute you entered the property. As an attorney, you should realize that."

There was a part of her that hated being spied upon, while a part was also glad nothing worse had been overheard in the car. That was a draw. But to attack her professionally was going way over the line.

"You understand no consent was ever given."

Gradeen fired right back, "Consent is implied."

"It's never implied. That is why it's called consent," Jillian argued.

Eric stepped between them.

"Look, both of you. Like Jillian said to me in the car, and everyone in this room just heard, we're on the same side. Your security apparatus is incredible and I commend you for it and thank you for the demonstration. But we didn't drive all the way out here so you could show off."

"My apologies, Ms. Stennet," Gradeen said, pausing long enough to ensure no damage was done. "Your associate is correct. Follow me if you will."

He led them over to a darkened area that resembled a small theater. Whereas most of the barn floor was concrete, here there was carpet and old-fashioned movie theater seats. Gradeen showed them to two seats in the middle of the second row and sat a row behind them. The screen flashed and then came to life. It was an *Agribotics Technologies* promotional puff film, basically a five-minute infomercial which droned on and on about the greatness of the company and its founder.

Jillian for her part was still riled. She despised having her knowledge of the law questioned. Eric sensed her aggravation as she dug her French manicured nails into the armrests. He glanced at her to see her jaw set and her teeth clenched. She was not letting this go easily.

When the long-winded advertisement was over, and the lights flickered back to life, from behind them Gradeen asked eagerly, "Any questions?"

Eric reached over to Jillian and, this time placed his hand on her forearm. It was a gesture that signaled, "I got this one."

Turning to talk over his shoulder, Eric said, "Earlier you insulted my colleague and now you've insulted us both. There was nothing of import in that tripe that we haven't already seen. We, your defense team, need to understand what you're doing out here. What are you protecting? Why such elaborate security? Everything we learn is privileged and thereby protected, so let's get down to business."

Jillian's gorgeous silver eyes went almost red like laser beams wanting to burn two holes through him. Maybe in the personal injury world you spoke to clients in this manner, but not in criminal defense. She turned to begin apologizing, but Gradeen hadn't taken the verbal lashing as an affront. He nodded solemnly, as if accepting his scolding.

"You're right . . . again. This isn't a public relations visit, nor are you two prospective investors. What say we go outside to get a practical application demonstration of what we're developing here? Do either of you have an issue with changing into more appropriate clothing. It's muddy today."

By more appropriate attire, Gradeen meant nothing more than rubber knee-high boots instead of shoes and white lab smocks over their current clothes. Jillian mocked Eric for tucking his trousers into the boots, while he chided her for appearing so much shorter without heels. Her smock was so large that it covered everything, all the way down to the top of her boots. With her dark hair piled atop her head, and the long smock almost to the ground, she resembled a Geisha girl. I looked forward to the mud or boots making her take choppy steps.

Gradeen led them down a path behind one of the other barns, explaining as they went what they were about to see and the graph theory behind it. He did a few minutes dissertation on the need for algorithms to ensure fuel efficiency, even including the Chinese Postman Problem. This mention made Eric smile. Gradeen then went into Eulerian circuits and polynomial time. His explanation was far more detailed yet easier to understand than the internet version from a few days before.

As they found a comfortable spot from which to observe, Gradeen prefaced everything by saying, "Bear in mind, I use tractor when I mean any type of farming machinery because it's easier for nonfarmers to understand, but a *Swarm Farm Platform* includes all farming implements."

He positioned both his visitors in the boots and smocks so they could see what was happening. He pointed to an area for Eric to look while taking an inordinate amount of time standing behind Jillian and aiming her shoulders to get the optimum viewing angle.

The first field visited was nothing more than plowed dirt in the shape of a large lightning bolt, kind of an isosceles triangle with an offset parallelogram above it. In the brown field, down near the tip of the lightning bolt was a brown tractor. Gradeen explained that each post where boundaries of the field joined had been outfitted with laser receptors. The tractor had lasers and sensors above the four wheel-wells which projected outward, directing and protecting the tractor the same way new cars use sensors to avoid other cars.

He explained that while there were similarities, unlike the development of the self-driving car, self-driving technology for farm machinery was already upon us. He agreed with Jillian that there were fewer safety and liability hurdles to overcome with tractors in fields and away from people than cars on busy roads, but they still were not quite to market with the tractor concept yet.

He said, "Even though we're not there, we can see it from here. That in itself is progress."

A tractor contained a preprogrammed algorithm to plot its path. The lasers on the tractor would then reflect off the receptors at the corners of the field, turning the tractor until it picked up the next receptor. The lasers bouncing off receptors continued until the field was plowed or harvested or whatever.

He spoke of the next development as being nothing more than a rate-times-time-equals-distance problem, with the same lasers and receptors there as backup. In one scenario, since soil conditions can slow the tractor, affecting both rate and time, the receptors tell the tractor where to turn. It's that simple.

In *Scenario Two*, under perfect soil conditions, the lasers and receptors calculate the distances, and the algorithm works backwards to derive the optimum speed in regard to fuel-efficiency.

While it sounded like science fiction to us, this technology was already being considered first-generation by Gradeen and his contemporaries. The world was catching up, so it was time to protect these steps before stepping further.

As the three of them walked to another nearby field, it became apparent why the need for the boots. The rains from the morning before had turned the brown dirt path into mud. When they finally arrived at the next viewing station, Jillian placed her hand on Eric's shoulder without asking and used a stick to clear mud from the bottom of one boot. It was such a natural and unrehearsed act that it caught Gradeen's attention. He looked at Eric with a newfound respect, while Eric just shrugged, thinking about Teddy and third grade.

Gradeen explained that this field and one of the barns they were yet to visit were the reasons for the heightened security. This too began with an algorithm, but there were no lasers or receptors, no external markers on the fence line or boundaries. Also, nothing different had to be done to the tractor externally. Everything was managed internally, through something he proudly dubbed his "Magic Box."

He described how this dirt field was traversed using preprogrammed GPS coordinates in conjunction with the *Magic Box* installed in the tractor's internal brain. He apologized for not having a better name but rationalized that you should name something based on what it does. The *Magic Box* not only steered the tractor per the preset GPS markers, but these markers could be remotely changed and the box would accommodate and adjust, altering the path on the fly accordingly.

The statement carried such pride that Eric thought they'd finally discovered what was worth the extensive protective measures. It had to be the *Magic Box*. He'd read about similar GPS technologies while doing his research, but the ability to make changes remotely was groundbreaking.

"I've familiarized myself with *Swarm Farm* theory, but I've not run across any mention of the *Magic Box*."

Eric waited for him to turn toward him and asked, "Is this your Holy Grail?"

Gradeen smiled and said condescendingly, "Too bad that name's taken. Our *Magic Box* is so revolutionary that we foresee it being a game changer."

Eric considered asking who he meant by *"We"* since most of his colleagues were either presumed dead or missing, but instead went a different direction.

"You commented on the self-driving car. Are there applications for the *Magic Box* with cars?"

"Yes and no. The agriculture market has ninety-five billion in worldwide sales. Our pro-forma estimates that once to market, in just year-one alone, we can add about one-half of one percent of revenue to that number."

Jillian was the first to the math. "Four hundred and seventy-five million."

"At a minimum. You currently see the auto market is of no real interest to us. Add the costs associated with the long road of rules and regulations to approval here in the states, coupled with the fact that there are several variables in auto. Each model would require its own version of the box. Besides, we've tried it on a research basis here. The success has been limited."

Gradeen added, "It's not to say *Magic Box* technology won't one day be in passenger autos. It's just that that day won't be tomorrow any more than it will be ten years from tomorrow."

Jillian and Eric let this sink in for just a moment before being interrupted by Gradeen adding, "And there is nothing humanitarian about self-driving cars. That won't help feed the world."

The self-serving remark made Jillian's skin crawl. She didn't outwardly vomit, but her expression suggested she may have thrown up a bit in her mouth.

She'd warned Eric earlier about the man's desire to be painted as the great benevolent being, doing the greatest good for mankind. Supposedly his father shoveled the same manure. But four hundred and seventy-five million dollars could do a lot of good. Eric had a feeling mankind wouldn't share in it.

Sensing their time might be limited, Jillian was on to a new topic.

"Outside of security, is there a *Swarm Farm* application for drones?"

"Definitely. Think about versatile options if you're monitoring a tractor's progress using eyes in the sky. Say for instance the drone spots a weed that needs attention or a plant that requires additional water and drops a marker. A remote operator can then pinpoint the GPS location of the opportunity or problem and send instructions to the *Magic Box* to either drive the weed into the ground, or water the plant.

"And think of this. Picture the first barn you were in. One operator can sit before a bank of monitors relaying inbound drone camera video and manage several tractors and fields simultaneously."

"Can you have more than one tractor in the same field?" Jillian asked.

"With the newest-generation *Swarm Farm* technology you can because each would operate independently. With the early models, you'd have collision issues because they would be sharing receptors."

Jillian asked, "Geographically how far removed can you be to still remotely operate the *Magic Box*?"

"We've been successful up to two miles from a central base, but the drones offer us the chance to extend our distances geometrically."

Then she asked, "How big is your *Magic Box*?"

"Come on. I'll show you."

As they walked back into the brown area between all the brown buildings, they discussed the idea of some other responsible party having committed the crime of which he stood accused of conspiring. Jillian had already done this dance with him several times before, so they agreed on the drive out that Eric could try his hand. He started with Olivia Jacobsen, calling her the *Typhoid Mary* of sorts, the person who had allegedly set off this chain of events.

Gradeen claimed to remember meeting the newswoman, but he had no idea what she may have uncovered or how. He did acknowledge being familiar with her from the Channel 6 but denied ever being a regular viewer. When asked if she knew DeBisshop, Gradeen hesitated before confirming it. He may have the poker face Jillian had referenced but he didn't appear to be an adept liar.

He proved this by clarifying, "She and Arthur had a business relationship."

"But DeBisshop knew all about your *Magic Box*?" Eric asked.

"Of course," Gradeen huffed, implying the absurdity of the question.

"Then who's to say he didn't whisper something to her. She might never understand what she had, but whoever told her may have realized that having that knowledge made her a danger to them."

Gradeen seemed to weigh this prior to saying, "This is all speculation, but are you suggesting we try to hang all of this on Arthur?"

Jillian said, "Call it the first trial balloon. We want to float them out to see if any pop right away."

"Arthur is the first balloon?" Jameson asked. "What if she testifies that she's never heard of *Swarm Farm* or the *Magic Box*? Or Arthur for that matter?"

"We've already deposed her. She knew him," Jillian explained. "We'll want to do it again to ask these new questions. Based on her answers we then decide if Arthur's balloon pops or not."

"But we also feel there are other DeBisshop balloons out there if the first one fails us," Eric said.

As they walked further, they noticed that there were now two brown jeeps in the brown courtyard, bringing the number of armed guards to six. There were the original two from the first jeep, now these two in the second jeep and the two who had trailed them from a safe distance as they walked the fields. Where was the need for them to carry semi-automatic weapons?

"Jameson," Eric began. "Is something going on that we should know about, or are there always this many guards bearing weapons?"

"Don't worry. The security staff is intent on keeping those out, not keeping the two of you in."

This reminded Eric of Shane West's comment from a few days earlier about the security at their firm. He'd been equally ambiguous, yet threatening when he'd mentioned about protecting the lawyers, not prosecuting them.

Even with Jameson's laisse-faire attitude, neither Jillian nor Eric seemed overly reassured. Think about it. They were being watched from above with every word spoken between them being overheard and recorded. And now surrounded by armed security guards. And their host had casually mentioned for them "not to worry."

"Okay. Besides Arthur, what other balloons have you got?" Gradeen asked in the same calm tone.

At this, Jillian made stern eye contact with Eric and shook her head almost imperceptibly. She was telling him the name Thomas Gradeen had better not be uttered. There would be a time and place. This was neither. Even in her unspoken manner, he knew she meant it with the long "I" sound.

Eric acknowledged her and said, "What can you tell us about Randy Fuller? In your opinion was he capable of orchestrating something like this?"

Gradeen smiled at this. "You're starting with the two missing pieces?"

"Yes, but we prefer to think of it as starting at the beginning," Jillian said.

Gradeen considered this for a beat and said, "To truly to start at the beginning, wouldn't that be my father?"

They stood a distance from Jameson Gradeen and his armed guards, under the watchful eye of the overhead drones, two people in rubber boots and white lab coats having a heated discussion. They understood, however, no matter how hushed their voices, or how well covered their mouths, someone would hear every word.

"I begged you not to go there," Jillian said in a firm whisper.

"I didn't. He did. I was floating out stories like you were."

"Do you think he bought how I responded?"

"It's the truth. We have many other avenues we can pursue to defend him. We don't need to implicate his father in any manner."

Then with a sly wink of his left eye, Eric added, "Like you and Mr. McGraw told me, there's no reason to even investigate Thomas Gradeen."

She didn't grasp the subtle misdirection immediately, but once she did, she tried to return the wink but it was awful. It looked sleepy slow and awkward, more paralysis than deliberate, like maybe the first time she'd ever tried. How does someone not know how to wink? This beautiful woman with the amazing smoky grey eyes was unable to close one with the other remaining open without making it look as though it required a great deal of concentration.

"Exactly," she said almost robotically. "The last thing Mr. McGraw wants is an investigation of his friend. Jameson is our client, not his father."

About that time, almost with the mention of his name, Jameson Gradeen waved to them from the last of the brown barns and motioned them over. As they headed in his direction, they continued their murmured conversation.

Jillian went first, trying to keep her lips locked while speaking. It looked like bad ventriloquism and sounded worse. "Do you think someone could breach this perimeter?"

At least that's how it sounded.

He drew in closer to her ear and whispered, "Not without being noticed. I guess you could parachute in or cut through the woods."

"Does it strike you odd that they're hiding out here with all the brown, but there's a sign on the road directing people to the entrance?"

"That doesn't seem to make sense."

This time she whispered to him. "Do you think he's totally full of shit?"

Gradeen hollered out, "What are the two of you conspiring about?"

"He'll find out soon enough," Jillian said with a nod to the heavens.

"Just more stuff about your case." Eric had stepped a few paces away from her before yelling his answer.

"We'll have to set an appointment for later in the week."

Jameson had said this while turning to walk with them toward an open door on the side of the barn.

"Something's come up. I'm needed back into town. I'll leave you two in the capable hands of my new research director. Follow me. I'll introduce you."

He lead them into the last of the brown barns, but again no hay or animals. This barn was even cleaner and more hi-tech than the communication center. Whereas before there were security men with headsets in tee shirts, in here it was all one enormous antiseptic glass room with people in white lab coats. The air smelled of oiled machinery and processed oxygen. There was a noisy din coming from an industrial-sized air-conditioner in the corner which reminded Eric of the buzz and hum inside an airlock. Duct work sprouted from the top and ran in all directions like octopus' tentacles, several spilling down and hooking into vents under the raised floor. Inside, a small man turned as if on a swivel, heading toward the door when Gradeen motioned.

He looked like the guy you'd cast to play the evil Nazi scientist, with stringy white hair going everywhere like the air-conditioning ducts in the corner. He had what I call a vampire beard. You can't see it in the mirror and it doesn't show up on film. His stature was small, his paunch large. He had to be in his fifties with horn-rimmed glasses taped at the bridge worn down near the tip of his nose. There were several pens and a few items in the front pocket of his lab coat. His name did not hint at such, but I'd bet he smoked stubby cigarettes and have a German accent, saying things like, "Ve have vays of making you talk."

I'd have lost that bet. His name was Dr. Richard, pronounced like hockey's *Rocket.* He spoke with a heavy French accent. Despite his appearance, he knew how to use the language and its charm. He immediately went full charming Frenchie *Let-me-show-you-my-etchings* mode on Jillian. He gingerly balanced her hand in his and lightly kissed the back of it with an "Enchanté." He barely noticed Eric.

Gradeen explained Dr. Richard worked on similar technologies in Europe, clarifying however that nothing over there was as advanced as what they'd just seen. The doctor was introduced as one of the world's foremost authorities on remote application theory in autonomous field operations. Gradeen then instructed him to help in any way he could and to answer any questions. He thanked them for coming and said he looked forward to continuing their discussion later in the week.

Then Richard had the floor and Jillian all to himself to the point that Eric felt like a chaperone on their date. The man looped his arm in hers, leading her around the barn, apparently explaining everything and how it mattered in his work. Eric followed closely behind, struggling to hear any of their conversation over the din of the fans, only guessing as to the subject matter by where the man pointed and gestured. It was an odd sight. Jillian, much shorter than normal in her boots rather than heels, still had three or four inches on Richard. But he had her rapt attention.

After a leisurely trip around the inside of the barn, Richard showed Jillian to a chair and slowly and methodically removed her boots. It was weird and creepy at the same time. If he had made a move on her bare feet or calves, Eric would have interceded. Once barefooted, the mad scientist then helped her to her feet and they were up the steps and inside the glassed-in room. Eric quickly yanked off his boots, hustling up the steps to follow.

Once the airlock door sealed behind them with a loud hiss, the room was nearly quiet except for a continual lower decibel droning. Richard apparently came to the end of a story, causing Jillian to smile demurely and bring a hand to her mouth to hide a reserved laugh.

"Dr. Richard is a fascinating man, Eric."

This had been stated in an overly complimentary tone with a slight nod of respect in the man's direction.

"He joined the team when Dr. DeBisshop went missing. He says their paths crossed at a conference in Europe some years back."

"That is correct," Dr. Richard said, struggling with his English. "He was professor from Denmark who was leader in field. It is – How you say? – honor to be here to continue his work."

Eric asked, "Any idea what happened to your predecessor?"

The man looked up quizzically to Jillian. With a worrisome look he said something that sounded like, *"Je ne comprends pas."*

Eric watched in amazement as Jillian then responded to the man in French, apparently translating the question. Eric's mouth fell wide open. She spoke French! Fluently! It sounded exotic, almost erotic, causing him to swallow hard and look around to see if the other lab staff had the same reaction.

And when the two of them got going back and forth with the French, there was not one word that Eric could decipher, nothing about vanilla or cuffs, no dressing, no horns, no mention of fries. She spoke like a native, complete with hand gestures and that throaty laughter with sideways glances at Eric. He knew they were talking about him, but he was helpless to intervene. He could only hope that somewhere in the gesticulating and the *huh-huh-huhs* investigation business was being discussed.

This went on for two or three minutes, at the end of which she removed a business card from the pocket of her grey suit coat under the lab smock and turned to Eric. In English, she asked him for a pen. In amazement, he handed her one. She jotted her cell number on the card and handed it to Dr. Richard. He then again kissed her hand like a tiny French gentleman and then also kissed her business card like a creepy French pervert. He pulled a fat wallet from his back pocket and softly placed the card inside after giving it one more smooch. Eric couldn't get out of there quickly enough.

The scientist stared oddly at Eric for a beat prior to shaking his outstretched hand and then suddenly, the man morphed into a poor man's Charles Boyer. Chivalrously he bid *Au revoir* to Jillian and exchanged air kisses with her on both cheeks.

Once their boots were back on and they were headed across the compound to the original brown barn where they had changed out of their shoes, Eric spoke first.

"That was amazing. How long have you spoken French?"

Dead seriously she said, "What? I don't speak French."

"Then what language were you and Louis XIV speaking? And what did you tell him when you gave him your number? That guy is going to call you. You realize that don't you? He kissed your business card."

"Twice," she said with a wide smile. They walked a few more paces, and Jillian said without looking over to him. "I'm going to tell you one thing about me, so don't make a big deal about it."

"You know by now I'd never do that," he answered, trying to sound more earnest than excited.

While she wasn't completely convinced she could rely on his discretion, she shrugged both shoulders and stumbled ahead.

"My mother is French, born in France. I was raised speaking both French and English as a child."

"Really? That's cool. What about your father? Is he French?"

"I said one thing."

Her delivery of this line was so comically frigid that it stopped him from persisting, as she had intended.

"Well, you just made *Lucky Pierre's* day back there. Can you imagine how he must feel? Into his staid and boring scientific lab walks this stunning woman who speaks French. The old guy just hit the lottery. Oh, he's going to call you."

"He's a nice man, very polite, but I doubt he calls." Then sheepishly she added, "I kind of had to shut him down."

"How so?"

"He's French. Frenchmen see themselves as romantically entitled. He asked me to dinner and I politely tried to ward him off by showing him the ring. It didn't faze him. He tried for a lunch, or coffee and croissants some morning. He was persistent, so I told him you wouldn't appreciate that."

She casually threw out this last remark as if she were hoping to slip it by him unnoticed. Yet at the same time she flashed this crazy, adorable smile that seemed to be begging for him to catch it. And he had.

"Me? Why wouldn't –"

"I kind of told him the ring was from you. I'm sorry. I needed to back him down, and I . . ."

Even more stunned than earlier, he gulped. "You told him that?"

She reflexively cringed with her answer. "I did. Was that bad?"

There was a moment in here somewhere that he wanted her words to mean exactly what she'd said, exactly how she'd said them. It was two dimensional, out there on the surface, with nothing between the lines. Her words were her words. But a woman who doles out personal information a thimble-full at a time would not give relationship details to a stranger, French or not. She was never the kind to gush over any man to others prior to gushing all over him in the first person, especially when that man was an alcoholic investigator.

She was up to something.

And he finally understood her play.

Without winking – Thank God – she'd been able to convey that she was fully aware of the eavesdropping, yet realizing they had to talk about something so as not to raise suspicion. It was a cunning stroke of genius. Chances are if her conversation in the glassed-in room was picked up by microphones, which it most certainly had been, no one would understand it because it was in French. She couldn't now tell Eric everything they'd discussed, or risk losing the earlier cover of the foreign language. But the two of them had to talk about something. She'd chosen this faux romance for cover.

It was beyond crafty, and she knew it. Her delighted smile and dancing eyes were giving away how amazingly shrewd she perceived herself to be.

Eric regarded all of this while looking to where they were headed. They would have to continue this charade for at least a minute or more before they could get to their shoes. So, he did what any good fake boyfriend would. He stepped up to be the best fake boyfriend a girl could ever need.

He reached over and took her right hand in his left and said, "I know you are hesitant about the people at work finding out."

She looked to him in awe of his improvisational skills and how effortlessly he'd wrested control of their little game. Now that the proverbial shoe had so quickly changed feet, she became uncertain, almost reluctant, her expression turning toward discomfort as she looked up into his face. She feared how far he might go with this play-acting and wondered what little might be left of her shredded honor when he was through.

But she needn't worry. He continued talking, transitioning smoothly like a true gentleman on a Sunday walk in the park.

"You never explained the firm's rules about dating co-workers. When they find out we're a couple, if it becomes problematic, I'll leave the firm. You've been there a long time. *Donaldson, Clements* is your home. I'm the new guy, so don't argue. I'll be the one to go."

Sarcastically she scoffed, "Don't argue? Don't worry."

"What do you think McGraw will say when he learns?" he asked.

This whole scene was remarkable to her, both exciting and frightening. He was good at this. Too good. And very adept at thinking on his feet. But there was more to this. Was he merely playing along or looking to take advantage? His question about Mr. McGraw rang so true. He'd asked it in a manner that would work in this little drama, as well as in their real office life.

"What do you think McGraw *will* say when he learns?" he'd said.

It wasn't *would* or *might,* as if he were speculating. It was *will,* as though he was curiously asking as if an eventuality and knowing the Managing Partner would have something to say. But what? What were the rules on fraternization? She'd worked there for years and didn't know the policy on dating co-workers.

Eric regarded the ramifications of their playacting. Gradeen would listen in and find out about this and have no reason not to believe they were a couple. They'd explain it to McGraw so he wouldn't be blindsided. Then at the meeting later in the week to discuss trial strategies, they'd have to continue the charade. He'd gladly hold up his end.

He was again talking as they kept walking. "There's going to be a lot of upset suitors when they find out I won the Jillian Stennet sweepstakes."

There had been a time when she might have considered herself to be the prize in some big sweepstakes, a girl to be won. But those days were long ago. She was not a girl anymore and wondered if there might ever be another guy. She'd resigned herself to the idea that nowadays, a guy would be luckier to have her as his attorney than his girlfriend.

She regarded this and thought back to all the times he'd referred to the man in her life as lucky to be in that spot, to fill that role, to be with her. As she glanced to the big diamond on her left hand, she wondered if that remained the case? Or had it ever? Was all that luck which came with the big diamond now in the past tense, as sadly, now it seemed was the man who'd given it to her?

She'd had no choice but to move on, to make a life as a skilled attorney, focused on her job, her career and becoming partner. She was professional, driven and oftentimes cold. She's the ball-buster, a woman in a man's world. She didn't have time for distractions; she only had time for work.

And then, *Boom*, right out of nowhere, her work presents her with this distraction.

How could she explain her situation to him? Or herself? She'd been living a personal lie for so long it had become a second skin. To term it merely as "complicated" would not do her emotional mess true justice. And justice was allegedly her business.

Now she'd created this lie about the two of them to cover their tracks in the investigation, yet it didn't feel completely wrong. She'd roped him into playing along, and he was thriving in this pretense, behaving more like the dutiful boyfriend than the real one of her recent past. But if he was acting, it was very convincing.

All good lies are built on a modicum of truth, right? Maybe subconsciously she'd crafted the story not so much to shut down the Frenchman or to keep Jameson from overhearing their conversation. What if subconsciously she was gauging Eric's reaction to the possibility of something budding between them?

Jillian smiled at him before glancing up to the afternoon sky, her thoughts once more on balloons, yet not the trial balloons discussed with Jameson. Were they part of Eric's metaphor about his being a helium balloon bouncing around, about to disappear into the sky for good? Or was it somehow both? For the last few days, her world had been metaphorically chalked full of trial balloons. Who could criticize her for setting loose another?

She leaned into him as they walked quietly side by side, whether for the drone camera's benefit or her own she couldn't say. But she gave his hand an encouraging squeeze to reassure him that the string – his string -- was still wrapped tightly around her finger.

Almost reflexively, he squeezed back.

TWENTY-TWO

*N*either said a word until they were completely off the property and back on the county two-lane. Jillian had dropped the top on the BMW. While she drove, a paranoid Eric scanned the sky for drones. Once they were far enough removed from the prying eyes and ears and in the clear, Jillian could contain herself no longer. She pulled the car over to the side of the road and put the top back up to give their conversation privacy.

Pulling back onto the road, she explained Dr. Richard had been hesitant about answering questions not pertaining to *Swarm Farm*. She persisted, telling him that Jameson had said "any questions." Eventually, by her account, while the doctor was trying to wear her down romantically, she was wearing him down for answers. She'd won, but the tradeoff had been her number.

"I determined he might think of something else which we would find useful. It might give him an excuse to call."

Eric laughed at this. "He's back there right now concocting reasons to call."

"I'm okay with that. He's proven his worth already. He told me maybe a week ago, he overheard Jameson Gradeen on the phone. He's not positive but he thought Gradeen called the man Fuller."

"No shit? How'd you steer him around to tell you that?"

"I asked him if he was familiar with the names DeBisshop, Fuller and Steinhauer. He had a lot to say about the first. Only the mention of the phone call about the second, and nothing about the third."

"So, Fuller might still be alive."

She nodded at this and said, "The only mention of DeBisshop since he's disappeared has to do with just that. He said either no one knows what actually happened or no one is willing to speculate."

They stopped at the only stoplight in Edinburg. Rather than go straight toward I-55 and back to Springfield the way they'd come, Jillian turned the powerful car right, onto the inside lane of Highway 29.

"Where are we going?" Eric asked. "Why this way?"

"It's all right, my directionally challenged friend. You may have missed it on your GPS, but I know Highway 29 is a direct route back. I can get us home from here."

When he failed to reply, she glanced over to see he suddenly looked pale. Behind his sunglasses, she could see his eyes had closed, breathing in and out in short, shallow breaths like a Lamaze rookie. With an uncertain hand, he wiped at his top lip, the hand then slowly falling to pat the breast pocket of his suit jacket. It was like he was looking for his sunglasses before realizing they were already on. In a deft one-handed move, he ditched his tie and undid the top button on his dress shirt turning to stare out of the passenger side window.

"You okay?" she asked, her voice etched with concern and confusion.

"Yeah, sure." He wanted to sound lighthearted, the old Eric McKegney, yet his voice wavered unconvincingly.

She drove a bit further, the end of a Jason Mraz song on the radio, before asking again. Getting basically the same nonresponsive response, she tried to think what she may have done to bring about this drastic change.

"You sure you're okay?"

"I will be. Sorry."

Right there in front of her, he withdrew the leather wrapped, metal flask from an inside pocket. Without requesting permission, he brazenly unscrewed the top and took a swig. Maybe two. After a deep exhale, he replaced the lid and it was back in his inside pocket.

Now she was worried. Was his problem so bad that he looked visibly ill when he needed a drink? If that was the case, why did he look no better? How long would it take for his color to return? She flashed back to that Thursday night at Alford's when he ordered two drinks at a time. He'd not done that since in her presence, nor had his drinking seemed to be a growing problem around her. If anything, it seemed to be more under control, at least for a functioning alcoholic. But now this? It was barely three in the afternoon. What caused this abrupt change?

Without further thought, she continued with her recap of her earlier French conversation at the farm.

"Dr. Richard had also mentioned Monsieur Gradeen several times, and I thought little about it, until he then mentioned Jameson by name."

When he failed to react to this juicy tidbit as expected, she knew something far worse than his need for alcohol was ailing him. He'd virtually disappeared right there in her front seat. It was like she could extend her right arm and hit nothing. He was gone. Nonetheless, she continued explaining.

"Don't you see? Monsieur Gradeen is the father. Are you listening? Thomas Gradeen brought Dr. Richard over from France. The father replaced DeBisshop at the farm, not Jameson."

Still nothing.

Then a half-mile or so later, she saw the billboard, and it all made sense. It was old and rickety, made of wood, not steel or iron, from years ago, with a message painted on eight-sheet poster panels peeling like wallpaper in an abandoned house. She'd been able to read the message though. That's why he'd not originally directed them down Highway 29. It had nothing to do with where they were going and everything to do with where he'd been.

She glanced in the rear-view mirror to make sure she could slow without disrupting the traffic flow; she saw no one behind them. He felt the deceleration and turned from the window to look at her. She again checked the mirror before looking at him, her sunglasses hiding the watering in her eyes.

"I'm sorry about this," she said softly, her voice throaty and husky. "I can turn around and we can go back the way we came."

He was amazed how she had grasped his dismay and determined its reason without an explanation. Was it her compassion or cognition which was more impressive?

"It's okay," he heard himself say, a flat, almost dead smile creasing his face. "It's just up here a little farther on the right. Maybe revisiting my ghosts will prove therapeutic?"

"Will you want to stop?"

"Is that okay?"

She drove at normal speed for maybe another minute or so in silence, David Grey's Babylon in the Bose speakers imploring her to "Let go your heart. Let go your head. And feel it now."

But what was she supposed to feel? Once again with him she was getting ahead of herself. Her mind whirred with her work, with its expectations and their lies, with ghosts she was about to meet and balloons. Everywhere she looked her sky was full of allegorical balloons. How was she to let go of her heart, or her head? What did David Grey really know about shit anyway?

And then, there it was, tall and battered, shaped like an old Holiday Inn sign with the hunter green background and yellow arrow, complete with a sparkling star on top. The wording no longer mentioned being *The Nation's Innkeeper*. Instead it said Sangamon Suites Motel.

Her self-torture could finally be over, but his only about to begin.

She reached her hand over onto his arm and said with a forced laugh, "I can speed up and we can blast right past it. How about we do that?"

"Thanks. No. Just pull into the far end of the lot."

Sangamon Suites carried a notorious reputation, one that fit with the fact that two pretty people in a pretty car were pulling into the parking lot in the afternoon. Yet, unlike the other business sedans on this day, they'd pulled down to the north of the lot, far from the lobby with the see-nothing desk clerk and sheets available by the hour.

She went about as far as she could while staying on the pavement and threw the car in park. With one last check of her hair and makeup in the rearview mirror, she asked, "You want me to come with you?"

"Would you?" he asked in a small voice.

Eric walked solemnly, with his hands in his pants pockets. Jillian hustled to keep up, as she futilely tried to straighten her hair in the afternoon breeze. The few minutes leaving the farm with the BMW's top open had done irreparable damage to her up-do, so now she had let the dark hair fall past her shoulders, a few strands whipping against her face with the wind.

They walked together down the black-topped entrance across the aluminum culvert to the gravel shoulder of Highway 29. There was no traffic in either direction, so they stayed to the right, walking north in a single file. To their right was a drainage ditch with stagnant water as a reminder of yesterday's rain and a rise of grass and weeds up a dirt slope before a line of telephone poles supporting several wires. Farther up the hill, maybe ten to twelve feet at most, was where the woods began with heavy scrub bushes and trees.

Eric turned to say, "You know, this is going to be different now that there's a new reason why maybe she was coming here. Not easier, just different."

She followed him, gingerly balancing herself in her heels among the uneven gravel and glancing back over her shoulder to gauge any oncoming cars. From behind she watched him as he walked, hands still in his pockets, head bowed, suit coat buttoned against the breeze. It was more of a shuffle than a true stride, more cemetery than sidewalk, more pall than parade.

Up ahead several yards she could see what looked to be a homemade cross stuck in the ground, haloed by several wreaths of faded artificial flowers. At the base were two or three vases that once held real ones, plus a few votive globes minus the candle. There was also colored candle wax in heaps and piles dripped near stuffed animals at the bottom of the cross. This makeshift memorial was just across the ditch, partially up the slope before the trees. As

Jillian got closer she could read the name "Erin Haynes" and below it, she assumed had been the date of her death. Now, however, it was illegible.

She heard his sobs and the sniffling and felt helpless. His shoulders bucked as he lost control and fought to regain it. It was a heart-wrenching scene, his pain palpable and profound. She felt as though she could touch it, feel its thickness, like a cloud holding some kind of force or power of its own.

What was the proper etiquette in such a situation? Did she come up behind him with a light embrace to offer comfort, or was he better served by being left alone with his tears and his grief.

He answered the question for her by turning and wiping at his eyes under his shades with a thumb and forefinger. He then offered his hand to her, asking her to step up with him. She grabbed it, pulling herself in to stand by his side.

"How could I have blamed her?" he asked softly through his tears, more to himself than anyone.

She saw this as it was intended, a rhetorical question requiring no answer, or at least none she could supply. This was terrible for him. She could feel her tears welling up in sympathy, in empathy, or simply proximity. Then her tears flowed down her cheeks like rivers when he began to talk to Erin.

"I'm sorry. I was so . . . wrong."

The words caught in his throat to the point they were barely intelligible, but she understood. Jillian tried to look off to . . . anywhere. She felt as though she had no place here, like an intruder to a private, heart-tugging conversation. The raw passion in his voice proved to be the proverbial finger pulled from the dike and the tears gushed down her cheeks.

Then he sniffled hard and turned to her. Still choked with emotion and struggling to speak, he said, "I hated her for what I thought she did to me, to us. But I was wrong. She loved me and we were going to spend our lives together. I thought I was the victim. It was her. All the time, it was her."

Here a pickup slowed as it passed them on the other side of highway, going in the south direction. Eric pulled a handkerchief from his pocket and wiped his nose and again dabbed at his eyes. When the truck passed and the sound of the engine had abated, he spoke again through the sobs.

"I'm a mess since she left. She would not be proud of the way I've been carrying myself. I was so lost. I didn't know where to turn, and then every turn got me deeper into my mess."

After a slight pause, his voice lowered and he said, "I did love her, and I guess I still do. I hope one day I can prove that to her, prove I was good enough for her. I hope she can forgive me."

He removed his sunglasses and again wiped the handkerchief across his eyes and then turned to Jillian. He handed it to her, and she used a dry corner to dab at her incredible eyes, shimmering even more when she removed her shades. With a sad smile, she wiped the mascara running down the tracks of the tears from her cheeks, the white of the handkerchief now streaked in black.

She handed the handkerchief back to him and asked, "What can I do?"

"Will you just stand here with me for a second?"

She answered this by leaning her head against his upper arm and wrapping her free hand around their clasped hands. They stood there together, wordlessly breathing in unison, the breeze dancing through their hair. Every now and then Jillian would pull one hand free to get the dark strands away from her face, but other than that they remained still in the silent solemnity.

Jillian scanned the area, practicality overriding sentiment. How had this accident happened? What remained of the telephone pole that stopped the car and killed Erin was still there, fractured and splintered like a toothpick. The bottom remained firmly planted in the ground, pieces of the top hanging from the resisters attached to the wires. It was dangling like the string of a kite tangled in the wires. A newer, stronger looking post had replaced the broken pole, the color a deeper brown against the weathered remnants.

Eric spoke. "Erin's parents made this memorial. It used to be nicer. It had a great picture of her laughing, this crazy, excited look on her face. Time and the weather have taken its toll on all of this."

He crouched and tried to straighten up the vases and what was left of the flowers in them. There were a few cans and broken bottles near the base. He grabbed each and threw them up the hill into the woods. He did the same with a few larger rocks.

It sounded trite in her brain prior to saying it, and worse once she had, but she nevertheless asked. "Do you come here a lot?"

She could sense he was ashamed of his answer when he shook his head slightly and said, "Not as much as I probably should."

Then he stood and turned toward her, adding, "It might be different now. Before when I was under the impression she'd fucked me, it felt wrong to come here. It was hard to hate her and miss her at the same time. Does that make sense? And now . . ."

She understood. Before, Erin had betrayed him in his way of thinking, so it would have been disingenuous to mourn her. Now that might not be the case after all.

He said as if to no one, "I came out here for the first time the day after the wreck. It was maybe about this time on that Friday afternoon. I was supposed to be at Happy Hour prior to my bachelor's party, the day before my wedding. Instead I'm staring at the spot my fiancé just died."

Jillian closed her eyes and whispered, "I can't begin to imagine what that was like. I hope you understand how sorry I am for you."

"Thanks. But I don't really remember much of it. I was numb. I remember crying. A lot. I think I came out here to see the spot and maybe say goodbye, but also maybe to try to make some sense of it. Maybe determine what happened, you know, in case I could find someone to sue."

That line had brought the first wrinkle of a smile to his harried face, as the old carefree *Ambulance Chaser* briefly reappeared. Jillian, still with a hold on his hand, spun him slightly and pointed north, the direction from which the car had come on that Thursday night.

"Did you ever figure out how the crash happened?"

"Not definitively. The police stated Ritter was legally intoxicated and lost control, slamming into a telephone pole. But I remember seeing skid marks on the road. Ironically it looked to me that if he had not slammed on the brakes when he lost control that he might have gone off the road and up this hill."

He pointed to a cleared area behind them, between where they stood and the motel entrance. Jillian looked in both directions, judging the distances and imagined the speed with which they must have hit the pole to shatter it so.

She asked, "If they were going to this motel, shouldn't they have begun slowing down way back there?"

Again, she pointed back up the road, and said, "Think about it. If this was the destination and Ritter had allegedly been here before, wouldn't he know to slow down? The entrance is very well marked."

Eric glanced back to the hotel to see the enormous sign and then back to the north. There were no trees or billboards blocking the view of the old Holiday Inn sign. How could Ritter have almost missed so he had to slam the brakes? How fast was he going? How many pitchers of margaritas did they have?

Jillian was having the same thought and asked, "You did this for a living. Is there any way to determine how fast a car is going at the time of impact? Would it say in the police report?"

He thought about this and answered, "Normally police reports are vague. They use language like "Unsafe speed" or "Unsafe for conditions." They never speculate on the number. But I'll bet somebody calculating the length of the skid and the damage to that pole could have pinpointed the speed."

"By looking at what's left of that pole, I'd guess it was fast."

She waited for him to grasp where she was going with this, but when he once again failed to put two and two together, she got to four for him.

"Because if he was still going the speed limit right here, he wasn't going to this motel."

She looked from the telephone pole to the big sign, and the distance would not be as far as it seemed when seen through the windshield of a car going sixty-five miles an hour.

Eric followed her gaze and considered what she'd said. But if they weren't coming here, where were they going? What in the hell then was the "one last thing" Erin needed to do?

He felt the comfortable convenience of his personal version of the events slip away, being replaced like opening the next nesting doll. Every day, another opened egg revealed something new, another smaller egg. And every day they had to be getting closer to the truth.

Or were they?

And was that really what he wanted?

TWENTY-THREE

*C*onversation lulled as they walked the gravel shoulder back to the parking lot, now facing the sporadic oncoming traffic. Again in single file, Jillian now in the lead. She noticed a parallel row of telephone poles on the opposite side of the highway, their wires loaded with birds.

While glancing back she noticed Eric trudging along behind her, chin on his chest and hands in pockets. Every other step he kicked nonchalantly at a rock or other loose impediment.

"Hey," she said, sweeping her hair from her face. "You gonna be okay?"

Looking up he tried his best to smile and said, "Yeah. I will be. Thanks for doing this with me."

"It's my pleasure."

With this she turned and waited for him to catch up. She wrapped both hands around his left arm for support in her heels on the unsteady gravel and fell in step beside him.

"I hope you don't think this question is right out of left field, but do you know if Ritter was much of a drinker?"

"You wondering about his BAC?" This meant blood-alcohol concentration. "It was .08 or something around there."

"The legal limit in Illinois," she pointed out.

"So, are you going all defense attorney on me now?" he asked with a slight laugh. "I know he was cited for DUI after the accident. Straight into a telephone pole regardless of the number of margaritas often does that."

They took a few steps and she looked up to him and said, "I imagine you've run into this before, but you realize that .08 affects everyone's judgment and motor skills differently."

"Listen to you," he said with a laugh. "Are we parsing?"

"That's what defense attorneys do," she came back with a gorgeous smile. "I ask about his drinking to see if we can draw a conclusion about his tolerance level. Take you for example. For the last few days, I've seen you do astounding mental calculus and chances are you have been legally intoxicated the entire time. Not that I condone such behavior, but you function like you do because of your elevated tolerance."

"Plus, I'm a professional." When she didn't respond to this, he thought back to her initial question and said, "I'm sure I was around him at parties where he was drinking, but I don't know if he was ever sloshed."

"Any idea how long after the accident they drew his blood?"

It was as if he was now playing the prosecutor to her defense. "If it was still .08 when they finally tested him at the hospital, it had to have been markedly higher when he drove into that pole."

She heard herself say, "Best ally in a DUI case is the wait-time to be tested."

They curved together up the asphalt ramp and back into the parking lot. Rather than get in her car, she turned to lean against the driver's side door. He took his place on her left. Silently they stared across the highway and into the overgrown vastness of a field ringed by rusty barbed-wire strung on rotting fence posts. They watched blackbirds taking flight, their formation fighting against the breeze.

He reached into his inside pocket and pulled out the flask, without giving it a second thought. She finally spoke, and it was completely unexpected.

"I admire you. I admire how well you've managed the shitty hand you've been dealt."

This comment had stopped him somewhere between unscrewing the top and taking a drink. His hand holding the flask in this state of limbo, waiting for her to continue.

She looked over to him, isolated strands of lustrous brown hair blowing gloriously across her face and said, "And I admire the honest and open way you live. You're real. No games. No facades. Take it or leave it. This is who you are."

He had no idea where she was heading with this but perceived it as a preface of sorts to a topic she wished to discuss. Or dare he hope for something personal to be imparted by her, for outside of her French lineage, this would be a first.

He offered the flask to her. "Friends don't let friends drink alone," he said with a wry smile.

She took an almost imperceptible lean away from him and began protesting and waving him away.

"Just because that's the way you solve your problems . . ."

"Right now, I get the feeling we're about to work on yours. Being the gentleman I am, I'm merely letting the lady go first."

He said this with an emphatic bob of the flask in his right hand.

She actually looked in each of the four directions, as if she thought someone out here in the parking lot of a motel with rooms rented by the hour might judge or disapprove. She took the flask, testing its weight and balance.

"What's in here?" she asked, staring into the opening of the flask.

"Glenlivet. A fine single-malt Scotch Whisky."

She took a whiff of the liquor and scrunched up her incredible face, her nose wrinkling adorably. She brought the flask to her mouth and then hesitated, lowering her sunglasses, and turning her grey eyes on him as if all she needed was one more piece of encouragement.

"Scotch, huh?"

He was quick to oblige. "Go ahead. It's surprisingly smooth."

Jillian took a surprisingly healthy swig, similar to how he liked to tilt it back. She closed her eyes tightly. He watched as she was finally able to swallow, her face pained, like drinking sugar-free cough medicine.

"You call that smooth?" she said, the words coming out between gasps and a cough, the back of her left-hand wiping at her mouth.

He reached for the flask and took a similar gulp, showing no reaction whatsoever to the strong and smoky taste. He screwed the lid back on.

"Where were we? You were saying you admire me."

"You're authentic," she said plainly without flourish, as if speaking to one of the birds across the road on the wire.

"You cry and don't care who sees. You laugh at yourself more than at others. I'm not like that. I can't really laugh or cry. You're genuine. I'm fake. You live your life by your own plan. I live by someone else's. My path has been preordained."

He considered this and asked, "But aren't you the one . . .?"

"Oh, yeah. Go ahead and blame me," she said with a wide smile. "It's just that you already have more friends at the firm than I do, and you're like on day two and I'm in year whatever."

"I find that hard to believe."

"It's true." She shifted her weight and rolled her hip against the car door so she could face him, trying to keep her dark hair out of her face.

"You relate to people; they're drawn to you. It's like I wear people repellant. I don't have friends at the firm. I have coworkers, but no real friends."

"What about me?" he asked. "I thought I was your friend."

"You're the new guy. You're still in your probationary period," she said more as a tease than an answer. "No determination on your status yet."

"That's not what the Frenchie doctor thinks."

"That's right. And it was nice of you to volunteer to quit the firm if *This* becomes a problem."

She made a back-and-forth motion with the index finger of her right hand, implying "this" to mean the two of them, in whatever state that might currently be. She'd used this gesture previously when talking about the two of them.

"Length of service decision," he said matter-of-factly.

It was as if her mind was already elsewhere and no longer on seniority. She said, "My problems with the people at the firm are my own doing. I find myself in the unenviable position which requires I edit my personal content."

What? Was she suddenly speaking French again? Editing personal content sounded more like the sort of nonsense you hear about a websites. For her part, she noticed his confusion, reorganized her thoughts, and tried to better explain.

"You commented on it that first night. I'm a woman in a man's world. I'm rarely *the girl*. I'm one of the guys, forced to disseminate personal info with an eyedropper. I can't allow anyone to know private things about me which one day may come back around to haunt me. Say for instance, if that person and I are both up for partner. I can't afford to give anyone ammunition."

He regarded this comment as being sad, but quite plausible. He tried to place himself in her heels. *Donaldson, Clements is* a relative boys club. She'll never get to be one of the guys. She may profess to be, but it didn't work that way. Nor did she ever want it to.

"I purposefully remain aloof. Everyone perceives me as unapproachable. It's as if the other associates fear me and won't talk to me, but they're all guys, so who cares? Men are idiots. They walk on eggshells, like I've already got the sexual harassment complaint written up and just waiting to fill in their name.

"And don't think I don't hear what the paralegals say behind my back. That I'm a cold bitch. I'm formidable. Did you know that is the new politically correct way to refer to someone like me? Formidable. But I'm supposed to be the ball buster. It might even say that somewhere on my business card.

"I'm good at my job and I work hard," she was saying, growing slightly more agitated.

"There's not a lot of time for socializing. Plus on *Seven* it's frowned upon. Don't get me wrong. Everyone on the floor, all the married partners and their executive assistants are polite, but we're not friends. I'm not friends with my own assistant. All the partners' wives stare daggers at me. They fear I'm going to steal their husbands. Have you seen those guys? There's no chance in hell."

This was amazing. She was talking, spilling. Whether it was the little sip of Glenlivet or more the fact that she might be comfortable enough with him to open up, he didn't know. But just in case it was the former, he held out the flask for her. This time she never hesitated, unscrewing the top like a pro and taking a swig without the theatrics from the first time, save for some coughing. Then, as if returning to a stream of consciousness, here came more.

"I told you my mother is French. She's from the Languedoc-Roussillon region of France, down on the Mediterranean. She grew up in Montpellier, like Vermont's capital. She emigrated to the U.S. at age sixteen to perform with the Joffrey Ballet in Chicago as a prima ballerina. She was Madelaine Desmarais, which in French, literally means Madelaine who lives by the marsh. I have been able to speak fluent French all my life. And I've been to France too many times to count. My grandmother still lives in the house where my mother grew up.

"One of the sponsor families of the Joffrey Ballet then in Chicago was the Stennet's. They had a handsome nineteen-year-old son who took a shine to this exotic-looking Mediterranean beauty living in his home. When he graduated Law School and became established, they married. Have I mentioned that my father is also an attorney?"

"You don't really talk much about yourself," he offered with a half-laugh.

"Then you better buckle up and pay attention because chances are you're never getting me here again. So, as you can now guess, it's my mother's DNA responsible for my coloring and not the central Illinois sun. When I wasn't being teased for looking different they ridiculed me for being a ballerina."

"Could you have done it professionally?"

"I really think so, but my parents . . . I love my parents, but they are so diametrically opposed on almost everything. People wonder how they ever got together in the first place. Maybe it's yin and yang. They love each other and all us kids. My mother is all about the performing arts, as you might assume, while my father claims to be the grounded one. It was idealism versus realism. He eventually won, so I set my sights on a more practical profession."

Then, with more of a nostalgic flourish, she continued, "Mom taught dance after she stopped performing. She had a studio above a diner on Main Street. I spent my youth there. I thought I was a prodigy. Mom said I was good. Years later she admitted that was mother not instructor talking. I had the ballerina body-type attributes, thin physique and great feet, flexibility in the hips, back and knees, plus perfect hip turnout, better than one-hundred-eighty degrees. That's the outward rotation of the hip joint."

She added this last part as a way of explanation, which was good because our minds had gone off on any number of hip-related tangents that had more to do with a horizontal dance than a vertical one. Then her next topic nudged our minds further into the gutter.

"Then my body began to develop, and certain things came along." She said this with a self-deprecating snicker, nodding and glancing down toward her breasts under the grey suit jacket.

"There's a reason you only see flat-chested ballerinas; these things seriously get in the way."

She paused here with a sigh and said, "So, off to college and, at my father's urgings, on to law school."

At this, something changed. The laughs and lively animation evident when talking about her body changing and the hilarious gesture all slowly faded. She turned to the right to look away from him, as if embarrassed or afraid to face him. What brought this on? Was she somehow feeling guilty for not following her heart and giving in instead to convention? Had her father dashed her dreams of dancing? Had she retained some measure of regret because of it?

He noticed this. A blind man would have noticed the change, but thinking it might be some sort of an outlier, he tried to right the listing ship by asking, "Is your father still practicing law?"

"Semi-retired."

Her response while continuing to look away reinforced his suspicion there may be Daddy issues at play here. Yet he tried again to re-engage her.

"Do your parents still live in Naperville?"

"Uh-huh."

It was as if her personal history had run aground, or at least out of steam. The entertaining and free-flow narrative of her first twenty-some years had unfolded like a tantalizing striptease, each anecdote like the removal of an article of clothing. But before he could get to see everything, she again covered herself as her trip down memory lane entered a new no-man's land which was law school. What happened there that prevented him from now seeing her nostalgically naked?

Eric, like Jillian, was practiced in the art of getting people to talk, which is true for most attorneys . . . or even investigators. So, he tried to retrace her steps and get her back on the rails by asking about high school.

"Long time ago. Not much to tell," she said dismissively.

He nodded at this and took a sip from the flask, before again offering it to her. She turned toward him and shook her head almost imperceptibly.

Who was she kidding? This wasn't her. She couldn't try to be him, to live the carefree life, to drink from a flask on a Monday afternoon. She couldn't pretend to do what he'd do, talk about herself with no filter, no editing. While it was somewhat enjoyable and at the same time liberating, she could never be him. Why even try?

Just like mentioned about her parents, she and Eric too were opposites, but which of them was *Yin* and who was *Yang*? She was not wired to react to life like he was, to go with the flow. She was a doer. She acted. She set the pace; those around her reacted to her, to her script. Her's was a preordained life. Did this damaged guy have what it took to fit into her plan?

But what might that be? What masculine attributes was she seeking? Eric was handsome and funny, sweet and silly, smart and curious. He also carried enough baggage to need a Sky Cap, truly the butterfly with the broken wing as he'd described himself. She'd just visited the trigger of that hurt. And with all this, she couldn't shake the recurrent notion that this lost little puppy needed rescuing.

Maybe then it was time to change the plan, do a rewrite which included his saving, making a comfy spot for him because it was so god-awful lonely in here by herself. Maybe it was time to go completely off script and finally let someone in. No time like the present.

"On second thought, I'll have that drink," she said without looking at him.

With an equal amount of nonreaction or fanfare, he handed her the flask and said nothing. He did notice that this time, however, she took a more generous swig with no gasping or coughing.

She collected her resolve and stepped over right in front of him, gazing up into his face as he leaned casually against the back driver's door of her car. She watched her reflection in his sunglasses and tried on an anxious smile. She then placed both hands on his forearms near his elbows and drew herself to him, watching as he slightly cocked his head in hesitation as to what was coming next.

She whispered, "Remember when I told you my situation is complicated?"

"Uh-huh," he gulped.

"You're not making it any easier."

Before he could ask her meaning, she closed her eyes behind her sunglasses and moved her mouth toward his. Eric considered turning his cheek for a quick peck as done previously, but this was different, slower and more tentative. He too closed his eyes, lowering his head, preparing for a kiss on the mouth by this gorgeous woman, his mind racing in millions of new directions with billions of new possibilities. But rather than feel her soft lips on his, he instead felt her palms pressing against his chest. He quickly opened his eyes to see she was looking off to his left and pulling away.

"I'm sorry," she said immediately. "That was . . . God! I'm sorry."

"Were you . . .? But not on the cheek?"

She was mortified. "Yes. No! I shouldn't have . . . That was totally unprofessional. I'm terribly sorry."

He noticed her blushing and knew she was dreadfully embarrassed. He also understood there would be no joking this away. She'd tried to kiss him, wanted to kiss him only to then draw away. Either she reconsidered or lost her nerve, and that's with the long *I* sound.

He had no idea what to do or how to react, so he did the only thing he could, exactly what any good fake boyfriend would do. He offered her a way out, or at least something to blame.

As she continued her litany of apologies, he smiled widely and said, "Hey. It's okay. That's not you. That was the scotch. Trust me. It makes people do things they regret."

She'd stepped away, but then looked back over her shoulder, lowering her hands which had been hiding her rosy cheeks. She apparently accepted his reasoning with a pained smile.

"Yeah, that must be it," she said in a quiet and uncomfortable voice. Then her tone switched to a sense of relief, agreeing, "It had to be the scotch."

She quickly grasped the proffered lifeline, appearing to be momentarily snatched from her torment. While reeling her up, he offered her yet another motive for her behavior.

"If not the scotch, then sympathy. You're amazing. I can't thank you enough for coming here with me. This was very emotional and you're too nice not to care. I'm sorry you got caught up in all this, but I'll be okay. Thanks for all you've done."

She studied him, knowing lesser gentlemen would be more opportunistic. Hell, if she tried this with other men, they'd have hauled her up to the front desk to get an hour's worth of sheets and towels and may have been well-within their rights. She made the first move. But to what end? How had she envisioned this little scene ending any other way than badly?

She'd stepped up to that precipice, seemingly fearless of the height, only to then reevaluate her reasons to leap. That wasn't like her and her indecisiveness disappointed her. She'd reached a binary decision, a simple *Yes* or *No? Should I, Shouldn't I?* She'd decided *She should* and committed to that conclusion, only to change her mind. She was always the most decisive person; she never changed her mind. What had prompted this uncharacteristic behavior?

Had she pulled away because the thought of kissing Eric was a horrible idea which would lead to problems? Or was it a wonderful idea that would lead to a completely different set of problems? She glanced at the ring on her left hand wondering how it factored in.

Whether bad idea or good, wrong or too right, she'd inadvertently started and simultaneously stopped her futile attempt before it had actually begun in motion.

Part of her understood what happened and *why*, but it was coming from a place from which she was hoping to distance herself. It was her rational side, the practical side with the diamond ring and the promise upon accepting it. In this case it was making a great deal of sense, too much to be ignored. Her initial thought that there was no better time than the present had been totally baseless. While he might eventually be the right person, the place was totally wrong.

They were no more than fifty yards from where his fiancé had been killed eight months ago.

This area had to be swarming with haunted memories and ghosts, relegating him defenseless. That went without saying, yet it was her vulnerability which had been exposed. Had she also seen ghosts and been possessed? Or haunted?

Regardless, a return to reason told her simply there would be no immediate need to change her life plan. No rewrites to include Eric McKegney were required for this had been all in her imagination, all too emotional and none too real. Pursuing this now would be folly, purely romantic comedy fiction.

Yet, neither of them were laughing.

She'd nonetheless tipped her hand and there was no use denying it. God! Why hadn't she just given him another peck on the cheek?

Even after changing her mind, another light kiss on his cheek would've prevented all this wailing and gnashing of teeth.

And to make matters worse, his reaction to her bumbling attempt had been gallantry. He'd somehow appreciated her dilemma and made it clear that even though he might not completely understand, he wasn't overwhelmed by what happened. He'd even helped her wriggle off the hook. Instead of bombarding her with questions or inanely asking if she *wanted to talk about it*, he'd offered her a way out, an excuse.

Actually he'd given her two.

And in the neutrality and nobility of his gentlemanly reaction, not showing his cards, instead continuing to hold them close to his vest, he'd shown no indication of whether her feelings were reciprocated. He'd offered no hint.

She'd hoped for some sort of sign but knew she'd have to settle this personal tug-of-war without his help.

TWENTY-FOUR

*O*ftentimes when you overstep emotionally or make mistakes with your feelings, you can slink away or disappear into the background in hopes the target of said mistake will forget and eventually forgive. The same is true when leading with your heart and not your head makes you feel utterly foolish. Normally you have time to recompose and recover before again facing that person or reliving your shame.

Jillian Stennet was not afforded such luxury. She'd later refer to starting and then stopping the kiss as, "Making a complete fool of myself."

I had a better name for it.

She had no place to hide, no earth to swallow her whole. The person to whom she'd thrown the aborted pass sat right beside her for the torturous twenty-minute drive back to Springfield. Never before had the luxurious leather seats of her BMW felt so uncomfortable or confined.

To lessen this claustrophobia, or to distract from her humiliation, she'd let down the top and rolled down the windows. The wind whipping through the convertible tossed their hair and made conversation a challenge. Neither were able to hear a word said by the other let alone respond, as was her plan.

When the difficult moment from the no-tell motel parking lot eventually had passed and her incessant apologies stopped, Eric walked around the back of the car to get in the passenger's side. As they opened their respective doors, there was this split second where they stopped and stared at each other across the black ragtop of the Gran Coupe. They shared a singular moment which now seemingly carried contrary meanings.

He'd seen a glimpse of her that was more special than all the time with her to this point. She was sympathetic and caring about Erin, and then fun and engaging when talking about her past. She drank Scotch Whisky from his flask for god's sake. She'd been open, impulsive, almost improvisational. She was so real, so genuine, so enjoyable. God, the woman was fun.

But that all stopped so abruptly, and curiously at a major juncture in her life. Was it something to do with law school? Was it her father? Was it neither? Why did she insist on being so secretive about her past? What was she hiding, or hiding from?

And was she really going to kiss him? Why didn't she? What was up with that? It was like she missed. A *Kiss Miss*, I called it. Was there any significance with where that occurred within her timeline of life events? No answers were to be found at the Sangamon Suites.

Before either of them got in the car, Eric had said, "There's one other thing."

Without a word she stopped lowering herself into the car and looked stoically across the top to him. He had her full attention.

"Today was crazy. Back at the farm you and I kind of became boyfriend and girlfriend. I know it was a charade, just for show, but it seemed very real to me. I enjoyed it . . . playing my part. Maybe you did, too. I allowed myself to consider that it might be more than just for show, that it might be real. I don't know. Maybe you did, too. If you did, that might help explain a few things."

She failed to react. Saying nothing, her face expressionless like a cold-blooded killer.

Undeterred he tried something more. "And then *This* . . . here .. . you and me . . . also feels real. It may to you, likewise. But it can't be, can it?"

He was still mimicking her little back-and-forth gesture with his index finger when she threw a noncommittal glance and climbed behind the wheel.

He stood there for a beat, feeling like he'd just missed the *golden-est* of opportunities. She was actually going to kiss him. At the same time her timing was horrible. If that little scene had taken place anywhere else she may have actually gone through with it.

Kissing her is all he'd thought about since their first night. But what if she'd been messing with him? What if it was a tease, part of some shitty game? Could she be that conniving, that cold? Could anyone?

Jillian for her part had started the car, pondering his question, wondering, "Why couldn't this be real?"

There were a ton of practical reasons why it wasn't a good idea, but there was one other prominent explanation she had yet to consider. What if *he* didn't want it to be? What if he didn't feel the same about her?

Hell, what did she really feel? She watched him suspiciously, appraisingly, waiting for him to buckle his seat belt. Once she heard the click, she tore out of the hotel parking lot.

Now they were rocketing north on Highway 29, top down, radio blaring a song identified on the console monitor as "Doorways" by a band called *Civil Twilight*. She'd turned up the volume to sing along with the parts she knew. Eric was unfamiliar with the band and the song but seemed to get pulled in by the lyrics. Maybe what had just happened was serving as his frame of reference or that's what *Civil Twilight* had intended, but the song and the timing seemed incredibly appropriate.

To Eric it's about two people stuck in some sort of indeterminate state. They wouldn't commit to going in together even if it meant getting out of the cold. Instead they stayed in the comfy limbo of this metaphorical doorway, unsure what to do next. Do they leave separately or go inside together? The song ends with the guy asking why they continue to stand there and begging her to come in. It was an especially timely message.

When the song was over and a commercial for a Springfield bank played, he turned in his seat to look at her to gauge if maybe this song had been part of some bigger strategy. Call it subliminal messaging, or whatever, but she showed no reaction to having arranged this for him. Instead she stared straight ahead at the oncoming traffic, sunglasses now propped atop her head, the turtle shell temples holding her hair behind her ears like a headband. The small farming community of Rochester was approaching, so she slowed and reached over to turn down the radio.

To reestablish the boundaries and their respective places when it came to their jobs, in a bossy tone she said, "The little detour on our way back stays just between us. No one needs to know we stopped or what almost happened. Okay?"

She hadn't so much as glanced in his direction, making this pronouncement straight ahead through the steering wheel almost like she was admonishing the windshield for some unseen infraction.

He considered how best to play this and came back with, "That depends."

This time she turned to face him, her unbelievable eyes wide with suspicion. She asked, "On what?"

"You stop beating yourself up about what happened back there. And please don't apologize again."

At this she tried to smile before turning her attention back to the gathering traffic as they neared the small town's high school. The dismissal bell must have sounded recently because there were several cars and school buses pulling out onto the highway. Jillian, never having been described as patient, edgily tapped both hands on the steering wheel as he continued to watch her.

But he wasn't alone. Every guy in a car or a bus window was staring at her as they passed. Some may have been checking out the convertible, but Eric guessed most were more impressed by the brunette behind the wheel than the $65,000 worth of BMW.

She must have felt his eyes on her because she turned back again.

"What?" she asked, that playful smile flashing for an instant on her glorious face before disappearing. She'd intended to wallow in her embarrassment the entire return trip, but he'd have none of that. So she asked her question again.

"Nothing," he said with a shake of his head.

How could he explain it to her or anyone? She was such a living, breathing contradiction. It was more than the initial pulled in and simultaneously pushed away vibe. She'd now proven to be both soft and hard, a caring heart inside her formidable shell. She was like his flask, yet more intoxicating and addictive. Whereas the single-malt inside was protected by the hard metal of the flask, this woman too had an exterior of iron. She had her armor and, try as he might to chip away at it or possibly outflank her, he wasn't getting in until she decided to unscrew the lid.

It was about that time when the phone in his pocket chirped. The screen identified the caller as George Harrison, so he showed it to Jillian. With her left hand she reached for the door console and raised the windows, blocking the wind and reducing any exterior noise.

"Hey Sarge, how are things? What's up?"

Almost breathlessly, the big investigator said, "*Young Gun*, think I got a hit on Fuller."

"That's great. I was going to tell you that his name came up --"

Sarge interrupted him to add, "I mean right now. Tonight. Some Illinois Guard vets are part of a therapy group that meets Monday nights at a bar over in Decatur. I'm going if you think it's okay."

"You bet, Sarge. Good work. You know the age group we are looking for. See if anyone knows about him. Also, if you get over there before 5:00, use your cop contacts to see if anyone remembers him when he was on the force. We need to see if the Steinhauer connection starts there."

"Will do. When you comin' back?"

"We're on our way back now."

"Am I on speaker?"

"No. Why?" Eric asked suspiciously.

"How'd it go with the lovely lady lawyer?"

He looked to Jillian who must have sensed that the conversation had turned to her because she returned the glance, her grey eyes boring holes into him.

"I think we did a lot of good today," he answered evasively.

"You, *Young Gun*, are my idol."

"On the investigation, Sarge."

"Anything on the other front?"

"I'll tell her you asked."

"Don't you dare," Sarge fired back immediately.

At the mention of her, Jillian looked over at him with a quizzical expression. He covered the cellphone and said, "Sarge says hello."

With the phone back to his ear he heard Sarge saying, ". . . message for you here. That author you called. She left a local bookstore name that's got copies of her book about Gradeen."

He gave Jillian a thumbs-up and said into the phone, "That's great. I'll run by there and pick up a copy and start reading it tonight."

"Wouldn't you rather come to Decatur?"

"You can handle Decatur."

"You doing something with her tonight, ain't you, *Young Gun*?"

"And I'll catch up with you sometime tomorrow, Sarge. Good luck tonight."

"And good luck to you too," Sarge said with a knowing chuckle before ending the conversation.

Eric filled in the details of the call and when finished, Jillian saw that the traffic had dispersed. She rolled down the windows, cranked the radio and fired the engine of the big BMW. They were both pinned back in their seats, any further chance for conversation now gone.

TWENTY-FIVE

Decatur, Illinois, a town of about 75,000, is roughly forty miles due east on Interstate 72. Like every other metropolitan area in central Illinois it shares two things with Springfield, namely agribusiness and Abraham Lincoln. It also, however, has bragging rights on a third claim to fame to which no other city in Illinois can compare. I'll get to that here in a bit, depending how fast you read.

At age twenty-one, the future sixteenth president first settled thirty miles east of Decatur when he and his family moved to Illinois. That same year he gave his first political speech about Sangamon River navigation. It's said this caught the attention of the state's Whig Party leaders. And as you can probably guess by now, a statue commemorates the event. There aren't many things the man did or places he visited which don't have statues today. Long after his assassination he remains the most prominent presence in this part of the state.

The city is also a player in the world of farming. Agricultural conglomerate, Archer Daniels Midland, has its North American Headquarters here and is the city's largest employer. A. E. Staley's largest corn-processing plant was here until it was sold to Tate & Lyle, the British holding company which operates it today. Caterpillar Inc. also has a design and manufacturing facility in town for their wheel-tractor scrapers, off-highway trucks, and large mining equipment.

But it is A.E. Staley which holds the softest spot in the hearts of the long-time residents. Mr. Staley formed a semi-pro football team in 1919, the Decatur Staleys, employing players from his corn starch business. A year later the team was taken over by George Halas and moved to Chicago to become the Chicago Bears, a charter member of the fledgling NFL. In homage to those humble beginnings, the team's mascot to this day is *Staley da Bear.*

Suck on that Springfield.

These reasons combine to give rise to the city's motto: "Decatur, We Like It Here." It seems to fit much better than previously being referred to as the "Soybean Capital of the World."

Being an industrial city, Decatur has its share of blue-collar workers and railroads. These workers then frequent small neighborhood taverns, most of which sit on darkened street corners on inexpensive real estate down by the railyard. It was up the street from one such establishment, Spanky's, that Sarge banged away on his laptop, sending an email to Eric.

First, he explained in greater detail how he found himself in Decatur. As he worked his way through the list of the members of Fuller's National Guard platoon, he noticed on most that the area code was 217, which meant they were all from the surrounding area. This was not a surprise, since the unit prior to deployment was comprised of soldiers from Springfield, Decatur, Effingham, Champaign-Urbana and as far south as Litchfield.

"That's why it's called the *Illinois* National Guard," he typed complete with italics.

He'd been able to strike up phone conversations with some of the names on the list since he too had served. His deployment had been many years earlier and in Lebanon, not Iraq. He said he never came right out and asked about Fuller, instead he'd tried to engage them solely to see where it may lead.

A major topic of conversation among all veterans of late is the Department of Veterans' Affairs' medical care and extended wait times. It was easy to get people to open up on the phone, and what kept coming up was the excellent care offered at the Decatur VA Outpatient Clinic.

A quick call there, and a behavioral male nurse was soon talking about this support group he helps run. It meets once a month on the second Monday night of the month at a neighborhood bar. Sarge was told the guys have a few beers and play pool and darts and tell stories. Sarge promised no guarantees but thought between military service and Fuller's time on the local police force, someone would have something to say about the man. Whether anyone knew his whereabouts would be a different story.

Eric read the email and considered Sarge to be a virtuoso at working the angles. Did that make him a *geomitrist*? Or how about *Euclidocrat*? Did I just invent two words? Feel free to use either.

Eric went back to scanning through the Thomas Gradeen biography he picked up at a store called *The Book Knook*. Sadly, it was the last of a dying breed, the one-off brick and mortar book store. With online sales of books taking over, it's harder and harder for this type of business to survive, so they diversify. Not only was *The Book Knook* the place to go in Springfield for hard-to-find books, but now you could also get a cup of overpriced coffee while you examined the shelves. There had been five copies of the book in stock; four remained.

He sat with the book in his lap while sipping on Glenfiddich. He had a blank legal pad on the couch next to him, but it was serving solely as a coaster, for there was little of import in the book so far. The story itself was disjointed and dull. Gradeen didn't come across as someone to justify a biography, authorized or not, let alone a titan.

But what R.J. Harris' book lacked in excitement it made up for with bad writing. There was no linear structure like you'd assume with a biography, so it was hard to short-cut. Apparently no one had approved her outline for it was not following one. It didn't start with his childhood nor end in modern day. The timeline jumped all over the place like the story was being told with a shotgun; there was no way to go directly to the most fascinating chapters of Gradeen's professional life.

He considered since written as an *Unauthorized Biography*, it would be full of juicy gossip and unsubstantiated claims. Hardly.

Thomas Gradeen was the son of a farmer, active in the local chapter of the FFA -- – Future Farmers of America – and took over the farm upon his father's death. He married his high school sweetheart, who became Jameson's mother. Once he found success, he divorced her for a woman Jameson's age. That was public record, not disgrace.

Many of the pages were filled with meaningless tripe. He was a fan of the Beach Boys and Elvis. He liked James Bond movies; Sean Connery was his favorite Bond, but James Dean was his favorite actor. His favorite books were Mario Puzo's *The Godfather,* and *The Canterbury Tales,* by Geoffrey Chaucer, who some have called the Mario Puzo of his day.

Okay, I made that up, but just think what that tells us about this *Titan.* These two books were written over six-hundred years apart. One is credited with bringing the English language to mainstream literature, while the other did the same thing for the mafia.

Yet, who really cares? Where was the juicy stuff in the book? Why was this never authorized? Unless Thomas Gradeen didn't want anyone to know he was involved in any way.

The only sketchy thing about his business practices appeared to be he was an opportunist. Now, while this is not very dishonest, it's the only thing near scandal in the man's past. He bought a few struggling farms in deep financial trouble. Is that dishonorable or good business?

He also seemed to have an appreciation for the supply chain. Once operating these local farms, he invested in a seed company and a chemical conglomerate. He understood vertical integration, becoming his own best client. Then once he'd harvested product, he purchased grain elevators and a fleet of trucks and railcars to get it to market.

The book gave him full credit for the vision this took, but never broached the subject of his financing. Or how the labor to run it all was facilitated? There was a veiled reference to his position as landowner which may have implied sharecropping. The practice still exists to a small degree but it is markedly different than the *Forty Acres and a Mule* days. Today it's more a way to pay rent with produce, so the landowner is more heavily involved since he nets a percentage of production. This concept may have worked right into Gradeen's master plan.

Whether it does or doesn't, the book made no apologies for any of his means while celebrating all his ends. The man had gotten to the top. Little concern was spent if any were trampled on the way. The impression was also given that Gradeen would do almost anything to protect what he'd built.

This was the first pertinent fact Eric planned to write down when he was interrupted by his cell phone chiming a text alert. It was from Jillian.

"Sorry about today. I really enjoyed it and hope I didn't ruin everything."

He smiled widely at this, took a quick sip of single-malt, and typed a reply. "Thought we were done apologizing. Nothing close to being ruined. Enjoyed the hell out of the day."

Her next text read, "Can we pretend it never happened?"

He replied quickly, "What?"

There was a pause before her next text read, "Really?"

"Nothing happened." He waited to hit send and decided to take a chance. He had refrained from asking in person, but maybe texting might offer some distance, some anonymity.

He added, "Wanna talk about it?" tapped the arrow to send it on its way and didn't have to wait long for an answer.

She responded, "Not yet. Soon though. Texting is safer for now."

"Roger that. See you tomorrow?"

"Prep then court most of day. Sorry. Last trial. Maybe meet later?"

"Sounds like fun. Wanna tell me about your case?" He was groping, but he sent it anyway to keep her engaged.

"Domestic dispute gone awry."

"I'm sure you'll do great." Then with a big smile, he typed their code, "Business dinner?"

The text bubble showed she was already typing. "Maybe business drinks?"

"Already looking forward to it. Good luck in court." His one-hand one-thumb texting was improving, for he had made no mistakes.

Soon his phone chirped back with another message, "Good luck back. Good night, Eric."

All he typed back was, "Night."

Damn! She was amazing. He thought back to his initial comment to Teddy Grimes about her. She was almost more fun to talk to than to look at. The same could be said about texting with her. And the chance to gaze upon her was indeed a privilege. Then he laughed at Sarge's remarks about her sparking and "being open for business." Shouldn't her big diamond ring be regarded as a *Closed* sign? But what about the aborted kiss?

I reminded him that we were now referring to it as the *Kiss Miss*.

He reached for his scotch and stared at the face of his phone. After a deep breath he banged in another text. "Why didn't you just kiss me?" it read.

It never got sent.

He went back to the Gradeen Biography and immersed himself in several fragmented pages dealing with the man's relationship with his father and brother. It was getting late and he was wrung out from the day.

His laptop on the coffee table at his feet pinged with an incoming email. He considered ignoring it and heading to bed but reconsidered. The interruption would give him a reprieve from thinking about Jillian when he was supposed to be thinking about the Gradeen family.

He assumed it had to be from Sarge. That's the only reason he bothered to check it. What new excitement might have happened in Decatur in the last couple of hours? But there was no message. It was an eFax from a 217 number he didn't recognize as being firm or business related.

He clicked on the document, knowing if it was a virus it would never have gotten through the firewall, and his heart just stopped. It was an on-line story, complete with headline, from the society page of the State Journal-Record.

"Local attorney, Jillian Stennet, of the firm *Donaldson, Clements, Blaine & McGraw,* and of Naperville, Illinois, and Matthew Curry, of Washington D.C., are pleased to announce their June 4th nuptials, to be held at St. Simeon's Methodist Church in Naperville."

He stopped reading, in fact, surprised he'd comprehended a single syllable after stumbling blindly across the mention of the date. It never mattered what the rest of the story said. Damage was done. Jillian was marrying some guy in just over three weeks.

The floor fell away and he felt himself plummeting. The walls of his condo seemed to close in on him. Three weeks from Saturday? He pawed at his collar and tried to breathe normally. Was she going to tell him?

Suddenly back were the feelings of loss and emptiness, that gut punch again causing bile in his throat. He gagged on its mockery. He'd been hit by the same person who only five days before had come into his life to help rid him of similar agonies. Reflexively, the tumbler of single-malt ascended to his mouth and he gulped at it. This was betrayal similar to his original theory Erin was going off to screw Ritter. That narrative may have now been debunked, and here's more irony for you, that too had been by Jillian.

This somehow now seemed on a larger scale of duplicity, if not treachery. She was getting married in less than a month and hadn't bothered to tell him. Not only that, but she'd tried to kiss him. She hadn't seemed to find the ideal place to wedge that tiny tidbit into any of their flirtation.

How hard could that have been? It's not like there hadn't been a million places in their conversations to bring that up. Like maybe on that first afternoon in the conference room. "If you don't like anything I just said, there's the door and, oh by the way, I'm getting married June 4th." Or even today. "My mother was born in France and I'm getting married June 4th." It's not like she lacked ample opportunities.

Or how about, "Remember when I told you my situation is complicated? You're not making it any easier, so I'm getting married

June 4th." She could have whispered it while she was trying to kiss him.

But then again, what had really changed? He knew she was getting married, or he'd known. She was engaged. That damned huge diamond ring, her *Closed for Business* sign, should have been more guy repellent; it let everyone but him know she was taken. Therefore, he should know she's off the market, so why suddenly all this panic? Was it that the confirmed date now fostered this feeling of inevitability, of finality? Was it that *not* being aware of the date had maybe offered some glimmer of an illusion, some wiggle room for denial? Or was it the newfound suddenness, the three weeks?

Maybe. Maybe. Maybe.

It was in fact, all the above.

He thought back to her confusing comment in the Sangamon Suites parking lot right before she tried to kiss him.

"Remember when I told you my situation is complicated? You're not making it any easier."

Her comment now made even less sense. I suggested they were no longer standing in the comfort of *Civil Twilight's* musical *Doorway*. Limbo was over. In three weeks she was going inside with someone else.

$\mathcal{A}$ bit later, he and I had this long conversation about everything. He was aggravated, frustrated and intoxicated. So I asked his initial internal reaction to the faxed bombshell. I phrased it that way since I was present when he received it so I'd witnessed his outward reaction.

He called it straightforward denial, thinking initially that it's some joke. He questioned the unidentified source and the date of the story, rejecting both as possibilities, let alone factual. But it was. They were. All seemed probable. A June wedding for a June bride.

So then who was the incognito sender? He'd called the number and gotten the shrill beep of a fax machine in his ear. Had Jillian sent it? He doubted that. She'd shown today that she's carrying various engagement trepidations, but how would anonymously informing the reasons help her? This was cowardly. Wasn't she too stand-up to shoot him in the back like that?

More likely it came from someone else, like the guy she was marrying. That made the most sense. Maybe Matthew *Whomever* of Washington D.C. felt the need to protect his investment. Had he faxed this shot across the bow to get Eric's attention, to alert him to the fact that Jillian was off limits?

Regardless of *who* was on the sending end of the fax, it hardly mattered when compared to *what* was sent. This led Eric to mumble something along the lines of not wasting bullets on messengers.

Like he could hit the broad side of anything in his current condition. Believe me. Any and all messengers are safe.

He explained that this bad news had immediately been drowned as I might have anticipated. Or probably by now, all of us might have expected. He told me about the tumbler seeming to rise toward his mouth by its own power, but this wasn't reflex. It was alcoholism. This had become his response in every instance. Good news: Celebrate. Bad news: Drown it. Yet to be determined: Who cares?

He mentioned how his inner speech had always taken the voice of a female. It began with his mother or one of his older sisters, and then for a few years it was Erin. This continued since her death. But had the female speaking to him as his inner monologue now changed? He said he had the feeling before and asked me if I thought it possible that Jillian could now be that little voice inside his head. I asked if it spoke to him with an English accent for Teddy's sake. Eric found no humor in the remark.

I suggested that having met her only five days earlier, it would seem highly unlikely for that to be true. But if it was, then he was in a world of trouble.

He responded by telling me that's why the idea frightened him. After only five days, she'd invaded his being, casting a spell to the extent that now she was the little voice inside his head.

But had his voice of reason become a voice of treason?

He struggled with this predicament the way people struggle annually with the tangled chords of Christmas lights, in that there is rarely an easy resolution. He needed time before throwing them away and buying new ones.

And I can offer my friend both time and an accommodating ear.

We began with the given: Jillian Stennet is an astounding woman. She brings the total package of beauty and brains; aptitude and attitude; personality and possibilities. She was both so cool and so hot, but neither offset the other. Nothing about her was tepid. She was fun to look at and more fun to be around. And try as he might to deny it, he found something very alluring to the mystery in which she wrapped herself.

She was going to make someone a lucky man, but that *Mr. Somebody* was apparently never going to be him. Despite the *Kiss Miss*, or maybe because of it, he never really stood a chance.

We talked at length about leaning against her car in the Sangamon Suite's parking lot. He painted a vivid picture of what almost happened and then what did, drunkenly forgetting I too had seen it all. I suggested he put himself in her stilettos. Say he thought about kissing her only to change his mind in mid kiss. What would he be thinking? Or feeling?

This was an easy exercise since he'd thought about kissing her from that first Thursday night in the bar. His expression then went through an odd change as he seemed to reconsider.

"If I'm engaged and getting married in three weeks, I would not kiss me either. It would be totally wrong and completely unfaithful. I guess now I can see why she didn't go through with it."

I felt glad that I was able to grant some perspective.

"Then why do I start to kiss me in the first place?" he asked, laughing at the inappropriate pronoun use.

"You're a catch," I told him. I couldn't help it. I build people up.

"I'm a mess."

There was no point in arguing this. Instead we were on to asking why she hadn't told him about her pending nuptials. Obviously because she apparently didn't want him to know. Duh. That part was easy.

Then the question becomes *Why?* And for whose sake did she not want him to know about this other guy? Was it hers, his or the other guy's? In a curious way, two of the three vertices in this contradictory triangle benefitted from *not* knowing about the other. But that's how they work, structured on the principle of blissful ignorance. The three points rock along easily, frivolously, more like three collinear points than a triangle. In this case, Jillian's the middle point. She works to keep one from discovering the other's existence, because when that ignorance disappears, any previous bliss goes with it.

So, we dug into this deeper. I once again reminded that he'd been off the dating circuit for a while. He claimed it hadn't been long enough to become completely blind to women. He talked about the signals she'd been giving, the kisses on the cheek and then the kiss that didn't happen. I repeated that we were supposed to be referring to it as the *Kiss Miss*. He said how even Sarge earlier in the day had noticed she was sparking on him. I pointed out again that I had been there for that too.

He mentioned the faux romance she concocted to back down Dr. Richard, and the fun charade of pretending to be a couple when they feared someone was eavesdropping. Then she cried with him at the spot of Erin's accident. That wasn't faked. It felt so natural, so real, so possible, even though all along she must have known it could never be any of those.

We reviewed how she'd told him about growing up, about her mom and wanting to be a ballerina. He laughed about how she had talked openly about her hip turnout and more implicitly about her development, and how her father's practicality got her to law school. That's where her story abruptly stopped. Why? He had no answer for that.

Then the *Kiss Miss* happened. This time he had called it that himself.

He talked about what they called *"This,"* the thing budding between them. He even showed me the little back-and-forth gesture with the hand that she did, like winding something up between them. Whatever *This* was, unless he had totally misread the latest cues, *This* had momentum. *This* had velocity and direction. And then tonight, he finds out *This* is a bear trap set to snap on him in three weeks.

So, what then had she been referring to as *This*? And the *Kiss Miss*? What was her game?

Granted there were givens: she's extremely private, especially secretive and doesn't like talking about herself. But isn't there a major difference between being less than forthcoming about law school and not mentioning your pending wedding? Shouldn't she stop trying to kiss a guy long enough to tell him she's marrying some other guy three weeks from Saturday?

"What are you doing in three weeks? Business dinner?"

"Oooh. No, sorry. Can't. I'm getting married that night."

"Seriously? Am I invited?"

"Oooh. No, sorry. Can't. I tried to kiss you. That would be weird."

No shit! And she thought things were complicated before.

The huge, damned diamond ring informed the world of her engagement, but it was unable to broadcast the date. Shouldn't that somehow have been her job? Or how about her obligation?

Couldn't she see that he'd fallen for her? Or did she? Why had she done nothing to stop him, or at least to catch or cushion him? Or was she?

He'd fallen, hadn't he? I could tell. It had gone way past simple infatuation. What else would you call it when she dominates his every waking thought? And before you ask about the suddenness of this, and it only having been eight months since Erin, let's think about the *Rebound Effect* for a second.

Nowhere is there a manual or playbook for this. Hell, there aren't even *Rules of Thumb* to offer a suitable timeframe between the end of one relationship and the beginning of the next. Maybe Jillian was his rebound. Or maybe until just recently he felt he was jilted by Erin. Granted we're learning his outlook on her and Ritter is fluid, that maybe it served simply as a convenience. Had that solitary event, which now seems to be crumbling or eroding, nevertheless pushed him toward her? When you see Jillian Stennet and spend time with her, you realize you don't need a shove. A nudge will do.

I only offer this as a way to explain how quickly after Erin's death this might possibly happen, for Jillian had made him feel alive again. She had to be doing more than merely filling time until his next *Erin* came along, didn't she? He refused to believe his feelings for her weren't real, that they were temporary, borne out of loneliness and loss. Or that they were misplaced or misguided?

Then what about her? Maybe he'd misread the kiss, but didn't even the mere attempt mean she was falling too? Maybe tumbling would be a better word. Weren't they tumbling together, forward, in the same direction, tumbling toward *This*? Insert back-and-forth gesture here. She had to feel something? This tumble wasn't a solo act. Or was it perhaps less tumble and more tailspin?

He'd been able to rationalize the *Kiss Miss* by blaming it on scotch and then also on the emotional rigors of the visit to Erin's memorial. In doing so, he'd completely absolved her of any humiliation or shame. He'd even gone as far as to offer her a bit of bargaining room. Before climbing back in the car, he'd told her about how pretending to be her boyfriend had felt real. And he liked it. It was a kiss of his own, except with words.

He said, "And then this . . . here . . . you and me . . . also feels real. It may to you, likewise. But it can't be, can it?"

Now thinking about it, he wished he had rephrased the last line. Instead of "But it can't be, can it?" he should have said, "Or can it be?"

We agreed that phrasing sounded better, positive rather than negative. Even though I'd been there and already knew, I asked him what she said.

He answered that she had responded indifferently. He said, "It was as if . . . Oh, shit!"

I held on tight because I could feel we were again nosediving. What if she'd been angling for him to fall? What if she tricked him, coerced him, played him, drug him up the mountaintop and shoved him off? Had she expertly moved him around her wicked chessboard while all along he thought they were playing Chinese checkers? Was he some clueless pawn unaware he meant nothing and able to be sacrificed as a small part of a bigger picture? And if so, to what end?

These two paths then began to converge and I didn't like where I saw them heading. If she's pulling him along with all the teasing and the flirting, the coy smiles, and the light kisses on the cheek before the aborted one on the lips, knowing full well there is a looming deadline in a little more than three weeks, then might she seriously harbor doubts about marriage? Could she be needing him to verify or validate her decision? You know: test drive a car you don't like to make sure you love the one you're buying?

Okay, but tell him as much. No one understood second thoughts and doubts more than Eric. He admitted living and dying through that same firestorm. He'd told her of Erin's text.

"Don't hate me. Just have to do this one last thing. Then yours forever?"

If it's that, then was she auditioning the next Patterson Ritter? Did the queen have so little regard for her pawn that she intended to present him to her fiancé in that villainous role? Could she be that cunning, that evil to incorporate his pain into her wicked plan? Did she have that little indifference for Matthew *Whomever* of Washington D.C. that she'd use Eric to get out of her wedding? What better way than to blame it all on some other guy? Him, her perfect foil. As the textbook femme fatale she could then easily dispose of both. Her life would go on unchanged with minimal collateral damage.

Many less attractive women had charmed many a smarter man into doing her bidding.

Finally, after another tumbler of scotch, he asked for suggestions. I thought it was about time he sought my advice. I always find it serves everyone best to get to the point. I recommended a different approach, sort of a trial balloon of his own. Maybe the next time he sees her, rather than ask her or let her explain, he should just grab her and kiss her. After all, isn't that what she wanted today?

And I'm not talking about one of those little flirty pecks on the cheek. I mean really kiss her. Pull her hard against him and plant one on her, full on her open mouth. And mean it! The way John Wayne kissed women in old movies.

If she puts up a fight or pushes him away, problem solved. Trial balloon pops. Nice try. *This* turns out to be nothing after all.

But if she kisses him back, as I silently believed she would, then *This* gets real. He better take that finger making the stupid back-and-forth motion and wrap that balloon string tightly around it, because his wild helium ride is going to get a hell of a lot wilder.

And he's only got three weeks.

TWENTY-SEVEN

*I*t had been a petty move by a petty man.

Sarge didn't like what he'd done by sending the fax to Eric any more than he liked trying to rationalize his motives. As he alluded to earlier in the day, McGraw had detailed the fragility of Eric's ailment to him. He'd spelled out *Young Gun's* troubles and travails and his current drinking problem, stressing the firm's intent to ease him back into the game. But as it had turned out, Eric McKegney was not one to *ease* back into anything. He was both gunslinger and adept investigator, making substantial progress.

Therein lay the threat.

Former SPD Sgt. George Harrison had reacted, despite immediately taking a shine to his *Young Gun.*

When his duplicity is discovered, Sarge would simply explain his actions were borne of self-preservation. He'd mentioned about the failed marriages and all the alimony, even mentioning money as the reason he's still working. He had, however, conveniently left out the part about *Donaldson, Clements* being his primary source of income to supplement both his police and army pensions. He found it poignant that in the 21st Century four of-a-kind ex-wives still beat a pair of retirement funds.

Even with the sad shape of his financial scorecard, it had been a difficult decision to betray his new partner on the day of the partnership's formation. But if the *Young Gun* were truly as good as it appeared, future jobs would be going his way. Then again if somehow this investigation became derailed, and Sarge was the hero to ride in to save it, he'd be back at the top of the *Donaldson, Clements* job board.

Consequently, desperate times called for desperation faxing. Sarge wasn't proud of what he'd done, only proud of how he did it.

Like previous decisions in his long police career, in his small investigator's notebook he drew two lines in the shape of a capital T. The left column was *Good* while the other was labeled *Bad*. Some would call them *debits* versus *credits*, but Sarge had never been one to put on such airs. Ironically what was bad for *Young Gun* would be good for Sarge, so his T-graph had been from his point of view.

He appreciated Eric had a past, and while maybe not proud of where he was or how he got here, he made no attempts to hide it. That self-awareness had to be considered a strength for Eric so it went in Sarge's *Bad* column. But *Young Gun's* past could also be preyed upon, therefore a positive, finding a home with the *Good*. He had penciled in the word "Alcoholic."

He doubted all the tripe about the lovely lady lawyer being nothing more than a coworker and potential friend. Eric tried to deny everything and deflect like attorneys do, but Sarge had watched them interact at the morning meeting. There was something bubbling there. Was Sarge then to believe his eyes or what he was being told? The investigative eyes always prevail.

Plus, when she stuck her head into their storeroom office this morning, Eric had jumped. Maybe not to a world-record height, but certainly in speed of reaction. He offered no consideration as to the investigation's time. He was going to spend the day with "his friend."

Right. Make sure to do the little air-quotes thing when you read that part.

Sarge had jotted Jillian's name in the left column – good for him and bad for *Young Gun* – and underlined it two times.

June 4th was a bombshell since her wedding date had never been mentioned when Eric attempted to refute his feelings for the lovely lady lawyer. The simplest way for Eric to disavow everything would have been to state casually, "She's getting married in three weeks."

But he hadn't. It was readily apparent to a trained investigator that she was *Young Gun's* Achilles Heel. No better place to attack.

That's why in one way the fax pleased him as much as he imagined it hurt Eric. In another, *Young Gun* had become a victim of his own success, his only sin being good at his new job. But this new job threatened Sarge's current and future financial stability, so he had to be knocked down a peg if not completely replaced.

The fax was sent. The only concern remained when *Young Gun* discovered he'd been the culprit. Sarge knew he'd investigate; there appeared to be a bulldog intensity to the man.

Sarge also knew he'd thoroughly covered his tracks. He'd used an e-fax account registered to his most recent ex-wife. Oftentimes it was how he and J. Tyler had communicated when they wanted to stay inside the *Donaldson, Clements* firewall yet beneath the partners' radar.

And once Sarge explained the importance of needing her help, *ex-Mrs. Harrison the Fourth* would be sure to keep him apprised of any possible return faxes coming back, whether from Eric or anyone else at the firm.

This too could be seen as petty-minded, but he and his latest ex had become partners in several endeavors which would serve to be financially beneficial.

Too late for second thoughts now. What's done was done.

TWENTY-EIGHT

*T*here was a new resolve to Eric when he strode into his storeroom office Tuesday morning, one borne of decisions and determinations made running around Lake Springfield. As an aside, this made three days in a row for those of you counting?

He awoke from the crazy confusion the night before as a hungover, clear-eyed pragmatist. The world may not have changed overnight, but it looked different this morning. While maybe not rosy, there was a huge dose of realism.

What had the fax really changed? Nothing, other than things sped up, like someone somewhere had hit the proverbial accelerator. He'd known she was engaged, belonging to someone else, some Matthew *Whomever* from D.C.. It's just that now he knew it was in little more than three weeks.

So, the way it unfolded during his run, he had two options: try to stop it, or let it happen and be happy for her. He chose the latter, deciding not to interfere, not to be Patterson Ritter. Sadly, to accomplish that, he'd have to do what Ritter had not -- the chivalrous thing by bowing out. He'd wish her well and then say good-bye. What did the two of them have? Really?

Let me jump in here again for a second. Is it just me, or have you noticed Eric is really putting this Ritter guy through the ringer? When he and I met, Ritter was Satan, pure and simple. I get that. The man was evil incarnate with no redeeming values because of what he'd done. He was a complete dick.

Somehow, whether through deduction or now her duplicity, Jillian had been able to convince him that maybe Ritter's intentions with Erin were not solely sexual. Eric then temporarily eases up to the point where Ritter isn't a complete dick. Still a dick. He lets him up maybe because . . . maybe . . . What?

Maybe he didn't want to sleep with Erin, only to kill her so no one else could ever sleep with her? Maybe they weren't headed to that motel, but they crashed and she died anyway. Somehow, because of something equally inane, Ritter briefly gets a reprieve? Are we supposed to see him as a victim?

Now, he's drawing new parallels between the place Jillian has put him and Ritter. He remains reviled by the thought of being that guy. Ritter ruined his life, but Eric will not ruin the life of some guy he's never met.

So, I guess we've apparently come full circle. Eric is good. By comparison Ritter is Satan again, back to being a complete dick. Eric must then walk away from Jillian to not be Satan. Try to flowchart that stream of McKegney logic.

Anyway, while running, he realized in a way, Jillian is virtually no different than single-malt scotch. Forgive the non-sequitur and bear with me. Both are smoky and smooth and expensive, while both had filled a gaping hole in him when Erin died. And both had a current stranglehold on him. Whereas they were mental compulsions, only one thus far was physical. That would be the booze. Please don't tell him that the other being emotional might be much stronger and harder to kick. He's got enough on his plate already.

Now keep in mind, this was alcoholic reasoning, but he thought it should be easier to fight the non-physical addiction, the lesser of his two needs. His body would still function without Jillian, but it couldn't without liquor. If he could stay away from her and not see her, maybe he could kick her as a habit.

He'd have to disappear from her eyes. Those amazing smoky silver-grey eyes, translucent to the point you're afraid to stare into them, not because of what they might tell you about her, but what they might reveal about you.

His strategy boiled down to the proverb, "Out of sight, out of mind." What could be simpler? If you don't see her, then you don't think about her. Whereas before he'd lived and functioned in her presence, now he'd do it in her absence.

Oh-oh. He should have considered this scenario using a different location, because his very next thought had been yet another banal proverb. "Absence makes the heart grow fonder."

Shit! So, then which one is it? The two cliches counteracted each other, like lawyers arguing both sides of a dispute.

There was still part of me, however, imploring him to give her the chance to explain herself. I built upon that little sliver of his optimism which hadn't died with Erin, hinting that there could be a simple explanation, that somehow the newspaper story was wrong. A photoshopped hoax. Maybe she was unaware Matthew *Whomever* from Washington D.C. had planted the story as a practical joke. Or how about this? The story could be plain wrong. Stranger things have happened.

But the hardheaded Eric McKegney, he of the three continuous days of jogging, knew better. He knew he'd have to find a new way to forget about Jillian Stennet since he was already using alcohol to forget about Erin Haynes. So, to get his mind past the lovely Ms. Stennet, he'd throw himself into this investigation.

He glanced at his watch. It was still before 8:00 so he had almost half an hour before people would be getting to work. His plan had been to do a little more reading of the Gradeen biography, but he realized with the thoughts of *What's-her-name* dominating his mind, it was time to begin drinking. And just think, he'd almost made it to the start of the workday.

Rather than drink straight from the bottle in his backpack, he went to the kitchenette to make a cup of coffee. While the Keurig whirred and whined, dripping out a fragrant brew, he thought about the *Seventh Floor*.

If you were to look down through the camera of a drone, you'd see a long, rectangular shape with expanded corners and widened areas at the midpoint of the longer sides. I had used the turret analogy earlier; there are six of them. Think of it as the capital letter

"H" with those six major points, or an old-fashioned capital "O" with those little wings on the sides. Each of the corners houses a huge office with raised ceilings for the four general partners of the firm. If the letter is laid on its side, and the street front is the bottom, J. Tyler McGraw's office is the lower right corner. The lower left is Robert Garza, Labor & Immigration Partner. The conference room from Thursday's initial meeting at the firm was down by Garza's office, and the storeroom would be to the right from there, closer to McGraw's office.

On the backside of the building, or the top of the knocked-over letter, the corner offices belong to James Petrie, Litigation Partner, Jillian's direct boss, and Mason Harland, Corporation & Taxation Partner. Or is it Harland Mason? Junior Partners occupy offices on the outer edge of the building with windows. Associates fortunate enough to office on the top floor are then clustered around their bosses, but on the interior of the floor.

Jillian always seemed to be the exception to most every rule at the firm. As an Associate, she should have had an office in this inner area, if not a cubicle in the bullpen, not too far from this little kitchenette. But her office was on the back of the floor, in a very prominent spot right next to James Petrie, with floor to ceiling windows offering a nice view of east downtown. The way she had her office arranged, she sat facing the door with her back to the view.

Eric took his cup of Scotch Coffee and toured his floor. He didn't recognize most of the name plates on the offices until he got around to Petrie's corner. He knew Jillian was heading to court, so he loitered in her open doorway. Her office was smaller than his storeroom, but what she lacked in square footage she made up for in décor. Her furniture was modern and elegant, polished aluminum frames and glass table tops, all perched atop a carpet afloat on a bleached hardwood sea. Glass shelves protruded from a slatted wall on his right, decked out with feminine touches, like vases, trivets and other flowery displays. The opposite wall was all business, legal tomes crammed into mahogany bookcases.

Her black leather chair faced him with two matching office chairs with their backs to him, separated by a triangular glass-topped coffee table set to coax the chairs to aim almost intimately toward each other. The stacks of folders on her desk were aligned neatly as he might expect, the brushed aluminum accessories to hold pens or paperclips evenly spaced. There was a docking station for her laptop with a keyboard and monitor next to a desktop pad.

He pictured her holding a meeting here, nibbling on a temple tip of her glasses with legs crossed, swiveling her chair slightly back and forth, looking as if taking in every word. Then she'd notice him watching from the doorway and smile coyly. She'd excuse herself and saunter around her desk over toward him, hips sashaying on her approach. She'd undo her lustrous hair and let it fall, shaking it out as if in slow motion and . . .

He took a gulp of the coffee blended with sarcasm. Oh, yeah! This forgetting all about her was off to a great start.

TWENTY-NINE

*H*e'd thrown himself so deeply into deciphering the Gradeen biography and jotting down a few questions amid the inconsistencies that the alarm on his calendar had to remind him about his meeting with James Hoover. He'd worked uninterrupted, pleased with how much he'd accomplished, and how few times his mind had wandered to Jillian, or even to single-malt.

The law offices were right across the street and down the block from the Municipal Courts Building which also housed Police HQ and the Offices of Parole and Probation. This is also where Record Keeping was located. Eric decided to start there.

Records was down a sterile, cement-block hallway, accessed by a right turn after entering and going through metal detectors. There was a sign projecting from the wall, centered above a huge pane of bulletproof glass with two holes. The one about halfway up was to communicate with the workers inside, and the other was a slot and tray for payments and the exchange of documents.

This was Eric's old stomping grounds as a plaintiff's attorney, a home away from home. It felt odd to be back.

He stepped up to the window and informed a disinterested civil servant that he needed a copy of the Erin Haynes accident report, using the police ten-digit case number. The first four are always the year, with the remaining digits representing a code identifying the responding officers and their station.

Without so much as *How-do-you-do?*, the lady went to a computer terminal and banged in the number. All files are kept electronically so the process is to request a print copy, wait twenty minutes and then pay when it's ready.

"I have a meeting upstairs," Eric said. "Can I pick it up after?"

The lady pushed her glasses up her nose and said, "Got it right here. Been holding this for a while for you."

She slid an 8-1/2" x 11" manilla envelope through the metal slot where glass meets the countertop.

Surprised yet suspicious, Eric turned the envelope over in his hands and noticed it was blank except for a handwritten ten-digit number scrawled in the upper right-hand corner where postage would normally reside. He recognized it as his requested Police Report designation.

How'd anyone know he was coming? While this played through his head, he asked the number of pages and the cost.

"Says here it's paid for. Looks like your lucky day, Hon."

That's not how this worked. They always charged, and it was exorbitant. The small sign on the glass informed the public that while the first copy of the report was *Free,* additional copies were twenty-five cents per page per side. Most accident reports were a minimum of four to six double-sided pages, with multi-car accident reports sometimes costing ten dollars. In Springfield Record Keeping function is not a cost center. It's a profit driver.

Eric couldn't help himself, so he asked for an explanation. "You're telling me the report is already printed and at no cost to me?"

"Look, Hon, I just work here. Fewer the questions, longer the tenure. Call me your Gift Horse."

At this point you're probably expecting me to crack a joke about looking her in the mouth and the incompetency of the city's dental plan. So I just did.

The Offices of Probation and Parole are on the third floor, so he thought about taking the stairs and maybe opening the envelope in the privacy of the stairwell. Yet that little voice in his head, whether it was Erin or Jillian, said the report would only sidetrack him.

The Third Floor in the Municipal Courts Building looks like the floor where departments not important enough to warrant their own floor are placed. The map by the elevator doors had more names and arrows than a shopping mall, complete with the *You Are Here* red dot. The main office for Probation and Parole was at one end of the building. To get inside, you had to go through the main reception area to check-in.

There was a lady manning the only desk in the tiny foyer. Eric told her he had an appointment with James Hoover. She scanned a large grid sheet, the kind you'd use to reserve tennis court times. The parole officer's names were across the top like court numbers and time slots down the left margin. She traced her pencil over to Hoover's name and then down to the two o'clock box. Without moving her pencil, she glanced at a small digital clock on her desk. It looked like an egg timer.

"You're early. Have a seat."

This had all come out like one staccato blast, a run-on sentence. And she'd said this while pointing to a row of folding chairs without ever once looking up. If she died later in the day and Eric was asked to identify the body, he would only recognize the grey bun atop her head.

Rather than sit, he decided to read many of the plaques and posters on the walls. He rarely dealt with probation or parole, so he thought it might be best to familiarize himself with their procedures and practices.

One poster was titled "The Vision Statement from the American Probation and Parole Association," abbreviated as APPA. It read, "We see a fair, just, and safe society where community partnerships are restoring hope by embracing a balance of prevention, intervention and advocacy."

It also then listed "Key Values of this Vision," but he couldn't get himself to care enough to continue reading. He was here to find out what time it was, not to learn how the probation and parole clock worked.

There was no time to consider clocks or time, for James Hoover stood there with his hand outstretched. "Mr. McKegney? I'm Jimmy Hoover."

Taking the man's hand, he said, "Nice to meet you. Call me Eric."

"Nice to meet you, also." He motioned for Eric to find a seat and took an empty folding chair next to him. "You won't be upset to do this here?"

This struck Eric as odd, but he said, "Not at all."

Hoover appeared to Eric to be either a television evangelist or an old-time country singer, a poorly dressed version of Conway Twitty from the old "Hello Darlin'" years. He had perfect fluffed-back brown hair and an ill-fitting three-piece suit from the sixties, the kind with big lapels and tiny pinstripes. His shirt needed a tighter collar and his tie needed a smaller knot.

"Why did I assume parole officers wore uniforms?" Eric asked.

"In the old days, we did. Now, we go plain-clothes. Our clients find it to be less intimidating."

Hoover leaned in closer to add, "If you ask me, we do it to be seen more on equal footing with detectives rather than beat cops. But without the relationship with the police, our job would be impossible. Think of it this way: cops spend their time getting offenders off the street, while we try to keep the rehabilitated offenders in the community."

Eric regarded this and asked an obvious question. "But aren't those more or less diametrically opposed."

"You see that too?" Hoover asked, phrasing it more as a statement.

"We work within the confines of a given reality. We're responsible for over five million adult offenders, most have served time. Police have the power to choose who they arrest. We have no control over who ends up on our caseloads. But working together we're responsible for keeping offenders from committing new crimes, which keeps them from creating new victims.

"My job is to ensure my clients comply with the conditions of their court-determined supervision, while fostering social behavioral change. It's a short and long-term play when it comes to probation and parole and public safety."

He had wrapped this up succinctly then explained why.

"I don't mean to give you the bum's rush. I apologize. I did do as you asked and gathered up what I could find on Mr. Steinhauer. What I am at liberty to divulge at least."

He stood and walked to the front desk, where grey-bun handed him a manila folder without looking up. Maybe she was in witness protection.

"Have you got time for just a few questions?"

"Just a few? Sure."

He did not retake his seat, so Eric stood also and took the folder, placing it under the accident report envelope.

"As I mentioned on the phone, Mr. Steinhauer remains a loose end in a case I'm working. We have police reports on his murder in St. Louis."

"I did not see that coming. That was terrible what happened."

"But we are having a difficult time tying him to what may or may not have happened here. Can you give me some background? What kind of guy was he when you dealt with him?"

"He was repentant. He knew he'd made mistakes. He understood the rules and was looking for a fresh restart. He wanted to avoid recidivism. He was one of my model parolees."

"In a report I read, you wrote that you'd monitor his progress to keep him on the right track. Were you able to do that?"

"My caseload numbers are daunting. If I had, there would have been updates in his file somewhere."

"Understood. Did Freddy ever mention the name Cindy Wright?"

His eyes lit up as he said, "He did. Poor guy thought he could save her. I tried to convince him girls like her are a lost cause. He would hear none of it."

"Girls like her?"

"She was a prostitute. He referred to her as a lady of the evening, like that dressed up what she did. He admitted to me she was also a user."

"Would he have maybe gone to St. Louis looking for her? Maybe to save her? Is that why he was there?"

"It wouldn't surprise me if he knew she was there. He had a thing for her you know . . . I don't see it a lot. That's why I remember it. That's the kind of guy he was."

It was time to add her name to his list.

"Okay. Just one more question. Did Freddy ever mention the name Randy Fuller? He was a one-time Decatur cop and then worked security here in town. He worked for a man named Jameson Gradeen."

Hoover answered this one after a few beats of hesitation. "Freddy once told me a story of how he got in trouble when he was younger. It was in Decatur. A local cop was somehow able to keep him out of the system. I tried to look into it and found nothing. If it happened the way Freddy said, there would be no report anyway. I assume it's possible that it's the same guy."

"He used those words? "Kept him out of the system?""

"He did. I remember that he made it to sound like a quid pro quo."

The Springfield translation of the Latin "quid pro quo" in this instance is, "I keep you out of the criminal justice system now, and one day you kill a TV reporter for me."

No more questions, your honor.

$\mathcal{I}$t was a successful day for the investigation. They'd maybe established the link between Fuller and Steinhauer. Sarge had called Eric late in the day to say he'd uncovered a possible former Illinois Guardsman who might unknowingly lead him to Fuller; he was currently tailing him around Decatur after work. But the most successful accomplishment had been his ability to avoid Jillian.

Her first text had come around four o'clock when she'd finished with court for the day. She remarked about needing a drink. She asked if he'd meet for a business dinner. He replied via text that he was perusing Erin's accident report.

This exchange had bought him enough time to get away from the office, knowing she was probably on her way back. The plan all day had been to keep her out of sight, hence, out of mind. That was going to be almost impossible if she could stop by his storeroom unannounced at any time. Her next text had come while he was driving. Against everyone's better judgement, he read it. It was while he was stopped at a light. I promise. He was still texting and driving, while drinking and driving. A maximum quantity of infractions.

She mentioned how she'd stopped by his office and asked where he was and what he was doing?

He returned this text, telling her he was meeting Teddy for a drink, omitting that it promised to be several. He was purposely vague with his whereabouts. His next text to her mentioned that the accident report was "driving him to drink." Like he needed a reason.

But as he waited for Teddy in the lobby bar of the Wyndham Springfield City Centre, his first cocktail on the way, he undid the clasp on the envelope. He'd been carrying it around all day, sporadically reading a page now and then.

The state of Illinois uses a form with bold lettering across the top reading "Official Illinois Traffic Collision Report." There's case number and reporting agency, which was Sangamon County Sheriff's Department, and three boxes across in the upper right corner. The first box is "Motor Vehicles Involved," and there was a number one typed in the box. Next was "Number Injured." This answer was two. The final box asked, "Number Killed."

Seriously. That box exists.

He knew what it said, but he couldn't get himself to read it. His eyes would not travel far enough to the right. It wasn't like it was going to have her name typed there, but nevertheless he covered it with his thumb. He didn't need to be told Erin was gone; he was reminded with every drink.

And here came another. He paid little attention to the cocktail server as she placed his tumbler of Balvenie single-malt on a cocktail napkin near his right elbow. He thanked her without looking up from his reading, never noticing that she was a well-put-together blonde, maybe mid-forties, attractive with a sly twinkle in her eye which implied she'd be fun if it benefitted her tips.

After a slug of courage, he continued with the accident report because, in an odd way, it was like the feeling of inevitability when reading about Jillian's wedding. The ending held no surprise. He knew he'd get there eventually, so maybe just seeing it in print made it real, final. He hadn't needed confirmation, but here it was.

The next few boxes on the report were date, time, location, and weather. He already knew these by heart, so he skipped down to Section Two, the cars and drivers. In this case, there was just the one, so "Ritter, Patterson Hawkins" was listed as driving Unit #1 with one other occupant. There was his address, but his phone number, birthday and driver's license number were blacked out. Eric knew police do this as a matter of privacy, a routine to keep those in possession of a report from calling those involved. This precluded other drivers -- as well as *Ambulance Chasers* -- from harassing those recently involved in accidents.

While that makes sense from a protection and privacy angle, it always slows down the process. Claims adjusters must reach out by mail to those involved, asking them to call a number to make a recorded statement. After one week if there has been no reply – and there rarely is -- the adjusters then skip-trace the names to get phone numbers and place the calls themselves. If an accident has several cars, or the person deemed at fault either has no insurance or no desire to make a statement -- oftentimes both -- this process can drag on for weeks before a claim is started let alone resolved.

In this case, Ritter's BMW Z3 Roadster, color silver, with the license plate and VIN number listed on the form, was covered by Farmers Insurance. The policy number and agent phone number each had their own little boxes. It was listed that the car had been removed from the scene by Springfield Towing. They had the county contract.

At the bottom of the front page was the information about the investigating officer, his name, badge number and the supervisor who reviewed the findings.

Instead of reading the section about deployed airbags or the driver being transported via life-flight from the scene, he fanned through the pages to the back, to the diagram. This drawing, and the narrative which follows, is the single-malt Scotch of an accident report, in that it fills the need for substance and is addictive in its own way.

Picture an aerial diagram of the four lanes of Highway 29 running vertically on a page. There is a little cut-and-paste representation of Ritter's Z3 in the far-right lane, which in this case is on the left of the page, with an arrow pointing down, indicating he was traveling south. This arrow then veers sharply to the right on the page, or Ritter's left, crossing both lanes of oncoming traffic. At the end of that arrow is another little cut-and-paste Z3 Roadster and a starburst where the car contacted the telephone pole. Dotted lines on the diagram represent two slide or skid marks into the pole.

The scale of the diagram is such that it covers two hundred yards with no landmarks listed. It shows that the entrance to the Sangamon Suites motel is still another twenty or thirty yards down toward the bottom of the drawing.

So, what might he be missing? His inability to derive an answer prompted his visit to this bar. And the person to answer it just entered.

"*Shake and Bake* back together."

Teddy announced this loudly, arms spread wide as he approached the high-top table. It was an old *Talladega Nights* reference to the nicknames of Ricky Bobby and Cal Naughton, Jr..

Eric jumped down off his stool and gave him a bro-hug.

"Thanks for coming. Remind me. Which one am I?"

"Thanks for the invite." Teddy climbed up onto the stool across the table and said with a laugh, "I don't remember which is which anymore."

"It's been too long."

"No shit, man. Pick the one you want. I'm good with either. I see you started without me. I hope you haven't been here long."

"Not at all. This is my first, and lately, I seem to always start alone."

They laughed at this too, although it was too real to be humorous. Teddy gestured to get the attention of the waitress. She waved from the drink station of the bar that she'd be right there. While waiting, they traded quick snippets of life at *Donaldson, Clements* the way people might casually discuss weather that never changes. Neither learned anything they didn't already know, but they felt the need to start somewhere.

The waitress stepped over to them, flipped her blonde hair behind her shoulders and introduced herself as Veronica. Up close she had big brown eyes and bright red lipstick framing an engaging smile. She balanced her serving tray on the back of a stool between them while placing an embossed cocktail napkin in front of Teddy.

The young attorney made no attempt to conceal that he was trying to look down her low-cut top when he gushed, "Well, hello, Veronica."

"Who might we have here?" she seemed to gush back, probably already calculating her tip.

"Theodore Grimes, Esquire, but call me Teddy."

"You're a lawyer. It's nice to meet you, Teddy. What are you having?"

He pointed across the table and smiled widely while saying, "I'll have what Eric is having. I'm assuming it's a single-malt?"

"Balvenie," she informed him. "Might we be two scotch connoisseurs?"

"Everything I know I learned from him," Teddy said.

She stepped directly next to Eric and asked, "You're the aficionado?"

"Let's call it that. People have a lot of names for what I might be."

"Are you also a lawyer?"

"Let's just go with that, too," he said, hoping to stave off any drawn-out explanations of the finer points of his current employment.

"I'll be right back with your drink." Then to Eric she asked, "Are you going to want another one yet?"

"Not yet. Thanks, though."

Teddy chimed in, "If we both order at the same time we'll only get to see you half as much."

"Oh, you two are going to be trouble."

Teddy waited for her to get out of earshot and leaned across the table to ask with a smirk, "You think she'd go home with me?"

"She'd be a fool not to. You want me to ask when she comes back?"

"Would you? I'm kind of shy."

And it went back and forth like this until Veronica arrived with his scotch. It struck Eric as amazing that it had been at least six months since spending time with Teddy, but they fell back into the easy rapport they'd always enjoyed. Teddy would say preposterous things. Eric would play along, replying with dole comments. He had always regarded their dynamic as the classic younger brother – older brother. Teddy was like a precocious kid with ADHD, jumping all over the place, while Eric played the mature, steadying influence.

Tonight was like they'd seen each other every week in the last six months, in that once it got rolling, there were no lulls in the conversation or the laughter. Pretty soon Veronica too had joined in. At one point she actually pulled out one of the other two stools around the high table and sat between them, the three of them continuing the flirting and the innuendos.

Teddy's chance with her was looking doable.

As the bar began to fill with hotel guests and other white-collar workers having drinks at the end of the day, Veronica got busier so they didn't see as much of her except when they needed a refill. So Eric broached a new topic.

"I didn't call you just to meet you for a drink. I need some help."

Teddy never hesitated. "Name it, man."

He slid the envelope toward him and said, "This is Erin's accident report. Look at the diagram and tell me what you think. You were always better at making sense of these than me."

Eric explained the problems he was having. He wondered what conclusions Teddy could draw from the fact that Ritter had been in the wrong lane to turn left. Also, why might he have veered so violently before the turn-in?

Teddy was looking over the pages of the report as Eric spoke. Once his questions had been voiced, Teddy began to summarize the pertinent section near the diagram. The reporting county deputy began the three paragraphs of his narrative, setting the stage upon his arrival.

"Police, fire, and paramedics already on scene. Powerlines on the east side of Highway 29 down. Illinois Light and Power notified. Pavement dry. Neither passenger interviewed. Driver life-flighted. Passenger DOA. Next of kin identified, but not yet notified. The Roadster equipped with *ACN* -- Automatic Collision Notification -- which notified 9-1-1 of crash. A passing motorist did likewise. Woman remained on scene to answer questions. Hadn't witnessed accident, only aftermath."

The deputy took measurements and made estimates as to lanes and location of Ritter based on the skid marks and the angle of impact with the telephone pole. Then prefacing his conclusions simply as speculation based on factors earlier discussed, he estimated Ritter had lost control of the car while traveling above the legal speed limit of 65 MPH. The driver's initial response to loss of control had been "a heavy application of brakes," hence the skid marks. He also speculated it was the driver's quick recovery from the slide that kept the BMW Roadster from rolling.

The report's last paragraph was apparently added afterwards. It made mention of the driver's BAC of .081, blood alcohol concentration just above the legal limit of .08. He also mentioned the paramedic's statement of the blood test on the driver being taken over an hour after life-flight to the hospital. Based on this info, new conclusions were drawn that Ritter's intoxication was not merely a contributing factor to the crash; it had been responsible.

Teddy asked, "Any suits filed on this? Erin's parents retain counsel to sue Ritter as the tortfeasor? Would they? There's a wrongful death or vehicular manslaughter case here."

Eric had wondered the same, but how would he find that out without seeming unprincipled? Or worse yet, ghoulish? There was still time, however. It hadn't yet been nine months. In the State of Illinois Mr. and Mrs. Haynes had up to two years to file their claim.

And why, as merely the aggrieved fiancé, did Eric have no legal standing to sue? If the accident had occurred just two days later, he could sue as the husband. But as just an *Ambulance Chaser*, with no conclusive connection to Erin Haynes in the eyes of the court other than a promise, he could only sue on someone else's behalf. No one had called.

"The fact that I can do nothing pisses me off," he said in a soft tone which belied his anger. "I've been neutered by the court and castrated by Ritter."

"I thought that's why you refused to pick this up." Teddy said this while handing the report back to Eric.

When Eric slid the report back into its envelope, he noticed something he had missed. On the very back, what you would only see if the report were face down, was a stamp of the word "Paid." This in and of itself was not surprising, but right below it was the handwritten date "March 24." That was two months ago. Was it just the scotch or was there something about two months prior that kept reoccurring in all of this?

Teddy looked to his left and then to his right prior to asking, "Ms. Stennet seen the report?"

"Why would you ask that?"

Teddy sighed in exasperation. "I got tired of waiting for an opening to bring the conversation around to her. You're working the same case. What's she doing right now? Text her. Invite her. Tell her I'm buying."

Eric was unsure he'd ever seen Teddy this excited. "I'm not doing that."

Teddy reached across and grabbed Eric's cellphone. "Then I will," he said.

Over Eric's objections, he stared blankly at the screen and read Jillian's latest text aloud.

"You okay? Haven't heard from you. Almost six and still at office. Are we doing dinner?"

"Give me that." Eric reached wildly for his phone only to miss.

"Shit, man? Dinner with Jillian Stennet? What are you doing here?"

"It's complicated." He smirked at this, echoing how Jillian continually referred to her situation. He then added, "I'm having drinks with you."

"That's your loss. I'll tell her you'll do dinner tomorrow night."

Teddy actually began typing in the letters, so Eric came around the small table and violently grabbed the phone away from him.

"Dude, I was fucking with you. I wouldn't do that."

Teddy took exception with Eric's reaction and asked the reasons behind it. When Eric failed to respond, he asked again. After the fourth or fifth attempt, Eric finally relented.

Solemnly he said, "She's getting married June 4th."

"Seriously? Three weeks? How come no one at the firm's talking about that? Is it possible no one's invited?"

Eric tried to laugh but it was futile. "She's not telling anyone?"

"What about . . .?"

Eric was already shaking his head. "She hasn't told me. I mean, we have this incredible chemistry, this fun back and forth thing, so you think she'd have told me simply because we're supposed to be friends. That huge ring should have warned me off."

Now keep in mind Teddy Grimes is a lot of things, but understanding and empathetic have never been two of them. Nonetheless, after watching Eric's response, he asked a question in a caring and curious voice.

"What's changed? It's all still very innocent, right?"

"Until yesterday."

"Are you shitting me? What happened yesterday?"

Then Eric did something he swore he'd never do. He told him. He said she'd tried to kiss him but pulled away at the last second. I reminded him, at the same time pointing out to Teddy, that we are referring to it as the *Kiss Miss*. When Teddy asked for particulars, Eric told him everything, explaining his suspicions as to why she may have done it.

At this point Eric swore him to secrecy, and Teddy pantomimed raising one hand placing the other on an invisible bible. Eric knew he wouldn't tell anyone. Teddy knew that too, but he was going to get another round so they could hash all this out. He waved and whistled to get Veronica's attention.

On a side note, cocktail waitresses hate it when you whistle at them.

"Have you made any similar moves on her?"

"Nothing that overt. I've maybe said more than I should a time or two . . . some things not completely PC, but she's so cool she'd just laugh and swat them away. We do flirt like crazy."

"What would have happened if she *had* kissed you?'

"Seriously? I would've kissed her back."

"Good answer. How close did she get?"

Eric held his palm a few inches from his face. "About here."

"Her hands were on your arms. Where were yours?"

"What? At the end of my arms. Nowhere."

"What would you have gone for first? Ass or maybe her hair? God, she has a great ass. And great hair."

"What is wrong with you?"

"Where would you have put your hands?"

"I don't know." Eric couldn't understand why he was playing along with this crazy game, but he said, "Maybe her upper arms."

"Good idea. You could get a little side boob. What color underwear you think she was wearing?"

"How in the hell should I know?"

Teddy apologized for all this, and for jumping all over the place with his questions. Silence descended on the table as they both surveyed the room. Most of the stools at the bar were now occupied as were the remaining high-tops. A few of the tables had been pulled together to accommodate a larger group of local office workers, men and women in equal numbers.

Teddy broke the silence. "You're not going to like what I'm thinking."

Eric sighed. "Can't be any worse than what you're saying."

"That's funny," Teddy chuckled.

"I'm not sure I like what I'm thinking."

"You mean that she's playing you?"

"Wait. I figure I'm being played, but what are you talking about?"

"The movies, man. She asks you to kill her fiancé and then fakes her own death. As the final credits roll with you in prison, she's drinking Mai Tai's on a tropical island. Why? What are you thinking?"

"Not that," Eric said with a harmless snicker. "She's not playing me to kill the guy. At least I don't think. Maybe she's using me to run the guy off, like she doesn't want to get married. If the dude finds out about me, then possibly he'll call off the wedding so she doesn't have to."

"How'd you find out?"

"I got a wedding announcement anonymously e-faxed."

"What? You don't know who sent it?"

"That's what that long word with all the syllables means."

Teddy regarded all this and waited while Veronica delivered the next round. After another exchange of harmless banter between the three of them, she hustled off to take care of a large guy seated by himself nearby. He was sitting with his back to Eric, but his frame and shape reminded me of the man on the patio of the Italian restaurant the other night with Jillian.

"You're afraid she's wanting to *Patterson Ritter* you, aren't you?"

"I am. I told her that story the very first night. She's been able to change my original thinking on what he and Erin were doing, but it's possible she wants me to be her way out of the engagement."

"How can you be sure she wants out?"

Eric considered this. "I guess I can't."

"What if she's maybe looking for a last fling? If you're unwilling or unable, I'll volunteer. Least I can do for you since you're my friend."

"Oh, you'd be doing that for me? Not for yourself?"

"Kind of guy I am. Don't get me wrong. I'd also be doing it for her."

Eric laughed. "I had forgotten how truly selfless you are."

"I am. With me it's always about others." They exchanged chuckles at this and then Teddy said, "Let's get back to June 4th. If that's truly her intent, to use you to get rid of fiancé dude, shouldn't she let you know the time frame?"

This was another good point. "You think I'm way off-base on this?"

"Don't know. What if she wanted to kiss you solely because she wanted to kiss you? I can see that. You know I've always thought about it."

Teddy always joked about this with men, so the comment was harmless.

Eric simply replied, "And you'd be doing it for me, right?"

"Of course. Selfless. Remember. But what if she wanted to know what it would be like?"

"Then why didn't she just do it?"

"Because she's a beguiling tease? I don't know."

"Beguiling? Teddy Grimes uses words like beguiling?"

"Wanted to make sure you weren't the only one using big words."

Eric buried his face in his hands with the remark. When he glanced up Teddy asked what he was thinking.

"If she truly intends to hook me, play me, then she can't kiss me. She has to continue leading me on, and what better way to --"

"Wait! One thing we're missing. If she wants to hook you, regardless of why, pretending to kiss you is not the way. Letting you take her to bed is the best way. That's how they do it in the movies."

Eric regarded that any manipulation may come in a series of steps. Start with flirting, then the *Kiss Miss*, then a real kiss and then . . . Before that point she'd have already have him hooked. He might be helpless to do anything to stop her.

"God! I wish I were you," Teddy said with urgency, leaning forward with both elbows on the table. "Trade me. I'll let you have Veronica."

"Our waitress? Is she really yours to trade?"

"Not yet, but she knows it's just a matter of time. So we'll trade?"

"Jillian's engaged!" Eric had said this loudly, so he self-consciously looked around and then said in a lower tone, "She's getting married in three weeks."

"I have no problem with that." Then Teddy's expression became serious as he continued, "She's having second thoughts. That's all. You did too, right?"

"I did, but it was only a fear of marriage, or maybe Erin's family, never of Erin. I never once considered using anyone else to cause Erin to end it."

"You think she's doing that to you?"

After a pensive sip of his scotch, Eric answered, "I don't know."

"And you haven't spoken to her about any of this?"

"No," Eric said emphatically. "Unless she sent the fax, she doesn't know that I know."

"So we're back to that," Teddy said before a gulp of Balvenie.

Eric considered everything from this circular conversation and realized they had indeed returned to where they began. He rubbed a hand under his chin and tried a different approach.

"Don't you think that it is more than a coincidence I got the fax on the same day as the *Kiss Miss*?"

Looks like the name is catching on.

"That is suspicious," Teddy agreed. "Was it through the firm VDI?"

"Yeah. I think so. I had my *Donaldson, Clements* desktop open."

"That means someone at the firm sent it to you."

"You mean like her?"

"Can't say for sure, but the VDI firewall is virtually impenetrable." Teddy then smiled this crazy expression and asked, "See what I just did there? *Virtual* Desktop is *virtually* impenetrable?"

"That and beguiling. You've become a wordsmith," Eric said dryly.

"Don't forget. A selfless wordsmith," Teddy corrected.

"You're sure that the fax came from inside the firm?"

"I am. I tried to get a football point-spread sheet faxed to me by my bookie, but it was blocked."

"And that had nothing to do with gambling being illegal?"

"There is that, but I was told the firm's VDI blocks any emails or faxes from unrecognized sources. So maybe it's not internal, but certainly recognizable by the system. It's somebody who's faxed before."

This information eliminated fiancé dude, but virtually no one else. Eric couldn't shake the feeling that the timing of the two events had to make Jillian the prime suspect. But why?

Was she capable of such games? How much did he really know about her, and why had he investigated everything but her?

THIRTY-ONE

*H*e left Teddy around eight to dive into Jillian's history unsure whether his friend had a chance with Veronica. Teddy asked what time she got off and she'd told him, but Eric didn't know when that might be. Frankly, he didn't care.

This was a common occurrence in the history of drinks for *Shake and Bake*. Rarely did they leave together. Teddy, the unashamed cock hound, sported a better than average won–loss record. And while he might act the opposite, he was a grownup who could fend for himself. Regardless of what happened, whether he scored with the waitress or anyone else, Eric knew he'd hear about it in the next day or two. And they would no doubt be meeting for drinks again in the near future.

Leaving the hotel through the lobby revolving door after a quick stop in the men's room, Eric pulled out his phone to read three texts from Jillian. He'd yet to reply. The first was the one Teddy had read aloud about meeting her for dinner. That ship had sailed. The second was something about an appointment with Jameson Gradeen Friday morning at the firm. The third and final had come just a few minutes before. She hoped he was having fun and asked him to touch base on his way home. What though was he supposed to say?

There wasn't much activity under the wide expanse of the covered entrance driveway. This should have been expected, for who checks into a hotel on a Tuesday night? Particularly in Springfield. A uniformed bellman helped a well-dressed arriving guest with his expensive-looking luggage near the open trunk of a cab. Eric acknowledged both men with a nod while the driver hollered a greeting through his open window. He did know most of the city's taxi drivers.

He'd parked on a surface lot across the street and around the corner from the hotel, so as he walked to his car he regarded how best to text Jillian. He went around the taxi and down the slightly inclined sidewalk paralleling the U-shaped driveway. He knew he had to remain evasive and aloof, not tip his hand about June 4th. There was a stubborn streak in him that demanded she tell him herself. She owed him that much, dammit.

It was a beautiful early summer night, a light warm breeze, stars bright in the moonless sky. He typed he walked, glancing in both directions before crossing diagonally across the deserted street at mid-block.

"Leaving and heading home. Hope you're still not at work. Will –"

"Look out, Mister!"

The warning had come from behind him, back from the direction of the hotel. It apparently was the bellman. Eric looked up from his phone and turned toward the shouting to see the bellman pointing in panic down to the right. He looked in that direction and saw a pickup truck with headlights doused cross the dotted line down the middle of Adams Street. It was bearing straight toward him. His first thought was the driver might be having a stroke, so he calmly stepped backward onto the sidewalk, giving the truck ample room to recover.

It was odd that an alcoholic, leaving a bar no less, would immediately jump to the conclusion of a medical emergency and not drunk driver. Granting the benefit of the doubt, perhaps? Or is it more an honor among drunks?

His sentiment was brief, for it quickly occurred to him this was intentional; he was the target. The truck accelerated loudly as Eric turned back toward the hotel's driveway, dashing in and out of the illuminated cones of the street lights. The taxi driver who just before had said hello was exiting the hotel, his cab blocking the driveway from that direction. Eric braced his left hand against the cab's hood with his phone in his right hand and stayed on the sidewalk. The shocked driver laid a long blast on his horn.

The pickup expertly avoided a row of concrete bollards topped with LED lights on the sidewalk by keeping the right-side wheels in the street. He jerked back onto the sidewalk and was not as lucky dodging a large decorative wooden planter barrel or its matching twin. The pickup took out both and barely slowed, splinters of wood and potting soil flying high into the night sky.

Glancing back over each shoulder as he ran, Eric cringed from the explosion of wood and dirt. He weighed his options, calculating that the street gave the truck the advantage. He instead turned left away from the street and back across a grass island toward the hotel entrance, slaloming between three flag poles in front of the hotel. He then stumbled, barely brushing a shoulder against the far support column holding up the large entrance overhang. He was knocked completely off balance, falling to his knees in the damp grass.

The pickup seemed to correct itself but continued down the sidewalk, totally destroying a small wooden pedestrian bench and an ornamental street lamp. When the pole went over and the glass globe loudly crashed to the concrete, sparks flew and popped. The truck returned to the proper lane of Adams Street and sped off. Maybe a block or more down the street, it turned its headlights on in time for Eric to see the taillights disappear around a distant corner.

And just like that, more quickly than it had all begun, it was over. Eric was relatively unscathed, save for being winded. His dark blue suit would need a trip to the dry cleaners to rid it of grass stains. He collapsed on his butt in the grass, taking inventory. His hands were wet and muddy, while the same was true for his phone. He glanced at the screen to see his unfinished text too had survived the ordeal.

People from inside the hotel came running toward him. Whether they'd seen what happened through the many windows of the lobby or had heard the chaos of the sidewalk decoration being obliterated no one could say.

The first person to Eric was the bellman.

"Are you alright, young man?" he asked, also out of breath, but more from age than exertion.

"I will be. Thanks for the heads-up."

"You bet. Didn't like the way that was shaping up."

"You may have saved my life."

"Not hardly. Did you get a look at the driver?"

"Not really." Then he laughed and, in a perfect display of gallows humor, said, "I can tell you what the truck's grill looks like though."

"I'll bet you can." He laughed likewise and then said, "That didn't look like no accident. That truck was hunting you."

"You mean on purpose? No."

Eric knew that it had indeed been on purpose; there's no way it couldn't have been, while conceding as much to the bellman would lead to a police report and questions. Plus that would take a great deal of time, time that Eric didn't want to concede. Playing it off as unintentional or accidental would get him home faster. Before he could say anything, both men were surrounded by curious onlookers.

Everyone wanted to know what had happened and if Eric was okay. Some of the evening revelers went to survey the damage to the planters, the bench and the street lamp, jumping back and laughing at its shooting sparks. The sidewalk in front of the hotel looked like Panzers had come rolling through.

The bellman hauled him to his feet and helped brush the grass clippings from his suit coat and pants. Eric noticed that he had everyone's attention so he attempted to spin his own version of events.

"I'm not sure what happened. I think wrong place / wrong time. That driver was either drunk or ill . . . maybe even a stroke. Probably a stroke. His truck inadvertently swerved up onto the sidewalk right where I was. Luckily he corrected himself before he hit me or anybody."

"Can you identify the driver?" someone asked.

"Not really."

"How about the truck?"

"White pickup. Menacing grill."

While saying this, Eric glanced to the bellman who gave him a questioning glare. He'd witnessed the entire event and knew this had been no drunken accident or medical emergency. He was standing and conversing with the taxi driver. It was evident that neither was buying Eric's story.

Meanwhile, the questions kept coming.

"Did anyone get the license number?"

"Did anyone call 9-1-1?"

"Are you sure you're okay?"

Eric again got the crowd's attention. "Listen, folks. Thanks for the concern. I'm fine. Go back inside and enjoy your evening."

He shook a few hands and accepted a few well-wishes before the crowd dispersed. Pretty soon it was just Eric, the taxi driver and the bellman. He again thanked them both, shook their hands and bid them a good-night.

"Young man," the bellman began. "You realize that weren't no accident?"

Eric chose not to answer, feeling a bit guilty for implicating the man in his less than truthful spin of events. Instead he nodded his head quickly.

"You know who it was?"

This time Eric shook his head just as quickly.

"You at least know why he done that?"

This was a particularly good question, but how was he to answer? What had he learned which might make him dangerous to somebody? Or anybody? He was no threat. Why would someone need to silence him? All he had done is delineate random dots. There were so many he was yet to connect. Or had he? Had he accidentally gotten closer to some evidence than first regarded?

His thoughts went to Olivia Jacobsen, the television reporter at the heart of his investigation. She too had been targeted for reasons unknown to her. It was her inability to solve that puzzle which had cost her a job in the Springfield market. She had been relegated to Moline and forced to change her name. Did the same fate await him?

Finally Eric answered, "Not completely."

"Well, you best figure it out. You might not be so lucky next time."

At this the taxi driver asked, "What do you do for a job, my man?"

Rather than try to explain the minutiae of his current situation, he simply answered, "Attorney."

"Well, that explains it," laughed the taxi driver. "Who wouldn't want to run over a lawyer?"

THIRTY-TWO

On the drive home I reminded him that he hadn't yet returned Jillian's text. This would aggravate her. It had been over an hour and she was not a patient woman. We went back-and-forth, wondering whether he should tell her about the pickup, agreeing it would be best if she not know. She'd ask *Who?* or *Why?* He was unable to answer either. But he had to text something, right?

He waited until safely in the garage under his condo, having promised me and himself that he would not see her tonight. He crafted the following evasive text and read it aloud for my approval.

"How's this sound? Sorry about business dinner. Just got home. Fun catching up with Teddy, but he's exhausting."

Without waiting for my opinion, he sent it.

Her reply had come before we were upstairs and inside the condo. "Glad you had fun. Can I call you?"

Where some would see this as a natural part of the investigation, or possibly a veiled romantic overture, he didn't. Frankly, it pissed Eric off.

"Is she fucking with me?" he screamed to no one and everyone. "No! I don't want you to call me. I don't want to talk to you unless you're going to tell me about getting married in three weeks! Is that too much to ask?"

But for all his gruff and macho exterior, and his pleas for honesty, I could sense that he'd like nothing more than to send the word "Yes" or even "Please".

Or maybe call her himself. How great would it be to talk to her, to hear her voice? But we both knew that this would cause more problems than it would solve. He'd stood firm all day. Time to draw the line here. Now.

He calmed himself and texted back, "Not tonight. Need some sleep. See you tomorrow?"

He explained that he had put the question mark at the end so that it left the possibility open that he might be unable to work her into his schedule, suddenly playing hard to get. After all, he'd made it through one full day. Who says he couldn't do another?

Her reply was quick. "Hope so. Missed seeing you today. Don't want to do same tomorrow."

These were not the sentiments of someone marrying a different guy in three weeks. This was the emotion of an amazing woman who cared deeply for him. He wanted to run to her right then and believe whatever she'd tell him.

Then why was she marrying someone else and hadn't told him? There could be only one answer: Teddy was right. She was playing him, begging for him to interfere, to be her way out.

We could have gone on back and forth on this forever. Will she? Won't she? Does she? Doesn't she? She was either the gorgeous, sweet girl about to get married who wanted him as a friend, or she was trouble. He so wanted it to be the former, but that didn't lessen the animas he carried for continually being lead on. Nor did it slow his alcohol intake.

As I am wont to do, I steered our conversation toward the darker, primordial side, ruminating aloud about payback or what he might do as retribution. Most were primal and carnal; all were base and vile. The unseemly phrase "grudge fuck" was first uttered. It was only once and by him, not me. Yet there, deep in his eyes, I recognized that visceral hatred I thought he saved only for Patterson Ritter. I was concerned and suddenly quite confused.

He was not as drunk as normal, yet by now almost livid. It seemed peculiar to me, that even after reviewing the messy details in the accident report, then Jillian's borderline romantic texts, his anger remained seemingly directed more at her than Ritter. This disconnect bothered me. She'd merely lied to him. Actually, she hadn't really done that. She just hadn't been truthful.

Whether by accident or intent, Ritter had killed his fiancé just two days before their wedding. To me that was far heavier on my scales of justice. These two sins were hardly equivalent. Hers was merely venial. Ritter's mortal.

He recalled his reason for ducking out of the hotel bar earlier. Why had he waited until the sixth day of knowing Jillian to do background on her?

The first internet hit, not surprisingly, was the firm's website. He clicked through meaningless legalese and stock photos of fresh-faced models seated around conference tables until he found the tab for staff. The first section was *Partners*, with a photo of a bunch of rich old white guys with J. Tyler McGraw. Then there was an individualized portrait and biography of each. The next tab down was *Junior Partners*, so he ignored it and clicked on *Associates*.

There she was.

Her photo was the same from last night's newspaper article, but in full color and without the pulpy look. What last night looked to be a grainy was not so in color because of her eyes. In the black and white of newsprint, they looked like anyone else's, but here in full color they were incredible. They had to be photoshopped because that vibrant shade of silver-grey didn't exist naturally.

She was dressed in a black suit with a puritanical white ruffled blouse closed to the neck, wrapped in a royal blue scarf. Her hair was piled atop her head expertly and she posed with her shoulders at a forty-five-degree angle to the camera while staring straight at it. Her legs were crossed and her hands folded on her knee, left over right to display the huge diamond ring.

Shit. That thing was everywhere. We get it! She's engaged!

Her bio read similar to her recited resume' from that first night. Born and raised in Naperville; High School Valedictorian; graduated Northwestern with honors; top of class at University of Chicago Law; Law Review and Moot Court; *Donaldson, Clements, Blaine & McGraw*; member in good standing of the Illinois Bar Association for eight years.

He stopped reading and started doing arithmetic. She wasn't thirty-eight like he had deduced on that first night at the bar. She was barely thirty-three! Her goal to be partner was not by forty, but after being at the firm for ten years, by thirty-five. Hell! Among everything else, all her attributes and activities, she was also an overachiever. Of course. Partner by age thirty-five was a serious accomplishment. Did he admire her more for this or that she'd let him think she was thirty-eight years old? He overshot her age by five years and she'd said nothing. Don't women argue and fight to stay young? She'd let him believe he'd done this incredible job of deduction, when he'd been blindly guessing ages like a carnival barker, but less accurately.

But rather than pointing out he was wrong, and claiming her carnival prize, she'd let it pass. Why?

There was no mention of her marital status on the firm's website, so he went to Facebook. Not surprisingly for someone who claims to edit her own personal content, she had no Facebook page or Instagram. He found her on LinkedIn. Her page was very antiseptic – name, rank and serial number only and no photo. There was a mention in a State Journal-Register story about volunteering for a Puppy Rescue, with a photo of her in action surrounded by a bunch of dogs. There was another story in a later edition with a mention about her serving on the board of a local nonprofit animal shelter. Then a few more clicks, a few photos of her at charity events or fundraising walks, and he was again face to face with the newspaper wedding announcement.

Unlike last night, however, he took the time to read its entirety. Fiancé dude turned out to be an attorney named Matthew Curry. He seemed to be a nice enough guy, but how would two attorneys, one in Springfield and one in D.C., get together in the first place?

This question served as the impetus to put his deductive prowess to the test. He started with the given: they might have law schools and/or law firms in common. Or was it under-grad? Or maybe even the same home town or shared time in Springfield? What if it was all, or none?

This was exhausting. Plus, he was getting nowhere. There was, however, one other thing he needed to research while his laptop was on and open.

I asked what he was up to and he answered without taking his eyes from his screen.

"I was almost run over by a truck tonight. Don't know why. Time to change a few things in my life."

THIRTY-THREE

Eric awoke feeling no worse for wear after the incident the night before. There was no mention in Wednesday's newspaper of the attempt to run him down or the damage done to the decorative items on the sidewalk. Either it had happened too late or was considered completely un-newsworthy.

I guessed it to be both.

He ran the trails around Lake Springfield, mentally planning out his day. Again, as it had been the day before, at the top of his *To Do List* was "Avoid Jillian." Number Two was new and could have been #1A. It said, "Watch out for white pickups." After those, everything else on the list could be grouped together as "Do Investigation Stuff" -- two specific and the rest general. And of the specifics, Jillian had occupied his running thoughts when he wasn't peeking over both shoulders.

He got an early text informing him that she was back in court, something to do with her domestic dispute case. She thought she'd be finished by lunch and asked if he wanted to meet. She'd played off their little code referring to it as a "Business Lunch."

How was it possible for him to hate someone he cared so much about and who appeared to care for him?

He recalled Monday in her car on the way back to town after they'd slowed for the school traffic in Rochester. Following one of the more uncomfortable exchanges for either of them in the motel parking lot, she'd eliminated any chance of further conversation by rolling down the windows and speeding up her BMW. Eventually she slowed upon entering town and the silence seated between had begun eroding them both.

"Why criminal defense?" Eric had asked.

She'd been surprised by the question, for she looked at him and answered, "I don't know. Why personal injury?"

It was the ideal lawyerly response – answering a question with a question. Eric then did the same.

"You want the truth, or the career-fair answer?" he asked.

She dropped her chin and raised her eyes, flashing a cockeyed smile and said, "I'm guessing I know the truth, but I'm dying to hear how it's spun at career fairs."

He never flinched, instead reciting his canned response as if a public service announcement.

"Personal injury attorneys fight to right the wrongs of injury, whether physical, psychological or economical, resulting from negligence of another person, company or any entity."

"You make chasing ambulances sound very noble," she mocked.

"Did I mention it also pays very well?"

"And the truth makes an appearance."

He chuckled to himself at this and leaned back against the head rest. As if reminiscing wistfully, he said, "I wasn't always so mercenary. I started out in Public Interest law. I wanted to help people, maybe make a difference and change the world. But the world doesn't change overnight, nor will Springfield. I decided to make some money while I wait."

Jillian regarded this and asked, "Any desire to go back?"

"Public Interest? None whatsoever."

Rather than elaborate, he waited for a few adolescent boys in the crosswalk ahead of them, loudly hooting and hollering to get Jillian's attention. She reacted as if she didn't notice or was numb to such nonsense.

"Your turn. Why criminal defense?"

"Besides the fact that I'm incredibly successful at it?"

She had completely deadpanned the remark, but he spotted the return of that spark of sass and attitude in her amazing eyes.

"Yeah. Besides the obvious."

"To be honest, oftentimes my reasoning changes depending on the case." This came with a slight hesitation as she considered how to continue.

"I enjoy the lofty ideals: the accused entitled to his day in court. He deserves a competent defense to even the balance of power within our justice system. I level the field. My job is to keep the balance from being too heavily skewed toward the government. The deck is stacked against the accused, so criminal defense is for the protection of the everyman. Innocent until proven guilty."

Eric nodded his head while saying, "Now that's a noble answer. I'm glad I asked. Thanks."

"I'm glad you asked too. I was beginning to wonder if you were ever going to speak to me again."

She smiled with this remark, yet Eric noticed more truth than cynicism. Maybe it was relief. She no doubt was wounded by what she started but never finished. It had been self-inflicted, but a gaping wound nonetheless. Now here she was putting on the brave and genial face, trying to smile through her shame as though nothing happened.

At the time, sitting next to her in her car, he'd established she was going to be fine. She – they -- would recover from this slight embarrassment and things would go back to the enjoyable way with her.

Now a day or so later, none of what had happened between them on Monday even mattered, for he was the wounded one. Possibly mortally.

Maybe she was playing him. Probably not so he would kill Matthew Curry and she'd fake her own death. She may nonetheless find herself drinking Mai Tai's on a beach like Teddy suggested. But what if it's for professional rather than personal reasons? Either way she'd rely on her womanly wiles because she had those in Spades. But what professional motive might there be?

On his run, he thought of their inane Parking Garage Pact borne from her suggestion that someone, most likely McGraw, might be working against them; they might not all be pulling in the same direction. He'd witnessed nothing which might suggest such behavior – no infighting, no personal jealousies, nothing but teamwork. Their client, Jameson Gradeen, also seemed to be on board, contributing to his defense with a willingness to help. The only blemish in this rosy picture of cooperation was the unidentified fax.

That's why his first stop on Wednesday morning had been to the firm's IT Department on *Five*. Eric hadn't visited this floor since his onboarding Friday morning. The IT area is not so much an office, or group of offices, but more of a big open room just off a hallway from the firm's main lobby, through a door marked "Employees Only." Eric used his credentials dangling from the lanyard around his neck to open the door.

There are three cubicles against one wall for the staff and long tables spread out for doing necessary repairs. Under low-hanging fluorescent lighting, Eric saw laptops and docking stations, monitors, keyboards, desktop printers and desktop phones all spread out like hospital patients awaiting triage. Every item bore a brightly colored Post-It note looking like price-tags at a garage sale.

On the wall opposite the cubicles were shelves of servers all interconnected with colorful cables, red and green lights flashing and blinking. These were mainframes, obviously making this small room the nerve center of the building.

Shane West, the bearded tech who helped Eric log on to the firm VDI, had his back to the door, tinkering with one of the cables. Over his shoulder he shouted, "Be right with you."

"Take your time," Eric yelled back, surveying the working area.

In one corner he noticed a large stand-alone copier/printer with all its doors open and few computer boards removed and resting on top. In another were two or three tower systems with oversized monitors that would make for an intimidating workstation. He thought he might have remembered seeing such a set-up in the lobby behind the security command center.

While he waited to visit with Shane, he couldn't help but overhear a phone conversation coming from one of the cubicles. Swear to God, the IT guy asked whoever was on the other end of the phone if they'd, "Tried turning it off and turning it back on again?" A line right out of Computer Repair 101.

"Mr. McKegney, right?" Shane West asked, walking over to him.

"Yes. Call me Eric."

"You bet. What can I do for you? Everything working okay up on *Seven*?"

"It is. That's not why I'm here."

Shane West invited him to follow him to his cubicle so they could visit in more privacy, but Eric told him he only needed a minute or two to ask a few quick questions.

He started with, "What's the technology that allows a laptop computer to become a fax machine?"

"Sending or receiving?"

Eric was taken aback by the question and his unnerved expression must have alerted the tech to his dilemma. He answered solely with an exaggerated shoulder shrug.

"It's pretty much the same either way," Shane said, answering his own question. "All the magic happens right here in this room. Our domain name is *d-c-b-m-fax mail*. It's an abbreviation of the firm name. In your email you type in the fax number and the "at" symbol then *dcbmfaxmail.com*. The email data gets translated to send across a phone line. If you start with a fax machine, we translate the data in the other direction to open it as an email. Does that help?"

"Yes," Eric lied. "I got a fax from this number. Can you tell who sent it?"

Shane took the yellow legal pad sheet with the 217-area code number on it from Eric and asked, "Have something to do with the case you're working?'

"Yes."

In the strictest definition of the word, he'd again lied. He could have danced around the fact that it had to do with his boss in the investigation, but he chose not to go there. That would be splitting hairs. Besides, why should it matter whether it was business-related or not?

"You do realize that you can trace a fax number the same way you trace a phone number?"

"Of course."

Okay. Now that was the third lie in a row. Teddy had gotten him so overly concerned about how it could have gotten past the VDI that he never once considered just using a reverse trace to find the source.

Shane regarded the paper in his hand and asked, "You run the number?"

He wasn't continuing down his road of dishonesty, so he said, "Look. No. I have no idea what you told me. No. It's not related to my work, but that could be considered a gray area. And no. I never thought of just tracing the number. I did call it and got *beeped* in the ear. I'm sorry."

"No need to apologize."

"I'm probably the least tech-savvy person here at the firm."

"You'd be surprised," Shane laughed. "Tell you what. I don't care what's gray or not. We'll look into this, but don't expect anything today."

"No. That's great. Next day or two would be fine. Can you do it yourself?"

"Now I'm very intrigued."

"It's just that I'm guessing you're going to have to view the fax to do this for me and I don't want the whole firm to know."

"I wouldn't have had to look but will now for sure." He smiled and handed the paper back. "Jot your cell number on here and I'll call if I learn something."

"Then I can count on your discretion?"

"Attorneys aren't the only people in this building forced to keep secrets."

The comment initially startled Eric, but it shouldn't have. It should come as no surprise that workers in the firm's nerve center might inadvertently stumble across all kinds of crazy shit that no one wants to get out. Just a browser history alone could be blackmail material.

Eric thanked him again and dashed up the two flights to his storeroom office on *Seven*. He cleaned off the white board and jotted down the name of everyone involved in the investigation in order of importance, from Ann Flannery and Patrick Weathers to Freddy Steinhauer and Thomas Gradeen. Each player then got his or her own manila folder with the name printed in blue Sharpie on the tab. He had his reasons for doing this, and that became evident when he saw that the folder labeled "Cindy Wright" was almost completely empty. He found the name and phone number of the investigative detective in St. Louis, put it in her folder. He gathered up Freddy Steinhauer's folder in his backpack and was out of the office before lunch. Thankfully no text; court must have run long.

The St. Louis piece of the investigation had troubled Eric. Something didn't seem right. Then the day before Steinhauer's probation officer had mentioned Freddy possibly feeling the need to save Cindy Wright. There was no way to know for sure, but that may be why he was in St. Louis.

But why did any of this matter? Who cared why he was inn St. Louis? The facts were that he was found dead with a Cinderella mask. What information might Cindy Wright have been able to add to this folder? According to the file, that was a question for Detective Timothy Benjamin.

Benjamin worked out of the St. Louis Police North Patrol Division on Union Boulevard. Eric sat in the front seat of his Jeep Cherokee in the firm parking garage and dialed his direct line from the folder. It was answered on the first ring.

"Metro P.D., Benjamin." The greeting had been curt and blunt. This was obviously a busy man.

Eric introduced himself and asked if he could have five minutes of the man's precious time, to which Detective Benjamin said, "Take all you want. I've had it. What's new in the Land of Lincoln?"

The change in the man's demeanor was stark. He'd decelerated from sixty to zero in record time.

"Like I said, I'm following up on the Freddy Steinhauer murder. There's not much in our files about Cindy Wright. I'm sure she was questioned. She's allegedly the reason he was in your part of the world."

"Shit, man. Do you know how many of these things I do a year? No. There's no way you could. Sadly it's a fuckload. Pardon my French."

Eric could hear the shuffling of papers and the squeaking of a desk chair in the background as Benjamin asked him to hold for a second. When he came back on the phone he said, "Listen, Lawyer man. I go on lunch in thirty. You got a case number?"

"I do," he said prior to reading it to him from his file folder.

"What say I pull the case files between now and then and call you back?"

"You'd do that? That would be tremendous. Thanks."

Eric gave him his cell and rang off. While he waited for his call back he took a quick nip on his flask and ran a Google search on the number of murders in St. Louis. The descriptive "fuckload" was not used, nor was it mentioned of being French in origin. Some of what we did learn was no less frightening.

Here's one: St. Louis has the highest per capita murder rate in the country. They don't have the most murders, but the most per person. Because of this, I pointed out if St. Louis had more people, then they'd actually have less people. I'm not one to show off, but that little tidbit blew Eric's mind.

Here's another fun fact: St. Louis and Baltimore are the only two cities in the U.S. that are not also in a county. The St. Louis city limits run from the Mississippi River on the east and then St. Louis County sits on the other three sides. The city is virtually landlocked, so they weren't going to get many more people. This explains why the city has a population of under 320,000 and shrinking while the county is close to one million. This might also explain why St. Louis

County employs its own police force, as does each of the surrounding municipalities.

The Gateway City is only one hundred miles from the Illinois Capitol, hour and a half straight down I-55. In terms of size and crime statistics, however, it might as well be a million miles. That's why folks in Springfield regard St. Louis as a nice place to visit but --

His cell phone rang with a 314-area code and he immediately picked it up and identified himself.

"Counselor," Detective Benjamin said, again sounding relaxed and almost casual. "I've got the case file right here. What can I do you for?"

"That was fast. Do you have a statement in there from Cindy Wright?"

"She's pretty well known around our parts. I would have needed a two-wheeler if you wanted her files."

Then Benjamin began to review the facts surrounding Freddy Steinhauer's murder. He confirmed the date and time and place, plus the means – two shots to the chest, referring to it as a "Double Tap." They discussed the ballistics and that the murder weapon was never found. All this reinforced the investigation by the Springfield P.D. report of the same shooting.

"Here we go. Witness statement Cindy Wright. You know she's a pro?"

"I do. Sounds like she might be a busy one at that."

"You got that right," Benjamin said.

The man lacked any semblance of nuance; he got straight to the point. He was chewing on whatever he was having for lunch while skimming through the statement. Every now and then between bites he would read something aloud.

From what Eric could gather Cindy Wright had been less than forthcoming with information due to the fact that she'd seen her fair share of police tactics. These had made her untrusting. She hadn't witnessed the shooting. One of the other girls whose name Eric didn't catch recognized a dead Freddy Steinhauer as the same guy who the day before had come asking around about Wright. She then told Wright who then went to the morgue to identify the body.

"Was it a robbery or made to look like one?"

"Nope. Says here wallet with $40 cash, car keys, employee work badge for a warehouse up by you were all on person."

Eric asked, "What was the name of the other girl? The one who recognized Steinhauer?"

"One Mary Anne Tower."

"Is there any way I could talk to her?"

"Afraid you were going to ask. Deceased. Cause looks like O.D."

"What about Cindy Wright?"

"Was told we haven't seen that much of her lately."

"Did she change her ways?"

Benjamin laughed and said, "Or her Patrol Station."

"Okay. Thanks. Any more in the file?"

Again he did the reading aloud and chewing thing while Eric tried to catch any crumb of information which might fall out.

"Let's see. Wright didn't know anything about a Cinderella mask. Claimed to have not seen Steinhauer in over five years. Was surprised that he would have come looking for her. Tower told her Steinhauer said someone had called him saying she was in the STL."

"Wait!" Eric interrupted. "Say that last part again."

Benjamin chewed some more then swallowed. "Looks like Wright stated Tower told her Steinhauer had come to St. Louis looking for her because he'd gotten a phone call that she was here."

"Really?"

"And before you ask, Counselor, my file don't say who made that call."

"That's okay. You've been a great help. I can take it from here. I think I might know who did."

THIRTY-FOUR

*I*t had been a long day by the time Eric got home. I jokingly described it as a day spent playing *Hide and Seek*, in that he was *hiding* from Jillian while *seeking* the truth in the case against Jameson Gradeen. And while maybe it was a stupid remark, and I'll admit mine are not all pearls, he was winning at both, for he'd discovered a brand-new hiding place. Not that he needed it.

There was no text or call from Jillian all day, which was a stark departure. It's exactly what he hoped for, exactly what he claimed to want. Why then did it make him miserable? Maybe he'd gotten too good at hiding when he really wanted to be found, or in the least, continue being seeked . . . or sought.

He pulled his Jeep Cherokee into his garage and walked to the entrance to the complex to get his mail. Why they couldn't put the mailbox on the other side of the entrance so he could access his box without getting out of his car he'd never know. Maybe they feared head-on collisions. Makes sense.

Lake Springfield glistened on the near horizon while fluffy grayish clouds stood stock-still in the darkening sky portending rain in the forecast. He flipped through his mail, and for the first time all day, realized it was Wednesday. That meant a visit from *The Girl from across the Courtyard.* She'd completely slipped from his mind. But tonight, he knew she'd be back at his door, knocking persistently.

There seemed to be a duality to everything now. Part of him looked forward to letting her in, while another part no longer wanted anything to do with her. That part wanted to do the right thing and stop this, but the part with the drunken inhibitions wanted to do what was wrong. So wrong. And with Jillian no longer a possibility, maybe it was the perfect time for a Wednesday. The Stephen Stills song rang through his mind. "If you can't be with the one you love . . ."

And just as if the songwriter had her in mind, Lorrie Ann was sitting on the front steps of her walkup stairs. Eric laughed to himself when he thought about how his golf buddies would call her a *Pitching Wedge* because she works best from over a hundred yards out. He knew there would be no way to get inside his condo without speaking to her, so maybe time for a different approach.

"Hi, Lorrie Ann" he said loudly on his approach.

"Hi, yourself."

The surprise evident on her face could have been for any number of reasons. Take your pick: he seemed congenial, or at least polite; he didn't appear to be intoxicated; or he called her by her name. These three things never happened by themselves let alone in concert. Normally she'd knock. He'd open the door a slight crack, forcing her to negotiate her way in. She'd oblige by saying or doing something erotic or obscene eventually wearing him down or, better yet, firing him up. Ultimately the horny Eric let her in.

And she never supposed he knew her name.

"Happy Wednesday," she said cheerily.

Eric stopped a few feet from the bottom of her steps, quit paying attention to his mail and said, "Yep. It's Wednesday. Are your kids with their dad?"

Who was this new guy and what had he done with the old one? Now he even recalled her ex-husband's visitation schedule, let alone that she had kids?

"What are you doing sitting out here? Do you do that often?"

"No. I'm just watching the weather and, I . . . I was waiting to talk to you."

"Really? Everything okay?" He waited for her to nod a reply and asked, "What's up?"

His gracious response surprised them both, but this was the first time he recalled seeing her up close through reasonably clear eyes in relative sunlight. She looked a lot different, maybe not necessarily better but certainly no worse. She looked more grownup or mature. Her eyes were darker and bigger, her dark hair down and frizzy, as she twisted her fingers through it.

Her choice of clothing had not changed. This evening again it was as if she'd been working out. She wore a snug pink tank over a color-coordinated sports bra that looked to be doing double duty and grey leggings with a subtle pink pattern. That was the only thing subtle about her outfit; she apparently didn't want anyone's imagination to do any heavy lifting. She was barefoot and stood, bouncing nervously up on her toes.

"You sure you have time for me?"

"Certainly. You want to sit down for a second?" he asked, walking over and plopping down on the third step of her front stoop, his long legs stretching out to the ground.

She tip-toed down and sat on the step next to him. "Thanks. I need to tell you something," she said in a timid voice.

"There's a few things I should tell you, too."

"There is?"

Forthrightly he said, "I've got a drinking problem, which I'm sure comes as no surprise. I've spent the afternoon touring a rehab facility not too far from here. Before it gets much worse I'm going to check myself in to get clean."

"When you doing that?"

"Not sure yet. I'm working again, and functioning rather well, but it's only a matter of time. It's going to get worse. I'll probably hope to finish what I'm working on before going."

"Rehab, huh?"

"Yeah. I'm not going to kick this by myself. I'm going to need help and even then it's not going to be easy. As a matter of fact, it sounds terrible."

"Who else knows? I mean, you've never told me personal stuff before."

"You're the first."

Before she could wonder why he'd told her before anyone else, she said, "Ohhh!" with the realization that rehab also undoubtedly meant the end of their little adult games.

"Yeah," he said with a wide smile, glad she'd read between his lines.

His crooked smile was warm and encouraging. She always thought of him to be roguishly handsome in a bad-boy-next-door kind of way, but now with his hair mussed and his tie ditched, he looked plain hot. Yet at the same time she knew this little talk was about to end *them*. That irony was brutal.

"I owe you an apology," he began. "I'm sorry. Because of my drinking I took advantage of you, used you and --"

"We used each other," she cut in.

"Maybe, but I really used you. I may have told you some of this before, and if so, let me apologize, but I need to explain."

And he did. He told her again all about how Erin and her accident had started him down the road of inebriation. He told her how he'd wrongly blamed Erin. He told her how new evidence may have recently come to light about her death, and there was a good chance he'd been completely wrong about everything. He told her without going into much detail that he was investigating this case for a local firm. And then he mentioned Jillian.

"Wow," was all she said once he had finished. She took half a moment at most to process everything and asked a question completely out of left field.

"What's she look like?"

"Who? Jillian?" He regarded her question as odd, but answered, "Brunette, early thirties, kind of pretty."

"Has she ever been here? To your condo?"

"No. Why? I doubt she knows where I live."

Lorrie Ann smiled coyly and asked, "Did you maybe just downplay your description of her?"

"What are you talking about?"

"There was a girl at your door today."

"Today? Here?"

"Yes. If this girl was Jillian, then brunette, early thirties, kind of pretty, does not do her justice. Kind of pretty? Better find your glasses 'cause the girl at your door was absolutely gorgeous."

"Jillian was here?"

"I assume it was her. I'm not the *Neighborhood Watch* but I see things. The girl at your door has never been here nor has any girl who looks like her."

"When was she here?"

"You didn't miss her by much." Then she paused before asking, "She's an attorney?"

"And a good one."

"I thought you threw me over for a runway model or something."

Eric took exception at this. "I didn't throw anybody over," he protested.

"I know. I know." Almost by rote she said, "The deal between us is that there's never been a deal between us." She made the quotation signs the second time she said the word "deal."

Eric couldn't recall this clever little saying, but I knew he'd said it. It was readily apparent by her robotic response it had been repeated between them many times. I knew this to be their so-called privacy pact. For his part, he knew they had one, but what else might there be that he couldn't remember?

"So, getting back to what I wanted to talk to you about, I'm sorry --" he began to wrap up his apology.

"We aren't ever doing what we do again."

It was a statement, not a question, void of any emotion, as if she'd expected as much or she was used to being on the wrong end of conversations like this.

"Is that okay?" He then quickly changed gears. "I mean, that's just the way it has to be. I have to move forward. The drinking and the stuff with you will have to become a part of my past. I'm sorry."

"I get it," she said without too much conviction. "Apologizing is a major step in the process."

It sounded as if she knew from personal experience, so Eric gingerly asked if she'd been to rehab.

"A friend of a friend."

Her answer hung between them, buoyed by a growing silence. She looked away and finally said, "At least you didn't say something bogus like you hope we can still be friends."

"You and me?" Eric turned to face her and said, "We could try to be friends, but we don't even really know each other."

"This is true," she acknowledged.

"I don't even know your last name, or your kids names."

Here she giggled and spun a finger through her hair again. "If we were to become friends, we didn't go about it in the normal way."

"Who knows?" he said with a light chuckle. "It might be a lot easier doing those steps in reverse."

Then she asked directly, "Is it because of her? Victoria Secret?"

He sighed and said, "No. Part of me wishes that, but no. She's engaged and I'm an idiot."

He needed to change the subject so quickly asked, "How long was she here? What did she do?"

Lorrie Ann shrugged her shoulders. "Let's see. She knocked on your door and then checked under your mat like she thought there might be a key."

"There isn't."

"I know. Don't think I haven't checked too."

He laughed out loud since she'd shown no remorse or embarrassment.

She continued, "After knocking, she turned and looked down both ways." She pointed to each end of the courtyard between the rows of condos.

Eric thought about sitting here, on the steps across from his place, and seeing Jillian on his porch. He could see it in his mind as if it were happening right then. It made him smile. But why would Jillian have come here?

"Did you talk to her?"

"No," Lorrie Ann said. "Women who look like her scare me."

"Same here," he muttered nonsensically. "You really think it was her at my door?"

"Victoria Secret? How many other gorgeous brunettes do you know?"

She had asked this with a light smile showing the slight gap in her teeth.

Eric again laughed, this time at her implication and replied with a wink, "Just you two."

And with that line, Lorrie Ann Rosenthal and Eric McKegney took their first step backward into friendship.

 t was almost nine. Eric was more sober than I'd seen him in a long time. It was weird in a way. Those days with Jillian, his drinking had truly lessened. It had. She'd occupied the void in his life left by Erin's death and previously filled by alcohol. To use her phrase, she'd busied his idled hands. Now after the first two days of trying to be without her, those same hands remained busy with the investigation, while his longings were now for her instead of booze.

And don't think the visit to the rehab facility hadn't changed his perspective. Yet sadly, just a few hours after the tour and a glimpse at the travails which awaited him, he was again drinking, but not necessarily pounding the single-malt. He'd taken to heart everything he'd learned but was miles past the point where he'd be able to just stop on his own. Why even try? Why not have health insurance pay for the professionals to do it for him?

I referred to this current place in his life as a sort of *Mardi Gras*. Detox and rehab, like the forty days and forty nights of Lent, would be here soon enough. Why shouldn't every day until then be *Fat Tuesday*?

He reluctantly agreed, so after a cordial single-malt, we turned to a deep discussion of why Jillian had stopped by his condo. And then what might have happened if there had been a key under his mat? Would she have let herself in? What might she have done inside? Was she looking for something besides him?

We were unable to absolutely answer any of those questions, so ventured back from that tangent and returned to the main one: Why stop by? No texts or calls all day. Why not? Was it because she'd realized he was hiding from her? He could avoid such attempts, whereas not a face-to-face confrontation.

I watched from the wrong side of his laptop, as he banged a few keys and clicked the mouse. After doing this for close to a minute, he stared at the screen intently, encouraging it along.

Then his face lit up and he yelled, "Gotcha! 417 W. Edwards St."

After a few more mouse clicks, he added, "The Historic West Side, near McArthur and Lawrence. Come on. Let's go."

I wondered what he hoped to gain by going to what I assumed was Jillian's home. Why did he want me to come? He took a big gulp, slamming the empty tumbler on his kitchen tabletop and grabbed his flask and keys.

On the drive Eric explained it's not his place, nor did he have any intention to stop Jillian's wedding. I was thrilled to hear this. He went on to say if she wanted his assistance getting out of the marriage, like maybe Erin had sought with Ritter, he'd address that problem once it became a problem. But right now, he was not jumping in the middle of this.

I pointed out that all indications were that Erin had not asked Ritter to do anything of the sort, and this new position on Jillian's wedding was a departure from his earlier stance.

Both remarks went completely ignored, as did my question: "What then are we doing?"

Eric was quiet, but not in a morose way. He was deep in thought, deciding, contemplating. Alcoholics, and all addicts for that matter, become extremely proficient at rationalizing, particularly adept at making deals with themselves. Eric's no different. His position on her wedding was evolving, as was his promise to not see her. But he could then rationalize or explain his promise had been, by strictest definition, not to talk to her in person. It was okay to see her today. And if she happened to be undressing when he peeked through her windows, that would be considered fortuitous.

So, I'd gone from traveling with a wedding wrecker to a Peeping Tom. I was hoping nowhere in a suit coat pocket did he have a stocking cap with eye holes cut out. Even without that, this had all the indications of not ending well.

The Historic West Side is north of downtown. Most of the three-to-four-bedroom homes were built in the mid-to-late 1940's when our boys came home from war. They began to deteriorate over time as houses will do. Around the millenium the neighborhood underwent a resurgence. Older homes were restored and refurbished. These two-story homes had good bone structure and basements, so renovating was easy. Two adjoining bedrooms became a master with a walk-in closet. Hardwood floors, granite countertops, and modernized appliances went in, and demand in this area went up. These houses had huge oak or maple trees in the yards and detached garages in the back. They were close to town, close to schools and going for close to a quarter of a million dollars.

Investors bought a refurbished home to live in, and one or two others to refurbish. Even long-time residents felt the urge to flip. But like everything else, some flips worked and some flips flopped. So neighborhoods were dotted with eyesores devaluing everyone else's rebuilds. Comps drove the selling prices down, and it looked like the area might resume its decline.

But then mortgage interest rates dropped, making expensive homes again affordable. The Historic West Side was back. People poured in, buying these houses as homes, not investments, and certainly not flips. This stability brought home prices back above where they were at the turn of the century.

Eric knew this because he and Erin had looked at homes around here.

417 W. Edwards St. was a beautiful home, with several baskets of multi-colored impatiens hanging from hooks on the well-lit front porch adding to its curb appeal. The lawn was a thick, deep green and expertly manicured in perfect circles around three enormous trees, two on the driveway side of the front walkway and one on the other. The landscaping included Japanese maples evenly spread throughout green groundcover on a bed of white rock. The house too was white accented in charcoal grey, and tonight, everything looked bright.

He stopped a few houses down on the tree-lined street and we got out. The street was wide, the sidewalk on the same plain as the street, like in a valley. Some yards sloped while others had retaining walls with steps down to the sidewalk to make the front yard level. Jillian's sloped up.

We stood on the sidewalk, facing her right neighbors home. Clouds were gathering and thunder was rumbling in the distance. We were a long way from home, with no rain gear and apparently no plan. But in Eric's defense, how many times do you formulate a voyeur strategy beforehand? He had to figure most depraved perverts just went with the flow, provided a flow was detected.

He pulled out his phone and glanced up and down the street. Jillian's was not the only house brightly lit on her side of the street, but the two on either side of her were not. At my suggestion, he put the phone back in his pocket. Then from a different pocket he pulled out another phone. He'd brought his own cell and the firm-issued phone. I knew what he was thinking. Jillian's caller ID would give him away on the firm phone, but if he called her on his personal cell, she might not know it was him.

But I thought tonight was look-but-don't-talk. Or had he meant talk-but-don't-look? He kept bouncing all over the place about what his promise really meant. That can't be it, though. We could talk and not look from the comfort of his townhome. We needed to get back there. I actually began hoping for rain.

He started through the shadowy darkness of the neighbor's front yard. Jillian had a wooden privacy fence around her large backyard, but there was an opening at the driveway instead of a gate. Maybe she tired of having to open and close the gate to get her car in and out of the detached garage. Whatever her reason, since there was no gate on the driveway, he could walk through into her backyard.

It was not nearly as well-lit back here as it was out front, the only light coming through French doors which opened onto a sprawling cedar deck featuring varied levels. It was when I was checking out the rest of the backyard that he stopped in his tracks and crouched slightly behind the deck's railing. That's when I also saw her.

She sat with her legs curled up under her on a posh looking couch in a cozy room that looked to be a living room or den. Her kitchen was to our left, her right. She fanned through the pages of a magazine by the light of lamps on end tables bracketing her white couch, plus a ceiling lamp that also doubled as a fan which wasn't turning. There was a coffee table and two wingback chairs on a subdued area rug covering wood flooring. Regardless of what she may have spent on the home's furnishings, she looked by far to be the most exquisite item in the room.

I could tell Eric was mesmerized. She wore an oversize cowl-neck sweater and leggings, all black and all the way down to her bare feet, one of which was tucked underneath her. Her black-rimmed glasses were on. Her hair was up, loosely piled atop her head in a casual manner that allowed several tendrils to escape and border her wondrous face. In one hand she had an Interior Design magazine that she clearly didn't need and a goblet of red wine in the other.

He watched her languid movements, picking up and setting down the wine glass, licking her index finger and thumb prior to turning a page, nibbling on a finger nail. Her red lips moved like she was singing or possibly humming along to some music unheard from outside.

Those pouting lips transfixed him. He couldn't help but stare as they were there one second and then hidden by the magazine the next, almost as if she were doing it on purpose to tease him. He thought about those lips brushing against his cheek the few times she'd bounced on her toes to kiss him. As he'd done for days, he wondered what it would have felt like if she'd gone through with the one on his lips.

She looked up for split second, as if she'd heard a sound in the backyard before returning her attention to Interior Design. It was in that instant that he saw her eyes, perfectly centered in the frames of her glasses and accented by the matte black of her thick lashes and arched brows. In this light, even from this distance, they were a lustrous light grey.

She set down her wine glass and reached for something on the coffee table. It looked to be about the size of a cell phone. It was a remote control, and as she aimed it to her right at something not visible from the backyard, the level of the music increased almost to where it could be heard. Her subtle smile told anyone watching that this song had special meaning to her.

Eric reached into his pocket and pulled out his two phones. He got her number off the firm phone and called her on the other. He heard the phone ring when she did and watched as she turned toward the end table on her left. She struggled to reach for her cell phone without changing her position. It was not the most graceful of moves for a former ballerina, but even awkward she was incredible. She got the phone, glancing at the screen before answering.

"Hello," she said, her voice up beat yet curious.

He watched her without saying a word, the phone's speaker held to his ear, listening intently to see if he could distinguish the song she enjoyed enough to increase the volume.

And then there it was. He recognized it immediately, that signature haunting jazz saxophone. In that instant, after just those few notes everything changed.

"Hello? Is anybody there?" Jillian asked into the phone from inside.

Then thunder clapped loudly, causing Jillian's body to react slightly on the couch. She tilted her head to one side and looked at her phone. Was that thunder in real life at the exact same time as thunder over the phone? Was that possible? For that to be, the other end of this call, and thus the caller, had to be nearby.

All of a sudden there was an enourmous dog standing at the door, eyes surveying the darkness of the backyard. Jillian got up and joined the guard dog. Flipping on the flood lights to illuminate the deck before opening the doors, both stepped outside.

Still talking into the phone, she said, "Hello. I know somebody is there. I can hear you." Then into the emptiness of the backyard, she asked, "Is anybody out here? Don't make me let go of my dog."

The dog, her dog, an aged and fluffy golden retriever, glanced up at her and seemed to imply she could let go if she wanted but that wouldn't change a thing. He had no plans to leave this deck other than to return inside.

Eric was already on the dead sprint back to his car, swallowed up by her neighbor's front yard shadows. He understood that he had one more stop to make tonight, for, as crazy as it might sound, Dave Koz's saxophone was now the new voice in his head.

anting from the mad dash from her yard, we were greeted by that rubbery concrete smell oftentimes preceding an early summer storm. We realized we had to hustle to stay dry. He told me there was one more stop to make, but I was unsure we could get in there at this late hour.

He drove silently, contemplating the ramifications of what just happened. It wasn't the relief of a prowler's narrow escape, nor the guilt for having watched her like a voyeur. It was far more than either. It was somehow both real and surreal yet seeming to make perfect sense at the same time.

All he could think about was the song and its meaning, plus the flood of memories it produced. And the timing. For Jillian to turn up the music at the same instant he was spying on her may never be explained. Somehow, though, he got it. The song was a message.

A long time ago it was Erin's priest, Fr. Holiday, who upon her death had asked him to fly in the face of all he'd believed, foregoing evidence or proof, and take things on faith. He'd asked Eric to regard her death as God's master plan. Back then, he couldn't find any way to conceive of such lunacy. God's grand plan had collided with his own. God won. He always did.

Erin was gone, and no priest would be able to explain why.

Eric lived in the beyond-a-reasonable-doubt world where faith and belief alone were never enough to sway folks. This inability to understand *Why?* more than any other factor, torpedoed his relationship with the well-intentioned priest. He reneged on his conversion, going as far in the opposite direction as possible.

But one thing the priest had told him stuck. He'd said, "Erin may continue to communicate with you, only through others."

And it just happened! He heard a song with an ironically coincidental title and understood it to be Erin.

That song had played the last time they were together, the last night they made love, the day before she was killed. Whether it was good fortune, or maybe by the hand of God himself, she'd reached out to him. He needed to see her to apologize in person.

Roselawn Memorial Park Cemetery was fifteen minutes at most. North on MacArthur and then east on Highway 97, across Highway 29 to Interstate 72 east toward Decatur. Yep. The same Highway 29. Twenty-five miles northwest of where Erin had been killed, she was buried near the same highway.

The cemetery hours were listed as sun up to sundown. Eric got out, saying it would only take ten minutes. When I reminded him of the hours, he replied something about it being too dark to tell when the sun might set. It was good line, classic alcoholic rationalization.

"I've got to do this. You coming?"

He closed the car door and slipped through a wide gap in the ten-foot-tall rod-iron fence hidden by large evergreens. It was apparent he'd done this before, so I followed, because that's what I do.

With the flashlight app on both of his phones fighting against the rain, we navigated the concrete paths like seasoned grave robbers. In the downpour we saw an inordinate number of flowers spread around the grounds. Mother's Day had been a week and a half earlier.

We cut between a few monuments, through a muddy area. His shoes were already close to ruin and his socks soaked up past his cuffs. He pulled the collar up on his suitcoat and found himself in a driving rain, facing her tombstone, suddenly with nothing to say.

"Hi, Erin," he offered quietly. "I heard the song."

With the help of one flashlight, we read her name and the dates of her birth and death etched into the knee-high marker. She would be forever twenty-nine, never afforded the opportunity to turn the *Big 3-0.*

He pulled out his flask and emptied it in one long gulp. There hadn't been much left. Closing his eyes to stem the tears, he began to speak aloud to the woman he'd privately savaged for the past eight months, yet if she hadn't died, would have become his wife.

"I heard your song. I recognized Dave Koz. I remember the first time we heard it years ago, and of course I remember the last. I figured you played it for me tonight, to save me from doing something incredibly stupid."

He thought about the irony of the song's title. "Just to be Next to You." He saw Jillian cuddled on her couch, wondering if the song was meant for him and her. In that vision, she smiled at him over the magazine, while he sat on the couch, "Just to be Next to Her." But that was not to be, any more than he would ever again "Just to be Next to Erin."

He was alone . . . and pathetic.

"I'm not good at this, Erin."

He yelled and sobbed into the darkness, wiping the rain and the tears from his face with an equally wet hand. Then with a gulp of breath, he jumped into the abyss, free falling with an emotional torrent of consciousness that wouldn't stop until he finally hit bottom.

"I'm not good at living without you, out here on my own. I'm scared. I miss you. I miss the feeling of your hand in the small of my back gently nudging me toward the right things. Toward goodness. I make mistakes without you. I go the wrong way, do the wrong things.

"I need you again . . . still. I can't stop drinking. This creates problems. I'm so lonely. I was banging this girl who lives in my complex and pretending she's you. Now this girl I work with. That's over. I'm seriously fucked up, but the worst of my sins is I blame you for what happened to me. To us. You didn't do anything. It was Ritter. It had to be.

"I shot right past innocent until proven guilty. You and Ritter were guilty in my eyes of doing that one last thing.

"I have your text memorized. For eight months, I've focused on the first two lines and not the last two. We were supposed to be together forever. Jillian pointed that out to me. She's the girl who I now pretend to be you. Does that make me worse than I already am? It doesn't mean I don't still wish I were with you."

After coming up for air, he gulped a huge breath and dove under again.

"You'd like Jillian. She's a lawyer too. She's the one you saved me from making an ass of myself in front of tonight. Thank God for you and Dave Koz.

"I can't figure her out though. Why can't all women be like you? No games. No grey area. Everything with her is grey. You ought to see her eyes. They're even grey too.

"I love you, Erin. Not past tense. It's present and future. I will always love you, but I need you to forgive me for what I've done to you and your memory. I stumbled upon this false path and I've walked it for eight months, because it's easy. No other reason. It's unfair to blame you but convenient for me."

Then he yelled loudly, the agony scratched in his voice, "Help me figure out what happened to you. Why did you climb in that car? What was that last thing you needed to do, Erin?"

He sobbed heavily and breathed deeply, trying to regain his composure, the rain pelting him.

He said more softly, "I'll figure it out. I promise. Right now, I've got this other thing, my first criminal defense, a conspiracy case. It's a mess. Their case is weak, but our guy's probably guilty. I don't know, but I'm told it doesn't matter."

He thought how Erin might prosecute his *mess*. The first thing she would do was get out of the rain, yet he stood stock still, the drops piercing through puddles and thumping off the sidewalk. But like the rain, there was a rhythm to this *mess*, a progression of steps, drops rather than dots to connect.

Would Erin have brought conspiracy charges against Gradeen? Based on the evidence, and the promise to the grand jury to decode the secret cipher by the start of the trial, was there enough here for her to decide to prosecute? She had never been a climber, like

Forrester. Lacking a personal agenda, was there enough here to move forward?

Let's say there is, and she goes forth with a trial. Would she go about it any differently than he was? He was supposed to be the prosecution practice squad, but would a professional prosecutor look for the same things he'd identified? She'd try to find both DeBisshop and Fuller. She'd hope to connect Steinhauer to Fuller. She'd already have deposed Olivia Jacobsen to learn next to nothing. Wouldn't she wonder what DeBisshop and Jameson Gradeen had emailed to each other in their secret cipher, or what the news lady may have missed that allegedly set this intrigue in motion?

Would a true prosecutor bother to investigate Thomas Gradeen, or was that maybe where their paths might diverge? Had he gotten off track considering the elder Gradeen? Was it a wild-goose chase? Whether misguided or not, no investigation into Thomas Gradeen means no inane biography . . .

And that's when it hit him. Again, like the rain, it started with an isolated drop.

Pow.

Then two more. *Pow. Pow.*

He felt that he had missed something, that it was right there for the offing, there within his grasp.

Pow. Pow. Pow.

What didn't he quite understand? Then the drops and sounds again became a torrent, the rain harder, the rhythm of his thoughts becoming a deluge.

Finally he saw it. It was right in front of him all this time, but until tonight he'd been so busy looking elsewhere that he'd missed it entirely.

He came to the cemetery "Just to be Next to Erin."

She opened his eyes.

THIRTY-SEVEN

The intermittent buzzing noise was coming from somewhere, vibrating the kitchen tabletop into Eric's ear pressed against it. He slowly and deliberately raised his head, pulling away the page of the legal pad stuck by drool to his mouth. He tightened and stretched his back and shoulders, his palms driving deeply into his eye sockets. The buzz sounded again and he realized it was his cell phone somewhere amid the clutter.

He found it under the fanned back pages of a legal pad, between an opened manila folder and a mug of tepid coffee. There was a glass and a half-empty bottle of Glenfiddich. Legal pads and torn-off yellow pages were everywhere, piled randomly or some stacked neatly. Was it just his imagination, or did every sheet seem to be either damp or crinkled like it had been?

The memories didn't fall into place of how he got here or what he was doing. His shirt was wrinkled like it had been air-dried and needed ironing, pant cuffs were rolled up, his feet bare, socks and shoes piled by the front door by two towels from his bathroom. He wore his still sodden necktie around his head like a warrior's headband. He'd gone to war last night, but who did he battle? Had he won?

Then he saw the Gradeen biography, with its strained spine and dog-eared pages, and it came back to him with a satisfied smile. Believe it or not, *Thomas Gradeen: Titan of the Prairie* was the key to cracking the email cipher. And numerous decoded messages were scribbled on sheets of yellow paper piled on the kitchen table.

Just as the FBI had speculated, the emails back and forth between Jameson Gradeen and Arthur DeBisshop were written in the classic numerical cipher style, with the messages transmitted in groups of three figures. But what they didn't know was the key.

The three numbers, separated by commas, are coordinates to a specific word in the text. The first number is the page, the second is how many lines down from the top, and the third is how many words reading over from the left. Bible verses work in a similar way. There, however, it is book, chapter, verse. It is still three coordinates to get you to the pertinent place.

With a numerical cipher, there's a number, a comma or a dash, a number, a comma or a dash, and another number to get you to one word. Then there's a space. Then three more numbers and you have the next word. It's a deliberate and time-consuming process to decode, but once you get rolling, the sentences start appearing as if by magic. The sets of numbers are punctuated as if they themselves are words. Several properly punctuated sentences flowing into each other and soon you have a paragraph. Two or three paragraphs and you have every word in the email.

The emails were in a "texting" style – bad grammar and worse punctuation. It was obviously an onerous project of finding each individual word on a page of the biography and then counting its coordinates. It had to be exhausting. Thankfully this difficulty in *coding* the message made *decoding* easier because the messages were short and the same three-number combination was used multiple times. Out of expediency, oftentimes a specific three-numbers were repeatedly used for the same word.

He'd started reading the emails from his laptop and transcribing the words onto a legal pad. That's when he determined battles won do not alone win wars. He'd broken a numerical cipher to reveal a separate and distinct code of words. The key was correct; the derived words were all in English, and they were all words, basically making coherent thoughts and ideas if not proper sentences.

There were, however, no names, or even proper nouns. Every mention that should have been someone's name or a specific place was another code, or nickname. Ironically enough, most of the stuff that he thought was idiotic and arcane while reading the book, all surfaced in his decoded cipher. There were *Godfather* and *Mario Puzo, Elvis, James Bond* and *The Princess* among others. There was even someone who appeared to be called *Canterbury*. And you can't write a book in Springfield without including *Abraham Lincoln* and *John Wilkes Booth*. But who was supposed to be who? Or whom? I don't know.

Neither Jameson Gradeen nor DeBisshop had been dumb enough to address the emails or sign them using their nicknames. In other words, an email from Gradeen to DeBisshop did not start "Dear Godfather," and then end with "Regards, Mario Puzo."

In some, there were email chains with a third or fourth party. Whereas Gradeen and DeBisshop did nothing to hide their identities as senders or receivers, these other two did. The sending and receiving addresses were anonymous Gmail addresses, which added another layer to the unknowns.

It was like sometime in the middle of the night, Eric had become World War II cryptanalyst Alan Turing. He broke Germany's Enigma cipher to discover the solution was written in German. Eric didn't speak German. So then, while getting one step closer, he was one step closer to what?

After working studiously through several recent emails, back about the time DeBisshop disappeared, he'd taken one legal pad and written down the names of the players. They included Jameson and Thomas Gradeen, DeBisshop, Fuller and Steinhauer. He added Olivia Jacobsen and Ann Flannery, plus Patrick Weathers, Ms. Flannery's companion the night she was killed. In a second column, he'd jotted down nicknames uncovered in the cipher, at least those reoccurring There remained a great deal of laborious work to determine who was who. That was about his last conscious memory; it had come around 5:30 in the morning.

According to the screen on his firm-issued iPhone, that was only three hours earlier. His workday had just begun, and yet he already missed two calls and a text from Sarge -- a shared contact for Olivia

Jacobsen's personal cell number. The man was good, but there was no time to dwell on that now for there was also a text from Jillian.

It read, "Morning. Hope you're okay. Miss seeing you." It appeared she was communicating again.

As he poured scotch into his coffee he regarded her text. Why'd she have to add that last part? Didn't she know that he was trying to forget her? Didn't she know how much he missed seeing her, too? But she'd been playing him, right? Plus, June 4th was now one day closer.

He began to formulate a reply when his phone rang.

"Hi Sarge. I see you've been trying to get ahold of me. Sorry."

"*Young Gun*, you a hard man to reach. You already hard at it this morning?"

He surveyed his kitchen table and its disorganization. He said with a slight laugh, "You could say that. Thanks for Jacobsen's number. How'd you get it?"

"That's what I do, man. Give her a shout, but that's not why I called you. I may have found Fuller."

"No shit?"

"Told you about the one dude from Monday night at the bar, right? Illinois Guardsman with the guilt-ridden smirk? I've been on him like an ugly sweater, and he met secretly in the backyard of a house with some guy I think is Fuller. There's just one problem."

"What's that?"

"Don't know what Fuller looks like."

Holy shit! Was that even possible? Sarge went to Decatur to find someone he'd never seen whether in person or in a photo. And he may have found him despite that.

"I don't know what he looks like either, Sarge." Eric's tone was a mix of amazement and apology.

They discussed ways to get a photo over to Sarge, many of the ideas running headlong into firm security firewalls. They both were accessing files remotely. Eric's laptop had authorization to get on the web, while Sarge didn't. Sarge was unable to pull up a photo on his laptop. Eric could email, but Sarge couldn't open an attachment. It went back and forth like this for a minute when Sarge had an idea. And in the excitement of the moment, he tipped his hand.

"I'll give you a number and then fax it to me."

"Good idea." Eric moved back to the table and flipped open his computer. "What's the number?"

Sarge immediately realized his gaffe and his need to keep his e-fax number anonymous.

"No. Wait, *Young Gun*. Gotta to be a better way."

"I get faxes. I'm guessing I can send them too. I've learned the technology is basically the same."

"No. How else could we do it?"

"What the hell, Sarge? It was your idea. What won't work about it?"

"A fax won't do the photo justice. How about you bring up a photo of Fuller from your case files and snap a cell phone picture and text it to me?"

"How is that . . .?

"It'll be quicker." Desperate to change the subject, Sarge said, "Let me tell you about Fuller, or the guy I think might be Fuller."

Sarge went into detail about how he'd peeled a vet from the herd on Monday night and stayed on him all day Tuesday with no joy. Then this morning, on the man's way to work, he turned down an alley and visited with someone over a chain link fence. Sarge was sitting in his car at the end of the alleyway, a few houses down, but felt he got a good enough look at the man to recognize Fuller once he had a photo for comparison.

While Eric went through the low-tech steps of texting Fuller's photo, we noticed he had the same military buzz-cut look of firm security. The man looked eerily familiar.

Eric explained to Sarge about using Gradeen's biography as the key to break the email code. It was an arduous process with three coordinates and breaking the cipher had revealed a new code of its own.

"Where'd you get the book?" Sarge asked. "Go get more copies so we can help."

"Great idea. It's at *The Book Knook* on East Washington. I'll run back by there today."

"Listen, we all put our heads together, we can crack your code. Grab one email from around a date where you already know what happened? Maybe try right around where the news lady was killed. If you know events around certain dates, your code words may pop up faster."

"Great thinking."

After a bit of hesitation, Sarge said, "I'll bet the lovely lady lawyer is good at breaking codes . . . and breaking hearts."

He'd added the last part with a low laugh, but Eric didn't comment, having completely missed the remark. Instead he fired off the texted photo.

"There it is. I got the photo," Sarge said. "Sure looks like it could be the same guy, *Young Gun*. What do I do now? How you want to handle this?"

Eric realized quickly this was not his decision.

"See if you can confirm, and then call Jillian or McGraw. Let them decide how to proceed, and whether to approach. Stay with him, Sarge. Don't let him out of sight. Your Guardsman may have spooked him."

"Will do. Sounds like a perfect excuse to ring up the pretty lady lawyer. Want me to tell her anything?"

With a deep raspy chuckle and an exchange of good-byes, Sarge hung up. Eric knew he too needed to contact the lovely lady lawyer. She'd be interested to learn about the cipher and Fuller. Maybe Sarge could fill her in because Eric had something else to try.

Heeding Sarge's advice, he found emails from mid-summer a year ago. This would have been right around the time Ann Flannery was murdered, the event which had precipitated the whole conspiracy case being defended.

The first email alone, from Jameson Gradeen to DeBisshop two days after the murder, took a full Scotch Coffee to decipher.

Jameson Gradeen had closed the message by saying, "News says wrong reporter killed. Thanks."

His reason for gratitude could not be derived from the context, nor could Eric determine anything of import from DeBisshop's response. He peeled back a few pages to review the timeline. The story of Ann Flannery's murder missed the newspaper deadline but made televised news. Her murder was reported in the Sunday edition, but the paper hit the stands prior to the "wrong reporter" angle being released by the police. Once again television had scooped the State Journal-Register, simply a matter of timing over reporting talent.

The same email referenced someone Gradeen called "The Idiot." So, Eric jotted down on his legal pad guessing that meant Steinhauer. This, however, proved to be a pejorative more than a code name, because *Stupid* and *Patsy* were also used in emails to denote Steinhauer. *Cinderella* would have made a convenient codename because of the mask, but she was nowhere to be found.

The only other proper names used in this specific email were *Bond, Elvis, Booth, Canterbury* and *Top Hat*, and the last was only included because of the implied importance given to it by Gradeen.

Chances were Steinhauer was either *Elvis* or *Booth*, and Fuller was *James Bond*. The latter would seem to make sense, "License to Kill" and all that. Plus, Fuller was the fixer; he'd allegedly been dispatched to eliminate Steinhauer, so his codename might not be too difficult to verify.

Canterbury, on the other hand, remained a mystery.

Eric was able to verify with certainty who was who on the victim side. No codenames were used for Flannery and Weathers, calling them "dead girl," and "her friend." Also, it was not too difficult to determine that Olivia Jacobsen's codename was *Barbara Walters*.

What was odd, though, was how a biography about a Central Illinois farmer turned ag-entrepreneur would include any reference to *Barbara Walters*. When Ms. Walters was mentioned in the book, it was said the original Mrs. Gradeen "slightly resembled a younger Barbara Walters."

This arcane inclusion gave rise to two new questions: Had the code been written using the book as the key? Or had the book been published solely to serve as the key after the code was written? The latter would explain a lot.

Either was immaterial. The breaking of the numerical cipher was arduous and draining, but certainly doable. Trying to match up the players with their codenames was becoming more of an exercise in logic.

See if this makes sense.

Down the left side of a legal pad he'd written the names of the pertinent participants. In a column down the right, were the reoccurring codenames and obscure references. Think *Barbara Walters*. Now logic would dictate that the author of an email – whether Gradeen, DeBisshop or the two anonymous Gmail accounts – would not mention themselves in the email. Therefore, a codename which appears in all the emails except those written by Gradeen, could then be assumed to be Gradeen's. Maybe this wasn't foolproof, but logical. Right?

Using this reasoning after hours spent decoding the chains that included the anonymous Gmail accounts, he'd concluded that Thomas Gradeen may be one of the unknown senders and could be *Lincoln*. Jameson was *Godfather*, but the fourth identity, the other anonymous Gmail sender, remained unknown.

And how did he not recognize DeBisshop's codename immediately?

Question: Who's the most famous resident of Canterbury?

That's right – *da archbishop*.

DeBisshop is *Canterbury*.

THIRTY-EIGHT

ase # 75-93654 US v. Agribotics Technologies yielded good days and bad. The same was true with the news. Today could considered one of the better ones, because of the email cipher and progress made with the codenames. Yet as it seemed with everything in the case, bad news would be sure to follow quickly.

It was like my old story of the villagers and the giant terrorizing them. The good news was the villagers finally killed the giant. Bad news was he crushed ten villagers when he fell. No real moral here. I just like telling it.

Eric regarded this while running. He was both villager and giant, a drunken man chasing something, while simultaneously being chased. He ran from and ran toward. He ran fast and he ran angry. Still, he could never outdistance his ghosts nor gain on his prey. It was like running on a treadmill, getting nowhere fast. He knew who he was running from, but who was he hoping to catch?

Or had they become one in the same?

He'd spent nine of the last thirteen hours at his kitchen table, diligently working to decipher the email code. There had been three hours for sleeping, an hour to run and recover. He was exhausted both physically and mentally, basically surviving and functioning on the caffeine, liquor and adrenaline.

He'd returned to *The Book Knook* to get copies of the Gradeen biography, as Sarge had suggested, only to find they were sold out. Just days before, there were four copies gathering dust on the same shelf, tucked back in a remote corner of the store. Today they were all gone.

When asked about it, the same clerk from Monday commented it "boggled the mind" that a book with no sales for almost a year would then sell out in only three days. She said the same person bought the four remaining copies. Her only description was "a linebacker-looking Caucasian dude in a white shirt and red tie."

Sure sounded like *Donaldson, Clements* security. But why? And how had the firm found out about the books? That had to be Sarge. Hell, it had been his idea to purchase the remaining copies in the first place.

So, then like almost everything else, this latest development gave rise to a minimum of two more questions. 1.) Were the books bought by the firm to help him decode the emails? Or 2.) Were they perhaps bought up by the firm to keep him from getting help decoding the emails? And if it was the second, again the question goes to *Why?* Call that one #3 or better yet, 2A.

To get his mind off this newest puzzle, he dialed the number Sarge supplied for Olivia Jacobsen. A suspiciously timid voice answered the phone.

"Miss Jacobsen?" he asked. "Or is it Miss Jacobs now?"

"Who is this? How'd you get this number? It's my private cell."

"My name is Eric McKegney. I'm with *Donaldson, Clements, Blaine & McGraw*. Our firm is tasked with defending Jameson Gradeen in the matter with which I'm sure you're familiar. I know you've made numerous statements and depositions. I've read them. I realize your time is valuable, but I hope you have five minutes to answer a few additional questions."

Eric understood that before he could sell any product, or in this case a new interview, he had to first sell the appointment. He'd laid it on relatively thickly, schmoozing would be a better descriptive.

There was still an edge in her tone when she asked again, "How did you get this number?"

"The firm has an extensive investigative section. One of my associates sent this number to me. I don't ask how. I just say, "Thank you," and dial."

She considered this and then asked, "What did you say your name was?"

"Eric McKegney."

After initial hesitation she asked, "Why does that name sound familiar?"

Eric answered, "Prior to joining this firm and this defense team, I was a personal injury attorney with my face on billboards and on a lot of television commercials in Springfield. Some may have even run during your newscasts. I tried to make it hard for people not to know me."

"That's not it," she said, as if she had paid no attention to his last line.

"How should I address you?" Eric asked, hoping to clear up the Jacobs / Jacobsen name confusion.

"Why do you need to worry about that?" she shot right back. "I haven't agreed to talk to you yet."

"This is true." He regrouped and tried again. "I'm sure you're sick and tired of rehashing this. I also know it was not one of the more flattering episodes of your journalistic career. What if I told you I might be able to change all that? What if I had a way to make this your story again?"

"I'm listening," she said simply, very noncommittal.

"Can we do it in person? I can be in Moline in two-and-a-half hours. That would be around three. What do you say?"

Now she sounded skeptical. "You'd drive all the way from Springfield for five minutes just to do me a favor?"

"Maybe my motives aren't quite so noble," he allowed. "My apologies."

"Are you maybe being compensated by the hour?" she asked with her first hint of humor.

"No. That's not it. I'd like to meet you. It's that simple. I'd like to sit down with you and try to understand everything you've endured in the last year. Then I'd like to bounce a few new things off you and get your impressions. That's all, Miss . . ."

To his surprise she then said, "Call me J.J."

"Great. Thanks, J.J. What do you say?"

While he thought this newest silence signaled her continued consideration whether to meet, she was instead calculating how she might be able to save him some time and a few miles.

"Do you get to Galesburg? You should. It's the birthplace of Carl Sandberg, the poet. There's a Starbucks right off Interstate 74. It's Exit 48. You can't miss it. Can you meet me there instead at two?"

"I can do that." His tone, initially rich with surprise then moderated when he added, "Thank you, J.J."

"Eric McKegney. Now I think I recognize the name," she said. "Weren't you engaged to that girl killed in Patterson's accident?"

He wasn't sure if he had ever heard Ritter referred to only by his Christian name, nor had Erin ever been regarded as *that girl*. And now he wasn't completely sure if Patterson's accident had truly been an accident, but there was no time to get into all that. Whether his dubious connection to Ritter would be why she'd agreed to see him, he wasn't going to let this chance slip by.

Softly he said, "That's right. My fiancé was killed in the accident that crippled Patterson Ritter. Her name was Erin Haynes."

"I'm so sorry for your loss." Here she hesitated a beat out of respect before quietly adding, "All that happened right about the time I moved here. Terrible business. That man had the world at his feet."

They reconfirmed the meeting time and the location of the Starbucks before hanging up. After a quick stop at his home to get his blue and black patterned blazer, he was back behind the wheel of the Jeep Cherokee and heading to Galesburg.

I pointed out that we were being followed by an old beater of a Ford pickup, similar to the one driving on the sidewalk Tuesday night. Even had damage to the grill. He glanced in the rearview mirror and chuckled at my paranoia. I considered it to be observant, but he had other things on his mind than the traffic. As he stayed left where Interstates 74 and 55 split just north of town, and the rusty white truck did the same, he continued mulling over the news lady's last comment about Ritter.

"That man had the world at his feet," she had said.

Had he? Really? And if so, how'd she know? Eric knew the Springfield media to be a tight-knit group, so maybe it wasn't that far from the norm that a television reporter and one from the newspaper would know each other. But her whispered manner made it sound as if it went beyond a casual acquaintance. Was there anything between Ritter and Olivia Jacobsen? If so, that surely lent some validity to her remark about his future.

Eric now knew, or at least believed, that he was dead wrong about Erin's intention on that fateful night. Could the same be said about Ritter? Why would someone with the world at his feet purposely drive his old girlfriend into a telephone pole? In his way of thinking, Ritter, the proverbial scorned lover had vowed if he couldn't have Erin, no one could. Had he somehow gone from home wrecker to murderer to . . . now what? Unfortunate victim of a terribly untimely accident? A man with the world at his feet?

Would such a man, who may have had a heretofore unknown relationship with a certain local news lady, forsake that future for vengeance? Had Ritter sacrificed everything the world had lain at his feet solely to punish Eric for stealing his girl?

And while the selfish alcoholic always views things by how they affect him, Erin remained the true victim here. Whether the comment was fitting or not, the same could certainly be thought about her. Hers was the true loss. Their shared future would have been equally as bright as Ritter's, or anyone else for that matter, had she not been killed. But she had. And this again brought him back around to ponder how things might have gone if she hadn't.

He and I had this conversation too many times to recall, most times over too many drinks for us to remember. It always begins something like this: If the roles had been reversed, if Ritter was killed and Erin injured, how different might things be? There's a philosophical quotient here, one weighing the pros and cons of death versus disability, or the other way around. While her death was absolutely devastating to Eric, it had ended his involvement. She had been horrifically cleaved from his side, but it was clean and overwhelmingly final, like lopping off an arm. It's horrible, but you learn to live with one arm.

The same could never be said for Ritter. His family continued to live with his injuries day in and day out. Eric had no idea of the man's current condition, nor had he cared to learn. He imagined there were times when Ritter's family, or Ritter himself, had prayed he and Erin could have traded places.

Eric never once had.

He and I have learned a great deal about each other in the last eight months, and Eric about himself. And while he might be hesitant to fully admit as much aloud, he'd never have stayed by her side if she was hospitaized for the last eight months. This is not to say he didn't love her, for he did. It's just that a bedside vigil is not what he signed on for.

He admitted once that since the phrase *'til death do us part,* had never been uttered in front of God and the church he felt no obligation. This was a very intoxicated man who back then thought his fiancé had been about to sleep with an old boyfriend. I can cut him some slack.

But if he were forced to choose between where Erin is now and where Ritter is, he'd take Erin. Both are terrible losses, but Ritter and his family continue to lose more each day. And after watching the man suffer for God-only-knows how much longer, he's still going to die one day. After a slow and persistent and painful tugging, that band-aid would eventually fall off. As hard as it is to say, let alone think, that day might be a blessing to both Ritter and his family.

Eric knew his stark version of *such a* blessing had come eight months earlier.

THIRTY-NINE

*T*here's one Starbucks in Galesburg, and as mentioned on the phone, it's hard to miss. It sits west of where Main Street ducks under Interstate 74, in the same building as a pharmacy and walk-in clinic. Eric sat at a table staring into his phone with a frothy green drink of something in a clear plastic cup bearing his name. When he'd asked how he might recognize her, playfully referring to their impromptu meeting as a sort of blind date, the news lady had responded with condescension.

"I'll be the one who looks like my publicity photo on the station's website."

It reminded me of the old days when you'd ask directions and a person would tell you how to get there. This has since been replaced by just telling you the address and then forcing you to use your phone to find it. Rather than tell Eric what she looked like or what she might be wearing, his phone had to do the heavy lifting.

So, when she walked in, he recognized her immediately from her head shot, ball cap, sunglasses and all, like she was trying to hide her identity. He glanced around the nearly empty coffee shop, her arrival not interrupting the other two patrons on their laptops. She waved to the only other coffee drinker whom she presumed was Eric. She then gestured that she was going to the counter.

From where he sat she looked pretty in profile, tall and relatively thin with a braided blonde ponytail protruding out the back of her cap. Her clothing was nothing elaborate or showy, more of a very relaxed business casual of dressy khaki Capri pants, an expensive white cotton top, the same color of her hat, and a pair of what looked to be expensive sandals.

She glanced over at him, removed her sunglasses and smiled pleasantly, the kind she flashes when the live-shot initially goes to her. While she's attractive, and few women on TV news nowadays aren't, she was no Erin, and certainly no Jillian. Instead she had that understated Midwest-small-market-weekend-anchor hotness.

He rose and took her offered hand as she approached his table. She has a Nordic look to her up close, with the angular features and bright blue eyes, and a porcelain doll-like complexion. After an exchange of pleasantries and a discussion about the ease of finding the place, they got down to what had drawn them together.

Eric began with this prelude, "As I mentioned on the phone, I'm with *Donaldson, Clements, Blaine & McGraw*. We're defending Jameson Gradeen. I've been added to the team, tasked to punch holes in our potential defense strategies. I try to discover what factually happened so we are better prepared to defend our client. Does that make sense?"

"It does," she said with a nod. "I can see the logic behind that approach."

Eric said, "Good. Now this entire crime spree from a year ago, and the resulting investigation, hinges on one thing. Sadly that thing is you."

"I am fully aware of that," she said, obviously exhausted from repeating this over and over, and possibly aggravated for now apparently having to revisit that meat grinder.

"I'll try to make this as pain-free as possible. I already know much of what I hope to discuss from reading through several of your previous depositions. At the time of Ann Flannery's murder, you were investigating Arthur DeBisshop's company for alleged dumping of waste?"

She perked up a bit at this question. "The *Agricultural Chemical Group* investigative report was the assigned story, but we never learned anything substantial. It was never going to run, nothing there. I felt bad because the coincidental timing of my story got Arthur in a whole lot of trouble."

"Arthur? Not Dr. DeBisshop?" This was interesting. "How would you characterize your relationship with Arthur?"

She smiled uneasily at this and said, "Boy, you are a lawyer, aren't you?"

"I'm sorry," he said, his upturned hands then reaching for his greenish drink wishing it were scotch.

He studied his name on the cup, wondering why they'd felt the need to do that when he was the lone customer at the counter. Her cup didn't have a name on it unless it was under the fashionable drink sleeve. He shrugged this off and took a big pull on his straw.

"Arthur was a lonely man," she was saying. "He was from Denmark. Did you know that? His wife had died recently and he was certainly isolated. Think about it, an egghead scientist with no social life. He had his work. Several times I thought he was inventing reasons to get us to come out there to talk to him."

"Do you mean the research farm?"

"At the station, we called it Big Brown or Brown University. Have you been out there?"

"I have. They told us everything is that color so satellites or drones couldn't detect depth or differentiate fields from buildings."

"Arthur used to say it was because they got a great deal on brown paint."

He noticed a light smile dance across her lips with the remark as her blue eyes crinkled into a squint. There was a genuine affinity for DeBisshop here that may have run much deeper than a business relationship or simple sympathy for a lonely widower.

"When was the last time you saw Dr. DeBisshop?"

"It's been a long time, not since I moved to Moline."

Since she hadn't entirely answered the question, Eric let it hang there in hopes she would fill in the blanks. This was another from the bag of lawyerly tricks. Extended silence breeds anxiety, and the only way for the deposed to ease that worry oftentimes is to resume talking. It worked.

"When it was first reported that I was the intended target, he was genuinely concerned for me and my safety. There was no reason since I had around-the-clock protection from the Springfield police. I was basically forced into hiding, almost like witness protection. They interrogated me for days, wanting to know what I knew which made me dangerous. They gave up since I apparently knew nothing."

She delivered the line with an odd expression and a self-deprecating gesture before adding, "Makes it hard to find work as an investigative journalist."

"I might know how you feel," he remarked, thinking about the white pickup truck. "Tell me more about Dr. DeBisshop."

Something he couldn't explain was percolating in the back of his brain, so he hoped more context might push it closer to the front.

"What do you want me to tell you?"

"You said he was a lonely widower. You've mentioned that you interviewed him at work. Was he the same person privately and professionally?"

She considered this for more than a beat. After a sip of her drink, she set her cup down deliberately and glanced to the ceiling.

"That's an interesting question . . . One I've not truly considered."

"I only ask because I've come to learn that very few people ever got to see both sides of him."

"No. I get it. I'd say he wanted to be perceived as the same person regardless of which hat he wore. I was able to get closer than most. He was genial and quiet most of the time, except for that one day at the farm. I overheard a heated exchange with the younger Gradeen. Gradeen apparently won the argument because Arthur under his breath later apologized and called him an *M-Fer*."

"DeBisshop did?"

"He did, but funny thing, I think it was all an act, the whole show done only for my benefit, the argument as well as the outrage."

"What makes you think that?"

"They were both looking in my direction the entire time."

"Did you ask DeBisshop about it? How did he explain it?"

"He didn't really. He kept telling me how sorry he was. I kept telling him it was no big deal."

"When was this? Do you remember how long ago?"

"Let's see." Her eyes again glanced to ceiling, contemplating her response. "That might have been around the time Ann was killed. Definitely prior to that, but I'm not sure how long."

"That's okay. Did you know the Gradeens? Jameson or Thomas? Ever interview either?"

"I certainly knew of them. Most of the media in Springfield do and cater to them. I've never interviewed either. Come to think of it, the episode I just mentioned was the only time I recall being around the son. I've never had the pleasure of meeting the father."

"What were your impressions of Jameson?"

"Don't take this the wrong way since you are defending him, but he seemed like a real prick."

Eric laughed at this and asked, "Is there a right way I'm supposed to take that? It's okay. I can see how someone might think that. I've met him."

She leaned forward, anxious to volunteer more information. "He gave me the creeps. He looked at me with this scary stare. More like a leer. Then later he's screaming at Arthur. I'm glad our paths never crossed again."

Eric considered all this, regarding how that was also Jillian's impression of their client. Then was on to a new line of questioning.

"Did Ann Flannery ever go with you out to Big Brown?"

This question too made her think for a long beat. "Not that I recall. She did ride-alongs with my cameraman and me from time to time, but I doubt if she ever went out there. The anchors stay near the studio out of necessity."

"Did you know Patrick Weathers?"

"Not really. He was relatively new in Ann's life. I think that night was only their second or third date."

"But you had met him?"

"Once. He came by the station to watch Ann do the news. He was amazed by the process of putting on a telecast. Very curious guy. He asked questions of everyone and appeared to really enjoy himself."

Eric decided it was time to again change course.

"So, let's go back to that day a year ago if you will. How did you learn about Ann Flannery's death?"

Here J.J. became sullen, her hands in soft fists coming to her mouth with her elbows remaining on the table. She sighed and looked toward the counter before turning back to face Eric.

"We all got a text from the station manager as part of a blast to the station employees early that Saturday morning. I immediately called and he's a mess, could hardly make sentences. I flipped on the coverage. I can't even imagine how difficult that was for our people to report on the incident because they couldn't release her name yet."

This is standard operating procedure awaiting a next-of-kin notification.

Eric asked, "So if there were no names, then there were no details, right? There would have been no mention of Weathers or the mask, and certainly no broadcasting of the question about Ann being on the news."

She nodded solemnly at this.

Eric continued. "How much later in the day did you get your call?"

It was apparent that this portion of memory lane would be a difficult hike for her. Her teeth began to work almost like a saw grinding back and forth into her bottom lip. Her eyes, before wide and bright, were now closed to stem tears.

"It was late in the afternoon," she said through the beginning of light sobs. "I remember looking at the clock. I'll never forget. It was 4:14."

Eric hesitated prior to asking if it was okay to continue. Waiting for her to acknowledge, he regarded how surreal that morning would have been, but her day took an even more terrifying new turn at 4:14.

""It was supposed to be you," the voice said."

Her words had come out in a frighteningly shrill register, as she now began to rock slowly, rhythmically, backward and forward on her elbows. Her eyes remained tightly closed as she sniffled and repeated the line.

"It was supposed to be you."

Eric glanced around the coffee shop and observed their privacy remained intact. "Did the voice on the phone identify himself?"

Her eyes popped open and she said, "No. He just told me that he killed the wrong news lady and now they'd be coming for him."

"But he didn't say anything about who "they" might be."

She confirmed this with a slight shake of her head.

"J.J., were you out with Miss Flannery and Mr. Weathers that night?"

Again she simply shook her head.

"Where were you that night?"

"At home. I went for a drink with coworkers after the ten o'clock broadcast but was in bed long before what happened to . . ."

Eric already knew all of this from reading her depositions, so he felt guilty for making her relive it yet again. This was groundwork to get to where he really needed to be.

"J.J., in the time between you got the text from the station manager and the call from whom the police believe was Freddy Steinhauer, you had to wonder why this had happened. You had time to consider motive in Ann's murder. As a reporter, what possibilities did you come up with?"

She looked at him blankly. He wasn't sure if she was offended or confused by the question, so he didn't wait to find out and plowed ahead.

"You said you know it was my fiancé killed in Patterson Ritter's accident. I got the phone call late that Thursday night from Erin's father. Sorry. Her name was Erin. Erin Haynes.

"I know the horrific devastation you experienced. I've been there too. Once you fight past the denial and the disbelief, and say prayers that it's a horrifying mistake, the mind goes to *Why?*. And in my case, it got there quickly even though eight months later I'm still not sure. I have plenty of ideas and theories, and some continue to change daily. Initially I needed to know *Why?*"

She was nodding along before stopping abruptly.

"Back up for a second," she said. "You said the call, my call, came from the man the police *believe* was Steinhauer. You don't agree?"

She was a trained listener to have noticed the slight inflection evident earlier in his phrasing. While he didn't want to break his flow to revisit that comment, he thought it only fair to backtrack for her benefit. Leaning back in his chair, he crossed his right leg onto his left knee and tugged at the open collar of his white dress shirt under his blazer. Then he smiled patiently.

"Freddy Steinhauer's name never entered the investigation until after he was found dead in St. Louis. Then working backwards through the chain of events, the police put him at every stop. He may have not been involved in any of this other than wrong place / wrong time."

"But what about the phone calls found on Steinhauer's burner cell? That's how they triangulated back to Springfield and Arthur and Gradeen, right?"

This girl was sharp; it was hard to get anything past her.

Eric explained, "I'm still working on the phone calls."

She considered this with a light sip of her drink. From her expression Eric thought she was having trouble staying on the same page. He adjusted his frame in the uncomfortable chair and leaned forward.

"Can we get back to the time between learning about Ann's death and the second phone call."

Whereas before this topic had elicited pain and tears, now she seemed more engaged. Excitement had seemingly replaced the difficult memories.

"I remember thinking initially it was a robbery or mugging gone bad, or like you said earlier that it was a horrible mistake. I was praying that it was someone else. But you're also right about trying to figure out *Why?*."

"Did the police ever ask you why you thought someone might have killed your friend?"

"Not once. All the questions by the time I was interrogated were only why someone might want to kill me."

"How would you have answered if they had?"

He considered his question and then rethought this approach. After a quick sip he rephrased his request as, "Tell me about Ann Flannery."

She barely hesitated long enough to give this any thought, as if it were right there and had been since they'd begun discussing the female news anchor. And when she spoke it was in a cheery tone of admiration, haunted with a touch of loss, or maybe emptiness.

"Ann was my friend. She was a mentor to everyone. That's how she wanted to be remembered. Not so much for her accomplishments, but more for people she helped. It was never about her or her dreams. It was about others and their wants, or the guidance they needed. And it wasn't just with reporters at our station. She'd help anyone. And often, it wasn't members of the media. It was just people. That was her journalistic legacy, helping people."

"How did she go about that?"

"You know those consumer report stories and the like? That was all her. If a viewer felt wronged by a company, Ann would go right after them. She was fearless that way."

"Had she angered or embarrassed any companies around the time she was killed?"

"Oh, no. And even if she had she was charming and gracious enough to defuse any issues."

"I've been around people like that," Eric said.

Then he asked, "Do you know of anyone she might have been helping around the time of her death?"

"I'm sure there was someone. She was always helping someone, but I don't know. I'm sorry."

When she glanced at a flashy watch on her left wrist for the third time now, Eric recognized he'd overstayed his welcome. He withdrew an old McKegney Law business card from the inside pocket of the blazer he'd not worn since and jotted down his new cell phone number on the back.

"I know you need to go, and I need to get back too," he said, getting to his feet. "I greatly appreciate your time and for meeting me here. I'm glad we got to do this. As you can see, we're investigating a few new angles. If any of them pan out, maybe you can be the one to report it. This could become your story again. What do you think?"

She was extremely skeptical of this and asked, "Why would you do that?"

He never hesitated. "Several people appear to have been used in this, but no one more than you. It ruined your career. At least in Springfield. I think you deserve the chance to redeem yourself.

"I'll contact you if I learn more. Then you can decide for yourself. Take my card and call me if you think of anything we didn't discuss that you might like to add, or anything you feel may be important."

"You'd do that for me?" Turning the business card over in her hand, she said, "I'll call you if I think of anything."

"Thanks for your time, J.J."

She looked up from the card and then showed it to him. She said hesitantly, "Do you mind if I ask what happened to your old firm? This firm?"

He tried on a plastic grin and answered almost reflexively, "After Erin's death, it didn't seem important to me anymore. Nothing did. She was coming to work with me when we got back from our honeymoon . . ."

"I'm sorry about that." Her words were equally and evenly spaced, heartfelt and considerate.

"And I guess sympathies are due you also because of the accident."

"I'm sorry," she said, her head tilting to one side.

Eric was caught off guard by this and considered how best to answer.

"You mentioned on the phone Patterson Ritter had the world at his feet. I just assumed the two of you were close."

As he held open the door for her, they stepped outside into the bright and sunny afternoon. There wasn't much activity in the parking lot. They watched a few cars in the pharmacy drive-thru and a FedEx truck making a delivery.

"I knew him," J.J. said without looking back to Eric. "We were never really close. It's just such a shame when someone is cut down in the prime of life. Like your fiancé, for instance. You said she was going to work with your firm. Patterson was leaving the newspaper for a bigger and brighter investigative gig on TV in Chicago. I never meant to imply anything further."

Wait! Ritter was going to work in Chicago? Shit! Maybe the world actually did lay at his feet. This had been intended in the literal sense and not simply a figurative notion. A television position in the Chicago market would certainly be something worth staying alive for. Maybe he hadn't purposely driven into that telephone pole.

All of his presumptions about Ritter were changing rapidly, spinning from one theory to the next and then circling back.

"I didn't know that," Eric heard himself say.

With no thought to the consequences, almost as if by rote, he withdrew his leather-wrapped flask from an inside pocket of his jacket and unscrewed the top. That's when he realized J.J. Jacobs, a news lady, was watching his every move. He shrugged off being caught by her and took a long hit of the single-malt, nonetheless. When finished, he offered the flask to her as he had done with Jillian.

She silently declined, disgusted by the offer. She put her sunglasses back on and said almost as an afterthought.

"Sorry to see Patterson wasn't the only one crippled by that accident."

He would have been offended if it hadn't rang so true.

FORTY

_T_he return trip went much quicker than the original drive to Galesburg, perhaps due in part to the amount of scotch poured into his empty Starbucks cup. Even an inexperienced drinking driver understands Troopers frown upon flasks and rarely suspect used coffee cups.

As Eric drank and drove, he wrestled with a sensation he couldn't quite explain. Before eventually climbing back into the legal trenches, these feelings were always along the lines of dread, portending bad things. It's like waiting for that other proverbial shoe to drop. In his early days of alcoholism, rarely was it ever a good shoe. But that was then.

As a fully functioning alcoholic with a newfound purpose, these feelings were different. It was still a forewarning, but it was no longer angst and anxiety ridden. It was more like an intuition. Scary, right? It seemed to be propelling him forward, inching him closer to something. What, though? Old dread had been replaced by new frustration because he couldn't quite figure out what was churning in his mind and where it was trying to lead him.

So he continued chasing.

He realized it had everything to do with J.J. Jacobs. It had to. There was the Gradeen email reading, "News says wrong reporter killed," and there was his just-concluded visit with the _right reporter._ There had to be a connection. She had to be involved. Could it be that the _wrong reporter_ was really the _right reporter_? Or possibly the other way around?

He recalled her story about the Gradeen and DeBisshop argument, both staring at her while arguing; this didn't somehow fit. Plus, it was the only time she'd claimed to ever be around Jameson Gradeen. If the dust-up had been staged for her benefit as suggested, to what end? And why then had DeBisshop been so quick to curse under his breath and apologize profusely? Was he sorry about what she saw or what he said?

On a broader note, did DeBisshop's seeking forgiveness mean he carried an affinity for her as she appeared to for him? Had he cared what she thought? Had he felt bad for her personally about maybe being played professionally, if indeed the disagreement drama had been all for show?

What if it hadn't? If the two had been at such odds at that time, why no other reports of heated exchanges or a falling out between them? Where are the angry emails? Or had they just not made it to the offices of *Donaldson, Clements*?

Maybe it had been all for show, but again, *Why*? Why would they want J.J. witnessing an argument between them? What preplanned purpose did it serve?

But what if they hadn't wanted her to see? What if she'd stumbled upon the argument and they were watching her to ensure she couldn't overhear them, or read their lips?

And how does thanking DeBisshop fit into this mess? You hire someone to kill someone, and they mistakenly kill the wrong someone. You learn of this and then feel obliged to thank your partner in crime?

Not hardly.

It's possible by remembering the email timeline this was the first Gradeen had heard about the mistake. Maybe he'd never intended to convey gratitude. It's hard to deduce emotion from someone's email with limited context, but maybe it was sarcastic, not necessarily *Thanks* as much as *Thanks for nothing.*

Not bad. I thought he might be on to something, but did that get us any closer to . . . *What?*

It was about here where I mentioned the same white pickup that followed us *to* Galesburg was behind us again. Eric's mind remained elsewhere, telling me there's lots of white pickups on Illinois highways or sidewalks. Off the cuff he reminded me that almost every farm in America has a battered white pickup. I didn't debate his so-called facts. Instead I pointed out that while this may indeed be true, this looked to be possibly the same guy behind the wheel.

Eric adjusted the rearview to take a quick look and then took a sip from his coffee cup. Soon thereafter he changed lanes and exited south onto I-55 back toward Springfield. The truck in question continued on I-74. Part of me was pissed I'd been wrong, but quickly relief overtook my misplaced emotion. Eric had not been the only one shaken by the sidewalk incident.

I mentioned we'd lost him, but he didn't react. His mind had ventured off to contemplate the latest bit of Ritter news. And as we have seen of late, Ritter was no longer the total dick anymore. What was he then? Was he back to being a victim? Eric couldn't answer these questions.

To him, Ritter was now an enigma, a dick who put him through the gambit of alcoholic emotions, running from *A* all the way to *B*. He'd hated him, then hated him even more. But could a guy with a TV job waiting for him in Chicago purposely drive his car into a telephone pole solely to rob Eric of Erin?

So the drive back to Springfield was occupied at one time or another by a dialogue about either Gradeen, DeBisshop or Ritter. Sometimes it was Gradeen and DeBisshop or Ritter, and other times it was all three whipped-up together into something which resembled a scotch-addled lather.

Things got quiet when he noticed an old rusty farm implement sitting in a field off to the right side of the highway. Like most of the state, the ground around it was flat for as far as the eye could see. It looked to be an older-model John Deere, probably out there for years, its tell-tale green and yellow colors faded and corroded. The larger back tires looked flat. The front tires were completely gone, nothing but metal rims choked by weeds. It was as if the field had been recently mowed except for a grass jungle around the tractor.

Eric understood the symbolic significance of this intimate pastural scene. He was the tractor. The weeds were alcohol, surrounding him, suffocating him. Seeing the tractor in the field made him think about Jameson Gradeen saying how, for simplicity's sake around nonfarmers, it was easier to refer to all farm implements as tractors. Eric was a tractor.

And he was stuck out in that field without working tires. Plus, those weeds weren't going to get mown on their own. This reminded him that rehab awaited, but that realization didn't keep him from taking another swig.

It was about this time his cell rang. He fished it out of his pocket, expecting the screen to reveal the caller to be Jillian. Instead it was a number he didn't recognize.

"Mr. McKegney?" the caller asked.

"It is. Who's calling?"

"Shane West from --."

"Hi, Shane. Did you find anything out on that fax number?"

"I did. The number is registered to Vernice Harrison." There was hesitation on Shane's part prior to saying the name as if he had maybe glanced away to read it off a sheet of paper.

Eric asked, "Bernice? With a B?"

"No. Vernice with a V like in Victor. It's Victor, Echo, Romeo. Sorry. What's N?"

"N is November."

Eric replied almost by rote since it was his birth month. His mind instead had stayed on Romeo, realizing that whoever Vernice Harrison might be, that fax had doomed any chance he might ever have with Juliet.

Shane asked, "Does the name mean anything to you?"

It hadn't initially, but when he gave it some thought it became clear. The sender was fucking Sarge. That bastard. He'd almost admitted as much when they argued about faxing Fuller's photo so Sarge wouldn't give up his e-fax number.

It made sense: George and Vernice Harrison. She was probably one of his ten or twelve ex-wives. As one of the firm's investigators,

Sarge would have already been inside the firewall of the VDI. There was no reason to expect the outside fax number wasn't securely inside also. It provided perfect anonymity.

That part had been easy to decipher. Sarge's motives, though, were a different story.

And Eric thought they were supposed to be friends.

ather than head straight back to his townhome, Eric exited the Interstate and detoured through town on South Grand Avenue. I asked where we were going, but he didn't answer. I hoped we weren't going to look for Sarge because that wouldn't end any way but ugly.

When I voiced my concerns, I was told "You'll see," and "To relax." Easier said than done.

Pretty soon we pulled past a Bank of Springfield branch and into the parking lot of a JC Penny. Were we going shopping?

Rather than take a parking spot near the store, Eric pulled over to the farthest corner of the lot. There sat a stand-alone building bearing a *For Sale* banner stretched across channel lettering spelling out the name *Faces*.

We'd returned to the scene of the original crime, where Ann Flannery was murdered.

Eric fished through his backpack and withdrew a fifth of Glenfiddich and a file folder. Inside the folder was a computer-generated schematic of what the responding police officers discovered on that late Friday night / early Saturday morning last summer.

It took a few minutes for him to get his bearings. The lines painted on the surface for the parking lot were different since a car dealer sharing the same parking lot had poached several spaces, their cars facing Grand Avenue. He ended up going to the front door and pacing off the distance to determine where the two bodies of the victims had been found.

Eric had never been to *Faces*. He and Erin had talked about going once or twice but never made it, for it wasn't really their scene. Their parents or grandparents maybe. After the murder, it was described as a *nightclub*. A more apt description would be *Supper Club*.

The difference between the two is the average age of its patrons. *Faces* was not a spot for rock bands. It catered more to a big band audience. Story was that's why *Faces* didn't make it. A nightclub can survive a shooting in the parking lot. It's almost expected and sometimes good for business. It's the exact opposite for a supper club. No one wants to dine and dance where people were murdered, even if it was outside in the parking lot.

Eric studied the diagram, looking around to picture how this scene may have looked on that fateful night. This called for imagination. He stood in a secluded part of the parking lot, a good distance from the front door. On a Friday night, there would have been several cars parked all the way out here.

None were here now. Nor was it dark. The light poles were evenly spaced, but there was no way to tell if all the lights were in working order, or how well illuminated the lot might have been that night, or whether lighting mattered. The drawing gave no indication.

He stood where according to the diagram it was estimated Steinhauer had stood, envisioning slipping out from between a few nearby cars and surprising his victims. He raised his arm as if aiming a weapon. Weathers would have been on his right and Ann Flannery more to his left.

Aloud he asked no one, "Aren't you the woman from the news?"

He then turned to where Weathers would have been standing and fired his finger gun. *Bang!* He spun slightly to the left and fired two more times toward Ann Flannery. *Bang! Bang!*

Why did this seem so strange? What was he missing?

Even the worst hitman in Springfield should know to take out the man first; he had to be deemed the greater threat. And yet Patrick Weathers is merely shot once in the shoulder and Ann Flannery mortally, two to the chest.

We know from Weathers' account of events he was shot first, but not fatally. Obviously, of the two of them, he was not the intended target. Yet then we learn later, Ann Flannery wasn't either.

How does Freddy Steinhauer make such a grave mistake?

Eric and I began a peculiar roleplay exercise. I became Freddy Steinhauer and he played the part of whoever hired me. We started with a simple question neither of us ever thought we'd consider, let alone voice.

"How much information do you give a hired killer?"

Say you want to kill Ann Flannery and hire me to do it. Wouldn't you ask if I knew the intended victim, or could at least recognize her? This would be for no other reason than eliminating the need to describe her? Maybe a photo is supplied and you tell me where she'll be and when to do it. But what else?

Take away questions about compensation -- the how much and how I'm being paid. What else matters to me possibly besides the getaway?

Nothing. The *Who? What? Where? When?* and *How much?* are all covered, but I still kill the wrong person.

Where's our disconnect? How'd our signals get crossed? Or better yet, who crossed them? If Eric's the guy calling the shots, it's not him. Or at least he'll never admit as much. So it has to be me, or better yet, Freddy Steinhauer.

Hell, he confessed as much over the phone to Olivia Jacobsen.

So Freddy fucked up; it wasn't bad intel. Wait in the parking lot and kill Ann Flannery when she and her friend leave *Faces*. His instructions could not have been clearer? But the simpleton nevertheless finds a way to screw it up.

Or did he?

What if his instructions were exact, word for word? Wait in the parking lot and kill Ann Flannery when she leaves the club. What if he was not an idiot but doing exactly as ordered?

Too bad no one ever got the chance to ask him.

J.J. just told Eric she was not at *Faces* that Friday night. She met coworkers for a drink someplace else after the late telecast. If she was truly the intended target, why was Freddy Steinhauer here that night? Why was he not wherever she was having drinks with coworkers?

Let's go a different direction and assume for argument's sake Steinhauer got bad information. Let's say he was told Olivia Jacobsen would be here. Or maybe the info was less specific, no names, merely the fact that his target was a lady from TV.

So does he ask her about that solely for confirmation, or was it too dark for him to tell on his own? Or maybe his vision was limited by the Cinderella mask, so he wanted to make sure he wasn't killing the wrong lady.

But wait. Pitch black or bright as day, seeing the world through a mask's eyeholes or even with closed eyes, didn't Sarge mention Ann Flannery was a sister, an African American?

His exact phrase had been, "She was one of us?"

Regardless of the instructions, whether thorough, partial or nonexistent, shouldn't anyone -- or worse yet, everyone – be able to differentiate between a mature African American of *Supper Club* age and a younger white girl who would rarely visit such an establishment?

But Freddy hadn't.

What if Freddy followed his instructions to the letter and when he reported the mission had been accomplished, he's informed it was the wrong reporter? Maybe that's how he found out. And that's how he knew he was *Dead Man Walking*. So if they – whoever they may be – were coming after him, he could at least warn Olivia Jacobsen. Isn't that allegedly why he called her?

But even if it all went down like that, Ann Flannery remains the intended target. Freddy's here that night because *she's* here that night. Olivia Jacobsen may have been nothing more than misdirection. Pay attention to the left hand so you don't see what the right hand is doing.

Eric seemed extremely excited by this possible new turn in the investigation until I reminded him of one thing.

Regardless of which reporter was targeted, we still don't know why.

FORTY-TWO

_F_inally home, he walked to his condo after getting his mail in an exact repeat of the previous day. There was a buzzing of the phone in his pocket. Without having to look, he knew he was getting a text from Jillian.

He read, "You need to let me in."

Radio silence had ended.

His first thought was to let her in, to bare his soul and tell her how he feels, but that could only lead to more heartache. After just one week, he was crazy about her. She'd possessed him, yet she was engaged to another man, getting married in three weeks. The best thing at this point was for him to stay clear. It would hurt to see her, to talk to her. She was not getting in right now.

He stared at the screen on his phone, considering how best to reply, or what excuses to trot out in his little dance of avoidance. While regarding possible new steps, three little pulsating bubbles told him she was again texting.

He waited and then read, "Please open the door."

It took him a second to comprehend. Here again was the battle between the _figurative_ and the _literal_. She didn't _figuratively_ want him to let her in; she was _literally_ at his front door.

From down the sidewalk he saw her turn dejectedly from his door and sit on his top step. It appeared as if this time she wasn't leaving.

He started toward her and stopped, just like everything else throughout the day, the starting and stopping persisted.

She wanted to talk, prompting a return of that feeling of dread. Tonight she was going to tell him about her wedding, going to drive home that final nail. This one right through the heart.

I reminded him, "Isn't that what you want to hear from her?"

Rather than continue to the door, he peered at her from behind a big oak tree in the common grounds. Thankfully she wasn't carrying a hammer, holding her cell phone in one hand and what appeared to be a bottle in a brown paper bag in the other. Outside of a serious expression and a large purse thrown over one shoulder, she looked as if she'd stepped right out of a woman's fashion ad, tight blue jeans tucked inside a pair of tan heeled boots, untucked white blouse and camel color vest under a blue and grey patterned blazer that accented her eyes. The cuffs of her blouse were folded back over the jacket sleeves, revealing many bracelets on one wrist and an expensive watch on the other. Her dark hair was down and wavy and swept back, flipping on and off her shoulders as she anxiously turned to survey her surroundings.

He ducked back behind the tree and sent a quick text. "Why are you here?"

His phone rang immediately and he answered it without a word.

"Come on, Eric. Let me in," she said, her patience sounding stretched.

She spun on the stoop to look at his door back over her right shoulder. It was then she spotted him.

He stepped out from behind the tree in the courtyard and she watched as he approached. She smiled uneasily, but it was nonetheless remarkable.

Soon he was at the foot of his five front steps saying, "Hello."

"Hi. How are you?" she asked, still seated and looking down to him.

"What are you doing here?" he asked.

He hadn't intended to sound put off by her presence on his stoop, but he quickly realized he had. Maybe pained would be a better descriptive. Here was the most beautiful woman he may ever know, at his door two days in a row now, and yet he found little pleasure in her unexpected company.

For her part, she looked off in each direction, then her eyes fixed on a place off over Eric's head. He turned to see no neighborhood watch snooping from behind her curtains.

"There's things you need to know," Jillian was saying.

Initially he thought it best to have their conversation right here on the stoop, to not let her in because of a million reasons. Yet with another glance back to Lorrie Ann's condo he reconsidered. He didn't need anyone spying on him and Victoria Secret.

"You want to come in? I wasn't expecting company, so the place is a mess."

She handed him a bottle in a bag. He helped her to her feet without releasing her right hand once she was standing a step above him. He liked being face-to-face. She too smiled at this altered perspective.

He released her hand finally to unlock his front door. He then held it open for her as she stepped up and in, her citrusy fragrance trailing behind.

Once inside, in one deft movement, she dropped her cell into her oversized purse and draped it over the back of a kitchen chair. She glanced around the condo still with packed boxes lining the walls. The decor was extremely stark and masculine, screaming for a woman's touch. She wouldn't change the high-end appliances or the granite counters in the kitchen or the hardwood floors throughout, however. She was in fact a bit jealous of his kitchen, but the spacious living room could use a few plants or stand-up lamps in the corners. As a living space, she'd have to concede it wasn't far from being acceptable. Although, as an office, which it apparently had become, it needed organizing.

Or maybe a leaf blower.

He slipped the bottle from the bag to see it was a French Merlot. He wondered if there was also a glass in her large bag.

She said in a small voice, "I wasn't sure you'd have wine. I'm not ready to switch to scotch, although I could use some of its misguided courage."

He nodded at this, happily picturing the glorious agony on her face after drinking from his flask a few days earlier.

"Want a glass or are you drinking right out of the bottle?"

She thought it odd that an alcoholic would be judging her wine habits but smiled and nodded that a glass would be appreciated. He said to make herself at home, as he stepped into his kitchen to open her wine. She did this by touring his living room,

There were no attempts at further conversation, both knowing it would be strained. Likewise there was no dance around the investigation's developments for that would get them nowhere. She sighed deeply into the new silence, realizing it was her responsibility to get any dialogue started. She looked to his kitchen, His back was to her as he rummaged noisily through a drawer for a corkscrew.

"*Mr. Somebody's* name is Matt Curry," she said in a sheepish voice.

Eric looked up from the drawer and stared straight ahead at the hardware on the cabinet door at eye level. Her words were like a bullet and she'd waited for him to turn so she could shoot him squarely in the back. It was cowardly to do him this way while allowing him to hide his look of wounded devastation.

But he knew all this. He may not have comprehended the last name when he first read it, but he knew the man had to have one. Jillian Stennet-Curry? Why then did this hurt so much? Was it because it happened to him before, that he lost a girl to a rival previously?

First Ritter takes Erin and now Matt Curry takes Jillian? Maybe it wasn't apples, or even oranges, but that didn't lessen his anguish.

She waited for the searching sounds of his hands to resume from the drawer.

Then she said softly, "Sarge told me he sent you a wedding announcement. He feels terrible about that, but . . . I'm hoping you'll let me explain."

But she didn't commence immediately. Her hesitancy was killing him. Still without turning to face her, he opened the bottle of Merlot and poured a glass. Then as he walked toward the table, he swirled the goblet in his hand and set it on the table. Her attention was drawn to the lone framed photo on the mantle above an immaculately clean fire place.

So this was Erin. Her headshot was gorgeous, she thought. Blonde hair and big brown eyes like he'd said, but there was a mussed quality to the photo. She wasn't really smiling. Her hair was far from perfect. There was something so real about her that made it impossible to look away. Instead she took it from its place and held it in both hands like she was reading a book.

He poured himself a scotch, leaning against the counter between two expensive and seldomly-used barstools. He watched her looking intently at Erin as she subconsciously ran an index finger down and across the glass.

"Is she the reason you didn't kiss me or was it Matt Curry?"

His question caught her completely off guard and brought her back to the present yet without a proper response. She recovered enough to replace the photo back on the mantle.

"I don't know. I can't explain what I was thinking . . ."

Her thought had more or less trailed off causing her to sigh heavily, smiling uncomfortably and walking to the table to take a big swig of her wine.

"I wanted to tell you Monday afternoon. That was the perfect time. You bared your soul. I started doing the same, but then I guess I lost my nerve. Now I realize that's why you're avoiding me.

"While I respect you for what you're thinking, you don't . . ."

At this she began to pace aimlessly. Maybe it was the comfort of being on her feet like in a courtroom, but as she walked, she began to talk. There was a detached sense to her story, as if she were communicating with a jury about a client. Eric and I recognized this as the same third-person strategy he always used when telling about the woman in the framed photo.

Jillian was very businesslike, her articulation crisp, her tone measured and practiced. At the same time, however, she stumbled out of the gate, struggling with her emotions.

"We met in law school. He was my professor, older than me. He'd been in private practice before deciding to teach. He was one of the most brilliant legal minds I'd ever encountered, destined for a long and distinguished career as an educator. I was smitten.

"Tutorial sessions and coffee turned into dating. We had to do it in secret. University of Chicago has rules against professors dating student. We were in love. In a crazy way, it was like if he were married and would leave his wife so we could be together. In our case, he wasn't. He had to quit teaching.

"Anyway, he does and takes a job here in Springfield in the State Attorney's office. Naturally I plan to follow him here the minute I graduate. We have this plan and our future is set. Then our forty-fourth president is elected, Illinois' own, and half the attorneys in Springfield follow him to Washington."

She reached for her wine glass on the table and resumed the pacing as her story continued.

"I'm a year from graduating, moving to Springfield. Matt goes to D.C.. It was to be only a few years. One term max. It was great for his career and we could rationalize it would give me the chance to establish myself here in Springfield. On a visit here, he asked me to marry him. I agreed . . . part of my grand plan. Female attorneys are deemed less predatory if married. I could envision life with him, what I'd learn from him. I knew he would challenge me professionally. Wherever we might end up, I was going.

"Anyway, one term in D.C. transitions smoothly into a second. The place must be intoxicating; no one wants to leave. Four years was renegotiated to six, I think we knew it would be a full eight. It no longer mattered. Two becomes four. Four becomes six. Six becomes never.

"Somewhere in those starts and restarts I went from being engaged to Matt Curry, to being engaged to the idea of being engaged. I liked it because it fit my preordained career path. No distractions, plus it was supposed to make me better partner material."

Here she kind of squinted and quickly added, "No firm wants a spinster as a partner.

"The wedding date, June 4th, was set over a year and a half ago. We did it that far in advance to give two busy people time to figure it all out, to move forward toward a date-certain goal. It was like we were a college project. That was the due date. We may procrastinate until the very last minute, but we both knew we'd be ready to turn into a married couple come June."

She stopped the aimless pacing and took a gulp of Merlot, sniffling, and looking off into the distance, somewhere toward the kitchen.

"But it won't be. We won't be. There is no . . . We are no longer . . . I know I realized it some time back. He has too. Being a thousand miles apart was never easy on the engagement, but the distance has proven valuable now. We can almost pretend nothing has changed since neither of us apparently feel the need to broach the topic of whether we're still engaged or not.

"The saddest part of all is that it just kind of went away, lost all momentum, died on its own. There was no declarative statement from him, likewise nothing from me. Certainly no fanfare.

"I may have wasted those years being engaged, but I don't see it that way. It allowed me to focus entirely on my work. I'm extremely good at my job. I love what I do, and the time will pay off when I become partner before turning thirty-five.

"We got engaged almost on a dream and then set a date as the means to an end, like a business arrangement. It was a comfortable fit for us, but neither of us really put forth the effort. Then neither of us wanted to be the first to want out. We entered a holding pattern and have been circling the drain this calendar year. I last saw him and spoke to him at Christmas, but . . ."

She looked down and then away. Whether out of embarrassment or simply to regain focus on her story. I saw it more as her way of starting to wrap it up.

"Yet since Christmas I've continued to wear his ring. I don't have to explain to anyone that I am no longer engaged. Or if I still am, or what happened, because I'm not sure how to succinctly explain it."

Here she tried to smile and anxiously added, "As you can tell."

She paused, giving her next words a great deal of consideration. She turned away from him, apparently unable to face him, but then almost immediately turned right back around.

"I know I should've told this to you sooner. I'm sorry. You deserved better from me. A lot better. You probably think I'm the biggest flirty flake in the world, leading you on one minute and then shutting you down the next. I'm sorry about all that. I'm not a tease and I hate women who are. I am sorrier than you will know, but I'm confused and conflicted, and this *is* complicated. I tried to tell you it was . . . As I also mentioned, you've not made it any easier.

"I've had more fun in the past few days with you than I've had in all the time of being engaged. It was as if you reintroduced me to myself. I liked it. I like the uncertainty, the anxious unknowns, the feeling in my stomach when I'm around you. The longing when you're not. I can't explain it to you because it makes no sense to me. No sense at all."

She spun the wine goblet in her hands.

"At first, I think it was sympathy for you and all you've had to endure. You're damaged goods. I wanted to rescue you. But there's more to it. You're clever and handsome and funny and . . . As crazy as it seems, I like being around you. I like you.

"This flies in the face of everything I've ever done or ever believed and I can't convince myself that I shouldn't. Instead, I like you a lot."

She grinned awkwardly, self-consciously. Closing one eye flirtatiously, she added, "But I also liked wearing the ring. It does a wonderful job of warding off the assholes."

Here she held up her left hand, no longer displaying the huge diamond as she warily wiggled her long and delicate fingers, a tan line visible on the ring finger. At this her body convulsed slightly and she bit her bottom lip to stop the trembling, tears sparkling in her gorgeous eyes.

I recognized it more as relief than anything resembling fear or uncertainty. She'd done it. She'd unburdened herself of almost five years carrying out this perverse pretense. Her charade could finally end, but with it went those years of comfort, five years of knowing exactly who she's supposed to be. Now she was no longer sure.

It was scary. She'd just stepped out into this vast unknown. But when she considered it, it was supposed to be; no major change comes without a little trepidation. She'd taken a tentative step out onto a frozen pond and she wanted this heart-broken, alcoholic, wreck-of-a-man on that thin ice with her. Neither knew how long before it cracked. But right now, she'd rather fall through with him than stand on the shore alone, engaged to an idea.

She also realized, however, that this was more than just a tip-toed step. This was a leap. She was putting herself out there for a guy, and for the first time in who-knows-how-long, she felt unsure. It was frightening, yet exhilarating and liberating at the same time, and her tears kept coming. She closed her eyes and bounced nervously up and down on her toes, wiping the tracks of her tears with her fingertips.

He shifted his weight from his right leg to his left and reached for his tumbler of scotch. He regarded what she'd said. He was either too scared, too stupid or, more likely, too much of a pessimist to grasp the implications of what she was telling him. He was frightened to connect these dots because of where they might lead, too confused, not seeing, like gazing through gauze. Then she removed any doubt, ripping away the veil for him.

She wrapped her arms tightly around herself broadcasting her insecurity, her vulnerability, opening her eyes seemingly with a new resolve, undaunted by her apprehension or her tears. Her continual weakness was nevertheless evidenced by a nibble on one fingernail. Her shoulders drooped. She glanced to the ceiling uncertainly and exhaled up, her dark bangs bouncing.

"I wanted to be in love with Matt, and for a while I did love him," she realized aloud more to herself than to him, the words choking on her emotions, catching in her throat.

"Yet now, here I am, going completely off my script and standing here in front of you."

Through a lost little girl smile, she added in a whisper, "I think this is the part where you're supposed to give me a hug and tell me I'm not making a huge mistake."

He never hesitated, walking right up to her, her eyes offering unlimited glistening possibilities as she stared openly up at him. He grabbed her around the waist, drawing her into him and kissed her. It was just like he and I talked about the other night. He kissed her and he meant it. He kissed her for keeps, and outside of an initial hesitancy or possibly more out of surprise, she never once hesitated or tried to push him away. Instead she kissed him back.

And she continued kissing him until her body folded into his, and their hug melted into a passionate embrace.

And *This,* complete with the little back-and-forth gesture, had taken on a completely new meaning.

FORTY-THREE

*E*ric admitted to me later, regardless of sounding clichéd, he thought maybe he'd dreamt the whole episode. Alcohol does that, tempers some memories while amplifying others. This one echoed loudly.

He awoke alone in a tousled knot of sheets, with no idea where Jillian was. Her clothes were strewn around his bedroom, so she hadn't left. He'd never been diligent about keeping his bed made, but it resembled a wrestling ring. He'd apparently been pinned, yet it had been the grandest defeat of his life.

He wasn't the kind to kiss and tell, never relating bedroom tales about Erin, and remembering very few with Lorrie Ann. This time, however, was different. He left out the more salacious details, instead going on and on about her scent everywhere, the pillows, the sheets, him. And as he lay there reveling in her fragrance, he recalled images and sensations that made him smile.

He'd laughingly labeled it like a dance, a clumsy ballet of sorts between an exotic French ballerina and a guy with two left feet. There was a sense of grace to each of her movements, borne from years of dance training and discipline, yet for his part, he lacked the rhythm to follow. Initially, they never found themselves in sync, but in this somewhere was the fun. It was awkward and almost goofy, but that was okay. They giggled at their own expense and at each other, rolling and almost grappling and all the while laughing. Maybe it was this comfort found in each other that had made it so enjoyable. Eventually, exhaustion found them both and entangled them in each other.

She'd fallen asleep first, her head on his chest, soft hair framing a face turned up to him. He so wanted to wake her if only to gaze into those eyes from so close, yet she seemed just as beautiful with her eyes closed. Her lashes were dark and long, her eyebrows perfect and symmetrical. She seemed so at peace, so comfortable in his arms, with long deep, contented breaths in and out that he could feel tickling his chest hair. He pulled her closer and snugged the sheet around them. They finally found a tempo, although in sleep.

He now wrapped that same striped sheet around himself like a toga and ventured downstairs to find her working at his kitchen table. He viewed her in profile. She was wearing his white dress shirt, sleeves rolled so it wouldn't swallow her completely. Her dark legs were crossed with her right foot bouncing regularly. Her hair was up, held with a clip from the back, her glasses on and a pen brushing against her lips, as she perused the Gradeen biography, jotting notes on a legal pad. Except for her near nakedness and a glass of wine in front of her, you'd think she was at the conference table in McGraw's office.

This is the part where he told me about his apprehension, his nervousness about things now being somehow different, that maybe their clumsy tango had meant more to him. Doubt would be a better word, and no one is immune from the dissonance of the unknown, or in his case the unexpected. They weren't in Kansas anymore. But when she noticed him and smiled, he knew such fears were unfounded.

Then his retelling got almost syrupy if not sappy. He told me how all along he'd considered her an exceptionally beautiful woman, and her lying naked in his bed had only enhanced that belief. Yet somehow, she looked better now. There was an almost larger-than-life component. Had she transformed or was he seeing her through new eyes? He struggled to explain it, butchering a flower-in-bloom metaphor and some other inane and uneducated comparison to works of art. At least he hadn't commented about her "glow."

He never said as much, but I knew the work of art to which he had been trying to equate was the girl in the framed photo on the mantle. He'd deny it if asked, but all concerns about doubt and difference, and even Kansas for that matter, all came back to her. Would Erin approve of what he was doing?

"Hi," Jillian said in an upbeat yet casual tone, looking up from her work. "I thought I'd let you sleep. Also, I borrowed your shirt. I hope you don't mind."

"Not at all."

A wise rogue, when asked his favorite woman's outfit, had answered, "My dress shirt." Okay. I'm that rogue, but the image proved the adage.

She held out her left arm, inviting him to join her. When he did, she leaned her head back so they could kiss. She was amazing, so relaxed without any second thought or worry about sitting at his kitchen table, wearing a barely buttoned next-to-nothing.

They kissed like they do it every morning. The rhythm missing in bed had apparently been in the kitchen the entire time. There was already a comfort, like an old married couple, and he had to smile at it.

"What?" she asked, suddenly concerned by his expression.

Still behind her, his hands gingerly placed on her shoulders, his eyes trying to get a glimpse down the unbuttoned shirt, he tried his best to explain the irony.

"When I thought about *this*," he began, removing one hand just long enough to make the circling gesture where she could see it. "I wasn't worried about the bedroom part. I was concerned about what might happen now. I didn't want it to seem awkward."

"Do you think it does?" she nervously asked.

"Not at all. It's like we've done the *morning-after* countless times already."

She tilted her head back so she could see him and smiled widely.

"First, it's not yet morning. It's barely ten o'clock. That is why I'm having a glass of wine. Secondly, my worries were the exact opposite. Maybe it's the way women think versus men. I knew this part would be normal. That's the thing about you. You are who you are, no games, easy to be around."

Here she averted her gorgeous eyes and added coyly, "And I'm thinking next time the other part will be better since it had been a while for either of us. We're both pretty rusty."

Ouch! While it may have been a long time for her, he'd been rehearsing on Wednesdays and every other weekend for a few months. And yet he'd been described as *rusty*. He'd have to up his game.

He said, "I'd describe you as many things but rusty is not one of them."

She laughed at this, the flirty giggle escaping from under her hand. "I'll count on your gallantry to keep those descriptions to yourself."

"Deal. Are you hungry? I realized I never ate dinner. Did you?"

"You can cook too?" she asked in what I'd consider a complimentary tone.

"I was only going to scramble some eggs. Would you like some?"

"No thanks. I'm fine." She gazed over at him for a beat before asking, "How'd you figure out this book was the key to the email code?"

"I'll tell you, but I don't want you to think less of me."

"It's already a pretty low bar."

She again laughed, but this time much more assuredly. Maybe it was the wine or a post-coital glee, but she was in a playful mood.

So he chuckled in spite of himself and forgot all about scrambling eggs. He told her about being in her backyard and hearing Dave Koz over her stereo, always one of Erin's favorites. He told her how he'd then gone by the cemetery and that's when it all came to him.

"It was almost as if the song was Erin's way of asking me to stop by so she could explain it to me."

"Why did you run off from my house?"

"The thunder gave me away and I was afraid you were going to sic your dog on me."

"Clint?" she laughed, seemingly at the absurdity of the idea. "He's a teddy bear. If he had any desire to chase you he was only hoping you'd throw a tennis ball for him."

He liked this idea and asked, "You two a package deal?"

"You bet we are." She'd never hesitated.

I observed that this was the first hint of a future for them. To this point it was all about their respective pasts, places they were coming from as opposed to where they might be headed. Neither seemed to react, but I'm guessing both noticed it too. And as was their natures, both hesitated around the edges without either stepping more deeply into *This* complete with . . . Well you know.

Jillian finally broke the gawking silence, saying she'd deciphered one more email and organized the others into chronological order. She mentioned the process would go much faster with extra copies of the biography.

"Funny thing. I went by *The Book Knook* where I picked up that one and they were all sold out. There were four on the shelf Monday."

"Who would buy four copies since then?"

"I wondered the same. I was told a large man in a white shirt and red tie."

She looked up, her perfect brows bunching and asked, "Firm security?"

"That was my first thought, but it doesn't make sense. It was Sarge's idea to get more copies. Maybe he told McGraw and he sent security? I don't know."

Then changing to a new Sarge topic, he asked, "Did he call you for advice on what to do about Fuller? He thinks he may have a positive I.D. on him."

"Me? No, but that's great news."

"He called to ask how I thought he should handle it. I told him to check with you or McGraw."

"That means he asked Mr. McGraw. Would he have told him you cracked the code?"

He considered this and answered, "That's the only thing that makes sense."

Wait," she said, removing her glasses and nibbling on one of the ear pieces. "Work through that."

They did it together. He tells Sarge about the book being the key. They assume Sarge tells McGraw when he called for instructions on handling Fuller. McGraw then sends firm's security to buy the remaining copies. They're all gone when Eric returns to *The Book Knook*.

Eric considered the unidentified fax and said, "I'm beginning to question Sarge's motives in this."

"I can't believe he'd do anything to impede the investigation."

"Maybe you're right. Afterall it was his idea to decode emails from around a specific date to help me determine who's who."

Jillian said, "Nevertheless, if it went down like we think at the bookstore, this throws suspicion on both Sarge and McGraw. If he sent security to buy the remaining books, how is that helping us?"

"Does McGraw have other teams working on the decoding?"

"No," she answered immediately. "I'd know if there were."

"If it was McGraw who sent security to the bookstore, and for the sake of this let's say it was, why hasn't he told us about the extra copies?"

"Because maybe McGraw doesn't want you to know."

Eric was having trouble following but noticed one thing. Jillian had begun to refer to their boss now simply as McGraw, no longer *Mr. McGraw*. It was as if once aspersions were cast, formality and respect due the man vanished.

"Why would he want to slow down the decoding of the emails?"

Her eyes widened and she banged excitedly on the tabletop. "He knows what's in them!"

"Wait. What?"

She sprang from her chair and started the aimless pacing again. The way the oversized shirt hung on her, he could tell she was wearing nothing underneath. *Not-a-thing.* Her sleek and tanned dancer's legs were making it awfully hard for him to concentrate. But she was doing most of the deductive reasoning for both of them.

"Either McGraw has broken the code or someone broke it for him."

Eric recalled the man's reaction to the Gradeen biography discussion at Monday's meeting. He already knew the book is the key to the code and that's why he'd downplayed it's importance.

"Think about it," she said, stopping suddenly. "If the firm's security bought the books to help, you'd know by now. Therefore we must assume McGraw wants to impede any progress on decoding."

"Isn't that obstruction of justice?"

"Technically it's spoliation of evidence."

Her clarification had come almost as a postscript, like she used the phrase every day. She resumed pacing.

"McGraw knows everything in the emails. He's taken precautions to make sure we only have one copy of the damned book. He knows this won't stop the deciphering, only slow it. The code is the Alamo, and he knows you're already breached the walls."

Eric smiled at the reference and leaned back in his chair. Finally he asked, "Do you think Gradeen knows McGraw broke his code?"

"Good question," she said slowly, regarding this idea for the first time. "I'll ask him in the morning."

"I'll have to ask. If you do, then he'll know you're helping."

"Good point." She then refocused and excitedly leaned forward. "Let's do this. You skip the 9:00 with Jameson. I'll make up some reason. That way the email subject isn't broached. My involvement with the code, and my presence here, will never come up. And you will not be missed."

He wasn't sure how that last comment made him feel, but she was already on to the next topic. She reached for a legal pad and paged through her notes to get to an empty sheet.

Looking up, she asked, "What are we missing? What's possibly here that McGraw doesn't want us to know just yet?"

"The known unknowns," he said.

She smiled at this and suggested together they review the email she'd recently deciphered.

"DeBisshop was the sender. Most of the talk centers around *Top Hat*, which according to your list is *The Magic Box*. That's Telemetrics, right?"

He corrected her on the pronunciation. "It's Telematics. They capture data from farming equipment in the field and transfer it to a centralized location in real time. The same technology is in newer cars. The onboard computers send diagnostics to the dealers or manufacturers similar to how tractors tell when maintenance is required. This is also the technology insurance companies use to grade your driving abilities."

She considered this and asked, "But it is a one-way street, right? Did you find anything about info being sent back to the tractor?"

He thought about her question for a beat and then said, "GPS coordinates only. Why?"

She leaned forward, elbows on the table, the barely-buttoned dress shirt gapping provocatively, and removed her glasses.

"You remember Jameson's description of his *Magic Box*? What if he's figured out a way to send explicit instructions in both directions?"

"He told us he's doing that. He's steering tractors remotely in a field."

"What if it is more than just steering tractors?"

She'd asked this with the tip of her glasses in her mouth. Not waiting for him to answer this question, she was again on to more.

"What if they can take it out of the field and onto the road? Or out of the field and onto the battlefield?"

He leaned across the table to glance at her notes. "Wow! You might be onto something."

"There are several coded mentions in these emails about *The Pentagon*. Who would benefit more from *Magic Box* technology than the military? Think about a robot army with automated trucks and tanks, no soldiers, all controlled from a central location."

"That's science fiction. From what I read, that's way in the future."

"What if Jameson has figured out a way to make that future now? It would explain a lot."

Eric piled on, "Like the reasons for all the security measures at the farm. I visited with Olivia Jacobsen today. I wish I'd known this prior to see if she or Ann Flannery were working on anything with a military angle."

"Regardless, who does Jameson see as a threat? If he's working with the Army, does he have to keep secrets from the Navy, or the Air Force?"

"What if it's not our military, but maybe a foreign one?" Eric asked. Then he added, "Or more likely from his competitors?"

Jillian agreed this made more sense. Corporate espionage versus corporate security was an oft-fought battle. Why go to the effort and the cost of building something when you can just steal the intellectual property? This would explain his overabundance of security. But is it worth having someone killed?

Eric brought up the one historical motive worth killing for.

"Think of the money they're potentially sitting on. Can you imagine how much we're talking about if they get military contracts? Any military. His four-hundred and seventy-five million dollars becomes walking-around money."

"Or even government funding for research," she said, leading in to another discovery. "This email from Jameson talks about funding already received. There is more than one mention of it."

"Olivia Jacobsen said nothing about any of this."

"Would she have understood what she had? If there's malfeasance, whether with government money or private money, would a reporter recognize that?"

This time it was Eric banging on the table. "What if McGraw's an investor? Or even a partner in this? He stands to make millions, while at the same time, if they're defrauding the government he stands to go directly to jail without passing *Go*. He can't afford to let anyone find this out."

She hated to discourage him, but there were rules. She hoped he understood McGraw could not be personally involved as both investor and legal counsel because of the conflicts inherent in such aberrant linkage. But she conceded he was on to something with the money angle. Profit can be a compelling motive.

Eric continued traveling down that road. "The partners own the building which houses your firm. *Donaldson, Clements* does not own the building. The partners of *Donaldson, Clements* do. The partnership is its own distinct legal entity. The partners could own shares in the Gradeen companies."

Again, he saw a two-dimensional investigation from a three-dimensional viewpoint. What would stop the partners from investing together as a group besides the myriad of disclosure statements required in such a convoluted situation? Maybe they'd use a shell company. At the same time, she considered she was a few years from hopefully being a member of that influential group.

"I think you might have veered a little off course here."

He smiled at her good-natured scolding and acknowledged his lapse in focus.

"But I'm close," he said. "It's right there. I can't quite get a handle on it."

She stood abruptly and grabbed him by the hand without another word, leading him and his toga back upstairs. After their dress rehearsal, it was time for the real performance.

Her motives were more than mere carnal pleasure, for she too was "getting close." Hers was a hope another sexual release might clear her head. Something was chipping away at her brain that she couldn't quite yet grasp. It had nothing to do with the firm's partners and their business ventures, and everything to do with motives behind controlling the number of Thomas Gradeen biographies.

Was it done to speed up or to slow down the deciphering process? If the latter, was it so Eric would get no help? If it were the former, from where would the help arrive? Regardless of how long it might take, whatever was in those emails would be coming out eventually.

Why then did it seem as if Eric would determine the timing?

FORTY-FOUR

She stared at the ceiling, Eric's head resting cozily on a pillow near her right shoulder. There was a smile with the realization that, after a few years' hiatus, she'd found herself back in the puppy rescue game. She hoped this little orphan might stick around for a while, but experience had taught her strays have a way of doing what they want. She could nurture him, offer him a warm bed, but that didn't guarantee he'd stay.

She'd initially dozed off after a better choreographed and incredibly aerobic grand performance and slept fitfully. Her dreams were haunted by fractured images she was unable to coalesce into a coherent picture. Now again awake, she continued fighting with the feeling that whatever she was missing somehow affected him more than her.

It all came back to the number of biographies. Someone, presuming it was McGraw, had gone to great lengths to ensure Eric possessed the only key to the cipher. But why? The only reason which made sense was there was something in there intended for Eric's eyes only. Whatever that might be, if any of her suppositions were in fact true, why couldn't McGraw just tell him? What secrets were the two of them harboring? She didn't enjoy being the third wheel.

While on the topic of secrets, she and Eric had made the tentative parking garage pact on that first night which now seemed like forever ago. They'd agreed if it came to it, it would be the two of them against McGraw. Regardless of the games or the maneuvering, the posturing or the backstabbing, they'd be on the same team. Was their pact still in force? Funny how things can change in one lifetime of a week. It hadn't been easy to get to this point, but now she felt as though she had to protect Eric, even if from her boss.

With all this percolating through her mind, she knew it would be impossible to fall back asleep. Orgasms always wound her up, and now after a short catnap borne of sheer physical exhaustion, she was wide awake. She slipped out of bed, found the still-buttoned dress shirt on the floor where he'd pulled it over her head and was soon back to work at the kitchen table.

This time she didn't randomly grab isolated emails leading up to the Ann Flannery murder. She knew exactly what she was looking for and right where to look. She might never be able to explain how or why, but she knew.

Her question was no longer *Why only Eric was to have the key?* McGraw could have done this solely to keep the remaining copies out of the hands of the prosecution. She would not put it past him.

The true question went all the way back to the beginning: *Why Eric in the first place?*

It seemed like an unusual arrangement at the outset. Who hires a personal injury lawyer to fill out a criminal defense team? The man had no criminal experience, let alone defending a client. Yet, McGraw insisted he join the team, despite her initial objections, forcing her to work side-by-side with a heartsick, alcoholic *Ambulance Chaser.*

And guess what. In less than one week, two unexpected things happened. First, he'd proven very adept at the intricacies of a criminal law investigation, and secondly, they'd ended up in bed together.

She cleared this from her mind and meticulously went to work deciphering the one particular email sent by one of the anonymous G-mail accounts to Jameson. It was quick and relatively simple, like a Connect-the-dot puzzle from grade school. Number by number, or in this case, word by word, she inched closer to the final picture, her sense of foreboding mirroring her progress. The sender had gotten lazy in that many of the coded words had come from the same page of the book. Her decoding was happening almost too quickly. She wanted to know the end result, yet at the same time not know; she wanted her suspicion to be right, yet also to be oh-so wrong.

At about three quarters of the way through, she realized there were very few new codenames; the principal characters were spoken of more in very general terms. *The Pentagon* was mentioned again, plus *Reporter* and *Top Hat*, which they believed to be the *Magic Box*. There was also a veiled allusion to *James Dean*, but nowhere in the notes was there any reference as to who this might be. Or who might be the sender.

She could see where this was going without having to finish and no longer wanted to go there. The idea sickened her, yet there was nowhere to look away. Who would have imagined anybody could do this?

She was still a professional; she would have to be. She dealt with terrible people before and had no qualms about defending them. Afterall, that was her job. Regardless of the crime, terrible people were entitled to a vigorous defense and a fair trial. Guilt or innocence never enters the equation.

As she had told Eric early on, "Because it never matters to the defense."

But that now sounded like naiveté since that was before all this. What she just learned was different and fatal, evidence ending them, ending *This* with the back-and-forth gesture, nipping whatever bud blossomed between them.

When she finished translating the email, the last of the many dots and words connecting to form a traumatic and surreal picture, tears filled her eyes. The whole concept of this was so unfortunate and sad, but everything finally made sense. *Why Eric?* and then *Why only Eric?* This one email answered both.

She took a sip of single-malt for courage from his tumbler still on the table, one hand covering her mouth, glancing up the staircase. This little bit of news would change everything for him, for them. Yet did it have to?

What if she deleted it and others around that time? Who would know besides her? McGraw would, but who really gets hurt? Wouldn't they have to thank her for burying it?

As an officer of the court, she never could -- nor ever would -- do such a thing. Ethics can be a bitch. Yet, on second thought, could she keep the awful secret from Eric? Would it spare him the news or deprive him the opportunity to avenge it? He would definitely find out. Of all people, Eric deserved to know what she'd uncovered. He'd earned it. In the end, it was only fair for him to be the one to decide the next steps.

Afterall, isn't this exactly how McGraw intended?

But this would no doubt put her and Eric on opposing sides, with her in the wrong. She's now complicit. Her tenure at *Donaldson, Clements* and projected career path, both now seemingly in jeopardy. She'd put in the time and could see herself a mere two years shy of a junior partnership at the most prestigious law firm in Springfield. She worked hard for it. She earned it.

Then this happens.

Could she summon enough moral outrage to leave the firm over this? Could she choose an alcoholic *Ambulance Chaser* over her comfortable professional home for those years? It was that black and white, that binary. Eric or McGraw?

She thought back to her parents, knowing what each of them would advise. Her mother, the dancer, the dreamer, would tell her to jump on and ride with Eric regardless of the final destination. True love is hard to find. The enjoyment and excitement are in the journey, the unexpected, the unknown. Go with your heart. Roll the dice. Bet on Eric McKegney. Choose love.

Her father, the practical angel, sat on her other shoulder, cautioning her to do the reverse. Falling in love is easy; staying in love requires two selfless soulmates. That man is trouble, an undisciplined alcoholic still in love with his dead fiancé. Try as you might, and despite your best intentions, you'll never change either of those. He'll leave you heartsick and alone. Life with him will lack the financial stability you've enjoyed at *Donaldson, Clements*. Get out of his bed, put that ring back on and act like tonight never happened.

She got up from the table and tiptoed back up to his bedroom. For good measure she brought along the tumbler of scotch and choked down another sip. From the darkened doorway he looked so at peace lying there, hair mussed and unshaven. She considered climbing in next to him while the opportunity still existed. For once he awoke, this serene little vignette would never again be. She realized then her father was right. Practicality again beat fantasy the same way law school had trumped dancing. Sorry again, Mom.

I couldn't argue with her choice. As much as I care for Eric, I mentioned if she leaves *Donaldson, Clements* over this, that door closes forever. If she gets dressed and sneaks out, her bridge with Eric would definitely be ablaze, but not yet totally engulfed. There's the chance over time that the fire might be doused and a new bridge rebuilt.

I promised to help her, yet it was disingenuous. I found myself in that uncomfortable position of having to choose sides in a breakup. I *really* like Jillian, but I like Eric more. Plus I've known him longer. We've shared a lot. It's not that I wouldn't like sharing as much with her, but she was stabbing my friend in the back. My loyalties lie with Eric.

So, having made her dreadful decision, she gathered up her clothes to dress downstairs. She took a long inhale of his dress shirt as she removed it, sadly taking in the starchy cologne aroma one last time. She dressed quickly, quietly. Then it was back to the table staring at the top sheet on a new legal pad.

She unconsciously wrote his name at the top, as if her note could be intended for anyone else. Then she struggled with how to say all she needed. She began with what she uncovered, telling him about struggling with the questions of his involvement.

She regarded this news as lethal, a nuclear bomb potentially in the wrong hands. Yet here she was, presenting it to him like a gift, wrapped with a neat and tidy little bow. She was handing him the means to blow up a number of people. She reminded him of the tremendous obligation which comes with such power. She wrote that she would disavow any knowledge of the decoded email and that it would be up to him to determine how best to handle the information. Her clandestined role in any decoding was now officially closed.

As almost a post script, or better yet, as the intro to the next part of her note, she added, "Maybe this is the best time for this to happen, because it changes everything for both of us. I'm so sorry."

Then it was on to the more difficult and heart-wrenching portion of her note. Here she bit her lip and wiped her eyes, rehearsing in her mind not only what needed to be said but also how best to say it. After her third forced-down slug of misguided courage, it went something like this:

"We both knew last night was inevitable. That doesn't lessen how much I enjoyed myself or what it meant to me, what you mean to me. Regrettably, it can never happen again, nor can we talk about it. What's done is done. I'm counting on you as a gentleman that no one ever finds out."

Sadly she closed with, "I'm so sorry. Good-bye, Eric," and signed her name.

Two isolated tears ran down her cheeks and dripped onto the legal pad near the bottom, tiny puddles being absorbed and spreading, darkening the yellow sheet. She'd offered herself to him a few scant hours before only to now rip herself away.

As she let herself out of his condo, the grey of the early morning rising in the east, she accepted her betrayal for the first time. She was slinking away rather than face him with no discussion of any possible third option. Unlike the dawn sky, her decision offered no grey.

And she would forever have to live with it and her cowardice.

Her father wins again.

FORTY-FIVE

*T*he commotion down the hall around the corner from Jillian's office on *Seven* began shortly after 9:30. She and Jameson Gradeen were on their second cup of coffee, having spent the last half hour discussing court dockets, pre-trial motions and the like. She felt as if she was on auto-pilot. It all seemed so contrived, so trivial, for her thoughts remained elsewhere.

She could see her client's mouth moving but was paying little attention. He was a pretentious ass, high on himself, above reproach. Jameson Gradeen liked Jameson Gradeen. You'd think his company had saved the world or something equally magnanimous. He was spewing his bafflegab all over her desk to the point that she fought the urge to hold her nose.

She had to bite her tongue because of the decoded email, the dirty bomb she'd left for Eric. She wasn't sure what might happen when she ran into him since sneaking out and leaving him the note. She wondered how'd he react to seeing her. Would he flash his sad smile or pretend not to see her, or worse yet, not know her? He had to understand her predicament. He had to realize the precarious place in which that email put her. Her Hobson's Choice. She'd been presented with limited options and chose career over him.

Across the desk from her sat the *winner* of that horrible decision. It had come down to her heart against her head, love-life versus work-life, more so defined as Eric v. McGraw, or more fundamentally, Eric v. Jameson Gradeen. *The Chosen One* now sat here drinking coffee in her office, staring at murder conspiracy charges, while all she could think about was the one not chosen.

The raised voices and doors slamming in the hall brought her back to the present. Gradeen was enjoying the sound of his own voice as people ran past her open door toward the uproar. She got up from her desk to close it for some privacy when her paralegal, Morgan, stuck her head in, asking for her help.

"It's your new guy. He's forced his way into McGraw's office," Morgan stated in a panicked tone.

This was a reaction she'd not foreseen. Eric could have aimed her nuclear warhead at any number of targets, but why McGraw for his opening salvo?

She turned in the doorway and told Gradeen, "Stay here, okay? Hopefully this will only take a second."

That was cock-eyed optimism. Following Morgan down the hallway, she could hear an elderly voice that sounded like a distraught Mrs. Brubaker.

"I repeatedly told him he couldn't go in there!" She was speaking calmly to the gathering crowd outside of McGraw's office door. Then more agitated and somewhat breathlessly she asked, "Should someone call security?"

Jillian had expected he'd do something rash, but this? In a world where men often shy from confrontation, it was no surprise Eric McKegney would go right at it like a firefighter into a burning building. And like her bridge from an earlier analogy, this too was blazing. She didn't think he'd physically hurt McGraw, but she hoped at least he wasn't wreaking of booze.

The yelling from inside grew louder. Jillian fought through the crowd of curious onlookers by telling everyone, "He works for me. Let me handle this."

She arrived to see Eric holding the smaller McGraw by the lapels of his custom-made charcoal suit jacket up against the wall behind his desk. He even had the little man off the ground, McGraw's Florsheim's nervously dancing as they sought purchase on the floor.

"You knew!" he said in a menacing tone to the Managing Partner. "You knew and didn't tell me! You knew they tried to have Ritter killed! Erin died in that wreck! They killed Erin and you knew!"

From where she stood, she saw Eric with his backpack still slung over his right shoulder, meaning he was so intent on beginning this skirmish that he'd not stopped by his storeroom. He had his back to her so she could not see his face, but she could see McGraw's. Surprisingly the older man didn't appear fearful or the least bit rattled. Granted he had both hands up defensively, trying to calm his attacker, begging for the chance to explain in non-threatening tones.

"Eric. Listen, Eric. I don't know what you are talking about."

McGraw's denials sounded clipped, almost rehearsed and fully enunciated. It was as if he wanted to make sure witnesses could understand every word of his claims of innocence.

Eric was ready for a fight. The last thing he wanted was to listen to reason. He tugged on the man's jacket and bounced the little lawyer off the wooden wall, causing framed photos of governors and local celebrities to crash to the immaculate carpet.

"They killed her! They killed my fiancé! And you knew. You should've told me!"

The Managing Partner calmly said, "I didn't know. I don't know whatever you are talking about."

"That's the only thing that makes sense. You knew. That's the only reason I'm here! It has to be the only reason you hired me!"

Other attorneys and even one or two partners barged their way into the office. Jillian turned and held out her arms to block them. She was able to position herself in the only path around the desk, her stern expression daring anyone to try to get by her.

"Let them go!" she said, repeating it every time someone new entered the office. "They're just talking. Everything's okay."

All the while, Eric's menace raged. "You used me! You set me up! They killed Erin and you knew!"

And through it all, McGraw was more persistent in his denials. His tone was restrained and controlled, his level of calmness extraordinary. The man was being held off the ground by the lapels of his suit coat and his expression looked as if he were at a poetry reading. And not one with the dirty limericks.

Security finally arrived. Two of their finest instructed everyone to clear their paths, tasers cocked and crackling at their sides. Like soldiers clearing a room, two of the largest, ill-humored men Jillian had ever seen in blazers and clip-on ties maneuvered cautiously around the desk, out flanking her. She immediately showed them her palms but did not step out of the line of fire.

This was an odd Mexican standoff. Security knew better than to treat her with anything other than respect and dignity. Bad news for them was she knew that too. She also knew the tasers were not meant for her. Therefore, she refused to back down or step aside, blocking any possible progress by either guard with her arms, as she jumped from foot to foot.

This is when McGraw spoke up, "It's okay. Stay back. He's not going to hurt me." Then softer and more directly he asked, "Are you, Eric?"

Eric glanced back over each shoulder, realizing he was surrounded. If he decided to go any way other than peacefully, it would be on the business end of fifty-thousand volts.

Softly McGraw asked again, "You're not going to hurt me, are you, Eric?"

In the man's tranquil eyes, Eric saw something which appeared familiar. It was then that he realized this was *the look*, that tilt and dip of the chin. McGraw was known for asking questions in a way that informed someone they already knew the answer. *The look*, the thing with the chin, was on full display, imploring him to fill in the blanks.

Eric considered what he'd learned from the email Jillian had decoded. It explained Ritter had begun to fancy himself as an investigative journalist. The email sender, Thomas Gradeen, had invited Ritter to the Edinburg farm for an interview. Then right outside the Sangamon Suites motel, Jameson Gradeen or one of his technological minions used the so-called *Magic Box* to take control of Ritter's car and crash it. *James Dean* had not been a code name of one of the participants. It was a verb.

The assumption could be made from this that the science was no longer mere theory and speculation. *Agribotics Technologies* and their *Magic Box* could not only receive telematic information from a vehicle. They could also send instructions, demonstrated by *James Dean*-ing Ritter's BMW Z3 into a telephone pole, killing Erin.

When reading and rereading the email, Eric recalled Gradeen's glibness at the farm. He commented one time they'd attempted it with a car. He claimed it hadn't worked, but had he been brazenly announcing right there that he'd caused the accident that killed Erin? Could he have known she'd also be in that car, or Eric's connection to her?

This meant Erin's texted "One last thing" was now something as innocent as accompanying Ritter to interview Thomas Gradeen. For all he knew, there was the distinct possibility she was invited along for no reason other than to meet the patriarch of Springfield's first family.

She told him not to hate her for it. Once she'd explained herself, how could he have ever hated her?

Tears flooded Eric's eyes as he released his grip on the man's suitcoat. McGraw again dipped his chin, this time things and events began to fall into line. Eric's mind rewound to two months prior and those random dots began to connect themselves.

McGraw talked to Teddy Grimes, asking about Eric's willingness to be an investigator. By then, someone had paid for his copy of Erin's accident report. That had to be McGraw. Then the Managing Partner conspired to make sure he had the only copy of the Gradeen biography, the key to the email code. All of this was done so Eric alone would discover the Gradeen's treachery behind the attempt on Patterson Ritter's life which ultimately took Erin.

It was hard for him to imagine Erin was dead because Ritter wanted to play *Woodward & Bernstein*. With this latest transformation from dick to whatever, among the speculation and myriad of theories, this never was one of them. How could it? Nor would Eric have ever gotten to this conclusion without all the help that came his way. Maybe Ritter had the world at his feet after all.

McGraw, for his part, had to know all this; that's the only thing which made sense, the only conclusion which could be drawn. The fact that McGraw saw to it that Eric got no help decoding the emails was purposeful, as Jillian had surmised, because he already knew what they revealed. This meant McGraw had been aware of Ritter's role at the center of this when Eric was hired.

Yet at the same time, if this was indeed the case, didn't it seem as if McGraw had gone to great extremes? Why would anyone devise such a complicated con game with so many moving parts? Wouldn't a less intricate machination have served better? Or maybe an anonymous note? How could McGraw have been sure that an alcoholic *Ambulance Chaser* would stay on the intended path?

He knew because he placed two or three people along that path to help.

Eric turned to look at Jillian, harried yet beautiful, bookended now by the two hulking security guards. She'd obviously been a helper, and the two-timing Sarge another. Had Teddy been the third? It was like Eric had been the blind man and they his seeing-eye dogs. They led him to the finish line, to this office, to this confrontation. But why so many gears and cogs? Why all the theatre and dramatics?

Why all . . .?

Then it hit him. How in the hell had he missed it? He turned back to face McGraw and gingerly smoothed the man's lapels and straightened the wrinkled suit jacket the best he could. With a wink, he let the cagey old lawyer know he understood.

"You're right, sir. I'm sorry. I'm not going to hurt you."

All along it had been something as basic as *Attorney/Client privilege.* Simple legal ethics prohibited McGraw from outright accusing either Gradeen of being an accessory to murder, nor could he whisper it to Eric or anyone else. After all, his firm had been retained as their attorney. Regardless of how McGraw learned about the Gradeen's involvement, the ACP, the privilege, prohibited him from telling anyone. If he was intent on seeing either or both Gradeen's go down, someone else was going to have to connect those dots.

Cue the drunken *Ambulance Chaser*. McGraw suspected Eric would be so hell-bent on getting his revenge that he'd not wait for the dish to cool, trampling any and all legal conventions. The genius of the plan lay in the fact that Eric had been hired not as an attorney, but as an *investigator*. While the ACP applies to the entire defense team, it could be argued as simple semantics: "There is no *Investigator/Client privilege*, Your Honor."

The Managing Partner had painted the greyest of grey areas and contracted the perfect assassin. Now he just had to hand him a weapon.

Still smoothing the man's lapels, Eric nodded with respect to the man's cunning and repeated, "I'm not going to hurt you. Instead, I need to thank you."

The old lawyer winked back, and in an odd way there was this momentary level of mutual respect. Both had jobs to do, one leading, one following. Eric felt as though a master puppeteer had expertly played him, while McGraw's eloquent smirk told him he'd thoroughly enjoyed having his hand up the young man's ass, working his mouth and arms.

J. Tyler McGraw's involvement in this case, his descent from on high, had been solely for this very confrontation. He'd orchestrated all this so Eric would draw the conclusion he just had. And if you are a fan of irony, try this on for size. McGraw had manipulated the *Attorney/Client privilege* to achieve his end, while at the same time being able to invoke the same fucking privilege to secure everyone's silence. Anyone who might figure this out, or anyone at the firm he might one day tell over cocktails, would be unable to do anything with the information. Was this genius or lunacy? Whichever, it worked brilliantly.

But McGraw's role in this little Kabuki theater was just beginning. The soft and fuzzy mutual admiration society moment ended abruptly. McGraw puffed out his little chest, threw back his tiny shoulders and transformed himself into a full-blown king of the jungle.

He roared at Eric, "How dare you lay hands on me!"

With this, he violently shoved Eric back and away, reestablishing his supremacy and yelling for security to remove the ungrateful son of a bitch from the hallowed premises.

He screamed loud enough to be heard in the hall. "I tried to help you! I gave you a chance when no sane man would! I tried to turn you legitimate, but you are never going to be *Donaldson, Clements* material."

As Jillian watched this scene unfold, the security guards eventually rushed by her and ripped the backpack from Eric's shoulder and riffled through it. Eric was compliant, arms outstretched, his face not showing defeat, but ironically perhaps victory. They removed his company-issued laptop, plus all firm file folders. They patted him down like a criminal and came away with two iPhones – one firm-issued and one his -- and a flask from the inside of his suit jacket pockets. One of the guards pulled a bottle of Glenfiddich out of the backpack and made a big show of holding it up for everyone to see.

"Let him keep it," yelled McGraw. "You are a drunk, Eric McKegney. There is no place at my firm for a man like you! You are fired!"

The bottle was returned to his bag and the flask back in its customary inside pocket. The two large men were joined by two more, looking like one guard short of being an offensive line. They formed a tight pocket around Eric and ushered him from the office.

McGraw, playing to the stunned crowd, spread his arms wide to convey he was king and this remained his dominion. He yelled out dramatically, "You come in here with unprovoked attacks and unsubstantiated charges. Have you nothing to say for yourself? No explanation, young man?"

Eric stopped and turned, still surrounded by four men much wider than him. He respected what McGraw was doing and had no desire to participate. The foundation was being set for plausible deniability. The lawyers in the room recognized the parlor trick for what it was. Anyone asked could testify that the new guy was drunk and attacked the Managing Partner without provocation.

"No. I have no idea what may have caused it," they would attest. "Did you know he was an alcoholic?"

To ensure the firm's sustained survival, the entire incident would be hung around Eric's neck, the drunken investigator with no respect for jurisprudence or the rule of law.

Instead of biting on McGraw's bait to play along, he was more interested in checking on Jillian. Her betrayal by leaving without a good-bye stung. Her note had then pretty well crippled him. There was no point in denying it. She'd hurt him badly, but he understood. This was her home and he couldn't drag her from it. Nor could he ask her to leave with him of her own volition.

Tears clouded her amazing eyes of silver blue, as she stood, one hand to her mouth and the one again wearing the big diamond ring on her hip. Her ivory skirt and blazer made her complexion appear darker by contrast and far more exotic. Even terribly distraught by what she'd witnessed, still confused and anxious about the ramifications to come, she looked amazing.

We were really going to miss her.

She'd made it quite clear that *This* with the little back-and-forth gesture was through. The return of the ring confirmed it. He'd never considered contacting her about his plan, for try as she might, she wasn't going to be able to talk him out of confronting McGraw. And any sane fool saw this ending no other way. This was his grenade to fall upon. Hopefully he'd shielded her from collateral damage. As she'd requested in her note, her role in this would remain a secret.

As their eyes finally met, he winked and deliberately mouthed the words, "Thank you."

Realizing he'd been unharmed in the melee, she finally forced a smile through her panicked tears. Unaware of the eyes in the room on her, she tried to wink back before going back to acting like an equally detached spectator.

Eric smiled at the scene, still unable to wink to save her life. You quickly close one eye while keeping the other one open. How hard could that be?

If, god-forbid, this was to be the last time he'd ever see her, watching her comically try to wink one last time was a fond memory to hang onto.

FORTY-SIX

Surrounded by his phalanx of security guards, the once-again-jobless Eric McKegney was ushered toward the elevators. That's when he saw him. Off to the side near the corner, just in the hallway leading back toward Jillian's office stood Jameson Gradeen, one of the men responsible for Erin's death. The two men locked eyes. It was an intensely personal stare from Eric that caused the asshole to reflexively look away.

Only two of the four large guards in their matching slacks and blazers stepped inside the elevator. Their instructions were to see him completely off the premises. When the doors closed, Eric casually hit the button for *Three*, mentioning his car was on that floor of the garage. When he stepped back to his place between the two large men, the image in the mirrored doors reminded him of glancing over his shoulder to see Jillian between the same two when all hell was breaking loose.

His reflection realized he'd become quite predictable. It seemed to shrug at the notion. He'd lasted only seven days back in the working world before being fired. It was probably due to being an alcoholic, among other things like assault and battery. I guess they should have seen this coming. He wasn't the most stable employee ever, but he was nothing if not predictable. So predictable in fact, that he pulled his flask from his inside pocket. He offered it to each of the guards before talking a big gulp himself. Not surprisingly, both declined.

"Did you see that skinny asshole in the hallway? He killed my fiancé."

When neither replied, he took another hit from the flask and asked, "If I had taken a run at him would you have Tasered me?"

"Would have had to. If it's the skinny guy I saw, you'd have killed him," the guard on his right in the reflection said. It was the one called Smith from his first day at the firm.

Eric chuckled at this and exclaimed, "Wow! You ever see anything like that back in that office?"

Neither guard responded, the one not named Smith returning his backpack. Eric slipped his right shoulder through the strap and asked, "Did anybody ever last less than one full week around here before?"

"I think you're the first," Smith said, trying to hide a smirk.

Eric said, "It's going to get pretty boring around here without me."

The reflection of both guards showed them trying to hide smiles. Nobody said much else as the elevator crept downward.

I wanted Eric to ask if they knew he'd slept with Jillian Stennet last night. That would get a reaction.

Would he ever see her again after her note and what he'd just done? Would she survive the fire storm he'd wrought on *Donaldson, Clements* as ostensibly was her plan? Hopefully he hadn't marred her pathway to partner in the next two years? That had been her stated goal since that first night, a night not seven nights earlier. How could he wrought this much shit in one week?

I was beginning to like that word "wrought." It sounded almost biblical, like something God would do to the Philistines. But back to Jillian.

He liked that she loudly protested his treatment in McGraw's office. Yet Eric knew she'd been relatively neutered; there wasn't much she could do. She saw everything through eyes focused solely on her legal future.

He just rained fire down upon the whole firm, and there had to be presumed guilt associated with her because of his association. Funny, but sometimes law firms are the hardest place to find "Innocent until proven guilty" put into practice. She may be found guilty of aiding and abetting. Or had they concealed their tete-a-tete sufficiently so none would suspect her involvement?

Would McGraw ever realize her true role in this? Would he find out she decoded the important email and question her loyalties? Eric hadn't; her letter made it clear her loyalties were to the firm and McGraw. The little *Dream Team* served its purpose. Without realizing it, Jillian had masterfully shepherded her lost little puppy exactly as foreseen. But she hadn't pulled him by the leash. It was more like she had let him go, like she threatened with her golden retriever.

"Don't make me let go of my dog," she yelled the other night when Eric was in her back yard.

But unlike Clint, Eric had attacked. She got him exactly where he was supposed to be, whether she realized it or not.

Eric's little scene in McGraw's office might have momentarily bumped her career off its track, but she'd get it back on. Or maybe his actions had cemented her position. Either way she'd be safe. She was a clever, talented lawyer. And besides, everyone on *Seven* regarded her as a delight to gaze upon.

After another big gulp, and another pass from his escorts – It was barely 10 AM -- he understood this time he'd have to stay away from her for good. They needed to put some distance between themselves for her to survive this.

McGraw used him to compromise both father and son Gradeen. How come? Once again that piece was missing. That nexus point, McGraw's motivation and/or reasons, from which all this sprang remained unknown.

Did Jillian maybe know? Should he be suspicious because she decoded the email precipitating the scene just concluded? Wasn't it also curious she just happened to stop by his condo last night of all nights? But she'd slept with him. Had that somehow also been part of this far-flung plan? He was starting to think like Teddy.

The elevator door dinged on *Three*. The two guards accompanied him to a glass door leading outside to the landing in the parking garage.

Eric broke the long silence by asking, "You guys get to throw a lot of people out of this building?"

"Keep walking," the one not named Smith replied, obviously not thrilled with this latest assignment.

Eric motioned in the general direction of his Jeep Cherokee parked far from where they stood and said, "I can take it from here, Gentlemen. Thank you."

"Off the premises," Smith said, repeating McGraw's instructions.

The parking garage is what is referred to by those in the business as a double helix design. Think of it like the staircase inside an apartment building. The office floors open up onto a landing area, but the cars park on the ramps leading up and down. These ramps don't curl like in many garages but are straight with two lanes of traffic and cars parked on both sides of each stair. It is all open-air, so sounds from any levels seem to echo and travel easily.

The air on the third level smelled of motor oil and trapped exhaust. They walked together and then turned right, beginning down the slope. Eric again pointing toward his car, the guards likewise repeating McGraw's instructions.

The guards' attention was drawn to the shriek of approaching tires coming from the level below them. It soon grew louder and closer, the squealing around turns indicating dangerous speed for a parking garage. The three of them saw a nondescript white Ford pickup with a damaged grill charging up at them from the ramp below.

Eric's initial thought was that the truck looked somehow familiar. It did, but before I could tell him it had tried to run us over before following us yesterday, I mockingly threw his words back at him.

"There are a lot of battered white pickups in Illinois, one on almost every farm."

As the driver showed no signs of slowing, Eric went one way and the two guards the other. I pointed out to anyone who might listen that we were a long way from anybody's farm.

FORTY-SEVEN

*J*illian considered a quick detour to the powder room to put herself back together before returning to her meeting with Jameson Gradeen. The tears in McGraw's office had wrecked her makeup, but she decided against a touch up. Out of expediency, a few Kleenex from a drawer in her desk would suffice.

Her client, seemingly disinterested by the commotion and eager to conclude their meeting in order to get back to his life, waited in the hallway. He leaned casually against a wall, a coffee cup in one hand and his cell phone in the other.

"Routine Friday morning?" he asked cynically.

She despised this guy and hoped she did a satisfactory job of concealing it. Maybe she could hustle him out, close her door and try to absorb what had just transpired and its effect on her future at *Donaldson, Clements*. Was she finished as a member of the Gradeen defense team? If so, hopefully her removal would be less of a spectacle than Eric's. She guessed after a thorough debrief, things would go back to the way they were *pre-Eric*. McGraw would probably let her again defend cases under the watchful tutelage of James Petrie.

The same was more than likely true for McGraw's own spot on his *Dream Team*. Both had played their parts to fruition and their roles could be written off the *J. Tyler McGraw Show*. Other litigating partners and juniors would be able to take it from here and take it to court.

Why then did she feel obligated to finish this meeting? Gradeen could be reassigned. She could be out.

With no clue as to the change in his legal fate within these hallowed walls, he followed her back into her office and plopped in the chair he'd occupied before the uproar.

He smirked like a man with a secret and asked, "Something to do with me?"

She thought he knew or at least suspected; his expression said as much. Nonetheless she explained in a stern voice, "He knows you killed his fiancé. McGraw also knew but hadn't told him."

Gradeen tried to shrug it off. "Oh, that? That was all my father's doing."

She couldn't believe he could be cavalier, let alone so callous. Regardless of who gave the order, or who was culpable, he reacted as if her comment meant nothing to him. He, or his father – She wasn't going to debate the point -- was now responsible for at least two deaths at a minimum, Ann Flannery and Erin Haynes. For all anyone knew there could be more, maybe DeBisshop, Steinhauer and/or Fuller. Yet here he sat, conceited and flippant, acting as if murder was a common everyday business occurrence.

Not discounting his total disregard for this latest bit of news, he appeared incapable of comprehending what effect this had on his conspiracy to commit murder case. This newest factoid connected the two confirmed murders with him as the sole pivot-point, not to mention his father's possible complicity. Could he be that evil or that clueless?

Jillian had already had enough. Plus, he was about to become some other poor litigator's concern.

"I can't deal with this today," she said. "If we haven't covered everything satisfactorily, would you be offended if I rescheduled you with an associate?"

"You're dropping me?" He seemed hurt by this.

"I'm guessing there will be several reassignments after what's transpired."

"Yeah, and your investigator friend will be looking for work." He said this with his smugness on full display. "Sorry to hear that. Thought you two were a team . . . in the office and out."

Jillian had always been accomplished at compartmentalizing, so she locked her feelings for Eric away in a tiny emotional box and persevered as if nothing in her life had recently changed.

"We *were* on the same team. It was your team."

He regarded this and said, "But this can't be good for you two."

She hesitated for a beat before sitting behind her desk, cocking her head and staring across her desk. "I beg your pardon."

"Oh, I'm sorry," he began, enjoying this little exchange. "I was under the impression after your visit to the farm that you two were sleeping together."

She thought back to the little make-believe they played for the benefit of the farm's eavesdropping capabilities. At the time it had been necessary cover and seemed a harmless little game, an enjoyable means to an end. They'd discussed how to continue the pretense and explain their motives when Jameson came to the firm for a meeting.

And now here was the meeting, while their little game had ended, crumbling like any optimism it had been built upon. There was nothing to explain to McGraw because her world had completely spun off its axis since that day.

Before she could respond, with wide eyes and then a wink above his tipped coffee cup, he said, "And then with you leaving his place early this morning."

His earlier remark shocked Jillian. This comment stunned her. She again cocked her head slightly, wondering if she had misheard him. How in the hell could he possibly know that? How could anyone? She'd been careful, hadn't she? Hadn't they? But then again, why would they have had to worry about being secretive?

Had he been following her, or staking out Eric's condo? Even if either of those were remotely possible, *Why?* What had he hoped to learn? And then how to use it? Did his family now have leverage on her?

"We were working late on *your* defense," she began. "I was tired. I thought it best not to drive home. He let me crash -- He -- I left early this morning to get ready for work, for this meeting."

"You sound a bit confused about what happened."

She did. She was, yet being a professional courtroom attorney, she was extremely nimble on her feet. For years she'd proven adept at dealing with the unexpected, that bolt from nowhere designed to change momentum in a trial. She'd always been able to react swiftly, accordingly. Although maybe it's not as much reacting as it's acting, playing to the jury.

She said, "It's none of your business, but we broke up. Last night. He ended it. I hoped to preserve my dignity by getting out of there. Then this . . ."

Incredulously he asked, his words evenly spaced, "He . . . ended . . . it? He dumped you? He got tired of being with you?"

Why was this so hard to believe? She'd never seen herself the way others had, especially men. She knows she's attractive compared to other attorneys, but she also finds flaws in everyone. None more than in the mirror. Why wouldn't a great guy dump her? Why should that surprise anyone? She's no prize, and if anyone doubted, she'd play the footage of her last five hours.

But why *had* she framed it this way? Why lie about this? Was it because she didn't want to try to explain choosing her job over Eric? Or to not be perceived as the heartless bitch she'd become? She'd mentioned *her* dignity. Was she really hoping to protect Eric's? Was she subconsciously building him up, knowing all along she'd shown him the door?

While Jillian wrestled with this, Gradeen leaned back in his chair and asked calmly, "I assumed he gave you that big ring. What happens now? You back on the market?"

"It's really none of your concern. Plus you're a client."

"Tough morning for him. He loses his girl and job in the same morning."

He let this sink in and then, almost as if counting a predetermined number of beats, Jameson added, "McGraw shouldn't have fired him."

"Eric left him with little choice," she responded more out of reflex.

"No. The firing exposed him. It forced my hand."

Forced his hand? What did this mean? That had happened maybe three or four minutes ago. Then she noticed the cell phone resting in his lap.

In a voice which masked her horror she asked, "What did you do?"

"But if he just dumped you then you might be happy about it. What better way to get even?"

"What . . . did . . . you . . . do, . . . Jameson?"

He was saying, "It wasn't really for you, but maybe you should thank me."

With urgency in her tone, she asked again, "Jameson, what have you done?"

Jameson Gradeen picked up the phone from his lap and glanced at it. With a simple shrug of his shoulders and a dead expression he repeated, "Shouldn't have fired him."

The cold look on his face repulsed her, yet in there lay her answer. It had everything to do with the respective locales of McGraw's friends and enemies. The Managing Partner had disregarded the adage, cutting Eric loose, placing him squarely in Jameson Gradeen's crosshairs.

There was no need to wait further explanation. She jumped up, kicked off her heels so she could run and sprinted toward the elevators.

he battered white pickup from any number of Illinois farms was right on top of them, braking into a slide, the bed fishtailing wildly to the left. Eric went one way and to the ground to avoid being clipped, while the two guards went the other. One of them, probably Smith, tried to protect him and got smacked by the truck's bumper, his scream bouncing off the cement walls as his hulking body was thrown into a parked car.

The Ford F-150 had successfully separated Eric from his security detail. The driver's door flew open and out jumped a man who moved around the front of the pickup toward Eric. He had both hands on his pistol and moved like police in the movies when clearing a room. He'd obviously done this before.

Eric scrambled backwards, thinking the guy looked familiar. He knew him or at least had seen him somewhere before, but where? Then it hit him. Shit! His was the face in the photo he had texted to Sarge. Shit! Shit! It was Fuller!

"Don't do it," Eric said, showing his hands and trying to remain as calm as possible as he struggled to get back to his feet.

"Stay down. It'll be less painful if you just take it."

At this he raised the pistol.

"Stop, Fuller!"

The guttural scream came from somewhere below them along the row of parked cars, reverberating loudly in the tight confines of the garage. It was Sarge! While rushing up the ramp, he began firing his weapon wildly, the bullets banging off the truck, the gunfire echoing loudly.

Sarge's shots pinged off the Ford pickup, Fuller ducking reflexively with each ringing *bang* and the flying glass from the windows of the truck. The uninjured security guard, not Smith, scrambled around the back of the pickup with Taser crackling. Fuller looked to his right, then back at Eric, who was trying to crab walk out of the line of fire. Fuller compared threat levels. Seeing the guard as a more immediate danger than an unarmed Eric, he turned his gun on him and fired two disabling shots in rapid succession.

From where Eric was, scrambling across the damp concrete through a space between red and black parked cars, he couldn't see who Fuller shot. He heard, however, the impact of the bullets. It sounded like taking a sledgehammer to a Thanksgiving turkey, with a splattering *schwack-schwack*.

He knew that Sarge had not been shot. The former policeman kept coming from the same direction, from behind the truck, screaming and firing wildly.

As Fuller stepped over to survey his handiwork on the guard, Eric used the driver's side mirror of the black car to pull himself back to his feet, backpack still slung over his right shoulder. He contemplated throwing it at his assailant and making a run for it. But where to go?

Over the sound of the other security guard yelling for help into his walkie-talkie, Fuller turned back to him, both hands still on the revolver in the police-taught firing position.

Then the craziest thing happened.

"Aren't you the lady from the news?" Fuller asked in an almost mocking tone, a light smile curling his face.

"Wait. What?" Eric asked, completely confused by the comment uttered in the midst of a gun battle.

Then the gun fired from pointblank range directly into Eric's chest, just as the bolts from a Taser struck and spasmed Fuller to the ground. The next shot of his trademark double-tap went high and wide, the bullet ricocheting off the concrete ceiling. It had been the other guard, his friend Smith, the one initially hit by the truck, who fired the crippling electric pulse from over the bed of the pickup.

Eric went backward and down hard between two the cars, liquid dampening his shirt, pain throbbing in his chest and screaming through his ears.

Sarge finally arrived on the scene, out of breath and panting loudly, pistol still at the ready. He immediately did a cursory check on all involved. Fuller had been neutralized by the Taser, his body madly convulsing on the cold concrete of the parking garage. Sarge kicked the man's pistol away.

He observed one security guard tending to the other when he heard his name echoing through the parking structure. He looked back toward the elevators and saw Jillian, standing perfectly still, frozen in shock, a hand covering her mouth.

She'd gotten to the parking garage in time to see a man with a gun aiming it into Eric's chest. Everything unfolded almost as if in slow motion. It looked like the two were having a conversation of some sort, but she could only see the gunman's back. She watched one of the security guards struggle to his feet, walkie-talkie in one hand and what turned out to be a weapon in the other. He aimed it across the bed of the pickup. For the first time in this harrowing unfolding scene she recognized a glimmer of hope.

But the man with the gun fired first, the boom quickly traveling the distance to her. She screamed about as loudly. Eric had been shot from no more than ten feet and propelled backward. The guard had then fired his Taser into the man's back, dropping him on the far side of the truck. He then screamed again into his radio while checking on the other guard.

"No, Miss Stennet," Sarge hollered. "Stay there please, Miss."

"What about Eric?" she screamed in panic. "Somebody check on Eric."

While sprinting up the ramp, Sarge too had seen Eric shot from what looked to be close range. Without having to check on him he knew whatever he'd find would be bad. He held up his hand as a signal to keep Jillian away. He needed to spare her from the blood and carnage, but most importantly the sight of Eric's body.

"No, Miss. Please stay over there. Call 9-1-1. Tell them . . . What floor are we on? Anyway, request police and multiple ambulances."

"It's *Floor Three*. Eric parks on *Three*," she answered distractedly. Then in an apologetic tone she added, "I didn't grab my phone."

She felt useless, helpless. The sight of Eric being shot had paralyzed her to the point she was unable to go back in for help, too scared to go forward to check on him. The macabre scene played out like something on television with the volume turned up. The noise of the echoing gunfire had thrummed through the tight confines of concrete and blasted in her ears.

Security guards rushed past her in waves of two or three, some carrying large red first aid bags. She wanted to follow them, wanted to help, but Sarge again yelled for her to call for help. One of the guards overheard and informed everyone paramedics had already been alerted.

She watched two guards tending to their brethren, administering aid on the ground at the rear of the pickup. The wounded guard had apparently been shot in the right knee. He remained conscious but in a great deal of pain, his grey slacks soaked in a syrupy red. Another guard with a first aid bag joined him to examine Smith, the guard who'd fired the Taser to stop the man with the gun.

She took a few tentative steps closer to the scene in her bare feet. Why had no one gone to the other side of the truck to help Eric? Was already dead?

"Sarge," she yelled, getting his attention once more. With a quivering voice she pleaded, "Can you please check on Eric?"

When he failed to move, continuing to stare in her direction without saying a word, Jillian added, "I'll stay over here. I promise."

She watched him say something directed to the security guards and turn to walk between a red car and a black car. She noticed him look down and then to his right and then to his left. The messily parked pickup, still running with the driver's door open, blocked her view of Sarge for a beat before he popped back up. He stood there, his back to Jillian, seemingly staring aimlessly at the concrete wall.

"Miss Stennet," he yelled, turning and now waving her over to him.

Stay over there and now *come here*? What was this about? Her first thought was that Eric wanted to say something to her before he died. But that dreadful thought didn't match Sarge's expression. The man was smiling. So she said a quiet prayer as she hustled to the ramp and then partially down it. She saw all the glass on the ground and froze, recalling she kicked off her shoes rather than try to run in heels.

"You're not going to believe this," she overheard Sarge saying. He turned toward her, again with a smile that didn't fit the circumstances.

"Not going to believe what?" Jillian asked, tiptoeing around the truck to look between the cars.

"*Young Gun* ain't here. I looked under all these parked cars. He ain't here."

"What does that mean? How is that possible?" Without giving him a chance to answer she added, "But I saw him . . ."

She'd been unable to finish the sentence.

"I did too. Fuller was almost as close as you and me," Sarge explained, waving his hand between them.

"He's not hiding behind a tire or something is he?"

Sarge considered this. "Guess he could be, but why ain't he coming out now that it's all over?"

She was extremely confused by what was happening, and where Eric could have gone. As she tried to put all this together, she realized Sarge had called the other man "Fuller." She turned and looked to the man on the ground by the pickup. His convulsions had stopped, but he was out cold and going nowhere.

"That's Randy Fuller?"

"Haven't officially I.D.'ed him but fairly sure. Been following that truck all morning."

She said almost as a second thought, "That's who Jameson called."

Jillian doubted the smug bastard would have hung around long enough to see how things turned out, so she saw no reason to dash inside and confront him. What could she do anyway? She was his attorney.

It did make sense though. Eric figures out that he killed Erin while trying to silence Ritter, so they would try to silence him. But had they succeeded?

After a few glances around them, she turned back to Sarge to ask, "So where's Eric?"

"You mean why ain't *Young Gun* laying here dead?"

Sarge pointed to the small opening in the wall between the parked cars. There was maybe a two feet high open area between the precast concrete supporting the level they were on and the supports for the roof above them. The open space slanted downhill at the same angle as the parking garage ramps.

Sarge extended an open palm between the red and black car and said, "After you, Miss Stennet."

Jillian walked to the wall, glancing down to see there was no noticeable blood between the two cars. Thinking this had to be good news, she stopped and turned to see if Sarge had observed the same.

He, however, was busy taking control of the scene, barking out orders. He told one guard to turn off the truck's motor since the exhaust was choking the wounded man by the tailgate. When the guard did, he came out of the cab with something he showed to Sarge.

Jillian took a few more barefooted steps and leaned out the opening. Even though they were on the third floor of the parking garage, because of the downward slope of the ramp they weren't a full three stories up. Then factoring in the landscaping mounds below with the bushes and hedges, it was quite possible that if he'd survived being shot, Eric could jump and survive that too.

Before she could report her findings, Sarge waved her over to the pickup. He was standing with the guard, both looking at a photograph.

Handing it to her, the guard said, "You should see this, Miss Stennet."

She found herself gazing at a candid close up of her and Eric, both wearing oversized white smocks and huge smiles. Eric's face had been circled in red. She knew it had been pulled from footage taken on their visit to the Edinburgh Farm on Monday.

As the sound of sirens could be heard approaching in the distance, her mind again rewound to that day spent with Eric. It was a happier day as evidenced by their expressions. Back on Monday they were both still flirting and feeling each other out, doing the little dance prospective couples do.

After the farm they'd visited Erin's memorial and drank scotch from his flask. She'd learned a great deal about him that day, and he about her. But as was customary, she more than he.

Although she learned a great deal about herself.

Right now, however, her sole focus was knowing one more thing.

How badly had Eric been hurt? And where was he?

Okay. Two things.

FORTY-NINE

The impromptu meeting in McGraw's office bore no resemblance to the Gradeen Investigation summit on Monday morning. The seating arrangement of the participants was eerily similar, but that's where any parallels ended. Sarge sat across the small conference table from McGraw with Jillian again between them. Opposite her was an empty chair. And as you may guess, the topic of conversation revolved around the whereabouts of Monday's occupant.

Back then all were buttoned-up and sharp, first-thing-in-the-morning fresh, ready to attack the day and the new week. Now it was the complete opposite. They were frazzled and drained as if the past days had instead attacked them. Yet, considering what two of the three had observed in the attached parking garage, they were functioning as well as could be expected.

It had been the craziest morning beginning with the showdown in this very office. Then things sped further toward the surreal out in the parking garage. The melee was hours earlier, but little of the exhaust had adequately settled. In that time, the two security guards had given corroborating statements to the Springfield Police.

The condensed version went like this: "A pickup ambushed us as we escorted Eric McKegney to his car. No. We don't know who was driving. Yes. Sarge may have saved our lives. No. We don't know where he came from. Yes. McKegney was shot from close range. No. We don't know where he is."

Lorentz, the guard not named Smith, was unable to substantiate the shooting claim since he'd been wounded and downed. He was resting comfortably at St. John's hospital after arriving via ambulance. Smith was checked by paramedics and remained under observation due to a possible concussion. Fuller had been revived and taken into custody awaiting interrogation. There was concern on the *Seventh Floor* that he might become talkative. Just in case, the firm had dispatched two attorneys to protect his silence.

Sarge continued downplaying his role. His statement included following Fuller from Decatur this morning and parking a level above the ground floor near enough to surveil him in the garage. When he started the truck and drove up the ramp, Sarge followed on foot. But Fuller was not leisurely driving though the parking garage. His truck had gone tearing up the ramp so Sarge thought it best to pursue him.

From that point he stated, "I ain't no hero. Just did what anyone else in my place would've did."

It wasn't grammatically correct but it exemplified the man's training and humility.

Jillian, for her part, had also been questioned as a witness, but had not been close to forthcoming in her statement. The *ACP* allowed her to conveniently omit Jameson's role in ordering the attack. She explained her presence in the parking garage solely as hoping to catch up with Eric, convincingly claiming she wanted to debrief her just-terminated investigator. Nothing more. She was credible; everything fit with the other evidence. The SPD never second-guessed her reason for being there.

They did, however, suggest an officer stay with her since she was also in the photo found in the pickup. She'd hear none of it. Her face had not been circled; this was no time to worry about her. It wasn't bravado. It was simply that she felt SPD's time would be better utilized searching for Eric than baby-sitting her. Plus, privately she knew if Jameson had wanted to hurt her, he'd missed countless opportunities earlier that morning.

Springfield's finest debated this with her, recognizing instantly they weren't going to prevail. The last thing they needed was another black eye if anyone else involved in this case went missing or wound-up dead. They were placated by Sarge. He proposed he wouldn't let her out of his sight. And except for her quick trip to the powder room, he hadn't.

He relished the assignment because she was a marvel to behold and be near. He couldn't get over how she could simultaneously look so exhausted yet so lovely. She'd been put through the ringer in that parking garage but came out the other side remarkably. Her makeup was a mess, but nobody cared. Her eyes were dewy with tears and shone a blue-gray like he'd never before seen. Her hair, which had been fixed neatly earlier in the garage, now looked more thrown-together, a quick and casual up-do with bangs swept to one side, a few tendrils hanging loose at her ears. There was blood smeared near the hem of her skirt and on one sleeve of her blazer from where she knelt to have a cut on her bare left foot bandaged. It had not been a good day to choose the ivory business suit.

With all that being said, and without setting foot in the parking garage, the morning's bloodbath had apparently been most damaging to J. Tyler McGraw. He was distraught and apologetic, taking total responsibility for what happened to Eric and his two guards.

"Why deny it?" he had asked of Jillian and Sarge. "This was never my intent, nonetheless all my doing."

For the last two hours he sipped from a tumbler of Pappy Van Winkle's bourbon pulled from a wet bar hidden in an office closet. He'd offered some to his guests, but Sarge declined and Jillian asked for scotch. Okay. Not really. Wishful thinking. They both declined, but the Managing Partner was never opposed to drinking alone while under strain.

In a rueful subdued tone he'd explained Dr. DeBisshop had surreptitiously approached him, stating fear for his life. He'd delivered a copy of the Thomas Gradeen biography, complete with a handwritten keycode explanations. Why DeBisshop had chosen this course, he claimed not to know. His instinct suggested the scientist was seeking protection.

Jameson Gradeen and his father suspected DeBisshop may have betrayed them and taunted McGraw, telling him there was nothing he could do with anything learned from the email code because of client confidentiality. Shortly thereafter DeBisshop vanished.

McGraw admitted to using Eric in this game to better control the Gradeen family but had no idea he'd connect the dots so quickly. He claimed the *Book Knook* was his only mistake, having never researched the possibility of there being a local source for the biography. He even confessed to sending a member of the security team by there to forestall any progress.

While on the topic of confessions, Sarge apologized again for sending her wedding announcement to Eric out of petty jealousy. He sought absolution for his impetuosity -- My word. Not his -- while acknowledging how the move backfired because Eric became hyper-focused without her as a distraction.

Jillian could only smile, recalling the chivalrous Eric not wanting to be Patterson Ritter and wreck her wedding. At the same time she wondered if not for that fax she would not have ended up with him last night. Her intention had been to solely explain her tattered romantic past as a fragile justification for her *come-here-now-go-away* behavior. Never had she expected them to end up in bed – twice. Or maybe had she. She wouldn't be able to honestly tell anyone her motives, for she herself was unsure.

But it had happened – twice. She'd absolutely enjoyed both times.

As unlikely as that outcome might have seemed when the evening began, the only thing harder to believe was that she'd choose her career over him. So with little other recourse, she'd sneaked out like a thief in the night without a good-bye.

Yet somehow Jameson Gradeen knew. How? And why was this important enough to mention earlier this morning? After she'd lied, telling him she'd been dumped, he made it seem as though killing Eric would be doing her a favor. Had the man completely lost his mind? Or like several other players in this ever-unfolding drama, was he also some kind of an evil mastermind?

This knowledge gave him weight on her. Not good. She was compromised. He'd leveled the playing field with her in a manner similar to that McGraw had attempted to do with his family. If Eric now did anything harmful or hotheaded with his new information, Jameson Gradeen could accuse her of complicity.

Then why try to kill Eric? Didn't this return an assemblance of control over Jameson back to her? He ordered the parking garage hit. She hadn't told the authorities, partly because she couldn't as his attorney. He was aware of this. It was his working knowledge of the *ACP*, according to McGraw, which had been the match strike setting this whole chaos ablaze. Yet the advantage was not completely his because, chances are, he was unfamiliar with the crime-fraud exception.

In a nutshell, it works like this: Since the privilege belongs to the client, it is his intent which determines if the exception applies. The *Attorney/Client privilege* may be disregarded when the client's communication to his attorney is in furtherance of a current or planned crime or fraud. In this case, that exception would allow her to report Gradeen's involvement in the commission of the crime perpetrated in the parking garage.

So then were their secrets of sufficient and equal weight to offset? Hardly. He might stain her. She could end him.

While Jillian reveled in her leverage, McGraw changed topics.

"If you're our young friend, what do you do next? What might he be doing now?"

Sarge just assumed the question had been asked of Jillian. He turned to face her, seeing her deep in thought, absentmindedly nibbling on a fingernail while lightly drumming the tabletop with another.

Careful not to reveal her involvement, she said, "We need to ask ourselves who benefits most from what he now knows."

Sarge jumped at this. "The families," he said enthusiastically. "His fiancé's parents, or maybe even the driver's family? We know anything about them?"

"You're being way too short-sighted," McGraw said to Sarge, the bourbon slowing down his speech and causing a twang like that of a southern gentleman. All he needed now was a sear-sucker suit.

"That won't do the damage he seeks." He then turned toward Jillian and drawled, "Might he be able to connect his fiancé's death to the case he was investigating?"

She glanced from McGraw to Sarge and then back. The Managing Partner recognized her trepidation and asked Sarge if he could run out and check with the local constabulary on any news about Eric.

"I get it," Sarge said, getting to his feet. "Can't hear no private lawyer talk."

When they were alone, Jillian said, "You know he's already connected Jameson not only to both deaths, but also to the attack on him."

"Agreed. So what's he do with all this newfound knowledge?"

She regarded this for a beat before asking, "Are you assuming he's looking to do damage? Is that what you're hoping?"

"At least to an extent it was." His response had lacked certainty, but not contrition. He had been busted, so tried his best to explain.

"Initially I counted on his need for revenge, in addition to his instability. I foresaw him as my loose cannon on deck from the outside since that's where he'd be perceived as a legitimate threat to both Gradeen's. Inside these walls he's as bound up as you and me."

"Jameson reached the same conclusion," she said.

"I gathered that. So it seems I made two mistakes. That and the bookstore. I seem to have underestimated the swiftness of our client's response."

McGraw regarded Jillian, doubting she understood his motives behind this. If she might, would she also one day appreciate the virtuoso stroke for what it was? This thought brought a self-satisfied grin to his aging face. And why shouldn't he feel gratified? He just used the firm's newest disposable asset to give *Donaldson, Clements* the upper hand in interactions with the Gradeen family companies. If things go according to plan, and his loose cannon reacts as hoped, he might finally wash his hands of the whole goddamned Gradeen family.

The other partners wouldn't be thrilled with that development, but the other partners didn't have to deal with the family and their "needs" on an almost daily basis. The progeny was a pretentious ass, the father just an ass. There was something to be said for having Thomas Gradeen as a client; McGraw relished the envious looks from other local firms, but the man was high-maintenance and rarely worth the effort. His kid had turned out to be worse.

Apparently the Gradeen's failed to comprehend with whom they tangled. McGraw hadn't merely leveled the playing field, he'd also turned the tables and momentarily held the advantage. What happens next is up to Eric, provided he's okay. McGraw and the firm's response would be a reaction to that newest situation, but he felt confident he'd maintain the power position.

Through the years McGraw's silence, like all attorneys, was always for sale, but never as part of a client's power grab. No one dictated terms to *Donaldson, Clements, Blaine & McGraw* as long as J. Tyler McGraw sat at the helm.

Yeah! That McGraw!

Jillian watched her boss smile for the second time without saying a word. She wondered what had elicited such a curious reaction. She considered they both harbored secrets and their mutual level of mistrust may never wane.

"What does young Eric do?" he asked, sipping Pappy Van Winkle's while casually reclining in his chair. "You knew him best. What are your thoughts?"

"I'd go to the newspaper. The State Journal-Record."

Her response had been quick, maybe too quick. It was as if she'd given this question a good deal of consideration. But what else might she be considering?

He still viewed her as friend-not-yet-foe, but her loyalties appeared to be tested as Eric was led out of this office by security. He could tell by her troubled expression there was more between them than simply two coworkers. Neither had reacted toward the other, except for that god-awful wink of hers, for that would have exposed their little *whatever* for all to see. The attempted wink told McGraw she cared about Eric. He'd noticed it when those crowded into the office apparently hadn't.

He marveled at his matchmaking prowess. It had been in the planning stages for some time, but had taken just over one week in practice, fast by anyone's standards. He never doubted Eric's reaction to her. It was the same as every red-blooded anybody. She's the whole drop-dead package. Then you add in the bounce of a rebound.

The unknown had traveled in the other direction. Would she reciprocate? Apparently she had, at least according to Pappy Van Winkle.

He'd done ample research on Eric and developed this crazy suspicion sparks might fly. Like the other partners, he'd given up hoping to stay up-to-date with the contemporaneous details of Jillian's personal situation, suffice to say it too was messy. Was the wedding back on again? Should he buy a gift? Was she even still engaged? Yet, also like all the partners on *Seven*, he felt the need to protect her, the firm's prized lady litigator, whether from others or from herself.

McGraw threw two attractive and emotionally brittle people into a volatile mix and was not surprised by the results. He obtusely compared it to a recipe with varied ingredients mixed together in what could only be described as a shit stew. Start with one part him, one part her, add a healthy helping of the Gradeen family and a dollop of good fortune. Preheat oven to *who cares* and bake for just under one week. When finished, remove, sprinkle with reprisal, and then drive the dagger right into the Gradeens' backs all the way to the hilt.

The Managing Partner of *Donaldson, Clements* had no name for his dish, but right from the recipe, the plan was clear. Keep both members of his little *Dream Team* moving forward with the investigation, whether on the same path or diverse ones. Prod them along to the pertinent email, and let things naturally take their course. They had.

Intertwining his fingers around the tumbler on his chest, he asked, "How come the newspaper?"

"Think about it. Where better to go to expose this? He puts a target on the back of both Gradeen's that the media cannot ignore, regardless of their stellar civic reputations."

She noticed this hit the mark with her boss but added nonetheless, "There's another reason. He answers what happened to their reporter. The accident was not Patterson Ritter's fault."

"Interesting idea," McGraw said slowly, as his voice now became gravelly. "But our friends at the State Journal-Record can't get him in the news until morning, if legal lets them print anything at all. I've gone toe-to-toe with a few of them. I doubt this would see print."

After a quick sip, he continued, "If it's immediate publicity or notoriety he seeks, why not television? He'll be the lead story tonight. And if he's feeling as magnanimous as you suggest, he can go to Ann Flannery's old station."

As McGraw drawled and droned about things Eric might do or places Eric might go and the legal ramifications of each, Jillian's phone vibrated with an incoming text. She hadn't recognized the number yet was proud of how well she'd maintained her poker face upon reading the message. McGraw continued his ramblings, clearly noticing nothing which piqued his level of suspicion.

"Excuse me, Sir," she interrupted, sliding her chair back to get to her feet.

"Yes, Miss Stennet."

He had said this practically with a genteel yawn, glancing upwards at her from an almost prone place of what appeared to be bourbon-induced relaxation.

Timidly she asked, "I need to leave the office for a bit. Alone. Would you have a problem with that? I promise I won't be gone long."

"Will you tell me where you are going?"

He had asked as if implying her errand was conditional, but she offered nothing with which to barter. Instead she fixed a steadfast expression, nibbled deliciously on her bottom lip and gave a defiant shake of her head.

"So the enigmatic Jillian Stennet would like to protect her privacy. I expect nothing less."

At this he smiled widely before taking another sip and added, "No. You go. I'll keep the troops here to make sure no one follows you."

"Thank you, Sir."

"Do me one favor, though," McGraw said, stopping her halfway out of his office.

"Please convey my apologies to our young friend. I firmly stand by my good intentions. Tell him I only hope one day our paths again cross on our respective roads to hell."

FIFTY

The text had asked simply, "Caesar Salad?"

She saw him from a distance, sitting alone at the same table from Sunday on the empty patio of Piozzi's. He looked almost unrecognizable with hair hanging into his frighteningly pale face, sunglasses poorly concealing huge circles under each eye. He sat in somewhat of an unnatural hunch, no tie, leaning into the table, staring into a half-full glass of scotch, the left sleeve of his suitcoat hanging loose. As she got closer, she saw his arm was in a sling.

He heard her approach and struggled to get to his feet. His expression too looked wounded, but a smile bloomed, barely hanging on like a battered door missing a hinge.

She ran to him on her bandaged foot, wanting to throw her arms around him and kiss him, but stopped short when he offered her his good arm. They awkwardly embraced for a beat.

Her reaction understandably confused him. Hadn't she made it clear *This* with the back-and-forth gesture was over and never to happen again? He'd read her note, and yet, here she was again in his arms.

It was at this instant that the same thought possibly crossed her mind so she quickly pulled back. She did reach out to caress one cheek, tears beginning to puddle in her eyes, glistening blue-grey and inviting, drawing him in.

"I was in . . . I saw what happened. I thought you were dead," she sobbed, embarrassed that she was unable to maintain her composure.

In a way this release felt like the night before, again unburdening herself. He was still alive, her anxiety becoming gratitude when last night's emotions had turned to relief.

She hoped to remain strong, almost businesslike, but this was impractical. The man had gotten to her, entering her life like a whirlwind, disrupting her staid and self-imposed solitary. In barely one week, despite her better intentions and an early morning decision, he'd done something to her. His death would have haunted her. A lot would have had to do with the fact that she was more or less complicit, but more pointedly, she would have missed him. Terribly. Regardless of what happened, she liked the possibility that he'd still be around.

"Thanks for coming," he said in a feeble voice. "I wasn't sure you . . ."

"Why would you think that?" she shot back instantly, feeling offended.

"After this morning . . ."

His voice sounded sporadic, alternating between weak and stout as he gingerly held her chair for her to sit. He had trouble pushing it in, apologizing repeatedly.

She regarded her damned note and the decision prompting it. "No. I'm the one who needs to apologize. I'm deeply sorry. It's just that . . ."

"I'm sorry, too." With a smirk, he added, "But I get it. Remember when I told you if it ever became a problem, I'd be the one to leave the firm?"

She wiped at her eyes and recalled his inane remark made that day at the farm when she first concocted their cover story of being the phony couple. It was absurd to consider then, but now . . .

"I hope you can understand my reasons," she said softly.

"I do. You have years there and days here. I'm sorry you had to choose."

"Me too." Her comment seemed to be almost in passing because she was quickly on to a more important topic. "How is it possible you're sitting here?"

He tugged his suitcoat more tightly across his left shoulder by poking his right index finger through a small hole in the left breast pocket. He wiggled his finger, exposing the white silk inner lining of his expensive tailor-made suitcoat.

"Bullet hit the flask. I guess it was like Kevlar."

He had announced this with the surreal smile of a man who just received the governor's pardon, actually not believing his good fortune.

He tried to laugh. "How's that for irony? Being an alcoholic saved my life."

He reached into the outside right-hand pocket of this navy suit coat and pulled out a mangled mess of metal with leather detailed topstitching that once was a working flask. It was the same flask from which she sipped Scotch a few days earlier.

It was 4-7/8" x 3-5/8" with a contoured curve to the width. There was a gaping hole in the convex front of the metal and leather, but only a deep protrusion on the concave side with a tiny opening. The mangled and flattened bullet remained lodged in the middle. It had punctured the metal upon entry but lost the necessary momentum to continue through to him. Instead it had only dented and perforated the second wall. It hadn't killed him, instead breaking the skin and maybe a rib or two.

"You lived because of this?"

She turned the mangled metal in her hands, amazed it could catch a bullet. She brushed it under her nose, anticipating a whiff of the smoky scent which scrunched up her face when tasting the single-malt. This smell was different, more metallic in a way she couldn't explain.

"So there's this warm liquid all over my chest. I just assumed it was blood. Hurt like hell. Like getting hit with a golf club. I opened my eyes and I'm staring up at the concrete ceiling of the garage. Everybody is screaming and it's echoing off the cars and walls. The sun was shining in through the gap between the floors and I reflexively went toward the light. Maybe I thought I was dead too."

"That had to be terrifying."

"You know the funny thing?" he began before hesitating. "I'm staring into the barrel of this gun and I was more worried about how much it was going to hurt. Dying never crossed my mind."

"Never crossed your . . .?" The astonishment in her question trailed away.

"It's hard to explain. It was like an almost dreamlike calmness. I understood now what had really happened to Erin. She could rest in peace. We both could. I realized I might be seeing her again soon."

He then added with an awkward whisper, "Part of me was okay with that."

He again felt uneasy talking about Erin in front of her. There had never been any basis for this feeling, but to him it always felt like talking about an old girlfriend around your new one. Maybe it signaled his admission that he was still in love with Erin. Maybe it didn't. Either way, he smiled at the absurdity.

She noticed his contented expression. She'd tell me later she knew from where it had come, or at least what prompted it. She also admitted privately that her job at the firm and her career were not the only things she feared might one day come between the two of them. Erin, too, was always going to be in the picture. Jillian understood, whether in the background or the foreground, Erin was part of his story. She belonged.

"Besides that, right before Fuller pulls the trigger," Eric began, rearranging himself in his chair. His voice again sounded strong with a touch of excitement as he continued, "He gets this odd look on his face and asks me if I'm the lady from the news?"

"What? The lady from the news?"

"Yeah. That's when everything fell into place for me. I've jotted it down just in case things continue to get foggy."

After a sip of scotch to help the pain he clumsily groped his right hand into the sling and withdrew a tri-folded sheet from a yellow legal pad.

Placing it on the table he chuckled, "You wrote me a note, so here. Don't think I still owe you one."

Despite his good-natured manner, she took this as an affront. "I've already told you I was sorry. What more do you want me to say?"

"You're right. That was uncalled for."

His apology hung there for a beat before a sad smile crossed his face. "I've thought a lot about this," he began. "I think we find ourselves in places neither of us could have anticipated this time yesterday. You realized it first, and the parking garage really doesn't change what's happened to *This*."

She offered a slight smile at his back-and-forth gesture between them, recognizing it now sadly suggested a different scenario. But he was right. They were on opposite sides when the day began, hence the reason for her letter. It was as if she built this metaphorical wall between them. Now it seemed too high to climb or maybe too thick to penetrate. Whichever, their chances of being on the same side of it appeared just as dim.

She asked, "Where's this leave us? Are we adversaries? I don't want that."

"Nor do I." He ran a hand through his hair to get it off his forehead and said, "Right now, though, we're still on the same team because I solved your case. I'm afraid you're not going to like it though."

"You what?"

"It's still a theory. It's definitely not exculpatory, but it explains a lot."

She then tempered her previous excitement and in a serious tone said, "Should we start with why I won't like it?"

He straightened in his chair and said, "What if I told you everything was a series of perfectly timed and perfectly executed predetermined acts?"

"You would certainly have my attention."

"Here's your headline: Freddy Steinhauer didn't shoot Ann Flannery and her friend. Fuller did. That's what he was essentially admitting in the parking garage. And another thing, killing the wrong reporter was never an accident. It was all part of the ruse. Ann Flannery *was* the intended target."

"Holy shit. Can you prove any of this?"

"Not completely. Not yet at least. I've only played this out in my head, and scribbled it on this paper, so if it's hard to follow or doesn't make sense, I apologize in advance."

"Keep going. I'll not interrupt."

With this she flashed that knee-buckling smile and pantomimed locking her lips with an invisible key. She then tossed the pretend key over her shoulder as she did nights earlier at this very table. He tried to laugh at her presentation but it caused a grimace.

"I decoded an email from a few days after Ann Flannery's murder where Gradeen tells DeBisshop that the media was reporting the wrong reporter was killed. He then thanked him. His gratitude confused me. Was it sincerity, or sarcasm? What had DeBisshop done for which he needed to be thanked?

"Then yesterday I met with the former Olivia Jacobsen, now J.J. Jacobs. She tells me the only time she'd ever been around Jameson Gradeen was one time at the farm when she was there to interview DeBisshop. She referred to him as Arthur, by the way."

Jillian reacted to this bit of gossipy news with a perceptive nod yet made no comment.

"She says at this meeting these two have this heated argument. They were too far removed for her to hear, but both men were looking at her like either they were talking about her or they wanted to make sure she saw. She thinks the entire scenario was staged. Then DeBisshop apologized profusely for what she witnessed. She also said he used very colorful language when referring to Gradeen.

"This could have been when they decided to introduce her as the wrong reporter. Think about it. A masked gunman approaches Ann Flannery and Patrick Weathers in the nightclub parking lot. He asks Flannery if she's the lady from the news so Weathers can hear it. He then shoots Weathers in the shoulder and Flannery in the chest, killing her but not him. Why?"

"It was so Weathers could tell the police about the gunman's *lady on the news* question, right?"

"Right. And he could also tell the police about the Cinderella mask. So they begin investigating what stories Ann Flannery might be working which made her a threat to somebody, anybody."

Jillian picked up the narrative. "But before they get too far, Olivia Jacobsen gets her call and the focus of the investigation immediately changes to stories she's working."

"Again, you're right, but only partial credit. The caller also tells her that he fears for his life since he killed the wrong reporter. So then when the man the police believe made the call is found dead it's like a self-fulfilling prophecy.

"Not only do I believe Fuller shot both people, but I think he made the phone call to Jacobsen. He goes to St. Louis, kills Steinhauer and leaves the Cinderella mask to tie it all together. Not only was Freddy Steinhauer never a party to this crime, but chances are also he never even knew any of it happened."

She considered this and asked, "What about his cell phone calls? They were triangulated to that hotel to implicate Jameson."

"The phone calls do tie him in. I'll grant you that. However, it could be easily explained as Fuller arranging their St. Louis meeting. Maybe he told him he knew where Cindy Wright was. It fit with the plan. The phone calls give Steinhauer a presence in the scheme, but if you look at the police reports, he's placed everywhere after the fact. Once the Cinderella mask is discovered in St. Louis, they work backwards from there to inject him into several pivotal points throughout the investigation."

She regarded this, but like all good attorneys, wasn't completely convinced. She asked, "But why use a reporter with existing ties to DeBisshop as your decoy?"

"That might have been what they were arguing about and why DeBisshop apologized to her. Maybe he realized they were dragging her into a mess and was apologizing in advance."

"They were both getting dragged in," Jillian said. "Once the investigative focus is off Ann Flannery and on Jacobsen, then it's also on DeBisshop and *ACG*. Why call attention to themselves?"

While this was a great question, he already had his answer ready. "What if DeBisshop was as much of a pawn in all this as Steinhauer was? What if Gradeen was always the one in control. If he called the shots, maybe this was a way to keep DeBisshop in line."

"So Jameson is essentially holding the reporter hostage," Jillian said. "She's Jameson's insurance policy. If DeBisshop cared for her as you say it seems she did for him, then he plays ball or something bad happens to her."

This was good. Neither of us had considered this.

She continued, "If true, this corroborates what McGraw told me about DeBisshop coming to him with the book as the key to the code. But what can we do with any of this?"

Her question was rendered almost rhetorical since the *Attorney/ Client privilege* would preclude *her* from doing anything. Besides, the truth rarely held bearing as to the ease or difficulty of defending a client, even one as unpredictable as Jameson Gradeen.

A waitress stepped outside to see if they needed anything. Jillian deferred to Eric. He considered ordering another scotch but realized he'd only taken a few sips of the one in front of him and waved her back inside.

Once they were alone again on the patio, Jillian grabbed for his glass and took a swig. With barely a reaction she said matter-of-factly, "He knows about us. Jameson knows I was with you last night."

Rather than ask the obvious question of *How?*, Eric instead asked, "Will this cause problems for someone who likes to control her content?"

She grinned at this, wondering how he remembered an offhand remark made days ago. This was always going to be a possibility with Gradeen. She had the crime-fraud exception and the expectation of being reassigned, so she pursed her lips and shook her head.

"What time did you leave? Did anybody see you?"

"I didn't think so. It was still relatively dark."

How did this make sense? And better yet how was it possible that anybody knew, let alone Jameson Gradeen? Was he watching the condo? No. That can't be it. Someone had to be watching Jillian. Or something.

"What are you thinking about?" she asked.

"Hmm? Sorry." Once his concentration returned, he said, "Could Gradeen be tracking you electronically, like maybe through your phone."

Her face dropped at this. "Our phones are secure, but my car isn't."

"Of course," he said. "We were at the farm in your car on Monday. If that's when he tagged you, then he knows we stopped at the scene of Erin's accident. That would explain how they made the connection between me and Erin and Ritter and why they took a run at me Tuesday night."

"What? Tuesday night? Why didn't you tell me about that?"

"I was afraid to admit I didn't know what made me dangerous." Trying to chuckle he added, "I didn't want to end up in Moline."

Jillian smiled at the Olivia Jacobsen reference.

Eric mentioned something neither had yet to consider.

"That means he knows where you are right now."

"I'm not overly concerned about me, but he might have also figured out you're here."

He noticed the distress in her expression and apprehension in her tone. He appreciated her concern, while his was only for her. The bad guys didn't simply tag Ritter's car. They'd taken control of it and crashed it. He couldn't bear the thought of losing someone else that way. He awkwardly reached over to the chair holding his backpack, unzipping a side pocket. He withdrew his keys and held them out for her.

"Maybe you shouldn't be driving your car for a while until you get someone to look at it. Mine's on the third floor of the parking garage. Drive mine."

Here he smiled. "It's a major step down in class, but you'll manage. And you can stay at my place if you feel someone is watching your home."

She took his keys and examined them before asking, "If I have your car what will you do?"

He looked away without answering, surveying the empty tables on the little deck and the hedgerow surrounding them for privacy. The loosely strung lights above seemed to sag more in the daylight.

He reached for the glass of scotch and took a sip, tasting the irony.

"I'm going away. The timing is right after everything that's happened. After I make one more stop, I'm checking myself into rehab."

"You are? Now? Why now?"

All their collaboration about Jameson Gradeen and the offer of his keys had chipped away at the wall she'd built between them. She'd also felt as though maybe it put them on the same side. And now he's leaving?

"There's a lot to consider with what I've learned. Ironically, you convinced me to investigate Erin's accident, and then you figured it out for me."

"But why now? What about Jameson? I'm still going to need your help."

His response came out as a half laugh. "I was fired remember."

"I can fix that. I can get you back."

"I can't ask you to do anything more. I appreciate everything. You'll never fully realize how much you've actually done. You pulled me out of my abyss. You plugged me back into the world. I'll never be able to properly thank you. You've done so much. I can't expect you to help fix me, nor can I ask. I don't want you to fix me."

Here he looked off again to nowhere and then added, "It's something I need to do. I have to fix myself."

God! This was all happening so fast, causing her emotions to veer off in diverse directions. Sure, she was disappointed, yet happy, upset but optimistic, sad for her and proud of him. He's getting help for the problem atop the growing list of reasons they'd never be together. Was this now somewhat of a glimmer of hope for the two of them? Didn't she want more than a glimmer?

"How long is rehab?"

"Insurance pays for thirty days."

With all this being said, his timing was not the best. But what was she going to do? Argue with him? How could that end any way but badly? Thirty days though? What was thirty days possibly waiting for Eric when she'd spent almost five years waiting on *what's his name*?

This couldn't be about her, though. This was about him. He exorcised many of his demons and made peace with Erin and their relationship. He found closure but needed time to work through it all. Maybe his timing was closer to perfect.

He asked quietly, "You sure you can handle Jameson Gradeen?"

She handed him back the ring of keys, thanking him for the chivalrous offer. Then she shook her head almost imperceptibly and said, "If he wanted to hurt me he had all morning. Besides, at least for now, I'm still his attorney."

She smiled at this, moving a hand from her chin to his warm cheek. It was a strange, sad sort of smile, but it didn't lack sincerity. She brushed a few wind-tossed hairs from her face with her other hand and stared right at him. The soft intensity in her eyes, a color now somewhere between silver and light blue, again offering possibilities.

He thought back to meeting her in the *Donaldson, Clements* conference room. That's when he was first struck by that optimism. Then the big diamond ring put the brakes on the idea. Now that flashing sign was nowhere to be seen.

"Will you call me when you get out?"

"Is that really what you want?"

His whispered question kind of hung over them like the strands of lights. The folksy sound of Italian music barely audible through the speakers, as the clattering sounds of the lunchtime dishes being cleaned was audible through the open windows. A horn honked from out front in the restaurant parking lot.

Finally from behind that great smile, she said, "Yes. I'd like that."

"You sure?"

"Yes, Eric. I'm sure."

"Great. That's my cab," he said with a pained expression.

"You're taking a cab to rehab? I'd be happy to . . . Let me take you."

"Then both you and Jameson Gradeen would know where I am," he offered with a sly smile. "I'm doing this by myself, for myself. It's probably best if we just say good-bye here."

She struggled with this and then admitted, "Okay, but can I say that this last week has been amazing?"

"It was," he agreed.

"What have you done to me?" she asked to no one in particular. "Before you, my life was ordered and regimented, scripted and methodical, and dull. I didn't realize how boring. This morning I'm drinking scotch and crying in your kitchen and now I'm playing hooky on a workday and drinking scotch again, but I'm not crying now. Instead this feels right, like somehow we're taking the next logical steps."

Eric struggled to get to his feet. She jumped up and grabbed his backpack off the chair, gingerly helping him slide his good arm through the strap.

"Do you feel that way too? Today was crazy, but this turned out okay. Don't you think?"

It struck her as odd that she sounded so unsure of herself. She was a woman who made decisions and then stuck to them. There were never second thoughts. She didn't know the meaning of the word "dissonance."

"If you say so." He tried to smile widely and said, "I can't wait for you to see me at my best."

"Thirty days though?"

"Only thirty days."

She gave him one more hug on his good side and leaned forward to give him a kiss. He turned, expecting it to be a light buss on the cheek like always before last night. Instead she stepped around and planted one right on his lips. When their tongues brushed against one another he thought he'd been tasered and had second thoughts about her letter and especially rehab.

But it was time to go. His cab as well as his future was waiting.

As she watched him trudge his way down the two steps from the patio deck, she hollered a question.

"What's the one more stop you have to make? Hopefully it's the emergency room."

Without turning, he said over his shoulder, "Think about it. What's my one last loose end?"

She didn't have to think long and should have expected nothing less. It made sense. With a devilish chuckle that she didn't know she possessed, she plopped back into her chair and reached for his abandoned tumbler of scotch. In one long gulp she drained it to the bottom.

Whatever in the world he'd done to her, maybe she could get used to it.

is cab pulled up out front of the large two-story home in one of the nicer upscale neighborhoods of the city. He asked the driver, the same one from Tuesday night at the hotel, to keep the meter running, telling him it would be five to ten minutes tops. Stepping from the backseat, he waved his good arm to a woman on the front porch.

She waited for him in the doorway, opening the screen door as he struggled to climb concrete steps leading up to her front porch. It was painted the same industrial garage-floor grey as the stairs.

"I'm Eric McKegney," he said through labored breaths on his approach.

"I know who you are. I've been waiting since you called." After a closer inspection of the man and the sling she asked, "Are you okay?"

"I will be, ma'am. Thanks for agreeing to see me."

She stepped aside so he could pass into the modern house and said, "How could I say no? You made a very compelling case. I must say, if half of what you said is true, you'll always be welcome in my home. Please come in. Can I get you anything?"

"No, ma'am. Thank you, though. I can't stay long."

For a large house, the entry was small, living room to the right and dining room to the other, second floor balcony almost directly above them. There was an antiseptic smell which reminded him of rubbing alcohol. From a room somewhere nearby on the ground floor, there was a rhythmic swooshing sound.

"Do you mind explaining again what you told me on the phone?"

"Not at all. As I mentioned, I was investigating the murder of Ann Flannery, for the law firm defending the person accused of conspiring to commit it. Within the course of that investigation, I learned a few details about Patterson and Erin's accident. To the outside world, the two women's deaths appeared to be seemingly unrelated tragedies. As it turned out, though, your son was the common denominator."

"How can that be?" She'd been holding a tea towel and with her question, she wiped it across her mouth.

"It appears Ms. Flannery was mentoring your son, teaching him tricks of investigative journalism, possibly in advance of his job in Chicago. They were working on a story dealing with *Agribotics Technology* and the military."

"That's right," she answered without being asked for confirmation. "That would explain the file folder. I couldn't make heads nor tails out of it but I do remember seeing that company's name. And the Department of Defense."

Eric considered this and wondered why no one associated with the Flannery investigation had ever interviewed Mrs. Ritter. But Ann Flannery herself had only remained the focus of the investigation for a few hours at most. No one thought to worry about Ritter once Olivia Jacobsen became the target. Plus, who might have known Ann Flannery was helping him?

"There's reason to believe that the killing of Ms. Flannery may have been intended as a message to whomever she had been mentoring. Your son."

She once again covered her open mouth with the tea towel. "Patty told me the lady newscaster's death was a random mugging."

"That's how they wanted it to appear, but I think it was a message. Either your son had been too slow to get it or too determined to heed it. We may never know. I'd like to think it's the latter."

While Mrs. Ritter appreciated the kind sentiments dealing with her son, she frowned and said, "But your fiancé died because of it."

Eric nodded at this and said, "Erin's last official assignment was as local liaison from the D.A.'s office to the Department of Defense. For all we know she may have played a greater part in all of this."

"And you're willing to take Patty's case?" she asked, excitement in her tone.

"I am, but let's allow everything to simmer for a bit before readdressing it. How about thirty days?"

"If you think." As she led him down the hallway of ceramic-tiled floor, she added, "Come on. You mentioned you were in a hurry."

As they neared Ritter's room, he noticed that the swooshing sound grew louder and the smell cleaner.

"Will he be able to understand me?" Eric had asked the question from a few paces behind.

"Yes and no. Some days are better than others."

They stepped around a tight corner in the darkened hallway and there he was, a mere shell of his former self in an adjustable hospital beds. He was still Patterson Ritter, but the man Eric remembered was forty to fifty pounds ago. He was gaunt and pale, his eyes hollow, almost vacant. His mouth was open, his head moving as if of its own accord, more of a twitching than conscious movement. His two arms, curled unnaturally with palsy at the wrists, seemed to be on strings, like a marionette at the whims of a novice puppeteer.

There were breathing tubes running under his nose attached to the noisy ventilator and an IV bag of clear fluid hanging from a permanent stand attached to the far side of the bed. Gravity-fed tubing ran from there, being held in place by a splint-looking device low on his right forearm. He looked so helpless, and he'd been like this for the past eight months.

"Patty," Mrs. Ritter said in a tone that sounded as if she was speaking to her infant son. "Look who's here. It's Mr. McKegney. Do you remember Eric? He was able to determine that the accident was not your fault. You did not kill Erin. Isn't that great news?"

At Mrs. Ritter's urgings, Eric picked up the story. "That's right. I now know that the Gradeen Family tried to kill you because you and Ann Flannery had uncovered an investigation by the Department of Defense into Jameson's company. They remotely took control of your car and crashed you into that telephone pole. They killed Erin. You didn't . . . They did this to you."

There was little reaction if any from Ritter. Maybe he hadn't heard or not understood. His head continued to bob and his hands danced randomly through the air. Mrs. Ritter had tears in her eyes when she looked from the bed back to Eric. Her effort to smile showed a combination of sorrow and delight, but mostly gratitude.

"We'll never be able to thank you. You're our conquering hero."

Eric nodded and said simply, "Ma'am, I'm not here to be made a hero. It's quite the opposite. I'm an awful person who wished awful things on your son because I thought he and Erin . . ."

"He quite loved Erin, you know," she said thoughtfully, sadly. "Come to think of it, we all did."

"A lot of us did."

She watched the contorted body in the bed turn his head toward them. Ritter held it there, his hands no longer moving, his wrists no longer bent.

"Look. I think he can hear us," Mrs. Ritter said in a muted excitement. "I think he understands that he didn't kill her."

"Ma'am, if he can hear me, there are things I need to say to him."

"I'll leave the two of you alone," Mrs. Ritter said, silently stepping out of the room.

Eric glanced back, as if looking for additional advice or encouragement, no longer wanting to be left alone. She was gone, however. He looked around the room with the one big bay window and the open frilly curtains. The bed was positioned in a way that he could look out at an old, rusty swing set in the back yard when propped up.

A television high on a shelf up on the wall was turned to Jeopardy, and my only thought was, "Let's try 'Awkward Situations' for two-hundred, Alex."

Eric sat in the only chair in the room, leaving him eye level with the bed railing. It was right next to where Ritter's left hand now lay limply on the bed.

He cleared his throat and began haltingly. "Patterson, it's Eric McKegney. Wait. I'm sorry. We've already been through that. I was Erin's fiancé. I'd also like to think you and I were friends because of her.

"I came here to do something I should have done a long time ago. I need to apologize to you. For the last eight months, I have spent every day loathing you for what I thought you did to me, hating you for what I believed you did to Erin. I am not proud of it, but I cursed you. I wanted your life to be a living hell. I'm so ashamed now that . . . Please forgive me. Please, forgive me."

Eric cried and coughed, sniffling back the tears and bracing his arm in the sling against his ribs. And then there was a hand on his shoulder. He glanced up to see Mrs. Ritter, wiping at her own tears with her tea towel.

He turned back to the bed. "Please forgive me, Patterson. I'm sorry for what happened to you and to Erin. You deserve better than this . . . better from me. I'm sorry I blamed you. I'm not a good person. I'm sorry I wished bad things for you. Awful things. I wanted you to know."

Ritter's hand slowly rose off the sheet and hung there by the bed railing.

"Grab it. Take it," Mrs. Ritter said, her voice trembling. "He's . . ."

Eric glanced again to Mrs. Ritter and stood, unsure of his next move. She motioned with her head toward the bed. He gently took Ritter's hand in his own. It felt cold and limp, yet wonderfully alive. There was the throbbing of a pulse, and when Eric felt the faint squeeze, the goose bumps chilled his arms. He closed his eyes tightly, but the tears rushed out, nonetheless. He turned to look at Mrs. Ritter who was making no effort to hide her smile or to disguise her own sobs.

"Thank you. Thank you both," Eric said, the feeling of eternal absolution lifting his spirit, making him forget his past eight months of guilt.

"I'm going away for a while. When I get back can I come see the two of you again?"

Mrs. Ritter dabbed at her eyes. Through a worn smile, she said, "You're always welcome here. You must understand how much what you've already done for Patty means for us? My son didn't do it. I knew he didn't kill Erin. We finally have someone to hold responsible."

Eric regarded her comment, for the first time seeing the effect of what he uncovered through eyes not his own. This woman had endured a pure hell for the past eight months so much worse than he. Hers was helplessness for herself and her son's guilt. Eric and Patterson Ritter were linked forever by the accident. They were no longer adversaries, however. They were kindred spirits, maybe one day to become allies.

"We need to keep everything said here under wraps. Are you okay with that? I will circle back with you in a month and we'll decide where to go from there. Is that okay? Can you wait thirty days?"

"We've already waited eight months. What is one more? I look forward to discussing it," she said with a cagey grin. "Here. See if this will help you."

She handed him a large brown expandable file folder with the elastic strap stretching and straining to keep everything inside. As she showed Eric to the door, she explained that it contained all her son's notes from his work with Ann Flannery.

"Has anyone else seen this? Does anyone know you have it?"

Mrs. Ritter shook her head and wiped her hands on the tea towel.

"Did you look through it?"

"Like I said, I tried. It doesn't make a great deal of sense to me."

"I'll make sure it gets to the right people."

"You are the right people. All along you were right for Erin . . . And now you'll be right for my Patty."

He waved to Mrs. Ritter one last time across the top of the waiting cab, realizing his day's duties were now complete, all loose ends tightly bound like his arm in the sling. And with that thought, he took a second to consider how close to death he'd come in the parking garage. Was it dumb luck or maybe a higher power that saved him? The expandable file folder seemed to presage the latter. Yet to what end?

He unzipped his backpack. To make room for the bulging folder he withdrew the half-filled Glenfiddich bottle by its neck, feeling its balance, its heft, ambivalent to its strength. The power of single-malt had been both good and bad. It had controlled his life for the past months, all that while inching him nearer to closure on several fronts. He'd go forward alone, however, his solo journey beginning at rehab.

Seeing this I reconsidered that maybe all along I'd been wrong about Eric's story. Maybe it wasn't the final act in an older tragedy but *Act I* in a happier drama, a prologue to the rest of his life. What if this now-finished tale merely serves as the *Set Up* for a greater story yet to be written? Could this end give birth to a new beginning?

This newest *Three Act Play* would lack any insecurely-tethered balloons or damaged butterflies, no demons nipping on his heels, neither ghosts nor guilt keeping him up at night. Maybe instead Jillian sans the big diamond ring might do that. We'll find out in thirty days.

And how great will it be to be back in the ambulance chasing game? His first real case in almost a year will be *Patterson Ritter, Plaintiff v. Thomas & Jameson Gradeen, Defendants*. The pages spilling out of the file folder made him virtually unbeatable. This gets his face back up on billboards, and maybe across the aisle from *Donaldson, Clements*. Or maybe even Jillian?

Wouldn't we enjoy that story? I'd love to be the one to tell it, however, I'll leave courtroom drama to the professionals. Besides, I'm done here. Eric doesn't need me anymore.

I taught him the internal stories we tell ourselves oftentimes differ from the truth but are never really lies. They serve a vital purpose to keep us upright, to help us survive and persevere. Maybe that's not a way to win, but to keep from losing you have to keep living.

I'd like to think I also taught him while someone never fully recovers from a devastating loss, carrying it with you becomes part of who you are. It may not define you, but it most certainly always describes you.

It's said certain things build character while other things reveal it. Death does both to the survivors. Who knows? Over time, you might be a better person when you come out the other side. It won't be easy. It takes time, and I foresaw just that likelihood for my friend.

After one final glance at the house, he tapped on the cab driver's window. Once it was rolled down, Eric handed me to the cabbie, saying, "It'd be a waste to pour this out."

"Thanks, my man. You sure?"

It was an unceremonial good-bye at best, but he was sure, as was I.

I'd like to think at times I'd been more than a mere crutch, an eight-month acquaintance. We'd been through a lot; we were friends, yet our parting proved easier than first feared. My feelings weren't hurt. Besides, his new resolve had me smiling. My friend's survival from this point forward is the most important thing to me.

Plus, there would be others. There always will be others.

As Eric climbed into the back, the cab driver looked at the half-filled green bottle and said with a laugh, "Where to, my man?"

I thought about it for a split second and said, "What say we drop him off, then go see what Jillian's doing?"

THE END

www.ingramcontent.com/pod-product-compliance
Lightning Source LLC
Chambersburg PA
CBHW032110310726
48972CB00001B/162